Race
to
Destiny

OLD THEAR

TIsroc

Strongmedjie

Silfr Mo

Knuts

Towers
OF THE
Horns

Rotte

Plains of S

Saurr-mode

Desert of Cinders

Castle Realmguard

Spikes
TO THE
Sky

Silfr Mo

ISBN: 979-8-89694-118-7 - eBook

ISBN: 979-8-89694-119-4 - Paperback

Race to Destiny

STEPHEN ALFORD

Book One: Race to Destiny

Table of Contents

Dedicated to my mother.

Carol Joyce Moore
who never read the whole story.

Special thanks to alpha and beta readers Jamie Sprenkel, Mark Schonebaum, Monica Smith, Karen Gleich, Quay Ngoc Tang, and Jessica Ketchum who talked me through roadblocks and made time to review this project.
Not to forget, James Hinshaw who inspired the creation in 1977.

PART
One

Grambol Doomsayer

"Har, Haggersath, that old Grambol is out of sorts, tilting around like a top an' rambling on about some sorta treasure in the fire pit o'er yonder."

Haggersath slapped his knee, nodding to himself as he rose from sitting on the large boulder. "Don't just stand there gapin' like a goat about to lose its head—take me there, Rock-Biter," Haggersath said. This was news he had been expecting.

Of course, the black, iron-bearded Captain Grölle was referring to Grambol Doomsayer. Grambol had a unique skill to find valuables and treasure and the like. Sometimes he could predict things to come. Other times he spoke through the heavy clouding of too much drink and a mind that teetered on the brink of sanity.

Grölle wasted no time turning back the way he had come. Haggersath was swift to match pace at the reliable captain's side. Haggersath knew Grambol Doomsayer had lived a long life—indeed, the old Dwarrow claimed to have witnessed much of their lore as it unfolded firsthand. Great tales at the fireside he oft spoke, many times too fantastic to believe. Nobody really knew his age—he claimed to be over three hundred years—but his ancient mind was curious and worked like a game of chance. He was a respectable one hundred and fifteen himself, at middling years.

Anything spilling from his mad mouth was as grounded as a spin at the wheel of fortune. With any luck, Jikseon, god of the Dwarrow, would steer the old Dwarrow to true riches and adventure this time. Sometimes he did, but lately his predictions had been empty fumes of harsh liquor.

Haggersath and Grölle hurried past half the company. Haggersath could hear the excitement around the fire even before they arrived.

Several of the company's common hammers gathered in a circle, murmuring with eagerness and watching Grambol Doomsayer. He was dancing drunkenly with his face contorting in wild, rapturous glee in the middle of the gathering. "Glittering, yes, sparkling…close! So close." Cackling madly, his eyes gleamed like polished aquamarine, flashing this way and that uncontrollably.

Haggersath groaned with displeasure at the lunacy and feared the worst. This was an episode of intensity beyond what most of them had witnessed from the ancient Doomsayer. Had the madness finally taken him? Just as Haggersath broke through the throng of Dwarrow, Grambol snapped back to himself, eyeing the gathering around him with dubious suspicion. He reeled, taking in the reality he had been slapped back into. His gaze stopped at Haggersath, with a sober gape that slowly spread to his typical friendly grin.

"Grambol, what did ye scrying eyes perceive for us this time?" Haggersath asked him without approaching. Haggersath extended his arms and half smiled at his old friend.

The surrounding Dwarrow leaned in.

Grambol Doomsayer smiled an odd stingy glint at Haggersath, as if Haggersath might steal away his most prized possession.

"An artifact, and close—very close." His voice held an edge of danger.

Haggersath frowned at him and glowered, pressing Grambol Doomsayer for more specific information. "Artifact? Bah! I've no will ta play yer miserly games.

Out with it, you old coot. What exactly? Waste no time with your guarded secrets—be exact."

Grambol Doomsayer pulled away, offended, his lean face rumpled. He gathered himself carefully before answering, "I...I don' know. Not fer sure." Grambol Doomsayer's tone changed to hurt confusion.

Haggersath, already annoyed with the tooth-pulling process, shifted and closed in on the Doomsayer menacingly, resisting the urge to hit the old Dwarrow.

Grambol Doomsayer backed away, his bright blue eyes blinking as if expecting a fist at any moment. "Wait! Wait! I dunno," he pleaded, scrambling back like a misbehaving dog. "I can say its impression be stronger than any I kin recall. This is big, Haggersath, my friend. It feels...well, foreign."

Haggersath paused, and Grambol Doomsayer recovered. When he spoke again, it was in soothing tones. "It's definitely not of Dwarrow construct. It has tremendous value—shook me bones an' beard like nothing I kin recall."

Haggersath dropped his annoyance. He relaxed his stance and felt his temper slip away. He let his voice become calmer now. "Yer talk smacks of jus' what we be needin'. How sure kin ya be, Grambol?"

"Sure?" Grambol Doomsayer chided, waiving one of his ruddy brownish hands with an air of dismissiveness.

Now filled with the confidence of a master divulging small bits of his craft to a naïve client, he added, "When have ye ever known me ta be *not* sure?"

Haggersath let a laugh quietly cross his yellow-bearded face. "Aye, Grambol, ye be right," he said softly, letting his greed seep out through his eyes and then his grin. "This be the one then."

"Aye." Grambol nodded and walked wearily away. Haggersath heard him say loud enough to hear, "But be warned an' remember, great worth means great danger. An' I do believe this be *very* great worth."

Haggersath spat, discarding Grambol Doomsayer's caution as pointless. They well knew the lands outside Tisroc, the area claimed by the Dwarrow, were notoriously perilous, and even the regions of Tisroc that were uninhabited by the Dwarrow teemed with wild things, namely the basilisks to the west of Strongmedjie. But Haggersath's troop had no reason to fear. They were heavily armed with hammer and steel—they were dangerous in their own right, and the wary would steer clear of them.

"We move at first light of day," Haggersath said, commanding the company. "Rest. May Jikseon bring us luck and a yellow Sun on the morn."

The camp settled into a slumber with a set of token sentries watching over them. As one, the Dwarrow drifted off.

CHAPTER 2

Mustering the Expedition

B right morning greeted the bleary-eyed Dwarrow. Cold air swept in off the jagged mountain slopes with icy fingers, penetrating the metal-laden, armored troop. Other races would likely shrivel and shiver, but not the Dwarrow. They welcomed the frozen blast, letting it invigorate their spirits. Sleepy grumbling quickly rose to raucous chatter over Grambol Doomsayer's curiously provoking message.

Winter was always harsh in the north, always bit through the bone—but cool air that had nearly lost its frosty edge had finally come to the land of Tisroc. Summer would rush in fast as it always did and chase spring away before it could be savored. The relenting of a seeming ice age could be nothing short of a good omen.

There was another good omen: Around the Dwarrow camp, a spitted tetrad of tough old goats were sizzling over open flames, hissing and crackling. The poor slow chevon were deemed too old to be of use to the herd and were put out by the alpha buck. The Dwarrow had welcomed them with hungry fervor and sharp knives. Thick wafts of smoky char and burning grease plugged the air. Aromas drew hard, pulling anticipation that soon roasted meat would satisfy growling bellies. This was much more a comfort than that crowded city they had left more than ten days past, but still, those tough beasts, their meat dried, would serve a meager meal for the road to come. Dwarrow were resourceful in all manner of things, feasting on the road notwithstanding. It was enough. For the Dwarrow, meat and marrow—no matter the quality or quantity—were just another good omen.

Haggersath woke in the shadow of Bolfath, a towering Dwarrow, if Dwarrow he was. He stood two full meters tall, likening to the tallest Man of the southlands. He was broad, too, boasting at least twice the girth of any Dwarrow in the company. But despite appearances, he was not a threat. He was Bolfath, Haggersath's bodyguard, and he was never far away.

Haggersath looked on in approval over his company of Dwarrow grimly quaffing exceptionally crafted

Siolvarin ale. It slopped around the sides of his own wooden mug. Years of use and travel had worn the seams, and it leaked. It was a lucky mug—and a good one. Haggersath might say it had been the best he ever had. Taking a long pull, much of the ale was lost as it dribbled out the sides of the mug, leaving only the telltale frothy streams stuck on his coarse, wavy, golden-slate beard.

Bolfath sat down cross-legged on the dirt across from him. Even sitting, the pale-skinned bodyguard was near as tall as Haggersath when standing his height.

"They be excited fer the news of treasure, Haggersath," Bolfath said. "Ya don' seem ta share the same fever."

Haggersath thumbed at the golden Alexandrite brooch mounted in the iron gorget about his neck. "I be happy fer the lads enough. Look at them now." He gestured his chin in the direction of the Dwarrow gathered, pointing with his full wavy beard. Bolfath followed with his eyes.

"Aye, they be itchin' fer a fight," Bolfath said, his face alive with excitement.

Haggersath let his face spread with a great toothy grin of reflective pleasure. "Ye be right, me friend. They work well together. But methinks it be the meat an' ale that makes them happiest."

As if on cue, Othro walked up to them bearing plates of steaming goat and small boiled potatoes for each of them. He was one of the eastern Dwarrow that made up the minority of the warriors under Captain Jarlsalt's escort assigned to Haggersath's expedition.

Othro let a grin break his battle-scarred face. "The boys be sayin' ya'd go hungry if'n we din' feed ya proper." He handed off a plate to each of them, and Bolfath popped a potato into his mouth with hungry gusto.

Haggersath gave a start as Othro's overfull white beard moved around his neck and two pink-red eyes flicked open to stare at him. Othro grabbed at the beard, pulling it away from his face. "I don't me ta startle ya, Haggersath. It only be me little rascal, Avalanche." He scratched under the chin of the pure white fox draped at his shoulders.

Bolfath laughed, launching bits of half-chewed potato out of his mouth. Haggersath smiled, shaking his head. He saw the pet clearly now. Othro had only scraggly patches of white beard. His deep scars prevented the beard from growing in.

"Har, now that be a good one there, Othro." Haggersath had never noticed the beard was not Othro's own before. Othro smiled and looked with soft eyes at Avalanche. "She be more than meets the eye."

Othro walked away, cooing to the fox. Avalanche, not wanting to miss a thing, propped herself up on Ortho's ringlet-mailed shoulder, looking back at Haggersath and Bolfath.

"He be a fine warrior, that one." Bolfath nodded, adding another potato back into his mouth. His large hands brushed bits of potato out of his flaming red beard. Haggersath had always wondered about Bolfath's beard. It looked to be made of fine soft fibers like an animal's fur. The hair of the Dwarrow differed from other hair in that it was stiff and thick and made of metal-like brushes.

"There be many good warriors with us." Haggersath grabbed a greasy sliver of goat and slurped it into his mouth. It was fatty, and the gamey flavor made him frown slightly. He realized he just wasn't hungry. He noticed Bolfath was eying his plate, having already cleaned his own.

"Ya gonna eat that?" Bolfath asked, his pale ice-blue eyes locked onto Haggersath's nearly untouched plate.

"No, it be yours." He handed the plate over. Seeing the eastern warrior only reminded him of the divide between eastern and western Dwarrow. He frowned, looking at the ale that had spilled over Bolfath's beard and dribbled over the big bodyguard's boots. Bolfath was too engrossed in his feasting labors to notice. That was when the crunching of footsteps approaching broke Haggersath out of his stare.

It was Captain Jarlsalt, the leader of the armed forces, handpicked by the Bornholm himself. Jarlsalt was a smallish young Dwarrow adorned in exquisitely worked, highly polished trusilver armor that was intricately painted black and trimmed in rich gold. A golden bolt of lightning was painted on the front; it split in ferocious prongs. The gaudy matching epaulets on his shoulders hung halfway down his arms, signifying a rank of nobility within the army of Strongmedjie. He carried his black-plumed golden helm at his side.

"Har, Haggersath," he greeted, ignoring Bolfath altogether. "What's yer plan? Do we move out as soon as me boys finish our morning repast?" He drew out a small blade and began working his nails, removing the accumulated grime under them.

"Aye, captain. Have them set a patrol ahead an' I'll send Grambol Doomsayer to the vanguard ta direct our path."

"So, ya don' know where we be goin'?" Jarlsalt said, a smile flickering over his lips like he had proved something of consequence.

This snit was always probing for weakness in Haggersath's leadership. He decided to ignore the jab. "Get yer boys on the move, Jarlsalt. I want ye to push along the road before the Sun peeks any higher above those peaks." He pointed north to the Silfr Mountains, as if Jarlsalt did not know where the mountains might lie.

Jarlsalt stopped working his grimy nails with his knife and smartly sheathed it. Jarlsalt's slick oiled beard still dripped at the sharply pointed end. "Ha! Already done. I dallied here for some time now, waitin' ta see ya off." His words oozed off his falsely smiling lips like dirty sludge. He tried to carry off some twisted picture of obedience.

Haggersath ignored the retort. Jarlsalt's typical passive defiance was of no matter and only served to make him look petty in the eyes of eastern Dwarrow. A good part of the company was made up of easterners. Only portions of Jarlsalt's command came from Strongmedjie.

Haggersath knew he shouldn't let it get to him. After all, smarmy attitude and unattractive face aside, Jarlsalt was also of an unreproachable lineage. He slung his title-less name about like it should mean something—sure, he was the son of the 38th Bornholm, ruler of the mountain city Strongmedjie, but he was the *16th* son, quite unimportant. Fifteen others stood in line for the throne, fifteen others he would need to outperform to be considered for the mantle of 39th Bornholm. Jarlsalt's exit came as a swaying turn on his military heel and the rapid short steps that made a comical spectacle all on its own.

"I be watchin' yer back when that one be about. But even I cannot be everywhere an' always." Bolfath had measuredly tempered his voice low. His thin-braided mustaches were still dripping with ale, and his breath was heady with goat. "Don't trust any of the westerners. But that one most of all."

Haggersath was more than aware of the ambitious danger and political clout Jarlsalt could muster. It did not get past Haggersath that the only look Bolfath had for the pompous Dwarrow was a stone-cold look of murder, but Haggersath could not be so obvious with his disdain. He always kept an eye on him and *never* trusted him fully, just as he *never* fought back with his own retorts.

But, still, he *was* the son of a Jarle, a part of the historic line of Dwarrow who have ruled the western kingdoms since establishing the Strongmedjie. Jarlsalt was very unlikely to rule the kingdom, but a post of power and prestige Jarlsalt obviously coveted.

"Yer speakin' me own mind, Bolfath. Let's get the lads on the move. At least he figured out that we'd be off early today."

Bolfath let loose a huge grin. "Hah, I knew ya'd know his ways."

They stood together, Bolfath tall as him and half again. Haggersath marveled at his good fortune to have him as a personal protector. Bolfath strode off, making short work of the pathway ahead, his long twin double-bladed battle axes crossed over his back.

Bustling up past the well-formed ranks typical of Dwarrow, Haggersath headed for the guiding party near the front of the column. Bolfath had disappeared off to the north. They soon found Grambol Doomsayer assembled with Mevindh-Gulbard and Diwolde Stonescraper in heavy conversation, discussing the pathway ahead of them.

"Stone and Sun grant you strength, Giftgiver," Mevindh-Gulbard spoke in his deep, even cadence. He was stroking his pale golden beard that was kept tucked into his belt. Mevindh-Gulbard was in the habit of acting more formally than the other Dwarrow. It was not an uncommon practice among Gulprąsts—he was of their order—who had powers granted by Jikseon, where they could convey his favor and occasionally perform outright miracles.

He looked every bit an emissary of Jikseon. Above the beltline, on the chest of the cloth, was the crest of the Gulprąsts: a circle of rope around protective runes with the amber-jeweled mace of their order at the center. Mevindh-Gulbard's rich yellow beard shined of pure gold and brimmed in the Sun. Clipped at his hip through a ringlet on his belt gleamed a bejeweled mace nearly identical to the one represented on the crest.

"Har, Gulpraşt, Jikseon guide yer pathway," Haggersath said, nodding to the Gulpraşt in his immaculate white and gold tabard. How did Mevindh-Gulbard remain so untouched during travel? Smiling to himself, Haggersath thought no more of the minor miracle. Then, he shifted to Grambol Doomsayer. "Have ye discovered where our target be yet?"

"Seems to me we be headin' mighty close to the ruins of Krath," Grambol Doomsayer began, sounding far more lucid in the morning Sun. He popped one of those tart berries he liked so much into his mouth, wiping his hand on his stained purple vest. He went on as he chewed, showing red-stained teeth. "Likely ta be findin' some kvalid to contend with in those parts. They'd have come fer sure after Krath's demise, swept right in like it be their own, and no one cared ta bother with that lot. So, they stayed."

Grambol Doomsayer was right; the furry scavengers infested anything neglected over time.

Haggersath laughed. "No matter, we'll scatter 'em like leaves in the chill wind. Never had use for that kind. Craven cowards they be."

Diwolde Stonescraper belted out a laugh. "Aye, they will die by my hammer." The Sun on his face made the splotches of varying shades similar to pluff mud in tone show on his dark skin.

Diwolde Stonescraper was a merry sort, usually tainted with ale but rarely harsher spirits. His uncanny knack at solving puzzles and knowledge of rock were well respected. Mountains and stone alike spoke to him like old friends.

Haggersath gave him a brief half smile. "I be havin' more important work for you. A Grýttr would be wasted fightin' when I have near fifty warriors ta do that work." Diwolde Stonescraper smiled, his cheeks raising the billowy brown beard that almost covered his entire face.

"You know yer rocks, an' that's a skill we will be needin' if we end up in those mountains."

Diwolde Stonescraper was a Grýttr, the title of those who were learned in the ancient ways of stone lore. Carefully guarded, Grýttrs' secrets were passed down through apprentices very selectively.

"As you say, Haggersath. I'll be keeping me hammer at me side an' me sword in me scabbard." The plain short straight sword at his hip looked like it had seen plenty of combat, but his choice of weapon was sharp on both edges. It was unadorned, a plain weapon for a plain Dwarrow. For close combat, the only kind Diwolde allowed himself into, it was an excellent choice. He also carried four various knives, sheathed for easy access in a tight spot, one on each limb.

The road out of Tisroc followed the sheer jagged and tall peaks of the Silfr Mountains on their southern side. Every slope face was rough and rugged like the Dwarrow who called them home. Much of central and eastern Tisroc was uninhabitable except for the most insistent creatures—yeti, goats, eagles, and yes, Dwarrow. But that part was far to their backs, and they had no intention of going there. Long gone from the skies over the mountains was the shine of bright chrome dragons playing in the firmaments over the snow-capped peaks. Over the years, they had vanished inexplicably.

CHAPTER 3

Haggersath Giftgiver

They had two days of good travel weather. Clouds gathered but seemed to do Haggersath's bidding as they faded off, passing southwest or disappearing altogether. The Dwarrow company's progress was not notable despite the good conditions. Jarlsalt did not share the excitement of Haggersath's Haseti and was tardy to begin each day. He called halts often, claiming that breaks were expected. It kept the spirits of the Dwarrow under his command high, and that was enough for now. The third day opened with low gray clouds that blotted out the Sun. The dew in the air smelled heavy and threatening as they marched.

A Haseti was what the eastern Dwarrow leaders called their closest friends. It was a trusted council and acted as the core leadership group. Haggersath considered Mevindh-Gulbard, Diwolde Stonescraper, Grambol Doomsayer, and of course, Bolfath his Haseti.

It was midday when Grambol Doomsayer turned a wild-eyed look to Haggersath and fervently began tapping at Haggersath's arm as if he did not already have his attention. "The skies are gonna break t'day. I seen it in me sleep."

Haggersath looked up. The skies thundered; black-gray clouds rolled in even closer as if an evil directed the sinister wind. Tears of an impending serious storm began dropping.

"Good that we be havin' a Doomsayer with us ta warn us of these kinda things," Haggersath said, holding back no sarcasm.

Grambol Doomsayer retorted, "Ya be lucky fer sure, Haggersath Giftgiver." He yanked at his cloak and pulled up his hood, then turned to tramp off, stretching out his normal short gait.

Wind kicked up, and the rain flailed with angry intensity. Haggersath deemed it a good time to break. He stepped over to find his captain of the soldiers. Jarlsalt wasn't far off, and Haggersath approached with Bolfath ever shadowing him. The tinkling of the silver trinkets scattered with leather strips throughout his twin-braided red beard let Haggersath know he was near without looking. Haggersath called out to Jarlsalt,

"Bring the boys under the mountain's shadow. We break fer camp."

"Aye, good, as ya like," he said, looking with narrowed eyes. "That sheer wall and shelf kin be some shelter." He pointed to the shelf sticking out just past the sparse pines. Under his breath, he muttered something about it only being a little rain.

Haggersath welcomed the break. He hadn't had the chance to sit down with his Haseti since hearing Grambol Doomsayer's news. They were all eastern Dwarrow. Bolfath, of course, was one he entrusted his life to. But Diwolde Stonescraper was a true friend. Grambol Doomsayer and Mevindh-Gulbard served in very different advisory roles.

Jarlsalt believed he was included, but Haggersath did not in his heart trust the westerner. He allowed Jarlsalt into his Haseti only as a necessary formality due his station. In fact, he was not trusted—by any of them.

Regardless, now they could hammer out a plan with proper Dwarrow precision. A plan was needed, too, as they knew the ruins would not be empty.

Diwolde Stonescraper had found a place for them under the slate shelf jutting from the mountainside that had a spine to separate the Haseti from the rest of the company. Rain pattered as Haggersath and the ever-present Bolfath arrived under the rock canopy. Bolfath had to crouch to get under the escarpment; he sat in the back nearest the mountain's foot, watching. Mevindh-Gulbard was pacing in deep thought back and forth, and Grambol Doomsayer was talking to no one in particular about nothing that made any sense. They were already there, waiting as if they knew Haggersath's mind. It was a fact that they did.

"Har, Haggersath," greeted Diwolde Stonescraper, grinning from ear to ear. His bushy brown beard speckled with glistening droplets from the rain. It covered the area where his mouth should be, and the movement when he spoke and the jolly mirth in the words were the only hints that he was the one speaking.

Haggersath tipped a nod to each of them gathered.

"Where's that little snit, Jarlsalt?" Haggersath looked around.

"Ye shoud'nta bother with him, Haggersath. He ne'er shows respect due to any of us," Diwolde Stonescraper said, waving his strong, grayish, mottled hands in the air.

Haggersath nodded an affirmation, saying, "He fucks off when he likes. But we need him, don't you forget—it is he who commands the warriors. An' the time will come when we need them."

Diwolde Stonescraper added, "He never misses a chance to fling it in our faces. We could find some kinda accident, couldn't we?"

"I could fix that problem with the slightest stroke of me pretty ax." Bolfath smiled menacingly, his throat chuckling with expectant opportunity. He had slipped one off of his monstrous muscled back and was petting it like a kitten.

Jarlsalt arrived out of the gloom. "Could fix what, ya big oaf?"

Barking out a laugh like a child surprised by a gift, Bolfath returned his ax over his broad shoulders. Jarlsalt jerked away, his bulging eyes revealing a fear that he could not hide.

"*Enough!*" said Haggersath, stepping between his bodyguard and looking down his beard fiercely at the tardy Dwarrow. "There's no time for hammer play among us now. We are not long for Krath." He leaned into an unexpectant Grambol. "Eh, Doomsayer?"

"No, not far, and I be sure our path lies in that accursed ruin." Grambol Doomsayer nodded slowly.

"Blast me bones, if luck were gold," shot Jarlsalt, putting his hand on Diwolde Stonescraper's thick armored shoulder.

"If yer luck were gold"—Diwolde Stonescraper pushed the hand off and leveled a glare at Jarlsalt—"nothing would change."

A murmur of scoffing laughs were shared at Jarlsalt's expense. He scowled at Diwolde Stonescraper.

"Last I heard, the place was crawling with kvalid and their like. Nasty rats they be," Grambol Doomsayer said, twisting his face. He then spat.

"My axes ache for some bloodletting. Fine sport they'll make." Bolfath reached behind, loosening them in their sheaths with naked exhilaration.

"You'll get your fill, Bolfath, but there's likely more than a few of those rats. We'd be wise an' wary watchin' our backs, fer there ought to be at least one tralkvalid in their midst."

"A tralkvalid!" Grambol Doomsayer said in surprise, waking from a daydream. Jarlsalt's mouth almost frowned with concern, and Mevindh-Gulbard breathed out a heavy sigh, stroking his long tucked beard.

Haggersath went on, "Even so, we may need yer magics ta cope with this, Gulprąst."

"As you like it, Giftgiver," Mevindh-Gulbard said. "I have not seen one in many years."

"Bah! Big rats, small rats, make no matter ta me axes," said Bolfath, letting his mirth shake the trinkets in his beard. His grin beamed anticipation.

"Ya kin have them all, far as I'm concerned," Jarlsalt said and then pointed up to the jagged deep-gray outcropping sheltering them. "It's big enough fer you easterners to huddle under, eh? What about me Dwarrow out there?" He pointed to the soldiers sitting in the rain. Then he shot a stare at Haggersath. "Let me boys wallow in the mud, will ya?"

"Good enough, I say," Diwolde Stonescraper muttered to the group. "An' why not?"

Before Jarlsalt could react, Haggersath gave way. "We jus' be makin' plans. Once we finish here, out we all go. A little mud is good fer us all."

Jarlsalt smiled in a way that made Haggersath regret accommodating anything to the weaselly captain. "Good," was all Jarlsalt said as he walked away. "Very good."

"Why'd ya ever try and make that bastard happy?" Diwolde Stonescraper asked. "Them westerners—they all be no good."

"Why do everyone say that?" Grölle had joined them. "I be western. I was drawn from the mountainside near the Strongmedjie. Strongmedjie be my home, but Dwarrow be Dwarrow, east or west."

Haggersath gave a nod of his head at the young captain's claim. "Dwarrow do be Dwarrow," he said with grave, solemn pacing. He bowed his head and muttered to himself, "Home."

No one spoke. They were not used to his sadness coming out. His heart ached at the thought. He looked with hollow eyes, one silver, the other golden, at Grölle. "You be lucky. I have no home." His words kept them riveted to his bleak voice almost cracking with grief.

"The Towers of the Horne, my home, suffered destruction more than a century ago. Gnomôk came in massed armies and threw down the glorious towers. Calls to the west, to Strongmedjie under the mountains, were met with a stolid silence. A meager few managed to escape the sacked Towers through secret tunnels under the mountains. I was with them, as was Grambol Doomsayer and Diwolde Stonescraper and our other kin. We suffered and were greatly diminished in numbers and in wealth. Our pride was damaged, and prestige crippled."

"But there had to be a good reason they didn't come." Grölle was looking confused. "Surely they did not want the destruction that happened."

"It be jealousy, lad," Diwolde Stonescraper said. "The Bornholms were always coveting the wealth the Towers had. We Grýttr are unmatched with our knowledge in gems and metals of the Silfr Mountains."

Grölle was wide-eyed upon hearing the reason for treachery. "No. It cannot be."

"Aye." Haggersath nodded sadly. He pulled off his ox-horned helm and sat down on a convenient boulder. He gestured for Grölle to do the same. Since there was no other boulder under the escarpment, he sat comfortably on the dirt.

Bolfath leaned on the wall, while Mevindh-Gulbard paced again as if verifying the veracity of the recounting. Diwolde Stonescraper stood at Haggersath's side, remembering his own accounting of the time. Grambol Doomsayer seemed a world away, staring at the rock wall and pointing his finger here and there like he was testing if it was real or not.

"I was one of the two Giftgivers who escaped death at the demise of the Towers. Yet when we came out the western side of the tunnels into Strongmedjie, we were served nothing but dishonor by the Bornholm who ruled the Strongmedjie. Me uncle died in the mines. I fared better."

Grölle shifted uneasily, but Haggersath continued.

"With the ruin of the Horned Towers, Strongmedjie became the greatest and only stronghold of the Dwarrow. After that, the Giftgivers of the Horned Towers and the Bornholm of Strongmedjie had a cool relationship at best. I found myself forced into the humiliation of serving the 38th Bornholm, who now ruled in Strongmedjie, without the respect due to my station."

Grölle frowned. "But you lead this expedition?"

Scoffing chuckles from the Haseti softly imposed their derision of his claim.

"An' why do ya think the Bornholm put Jarlsalt in command of all the warriors?" Diwolde Stonescraper asked him.

"Because he is a captain of Dwarrow at Strongmedjie. He is a leader." Grölle's answer came more in the form of a question begging for support.

"No lad. It be because the Bornholm wants ta keep the Giftgiver under his thumb. Jarlsalt be no real leader of Dwarrow. But he be flawlessly loyal ta the Bornholm."

Grölle looked on like he had been struck by Diwolde Stonescraper's revelation.

"It is the reason he be here." Haggersath took up the conversation. "The Bornholm needed me gone, away from the Strongmedjie. That is why he sent me off on this pointless mission. An endless quest for the Bornholm with the goal of finding so-called treasure. A liar's trick. Scouring the land in search of relics and such artifacts the Bornholm claimed were vital to their long history. In reality, they were merely things of small value.

It was a veneer just to keep me out of Strongmedjie. More reasons to diminish the title of Giftgiver and demean the leader of the eastern Dwarrow."

Grölle was sitting with his mouth agape.

"That's right!" Suddenly Grambol Doomsayer cut in with his excitable timbre, making not only Grölle but Haggersath and Diwolde Stonescraper jump. "But he did not count on me. The blowhard. Ha! I know treasure. An' we be findin' some real treasure that the bugger ne'er imagined. Oh yes. We be makin' him sorry fer sendin' me with them." As suddenly as he jumped in, he was once more distracted and plucked a small pickled fish from the jar he kept in one of his packs and slurped it up in a single motion. Then he returned to the wall, studying it intensely.

"That is why there be trouble between the east an' the west. But ye seem ta be made of eastern soil by yer ways." Grölle started to rise from the ground, looking affronted by the statement.

"Be at peace, lad." Mevindh-Gulbard spread his hands in an open way as if presenting something to be received. "It be meant as the highest of compliments from the Giftgiver. He praises your open willingness to use yer own thoughts and make sound decisions." He smiled a friendly smile at Grölle, and he let the tension go from his posture and face. "Like the one you just made."

Haggersath smiled too. "Good." He straightened his old leather jerkin, its straps of good bearskin loosely woven together and fastened with cold iron studs that never rusted. There were slashes across the leather at many places, but it had kept life and limb intact for years. It was a good, reliable piece and matched well with the rest of his armor, light for traveling. "Now rest up, me lads. Looks like the rain won' be lettin' up fer the rest o' the day. We will make an early rise of it in the mornin'."

The Dwarrow belted a few drafts before slipping into a rain-soaked slumber. The morning light beckoned their eyes open. Rain had poured through the night but left the air freshly cleansed, easing the burden of setting to the road posthaste. By midday the mud would dry, and the company could break to clean and dust off before continuing.

Jarlsalt and Diwolde Stonescraper led the troop while Haggersath and his looming shadow of a bodyguard were joined by Mevindh-Gulbard and Grambol Doomsayer. One of Jarlsalt's provosts, Grölle, headed up the rear. It was easy going, and with the wet night and mud behind them, Dwarrow spirits were better. After nearly a league of travel southeast, Grambol Doomsayer and Haggersath caught up to Jarlsalt where the road heading north met the trade way. By looking into the throat of the road, overgrown with vines crossing the path and pines towering on both sides, they knew it was scarcely usable. Past the greenery loomed wicked-edged peaks leading into the heart of the Silfr Mountains that were once Dwarrow lands. Nothing but gloominess emitted from the sheer rock walls themselves, drawing the Dwarrow deeper into the inhospitable climb.

Diwolde Stonescraper was feeling the rock wall intently. It was almost like he was searching for something there. "There be a sadness in the stone here," he muttered to himself. "This is not a place where we be findin' friends on the road."

"Fear of rock? Comin' from a Grýttr no less." Jarlsalt scoffed, a smile curling up on one side. "We Dwarrow of the west do not fear the mountains—they are home, though dark and deep."

"This be not your home, Captain Jarlsalt," Mevindh-Gulbard said, catching up to them. "This be eastern territory. Your like may well be less welcome than most. At least we were once known to the stone here."

"Maybe once," Jarlsalt spat, taking the Gulprąst's words as an insult. "Now it be a rat-infested ruin, an' methinks they be likin' the taste of easterners fer their meals jus' the same as us."

"It may be, captain," Grambol Doomsayer said, using his most sane voice. "But methinks Krath is where we need to be, an' this road be our road today."

Hard feelings hung in the air between Haggersath's other Haseti and Jarlsalt. Clearing the flora as they went took time and was hard work. In some places, the vines grew woody and proved a great hindrance. The winding path grew smaller as it rose steeply upward. Gray, billowy clouds grew closer as they went. Rain sat heavy in those clouds, ready to burst, but they kept calm and held their water. Still, dry weather did nothing to improve their slow climb.

Two more days of the drizzling gray hike had the Dwarrow casting dark glances at the mountains and skies instead of each other. Pine trees began to become more prolific near the mountains. Heady, resinous scents clogged the air with a dampness from the saturated gray clouds, pressing like a weight upon them.

Grambol Doomsayer signaled Haggersath. "We be close now. I kin smell the treasure through the pine resins."

"Ye be sober today, Grambol Doomsayer? I need yer wits about ya," Haggersath asked none too quietly.

He was met with a cackling laugh from his Doomsayer that told him all he needed to know.

Bolfath leaned into Haggersath. "Methinks he be better when he be pissed."

Haggersath moved to face Jarlsalt. "Have most of yer Dwarrow break their fast. Then set a watch. Last, I mean fer ya ta take a dozen ta look around the area."

"I know how ta set up a camp." Jarlsalt shook his head. He tugged the tip of his oiled beard. He lasered a sharp glance, purveying his annoyance for a long moment.

Haggersath waited. Was the 16th son about to make the challenge of authority so soon? He knew it was coming, but was he brash enough, ignorant enough, to try so soon?

Then, Jarlsalt smiled with a snicker before relenting. "As you like, Haggersath, as you like."

Jarlsalt moved off in his rapid tin soldier walk, moving his arms back and forth rapidly, taking small, hurried steps, and did as he'd been bid. What an absolute fool. He was glad it was Jarlsalt the Bornholm had saddled him with. He did not need to fear the spy becoming clever.

Peering through the sap-sticky pines, Haggersath and Grambol Doomsayer—and, of course, Bolfath—could see the crumbled walls that once protected the dead city. Krath's walls were never much of an obstacle at just three meters high at the zenith, with a narrow parapet to patrol. Now, a poorly structured array of broken ladders and rope span bridges attempted to link the gaps, allowing crude passage around the disintegrated rampart.

Lounging at the entranceway were four brown, furry, rat-faced kvalid, easily identified by their slender weasel bodies, filthy, black-clawed hands, and feet. Shabby, worn leather jerkins closely fit their long, lean builds, and over their backs were slung quivers holding up to a dozen crude javelins. At their sides were assorted handheld melee arms of varying quality from inferior to abysmal. One of them walked in circles in apparent boredom while the others rested on their bellies, scratching at the earth on all fours. On the wall, two more walked in patrol, stopping to look out into the forest now and again. They could just barely be heard sporadically chittering among themselves.

Haggersath whispered, "I count six. Do ya see any more?"

"Ohh, I can take 'em," said Bolfath, his voice shaking in excitement. He began to loosen his axes, his grin showing his teeth and the gaps of those missing.

"Ya don' know how many more there be," Haggersath said, calming the huge Dwarrow down.

Then Grambol Doomsayer chimed in. "Me nose tells me there be no more nearby. But I'd bet on many more coming if they heard a fight."

Haggersath knew he should have brought the Stonescraper instead—if not for judging the stonework, then for level thought. But leaving him to watch Jarlsalt was safer than tasking Bolfath with the job. He didn't want to have to return to Strongmedjie and explain the grisly death of the 16th son.

Once more confirming his assessment, Haggersath tapped on Bolfath's shoulder to relax the bodyguard's grip on his axes. The Dwarrow slunk back into the woods and made for their camp ten minutes down the road.

Back in the camp, Haggersath gathered his Haseti and Jarlsalt.

"I'll take the Gulprąst, Diwolde Stonescraper, and ol' Grambol Doomsayer with me," Haggersath told his contingent.

Jarlsalt nodded in understanding, then stuck his thumb in Bolfath's direction. "What about him?"

"Ya don' worry 'bout the likes of me. I won' be far if ye want ta kiss me axes." Bolfath began to chuckle at him.

"Right, he be," Haggersath continued. "Move the camp to the entrance of the ruins once we clear out that rat scum. Captain"—he returned his gaze to Jarlsalt—"you will provide me with eight of yer Rock-Biters."

Rock-Biters were the elite troop in Jarlsalt's battle-ready warrior company. Only sixteen of his forty-six Dwarrow warriors were Rock-Biters. Heavily armored and especially stout, Rock-Biters carried a reputation well beyond just another Dwarrow warrior.

Sending half of his best did not sit well with the captain, and he shook his head disapprovingly. "Ya think that be wise?"

"I command the expedition. Do as yer told."

Jarlsalt held his eyes in challenge, mouth twitching in contemplative thought. Haggersath was well aware Jarlsalt thought of him as a puffed-up token king of a broken house. Grambol Doomsayer had overheard Jarlsalt boasting in camp when he thought no eastern Dwarrow could hear: "Haggersath may be designated leader, but it was only a formality," and that "every Strongmedjie Dwarrow knows that the son of the Bornholm is the true leader."

Haggersath had grown tense at the defiance exposed in Jarlsalt's expression. Suddenly realizing he telegraphed his thoughts, Jarlsalt relaxed into a very forced grin—a grimace of obvious pain.

"Of course, Giftgiver, Haggersath, as ye like." Jarlsalt supplicated a forced pleasant chuckle in the delivery with his most servile grin. He released his distaste and delivered his orders (laced with obscenities) to the troop.

Haggersath's exploratory group sat nestled in the pines, observing the same shaggy weasels at their languid guard posts. They had moved around some, but they seemed slothful.

Mevindh-Gulbard placed a hand on Haggersath's epaulet. "Jikseon varda," his deep soothing voice spoke under his breath.

He repeated for each of the band in turn, granting a blessing from Jikseon. Their armor would be harder, their hammers denser upon impact, yet lighter in the hand to strike home, and their luck guided. Yellow magic blessed the entire vanguard.

Haggersath began orders for the assault, "Grölle, you take yer ferskeyttr of Rock-Biters an' go with the Doomsayer and Diwolde Stonescraper over on the right by that white rock next to the wall. Ya should be able ta get right up next ta their stinkin' hides. I want Bolfath ta follow ya halfway with another one. The rest o' ya will stay here with me an' the Gulprąst."

The leaders looked eager to have some hammer play, finally.

CHAPTER 4

At the Mouth of the Mountain

Aferskeyttr was the elite combat unit of the Dwarrow, made up of four Rock-Biters. They were deadly effective and operated as a single unit. Even after taking losses, they lost little effectiveness making adjustments or combining with another undersized unit.

"Once we be set, Bolfath, yer boys rush in and charge 'em. That'll scare the fuzz off their faces—and when they be decidin' ta fight or run, that is when Grölle strikes."

Haggersath took a breath, enjoying the moment with a friendly smile. This was something Dwarrow relished. All parts of battle. Planning. Doing. Looting.

"Bah! I kin handle them all meself," Bolfath rumbled. "Why I—"

"*Melt me beard—what is that?!*" Grambol Doomsayer's eyes were wide, pointing to the ruins. The kvalid lay crumpled at the gate, and arrows struck those on the scaffold—they tumbled off the wall. Arrows? His company didn't equip any arrows.

He squinted, half seeing something that seemed at first like it wasn't there, and then like it was.

From the other side of the trees, they came streaking in. They were tall figures running smoothly, lightly, and astonishingly quick. Their skin was a woodland brown; they had sharp, defined features and lithe bodies that moved smoothly as trees swaying in a stormy wind. How could it be? If so, they were far from their lands. Very far. It made no sense—but it could only be.

"Sylvan!" muttered Mevindh-Gulbard. "In Tisroc?"

It was hard to calculate their true numbers with the flow of their movement and shocking speed, with them weaving about one another showing an innate and extreme natural skill. Twenty? Perhaps twenty-five? They were upon the entrance before another breath could be drawn—quick as a lightning strike!

Haggersath recovered first. "Blast ye laggards, move!" He waved his Dwarrow forward. "Fergit the plan and damn yer eyes! Go, move!"

They moved, disjointed, as a jumbled mob of twenty, completely without the sleek cohesion the

Sylvan effortlessly displayed. As different as they were, a similar determination drove the Dwarrow at the ruins. They came upon the dead kvalid just as the arrows in their bodies evaporated into whisps of gray smoke. Those who noticed gasped in uncomfortable awe. Sylvan magic! The older, more learned Dwarrow knew that those arrows had returned to the Sylvan quivers to be used again, over and over, endlessly cycling.

"Nice trick," remarked Diwolde Stonescraper.

Far less impressed were Mevindh-Gulbard and Grambol Doomsayer; they traded an uneasy glance as they spat in disgust. To Mevindh-Gulbard, theirs was an unclean magic. To Grambol Doomsayer, the Sylvan just felt all wrong. Haggersath could see them both wearing expressions of severe distaste.

Haggersath led them up through the ruins of the gate where the fallen kvalid lay. Bolfath pushed on the rotted wood panels the kvalid had lashed together in an effort to secure the ruins. The gates crumbled easily and fell to the ground.

"This be a travesty." Diwolde Stonescraper sadly observed the condition of the masonry. He walked about, looking closer. He went about touching stones and mortar like they were precious gems.

Haggersath noted the buildings inside the walls were in no better shape, half crumbled and broken.

This place had been ransacked and gutted many times over. But there—to the left side of him, north and west a bit—was a dark, looming cave entrance to the mountain itself.

Haggersath turned to Grambol Doomsayer. "Which is the path, Doomsayer? And don't tell me to follow those woodland fools into the mountain if ye like the length of yer beard."

Grambol Doomsayer shook his head, a grim, sneering smile slowly appearing. "But it be so, master Giftgiver."

"Damn yer eyes!" Haggersath's heart sank, balking at the truth, and he kicked a rock into the ruined town. Maybe it wasn't the worst of the options, since he had just noticed movement in the ruined buildings. With the stone he kicked having ricocheted about, he may have drawn unwanted attention. Then he heard them. Chittering noises assembled and responded to each other over in the rubble of crumbled buildings.

"Kvalid in the wreckage there," warned Grölle. He pointed with his hammer.

A glimpse of the rats could be seen moving in and out of the ruins. A blink of another shape closely followed—was it just a trick of the eyes, as the shadow blended with the broken masonry? Or was it one of those Sylvan who got caught away from the others?

"Go! Move now!" rumbled Haggersath, hurrying his throng toward the mountainside entrance. They would need to go to the same entrance as those blasted Sylvan. Haggersath cursed himself for kicking the rock, even though it was not what drew the kvalid their way.

He heard Dwarrow battle cries and the clash of steel off in the direction he had sent Jarlsalt.

Haggersath and Mevindh-Gulbard waited in the clearing before the cave entrance, waiting for Othro and Bolfath to come into the clearing. He saw Grölle had held up his ferskeyttr with Grambol Doomsayer and Diwolde Stonescraper, the six of them posed for battle at the mouth of the mountain.

But it wasn't Ortho's ferskeyttr nor Bolfath that broke the clearing. Haggersath's blood raced. He felt—alive, so alive. Four of the rats came chittering and waving their javelins. They did not rush them at first. "Be ready, Gulprąst."

"We stand?" Mevindh-Gulbard asked, surprised.

"Aye, we stand. We wait fer Bolfath and Ortho." He was determined not to retreat without those two and the three Rock-Biters with them. "Jarlsalt be engaged fer sure. He has the numbers ta fight back this way though."

Then the four kvalid crouched and sprang. Haggersath pulled his hammer free, and Mevindh-Gulbard his bejeweled mace.

Haggersath saw the first javelin coming and moved as it rushed past his face. He heard another clink on metal and felt its deflected shaft ricochet off the armor on his back. "Hoho," he laughed out loud.

In an instant, they were upon the two Dwarrow. A rodent stench clotted the air with the bristling greasy fur of their enemy. Haggersath dropped his hammer hard on the unprotected head of the first to reach him. Hot blood shot in a spray that splattered them both. It crumpled at his feet, falling onto Haggersath's legs. His breathing was rapid and deep, fueling his desire for battle.

All three of the other kvalid had surrounded Mevindh-Gulbard, but the Gulprąst was nobody's doormat. He held them at bay. Haggersath brought his hammer crashing into the leg of the closest to him. He heard the crack of bone splintering, and the kvalid collapsed to the dirt.

Mevindh-Gulbard's mace smashed into the collar of the one farthest away, its squeaking yelp dying in its mouth as the mace dragged through the body clean and fast as any bladed weapon might. Haggersath smiled as he brought his focus on the sole remaining kvalid on the other side of Mevindh-Gulbard. That mace, driven with added force of the yellow magic, had hit the kvalid with the strength of an ice giant.

Sharp pain shot up Haggersath's leg, and he grunted, pulling back and looking down to see the kvalid he had just laid low biting and working to gnaw on his mail-booted shin. Its broken face was twisted even more when biting with broken teeth and only half its jaw. He fell back, landing hard. He cursed himself for letting his mind wander in battle. He knew better than to take an enemy lightly. Haggersath kicked the smashed head away with his free boot, apparently landing a fatal blow. The rat lay there motionless.

He heard the crunch of Mevindh-Gulbard's mace flowing through the bones of the last kvalid. He looked back at his boot and saw no blood. Gathering himself and coming to his feet, he tested his ankle and shin. Sore but undamaged.

"There be two more comin'," Mevindh-Gulbard said in a raspy tone filled with heavy breathing.

Haggersath looked up. They were dashing out of the ruins, running at them. Looking over their furry shoulders behind, they hadn't noticed Haggersath or the Gulprąst. At that moment, it became clear what they fled to escape. With a battle roar, Bolfath came bursting out of the ruins, his twin axes raised like scythes of death out by his sides. Behind him came Othro, the formation with the three Rock-Biters of his ferskeyttr fully intact. Othro saw Haggersath and flashed a grin in recognition. Avalanche came with them, happily trotting in their midst, pinkish red staining her fine white fur. The ferskeyttr turned as one and stood while Bolfath ran his prey straight at Haggersath.

Haggersath felt his blood surging, the exhilaration of the fight, and he braced for the oncoming kvalid. He leaned back as he drew his hammer with both hands up into the chest of the rat. He meant only to graze the chest and come full force and uppercut the jaw, but he misjudged the speed and distance. His hammer bounced the kvalid off its clawed feet, and he fell backward, slamming onto the ground as he catapulted the assailant over him.

Haggersath used the momentum to continue the roll and come up on his feet, warhammer at the ready.

But the kvalid lay there, chest bloody, the cavity ripped open. Wiping the blood from his face with a forearm, he looked for more. Mevindh-Gulbard stood tall and golden-bearded over the second kvalid corpse.

Bolfath slowed to halt in front of him, looking disappointed. "Har, Haggersath. Ye owe me one. That one should be mine." He leaned on an ax that he placed headfirst on the ground while the other laid across his shoulder.

"There be more Bolfath, plenty enough fer us all," Mevindh-Gulbard said and tapped Haggersath with his mace, then pointed to where Othro had placed his ferskeyttr.

Out of the ruins they came. One dozen. Then a score. Othro had his ferskeyttr moving in an orderly retreat toward them, but at double time.

There was movement off to the left. Haggersath shifted to face the new threat, tugging on Bolfath's ogrekaru cloak to join him. Bolfath moved to the flank on Haggersath's right. Haggersath knew it was getting desperate with so many coming out from so many directions. Maybe Bolfath could handle them all, but there would likely be casualties. The kvalid came into view, bleeding and badly wounded. They fell under the hammers and short blades of Grölle's ferskeyttr. All four were present. Haggersath was relieved to see Grambol Doomsayer and Diwolde Stonescraper in the mix, looking hale but harassed.

"Form on me." His order carried like thunder across the way to them. Grölle's ferskeyttr responded and moved his direction in good order. The two members of his Haseti ran casually to join him.

"Are ye well, Giftgiver? Ye have a gimp in yer walk," Diwolde Stonescraper said, his face dripping perspiration.

Before he could answer, stepping out of the ruins where they had just come from was another dozen kvalid. This was too many. They couldn't wait for Jarlsalt. Without him, the risk was just too great.

"Fall back ta the mouth of the mountain, lads," his order came. "Do it now and do it fast. We form up ta fight just inside." He wanted to bottle up the approach and limit the attackers that could melee them. It would do more than even the odds. If the rats were foolish enough to test them there, they could slaughter them whole.

They reached the mouth of the cave, twelve Dwarrow against some forty kvalid. None of them seemed to have suffered any wounds of consequence.

It was dark in the cave, but as they turned to see their pursuers, their vision seemed enhanced. Standing in the darkness of the cavern allowed a clearer view.

Two score of kvalid were now cautiously moving to just within javelin range. Javelins launched haphazardly from the kvalid clattered about the mountain. Only one managed to make its mark and felled one of the Rock-Biters of Grölle's troop, striking through his neck. There were not many weaknesses in Dwarrow travel armor—this was true bad luck. Blood shot from the wound—the Gulprąst tended to him immediately while the other nine Rock-Biters hung back in the shadows. Diwolde Stonescraper seemed to be focused on feeling the rock wall, searching for something. He was always interested in stone, even at the oddest times.

"Yer weapon would be of more use than that blasted wall yer fondlin', Stonescraper. I be down a Dwarrow already," Haggersath said to him.

"Ye be right." Mevindh-Gulbard rose up and stood from the unmoving Rock-Biter, a regret on his kind face. "He's gone ta Hrajaar with Jikseon."

The throng of kvalid had gathered and closed on the opening. They would reach it soon. Haggersath and his company were ready for the melee, their weapons poised. According to his calculations, no more than ten at a time could fit in the entrance. That would be a crowded assault. If they stood second rank, they might bring another eight or so javelins into play. But those were short and not made to operate as pikes or long spears. Even well-trained formation warriors would incur self-casualties employing this tactic with javelins. Kvalid were entirely untrained and did not fight as a unit.

Bolfath took a wide stance, a double-bladed ax in each hand. "Ah yes! At last!" His fierceness alone caused the kvalid to hesitate.

He was flanked on either side, Haggersath on the right in his studded leather armor and a two-handed grip on his battle ax. On the left, Mevindh-Gulbard stood tall in his bright armor brandishing an ornate bejeweled mace used by those of his order. A powerful glow of yellow gold pulsed around him, making his presence indomitable, while sending a resolute spirit through the Dwarrow, stiffening the company's bones.

Out from the ruins behind the cowering kvalid stepped—a tralkvalid. It was markedly larger than its cousins. Thickly hided, bronze, scaly skin acted as its own armor. Large fangs protruded from its drooling maw even when closed, emphasizing oversized rat-like features—a hideous sight. It towered, fearsome and commanding, at nearly three meters—taller than Bolfath. Quite unlike the slender weasels it led. The tralkvalid let loose a loud, dreadful yawp, causing the Dwarrow to check their courage. This in turn emboldened the kvalid, renewing their resolve.

"That one be yers, Bolfath," said Grambol Doomsayer with a nervous grin. Haggersath couldn't argue with that logic. He was best suited to dispatch the beast.

Bolfath growled, "Come ta me an' taste me axes. Ya won' be so tall when I cut ya in pieces."

They charged the Dwarrow, the tralkvalid at an unrelenting, steady pace, allowing the smaller kvalid to lead, obviously hoping to soften up the Dwarrow. Bolfath stepped forward, arcing his right ax to strike off the extended neck of the first weasel through the entrance. He swung, and the ax bit deep.

Diwolde had ignored Haggersath's directive and did not join the battle right next to him. He instead concentrated on drawing three-fourths of an hourglass with two fingers along the wall. The rock shined a whitish silvery line where he traced. The entrance to the mountain was outlined in a flash of pale white-hot sparks, and then, as suddenly as it flashed, the rock door slammed shut and it all went dark.

The sudden gasps from a few Dwarrow and the wet clunk of a kvalid head hitting the floor were the only sounds.

Starting slowly and building into an echoing laughter, Diwolde Stonescraper filled the empty quiet. "Well, me boys, that is that," he said, sounding very pleased with himself.

Haggersath laughed in turn. "I see what ye be doin' there now. Ya found the door, did ya?"

PART
Two

CHAPTER 5

Daoine Maithe

Just being in the woods again tugged at Aieren's memory—a memory he needed to rekindle from time to time. Musty air filled with the scents of life, moss and fungus giving off the unashamed aroma of fresh growth and final decay. The full cycle of a life in a single breath of woodland essence. One feeding the other endlessly. It was supposed to be like this. Morningsong was the goddess of the wood and all things Sylvan and fae. She had made it this way. Perfect, symbiotic, and eternal.

Aieren felt the smoosh and stickiness of wet leaves, tawny on the forest floor. They made a carpet together with dew and rain that spread as far as the woods spanned. They would lie there until time took them, and then they would feed the dark, loamy soil.

He marveled at the ancient, grooved bark on the great oak trees. Here, near the forest borders, only a few of the majestic, giant oaks remained—they were cousins of the first tree, the Ancient Heart, which dwelled deeper in the forest. More common among the borders were the flaky-skinned cedars with their flat boughs spreading out for shade like little pillows in the air.

This was the Daoine Maithe, and it was Aieren's home. A light breeze came rustling through the leaves, an old friend, long missed. He breathed deep, taking in the very spirit of the forest with an effort to join with it and become as one. He belonged here.

But then his own golden skin caught his eye. It was smooth and sleek and bore no semblance of the forests. It was utterly *repellant*. Who was he deceiving? It did not belong here. He did not belong here.

He could feel and smell with those ordinary pleasantries, but the caress of magic was all but gone. It had left him, and no matter how many times he returned here and tried to reach the Daoine Maithe, it was beyond him. He sagged, losing his feigned euphoria.

Aieren was once a Sylvan. Was, but no more. His legs grew weak and limp. He could no longer stand, and he slid down, filled with agony, aching with the emptiness of a newly lost love. He knew he was not alone. There were many others that suffered the same fate. Little good that did for him. It was happening to them all. Given enough time, it would happen to all Sylvan.

He lay, face slack, in the wet leaves of the forest floor. His breathing was shallow and racked silent, private sobs. The mystical forest of Daoine Maithe was slowly retreating to ruin, and with it, the Sylvan—one by one—found their magic fading with the death of every tree. Their skin would lose its bast, its semblance to the natural beauty of tree bark. It flattened and smoothed, becoming a dull gold, the color of decaying leaves. Horrid! Just like his.

His features, too, lost their once-handsome angles and ridges to become nearly identical to the soft, plain features of the race called Man. The transformation of a divinely magical being to a simplistic creature unable to even feel the most minute flows of magic—it was a tragedy. The Sylvan race was fragmenting.

Aieren had suffered this change into being a Galean—a Sylvan who lost their sense of magic—almost completely. His frame had become thicker, heavier, and less efficient. Sylvan possessed root-strong, sinewy muscles and bones that flexed and moved as trees do, but not a Gaelean; their muscles were thick, bulging needlessly, mushy like a waterskin, and their bones inflexible and brittle, like those of Men. Aieren lamented in self-pity—his skin had lost its exquisite kinship with rich red maple bark and became *this*! He remained, face to the forest floor, more miserable than ever. He could not return to the Daoine Maithe; doing so would kill him. Then again, maybe death was a better choice. He was filled to the core with a mixture of despair and vile self-loathing.

A cedar beetle picked its way carefully along the dead leaves, foraging its way to the next deliciously sappy cedar. Even its simple life held more importance and purpose than his pathetic existence.

Breaking tree limbs nearby snapped Aieren back to the moment. Something was approaching, fast. Something very large. Aieren got up on all fours. Wet leaves stuck to his face by their sticky composting.

Suddenly, it broke through the clearing. It was a tall creature, nearly three meters high. Standing on two rather slender, heavily furred legs, it bared twisted fangs that glistened wet, jutting out of its slavering face in a jeering, permanent smile. Patchy mottled brown and umber fur, mangy and matted, exposed bright pink, rosy skin where it was thinnest. Its oversized, pointy canine ears twitched upright, hearing something Aieren could not. If he were still Sylvan, he was sure he would have heard it too.

The terrifying beast was carrying a branch stolen from an oak, a full meter long. An iron band, twisting crudely up at its edges into cruel spikes, had been hammered to the top part of the wood, making a skin-flailing, bone-breaking mace. It wore padded armor woven together from a thick hide—who could tell if it was of an animal or Man, or even a Galean.

The beast nervously looked around before fixing its gaze upon Aieren. It was hard to tell who was more shocked to see the other.

"Ogrekaru!" Aieren exclaimed under his breath.

Saliva dripped in solid streams as it leered at him. It heaved its thick, wire-haired chest, gurgling a moist wail before it sniffed the air as if to identify what Aieren was.

Just then, two more ogrekaru broke into the clearing, nearly bowling over one another. One had a crude mace just like the first, but the other carried an iron spear. Both were wounded, arrows sprouting from their bodies. The first said something to the others in guttural tones, gesturing at Aieren.

The one with the spear did not hesitate and advanced upon Aieren with quick thrusts. Its aim was off target—ogrekaru were known for their poor vision, and Aieren could still move adeptly. He was no Sylvan, but Galean still possessed amazing quickness. His gently curved kindjal was out of its scabbard with a single automatic motion. Galean had used the glaive-like kindjal since before the demise of his stricken city. It was most slender where it met the scroll-shaped guard at the hilt; from the hilt, it expanded, curving up sharply to a weighty end with a long curl to the tip—designed for deep slicing. It was a formidable blade; when sheathed at the hip, it hung just over halfway down his calf. Naked steel gave Aieren confidence, despite the odds.

And the odds were certainly against him. Aieren would be hard-pressed facing even one ogrekaru, but three? Even with two of them wounded, it would be a challenge. Twisting to the side of the attacker, he slashed an off-balance cut at its outstretched arm. He felt the blade slicing through the fur and muscle, meeting a stop as it chipped into the bone. Black blood released and stained his silvery kindjal. It was slick and thick.

The ogrekaru drew back its wounded arm, slowed for the moment. He could not pause. Not with two more. Aieren continued spinning to the side, trying to avoid the rush of the other two, but his speed failed him. A Sylvan would have the speed and grace to make the move easy. But he was just Galean, and he stumbled. The pressure on his shoulder shot a shock of pain all along his arm, tingling so that he loosened his grip on the kindjal, almost losing the blade. The follow-through of the mace that had just glanced off his shoulder sent him airborne, spinning. Even just a grazing blow from the ogrekaru was enough to send him crashing into a stout cedar—pain washed through his back, white light flashing in his mind. Ogrekaru were tremendously strong creatures. He lay against the tree, unable to regain his breath.

"Dean deifur," someone called out in the clear, melodious Sylvan tongue—it was almost like singing. It called him back from being stunned, and he focused, seeing the three ogrekaru hastily advancing upon him. The Sylvan cries came closer, making the ogrekaru look over their heavy, wire-haired shoulders.

Arrows ripped through the air, striking the ogrekaru. One found the neck of the ogrekaru that had just hit him with its bladed mace, and it fell back, clutching its pierced neck with a taloned hand as black blood gushed down under its pelted armor. It let out a gurgling noise, and then it went to its knees, finishing with a thudding faceplant. Another arrow found its way through the padded armor into the left shoulder of the spear-wielder. It would have knocked the surprised ogrekaru to the forest floor, had it not used the spear butt to catch its fall. Two more swift, dark Sylvan arrows flew right through its back, and it went down with a breathy, heavy sigh. It lay still with its horrible grin falling slack.

The ogrekaru that had first found him panicked and turned with a leap to make an escape. Aieren's head had nearly cleared, so he bounded up and rushed after it—but with magic-driven swiftness, several Sylvan swept in ahead of him. Three of the lithe, bark-skinned protectors of the wood overtook the beast before Aieren could close. He felt the hotness of his shoulder, reminding him of the wound from the cruel mace. He was just close enough to see their long knives flashing, eviscerating the ogrekaru almost instantly. It collapsed on the forest floor, its pelt lying in scraps, lifeless from a hundred or more cuts. After only a few moments, the arrows evaporated into wisps of gray smoke.

It was then that they gave notice of Aieren. Smiling among themselves, they laughed gaily. "Tá dearmad déanta ag an bhforaois ort, Galean." They spoke in the Sylvan language, that much he knew, but Aieren could no longer understand Sylvan. The magic it took to work the language had all but drained away.

All three of the Sylvan were slender as the woods themselves. Such beauty made him envious all over, with their skin in woodland tones of trees, holding deep, hard textural contours like tree bark. With the battle finished, their skin slowly relaxed and became smoother, reverting to a memory of bark. It retained the same color that it had when they were in "battle-skin."

The hard bark-skin was as effective as mail and served as armor. Their hair was leaflike instead of falling in strands, with one green as new spring and the others radiating the vast shades of seasons into the growth of summer and the bounty of autumn.

The tallest one spoke to him in the clear common talk that all intelligent creatures learned easily from their earliest years. "Are you lost, Galean? This is the Daoine Maithe; there is no city for your kind here. This forest expelled you when you became unworthy—and by your look, that was quite some time ago." He held just enough smugness to make it clear the question needed no answer.

The other male sneered at him; he was not as tall but carried himself with the bearing of a lord of some importance. "Your stench was noticed half a league away, befouling our precious wood. We thought it was only the ogrekaru, but now it is apparent that it was you, an outcast. However, we are not without compassion. Since you once had grace, we will allow you to leave unmolested. But this offer expires with the wind. You should go now." He went to clean the black blood off of his long knives.

The female stepped in front of the two, her ashen-skinned arm forward, warding them from him. She intervened before Aieren could reply. "Be kind to him,

Belusan, Rommaith. Your own fates could follow in his tragic footsteps. The magic fades, and the forest will follow, as we have seen. In time, all Sylvan are destined for this fate." She said this with a voice of silvery beauty. It had been longer than he could remember since hearing the siren effects of a female fae speaking.

Aieren's face was twisted with seething odium. He knew their veiled insults. Her decency should have calmed him, but he let the gouging words sting. He shot back at the others, "You'd best listen to her wisdom. I am Aieren of Galee, a High Sylvan of the Daoine Maithe. This mistreatment and express slights I will not suffer without recourse. Know this: I will exact my due respect from your arrogant brown skins." Aieren brandished his curved kindjal, still bloody, with expert skill. He positioned to attack the largest of the Sylvan.

"Hold your blade, Aieren of Galee." The female spoke in a calming yet firm intonation. "Do not provoke Rommaith." She gestured at the larger of the two Sylvan, who seemed more inclined to engage him than listen to her. "We will escort you to the border of the wood so you may make your way back to Galee. This is no longer your place, no matter your former station."

Aieren pondered her offer. Rommaith seemed as tall as an oak, with powerful shoulders thick as some trees' trunks. His skin was now starting to turn to bark once more. He fingered his scian in its sheath. Leaning with an eagerness toward Aieren, his brown eyes blazed intensely. He let out a snort and seemed to contemplate whether to listen to the female or kill Aieren.

CHAPTER 6

Morningsong

The wind whipped up, drawing their attention as a gentle whirl began circling around Aieren. Then it moved purposefully away from him to the center, between Aieren and the Sylvan. The leaves rustled, and the slender cedar nearby swayed as if in a dance. It shook off the beetles that had gnawed upon it, making it both a feast and a home. It slowly took on a slight, delicate female shape. An essence surrounded the image with red, blue, and purple, shimmering between colors as it moved. She looked neither Sylvan nor Galean, but both all at once. The rustle settled, and the feminine tree spoke to them, a voice on the wind carried from afar. Distant and faint—yet clear as one spoken plainly in front of them.

> *"Be at peace, children of the wood, and*
> *fear me not. For I am Morningsong, and*
> *you are my children."*

Aieren felt a pang of longing pull at his chest. The lump in his throat grew to seize his breath. Morningsong! The goddess of all Sylvan. He sweated and felt his knees buckle; he fell to them before her.

The Sylvan had ceased paying attention to him and appeared to be struck with awe, for they all knew her to be who she claimed. She gathered their attendance as she continued.

> *"I will tell you the making of the*
> *world. For only the gods truly know the*
> *tale. Stories you may have heard by your*
> *counsels or elders bear some truth. What*
> *I say now is what was and is, for I was*
> *there, and I was of the making. I created*
> *you, my Sylvan children."*

Aieren could not look away; she held him to her. But he was not Sylvan, not anymore. He felt the lump in his throat suffocate him, and he could not breathe. Morningsong focused on him, a faint purple glow in her fair smile. She, for only a moment, flickered as a Galean. He understood then. He was included. All Galean were her children. The Sylvan did not seem to see the change as their reverence for her awaited her words.

> "When the world was complete, and the gods had been formed of the Sun. We were equals. We knew we were expected to populate and take custody of this world of Thear. We were five. First was Bruss. He was made of the yellow of the Sun, and he drew from the waters his children, whom he named Man. Much as he preferred to be, they lived on the land but loved water. It was a simple thing he made, but it was good.

> "Next came Jikseon. He was of red and yellow, having contrast rather than a single color of focus. He was rash and made the Dwarrow to rise up from the land, like stone and metals. They are harsh creatures and were made without thought.

> "I did not come with impatience as Jikseon did. I wanted more for my Sylvan than Bruss made for Man. I have both red and blue magic. They had not touched the blue, as they have no claim on it. Using

a delicate hand, I made from the wood, you—beautiful specimens of superior quality, the Sylvan. Your powers are far vaster than the singularity of the other races. You are my children."

Aieren saw her wipe a tear from her eye, so moved. He noticed the Sylvan bowed their faces to the floor in reverence. He caught a tear in the female's eye, streaming into the grassy dirt she kneeled in.

"Now, Christiemay said to me, 'What a divine race you have made. I can do no better in quality than you have shown, sister. So, let it be in quantity that I will flourish.' She created all the other creatures to populate the land. 'And they shall have many tasks. They will feed your peoples, but they will feast upon them as well. They will be useful to the renewal and the lives of all who live upon the lands. But they will exact a price. Theirs is as one being, though they are very many more than all other races.'

Christiemay was always wise in seizing an understanding of need, and she was wise in her choice."

Morningsong paused. She motioned with her slender wood-like arm, gesturing to the west. She shook her head sadly as she nodded, seeming to understand something she was about to reveal. Aieren became a little nervous seeing her change in approach. She was hard now. Like petrified wood, her face became sharper and angular, marring her beauty.

The silence after was a contemplative one. The Sylvan seemed to understand something more from the goddess's dissertation. Aieren had never known such an intimate relation to not only his own creation but all the other beings of Thear. Each of the gods had considered their creations greater than the last. But Aieren thought Morningsong had said five. Only four had created their races.

> "Aieren Rioga, you listen with a full ear. Noshid had not yet spoken nor made a creation to fill his heart. But he was of solely red magic, which is short of patience and quick to act. He was raging and spoke with the heat of anger burning his words. 'Forgetting me, my brothers and sisters, in your pomposity will be your undoing.' He was callous and called on us siblings with hate-filled anger. He addressed his grievances to us each in turn.

"'You leave me little, Christiemay, by taking so many creations to yourself. Because of this, I gather strength from your realm of the air and leave it as befouled as your selfishness makes me now.'

"He faced Jikseon next. 'My brother, you share the red magic. You, most of all, should have known better. I am fire, and I will scorch your rock and melt it to my bidding.'

"Looking at the creator of Man, he did not soften his tone. 'For you, Bruss, your waters will boil and dry up.'

"Then he lowered his fiery eyes upon me. 'Because of your hubris, Morningsong, yours will suffer the most. I will take special care to burn your woods with great glee and leave the charred remains as reminders for you to contemplate your worth.'

"Then he swept the fire over the waters and through the air, burning the wood upon western Thear, and creatures died while the waters boiled and the bitter *remains formed into his creation, the Gnomôk.*

"'My Gnomôk will be like me. They will shun your kind without trust. Their thoughts will be as mine, and they will forever hunt and be a bane upon your peoples.'"

Morningsong stopped again. It was as if grief had gripped the goddess. Aieren, too, was rigid with fear. Now he understood why the Gnomôk were full of wanton destruction. He had never seen one before, but he had heard stories of their persistent malevolence through the ages.

He became aware of the biggest of the Sylvan, Rommaith, punching his fist to the ground and speaking in his tongue. The other two tried to calm the great warrior, who had gone bark-skin for battle. Morningsong brought them back. Her voice had moved to a cold resolution.

"His act and creation were purely of anger and malice. Such blind bitterness was unknown to us until this act. Pure had been the Sun, dazzling with yellow magic emanating from its face and seeping the beauty of red and blue under its

golden blaze. But the evil that had now been spewed could not be withdrawn, and the Sun became blemished with patches of blackness. Its beauty was darkened.

"The shadowy spots appeared like sorrowful eyes, a grudge painted forever on its face. The darkness stirred with an evil maliciousness that weaved slowly within the stain. The Sun itself felt fury, affronted by the pain Noshid caused. The Sun, his altruistic creator, lashed out at Noshid. Raw as the Sun's core itself— the core of magic. Noshid's mind split— broke—and he was slung forth as a comet into Thear. He was cast to where he had made the destruction. Thus was created the Desert of Cinders.

"We feared the proclamations of Noshid. Christiemay foresaw the strife coming to their combined peoples. They would need our protection in their own hands.

"Bruss watched as Jikseon and I each began to work in our own fashion, investing our powers into something tangible. Bruss said to them, 'Come, let *us join together. We each alone are mere equals to Noshid. Together, we may make a thing beyond his ability and influence, something with which our children may fight back against his threats, for I can see in his wrath a coming terror.'*

"We joined together, pouring much of our power into the base of Thear, land of their creations. From the wood and air and rock and water we drew, forming a great crystalline Stone. Bruss, Jikseon, and I filled the item with raw force— yellow, red, and blue was the magic— leaving us drained and lesser than before. But Christiemay did this with restraint, holding back and steering, directing the forces to synergize into a greater power. At last, we stood back and looked in satisfaction at our creation. It appeared as a great jewel with many facets—flawless in every way. Blue and yellow light flickered in every face, glimmering with scant hints of red. It was truly glorious. The Destiny Stone."

It was a wonder, Aieren thought. A Stone with the power of the gods themselves, created for use by the peoples of Thear. For the peoples of the Daoine Maithe. For the peoples of Galee! He was too embroiled in his musing to notice the Sylvan. But Morningsong was not finished.

> "His evil had lingered on the Sun. It was now its own entity. From the blackness on the Sun, wispy dark fingers traced out with criminal speed, grasping the Destiny Stone. Taking us by surprise, we knew our peril as it seized the Stone in front of us. We three who poured much of our essence out in the making were unable to react. But Christiemay was still with much of her power and did not need to recover, yet she did nothing. She held back as we three did in diminished weakness and let the evil grasp the Stone. We saw the three shadows come and sweep it away, taking it to Thear, covering its light into obscurity and hiding the Destiny Stone from us."

She smiled at them. Aieren could not understand her smile. The Destiny Stone was gone. Apparently even the gods knew not where. There was no hope. This was terrible. To know there was an answer to save himself, to save Galee from this fate they had suffered, then only to have it torn away—it was devastating.

> *"I come to you now because the Daoine Maithe is in peril. It is dying, and the magic that has sustained it by my hand is failing. Noshid's legacy upon the Sun is coming into play.*
>
> *"We have made the Destiny Stone to salvage our creations. The Destiny Stone can bring change. It may perpetuate life. It can restore. Before we could resolve our individual desires for the purpose of the Destiny Stone, it was swept away and hidden by an undefined malice, the unwanted aberration that stains the Sun. While the Sun is the source of all magic and responsible for the creation of all things, including the gods, it is not indestructible. The black spots are eroding the Sun, slowly. In the hands of the chosen, the Destiny Stone may have the power to reconcile the blight."*

Aieren and the Sylvans listened in a trance, bewitched by the beautiful tree.

"The time for renewal is at hand. I know where to find the Destiny Stone. It has been revealed to all the gods, and I am not alone in this awareness.

Bruss, the father of all Man, knows. He is slow to move and is yet unconcerned, but he will find urgency in time. He would use the Destiny Stone to flow the waters and reascend the storms that impinge his Man.

"Jikseon, who made the Dwarrow from the mountain rock, is already working his way through his stubborn peoples. He would take the power for his Dwarrow and imbue the power of the gods into their crafting, with work in metal and stone.

"Christiemay lingers in the background, watching, as is her tendency. She will not reveal her hand openly and lays cunning traps with unequaled subtlety. Her agents meddle on her behalf, attempting to influence the other races to do her bidding, much as she once played her games with the gods.

"Finally, Noshid, though cast down and diminished in power, also seeks the Destiny Stone. He would use it to destroy all we hold precious. He must not be first to gain the Destiny Stone. He cares not for his Gnomôk, for they are expendable tools he employs in a pointless vengeance.

"While he is responsible for the formation of the taint upon the Sun, it seems to be beyond his control and of its own malicious will."

Morningsong paused, allowing them to think on what she purveyed to them. Then she turned specifically to Aieren.

"Aieren Rioga of Galee, it is you whom I appoint to bear the Destiny Stone to the Daoine Maithe and bring forth its power, for you were a Sylvan of high nobility before the fall of Galee."

Still transfixed, Rommaith curled a lip like he had swallowed something sour. He began to rise to his feet. The female looked confused and tugged at Rommaith's sleeve to get him to kneel again.

Belusan shook his head in disbelief. "No. It cannot be a Galean."

But Morningsong was their deity, and the goddess seized them with red flows of magic. Her kind face held a look stern like the roots of the first tree.

Her voice roared with the crescendo of shrill fae, trilling,

> "Do not doubt my commands. For I am supreme, and I alone hold your fates and that of the mystic wood in the palm of my hand."

The three shrank back, demure and submissive. Aieren did not feel the assault her voice brought upon the Sylvan, but he saw the effect as Rommaith crumpled to his knees. They fell with their faces to the ground.

> "Glenia Fìor-ghlan, Belusan Qûm-hachdach, and Rommaith Glè-luath shall escort and guard Aieren Rioga, the Galean, through his quest. It is he to whom I leave the fate of Daoine Maithe, and the fate of all Sylvan.
>
> "Be wary and do not think lightly about your course. The Destiny Stone lies in the ruins of the fallen Dwarrow dwelling Krath. It is guarded and will not be given

forth lightly. Aieren will know the way,
for I have shown him."

She touched his face with a gentle hand, and he felt calm. He felt the flow of magic course through him. It was not as if he remembered magic though. This was foreign. It opened his senses. He saw more clearly— and at a great distance. His sense of smell allowed the woods to fill his lungs. He felt the moss on the edge of the air as he inhaled. His skin was more aware of the slickness of water he could not see in the air. He heard Rommaith's heavy breathing as if it were his own. He was Galean no more. His Sylvan grace had returned, but he was not whole. He was not fully restored. It was enough for now. A taste. A tease. But he welcomed it.

When she withdrew her hand, he slumped and felt a loss. It was still there, but not as present or full as when Morningsong's touch was upon him. He understood her meaning. The Destiny Stone could provide what she showed him, permanently. It was the quest he must pursue, not only for himself, but for all Sylvan and Galean.

> *"Rise up, Aieren of Galee. Do not lament. There is no time for such indulgences. You have the initiative. I have struck first, but the other gods will follow and send their champions to seek out the Destiny Stone. Be swift and you will emerge triumphant."*

Aieren rose to meet her warm smile with his own melancholy thoughts lingering.

> *"Take these mounts. They are fervently loyal and fly like the wind. Now go and win this Race to Destiny."*

Singing a divine note toward the depths of Daoine Maithe, Morningsong called forth swirling colors, a nacreous red and blue that formed into shapes of four majestic unicorns stomping and stamping their hooves, causing shimmering blue and red sparks to fly like showers of glamor. The air crackled with a snap that echoed like a leather strap slapped against a hardwood board, and with that, the colors vanished, and the cedar was standing tall and alone. Morningsong was gone; the unicorns remained.

CHAPTER 7

Aieren Rioga

"We are touched by the goddess," the smaller male Sylvan said in apparent wonderment, his eyes open as wide as his mouth. Belusan was his name, Aieren thought. Yes, that was it. As if he was aware of his two long knives glistening wet with blood so dark it could be mistaken for black, Belusan wiped them on the fur coat of the nearest ogrekaru and sheathed them in the tough leaf retainers that were strapped at his hips.

Aieren was still experiencing the rush of his senses. Colors brighter, clearer—almost like waking up from a hazy nightmare.

"We have been granted such a great gift." Glenia smiled, her leafy mane shining both pink and green in the Sun. Yes, he remembered her name too. He could smell the elderberry scent upon her skin. It radiated over him faintly, delicate on the breeze. Time would be needed to get used to his enhanced senses again.

"So, what has this got to do with that useless brute over there?" resentfully asked Rommaith, pointing at Aieren with an accusing finger. He knew the harsh voice. For a Sylvan, it was not the usual pleasant notes of the woods but the loud creaking of wood under too much stress.

"Are you deaf, you oaken oaf?" Aieren stopped suddenly in mid-speech. They all were staring at him in some sort of disbelief. He was speaking Sylvan— the others had been speaking Sylvan—and he understood! His hand drew through his dark honey-blonde hair, letting it drop back past his wide, muscular shoulders. Understanding rushed in as a shock wave. So then, there was more to the touch Morningsong had laid upon him. He was by no means Sylvan, but he was changed.

"How?" Twisting up his sharp features, making him look angry, Belusan asked, "How do you know what we said?" His tenor carried no hint of anger though.

"I d-don't know." Aieren was as shaken as they were. He had replied in Sylvan yet again. "It happened when the goddess touched me." He let the words out without thinking. He was too busy staring at his golden forearms, turning them and searching for features of the arbor and finding only Galean.

Belusan said the obvious, "It is power Morningsong granted. It must be." He shook his pale green leaves like he was not really wanting to accept it. "We are charged by the goddess of the wood to escort and guard this... this Galean." Belusan nodded to them, expressing most of his attention on Rommaith. "It is repugnant, I agree. She has levied a queer fate on us all."

"Let us go then. She did stress urgency," Glenia said. Aieren could see her smiling with a curious anxiousness when he caught her eying the unicorns moving around playfully with each other.

Rommaith was grumbling, and then said, "Why? I have no need to follow this golden fool outside the Daoine Maithe. I am Rommaith Glè-luath. My family is akin to the Ancient Heart. I do not think she meant for us to go beyond the borders of our wood." He stood, imposing as ever, rooted.

Belusan looked at him with curiosity, like he had to sort out what he was hearing. He brushed at the forest-green tunic tied with a pale hemp rope. "You're not going?"

"Go if you wish, youngsters." He shook his head. "You have not seen what is beyond the Daoine Maithe.

There is nothing for us out there." He patted his chest with a large, heavy hand. "I will not go."

Aieren was astounded at the stubborn oak warrior. He had been commanded by Morningsong herself, and yet he would not do her bidding. He did not like this Sylvan. Something about him was feeling all wrong.

"Really, Rommaith?" Glenia took her attention from the unicorns, turning her head over her shoulder and laughing with a pretty smile. "You are afraid to go outside?"

"No." He almost took a step like she had slapped him. "I don't see a reason…I am needed in the northern homestead. My sire is an alternate for the Aìte Longotahce chair on the Council of the Leaf."

Aieren knew the Council of the Leaf. It governed the Daoine Maithe. His own uncle was the Galean chair of the council.

Glenia now turned to face Rommaith. "Your father, and an alternate at that." She mused a teasing look at him. "Oh Rommaith. An adventure. You would be doing the will of the goddess. Wait until he hears you were selected by Morningsong to lead her own quest to save the Daoine Maithe."

Rommaith now nodded slowly. "Yes. That would be something to fit the standing of our family." He began to smile.

Belusan looked to Glenia with a frown. "Who said that he was to lead—"

She shushed him with a wave of her hand. "If we manage to get into trouble, who will keep us safe?" She gestured with the back of her hand to Belusan. "Belusan, you are skilled in blue magic and illusion. You are dangerous fighting one on one. But in a pitched battle? He can fight many enemies at one time."

Rommaith was listening. Aieren was rather amused. She was good. She had him nearly convinced.

Glenia smirked with a laugh. "You can't expect our Galean to fight anything more than a frantic deer, can you? You saved him once already from the ogrekaru."

Now Aieren felt hot embarrassment. This just was not true. It was not necessary. Rommaith was already convinced. It was only worse when his enhanced hearing caught Belusan's snickering.

"Yes. You are right. I will lead you," Rommaith conceded. "But I am not a fool. You and Belusan did most of the fighting to save the Galean's worthless hide."

Aieren let the big warrior vent. Much as he disliked him, Rommaith might be worth the distasteful prejudice he brandished like a scian.

Lightening the mood, Glenia called out, "Look at them. Aren't they just a wonder of the goddess?" She was standing in the midst of blue and red sparkles cast off of the manes of the four unicorns. Their bodies shifted from a base of silvery white pearl essence to ripples of blue and red, sometimes seeming purple.

Belusan had joined her, reaching out and caressing them as they moved in circles, prancing as if on display. Much like horses in every way, they had their alicorn on the forehead equally distant between the eyes and the ears.

They played with the two younger Sylvan, the youngsters running and tagging a unicorn, then the unicorn would chase and frolic until it had come and tagged a Sylvan with the nuzzle of its stately nose. They did this until each had paired up and quickly mounted.

Belusan rode with a graceful swiftness only some Sylvan could attain. Rommaith chose the largest one the others had left for him.

"Galean! Move!" shouted Belusan over his shoulder, his voice light, and he was off. Rommaith was immediately on his heels.

Glenia looked with disapproving resentment at Aieren. "They are friendly. Do not be afraid. Besides, if you do not mount up, we will be too far behind to catch them."

He was still trying to put it all together. He was changed only a matter of perhaps an hour ago. He was struggling with the new sensations of life all around him.

He would have welcomed it before all this happened. In the forest when he was wandering, reminiscing of the wonders of being Sylvan. Now, here it was—at least in part—but even partially restored, it was not...not what he remembered it being.

But that was not all. He had seen—no, spoken with Morningsong. A goddess. His patron deity. She had given him a quest to save the Daoine Maithe. It was too much.

A Destiny Stone. Dwarrow ruins. Gods and champions.

He was only Aieren, the Galean. The son of an important Galean. But nonetheless merely a Galean. What was he doing here?

Glenia brought him back. "Galean!"

He flummoxed around, not sure of what she had said. He was dimly aware that she had been talking to him. "Take charge and let us be off," she said. He looked at her dumbly. "I said those things to Rommaith so he would come with us. I know you are the leader. Now, lead!"

He thought it a strange thing for her to say, but before he could sort anything else out, the unicorn behind him took charge of the problem. It kneeled down behind him and slipped headfirst under him and between his legs, careful not to gore him. Then it rushed forward with a gentle, skillful lunge. Aieren found himself sliding onto its back, and they were off before he could steady himself.

He gripped the white mane, which sparkled with some red but mostly blue glittering flashes. Only true magic could achieve how his unicorn flew like the wind as he caught up to the others.

There was no speaking as they rode. Aieren tried—he had so many questions, and these Sylvan seemed to have better understood the confusing dissertation the deity had delivered. But the blowing air swept all his words away. Sparkling trails of blue and red intermeshed, leaving a mystical stream behind the four riders.

The unicorns did not need direction; they knew their path. Attempting to steer them, he found, would only distract them and slightly hinder their progress. Urgency was the one thing Aieren understood without any doubt. Morningsong wanted action, now.

Restoration of the Daoine Maithe was another factor that caught his attention. What she meant exactly was unclear. Did this artifact, the Destiny Stone, have the power to restore the entirety of the Daoine Maithe? Would it even cover the expanse of Galee to the north and west? That would triple the size of the wood as it stood now. Would it reclaim the Plains of Sorka, where those rat-like kvalid now dwelled (when they weren't thieving and infesting other lands)? If it infringed upon the Desert of Cinders, it could mean the Daoine Maithe would cover everything from the desert to the Silfr Mountains, and east to the Jade Bay. What a wondrous realm that would be! Sylvan magic would once again rule the land of Thear.

When the forest broke and the land opened, it was to an endless, flat plain covered with tall, dark-green grasses. The Plains of Sorka. It stretched for thirty leagues in every direction from its center. The Rotte Hojle sat at the center of the plain like a festering anthill, spilling forth an endless stream of kvalid. They spread through the lands faster than the races of Thear could expel or extinguish.

Horses would be slowed by the tall thickets, but not the unicorns. They moved without difficulty at an unworldly speed that transcended the terrain. Did their hooves actually touch the ground? It didn't seem so—the ride was smooth as well as fast.

Over the Plains of Sorka they glided, its vastness quickly being swept away. They were only perhaps an hour from the Daoine Maithe when Aieren suffered weary pangs of hunger. When had he last eaten? When had he last slept? He could not think or remember while clinging to a speeding unicorn. He strove on in spite of his Galean frailties.

CHAPTER 8

The Plains of Sorka

"Stop. I need a break," Aieren said, using what he imagined was a commanding voice.

His unicorn shook its head, sending showers of colored sparks off its gloriously long white mane, and slowed its pace. The others followed suit as a single unit, slowing and stopping as one at his command. Aieren let out a breath of relief. He was not used to the strain of riding.

Riding the unicorns was easy at first. They took all the responsibility of keeping their riders on their backs, making it almost effortless. Still, even a smooth, easy ride like this wore upon him. He dismounted.

Rounding her unicorn back to Aieren, Glenia asked, "Why have we stopped?" Her voice was stern, and she frowned at Aieren, scrunching up her petite ash-tree features. "Krath is more than a day off, even with these glorious chargers." She relaxed her expression some. "Is something amiss, Galean?"

"I need to rest and eat," said Aieren. His plain, matter-of-fact manner caught the attention of the Sylvan. "Call me Aieren, please."

"What is the delay?" came Rommaith's deep, rich question. He looked tall and quite at home upon the large unicorn stamping its front hooves, reflecting its rider's impatience.

"The Galean says he needs to eat and rest." Glenia was biting back an amused smile.

She and Belusan clicked their respective tongues, sharing a look before each casting their own version of a disdainful look Aieren's way. Rommaith just glowered at the delay.

"Oh yes. I forget your kind must be nourished often." Belusan snickered at him.

"Aieren," Aieren said once again.

Magic sustained the Sylvan. Eating was only an occasional need.

"As you wish." Belusan tossed a sack full of large acorns to Aieren.

He made a clumsy attempt to catch it but missed; it landed with a thud at his feet. He opened the bag curiously, looking at the tree seeds. Biting into one, he gagged and spat it on the ground. Its bitterness curled up his tongue and nearly closed his throat, causing him to choke spasmodically. Near-hysterical laughter broke out among the Sylvan. He glared at them.

Once Aieren recovered his composure, he stalked away to forage out something more palatable. He had not thought the trip through. The Sylvan of course kept a bag of acorns or pinecones, as he had when he was Sylvan. But they would need no other food to sustain them.

But he, now a Galean, needed to eat regularly, like those of the Mannish race. He did not think to gather food and was never really given a chance to by the three Sylvan. Eating acorns was fine before, but he never really tried to do it once he became Galean. There were no more trees in Galee. Aieren remembered the beautiful maple woods that had once made Galee the envy of the Daoine Maithe. That was all gone now. He was hungry, and it gnawed at him. He had to eat.

Aieren had a difficult time scrounging around in the tall grass. Its leaves were sometimes sharp, and he was getting tiny cuts here and there. He heard the Sylvan lounging and singing harmoniously as he struggled.

If the mission was so important, why had Morningsong chosen him, a fallen Sylvan? He was so…uncouth. Why not Glenia? She was beautiful and graceful. Or why not Belusan? He was of noble stock and bore the true features of the glory of the Sylvan. He could tell by their tree heritage that both Glenia and Belusan were from the forest town Mulńntirna na Ban-dia deep in the heart of the forest. This was where the least regression had happened. The power of the wood was still strong in Mulńntirna na Ban-dia. Why would Morningsong not choose one from where her sway was strongest?

Or why not that great behemoth of a warrior, Rommaith? He was obviously from the old stock of the northern city of Aìte Longotahce, the center of Sylvan creation. He claimed to be a direct descendant of the Ancient Heart. The first tree was mere footsteps from the city—but no place was more in danger of losing its magic and becoming a wasteland as Galee had. The retracting woods closed on the city with every turn of the seasons.

But, no, Morningsong had chosen him. Why him? He never felt less worthy, less a Sylvan, than he was now. His form had grown. He was slower than any Sylvan. He—

Aieren saw a movement ahead and struck fast as he could with the smaller hunting knife from his belt. But he was too slow, and the pair of rabbits made their escape into the grasses.

"Damn my golden skin." He sat, hungry and dejected, a long time without a thought other than his personal misery.

Aieren was interrupted by a touch on his neck and over his shoulder, a slimy arm curling around his neck. He grabbed as fast as his Galean dexterity let him and pulled the snake's neck away, the flicking tongue close enough to touch his nose. The coils closed around his neck and began to strangle him. His eyes bulged as the snake began to squeeze, but his free hand still held the knife. Choking, Aieren rammed the blade up through the gullet of the snake's head, and it protruded through the top of the hissing, scaly mouth. It released its grip, falling limp. He moved and dumped the heavy coils from him.

He returned with the snake over his shoulder, as well as three leathery eggs he found from the nest he had been sitting next to when wallowing in self-pity (no wonder the snake assailed him). Holding it up like a trophy, he asked, "Who will make a fire? I did the hunting."

Squeamish looks reminded Aieren that when Sylvan did eat, which was rare, they ate only the produce of the trees and their growths. Meat was something he acquired a taste for as a Galean.

Nobody moved, behaving as if Aieren did not exist. Aieren huffed in displeasure, then gathered and piled some brush and varied dead branches that littered the Plains of Sorka. They were bones of the trees that once filled this place—a reminder of the once-great forest now forgotten by the lands. Aieren struck a flint against the stone he carried to spark a fire. After several tries, however, the brush failed to catch.

Exasperated by his helplessness, Glenia tilted her hand at the wrist without speaking a single word. A red flame flicked from her hands and ignited the piled brush. Aieren had to jump back to avoid being burned. He conveyed appreciation and irritation equally in the dark look he cast at her.

The Sylvan moved upwind of the fire to avoid the smell of Aieren's cooking. While the Sylvan kept their distance, Aieren ate with gusto, garnering malevolent glares from the haughty trio. He did not care. Once eating had been a rare intrusional need. But now it had become a pleasure. When he first felt the Galean need to eat, it made him vexed. All this time to do something just to maintain energy and life. But it grew on him. He enjoyed the taste of the food. The texture and actual mastication of his food brought delight. Creamy foods, those with a decided crunch or a resistant chew—this was the pleasure of eating.

He smiled to himself as he ate. The Sylvan did not own the best of everything in life. Ha! This was good. It may not taste as good as other food he had learned to eat, but it brought a satisfaction he craved.

Once finished, he stretched out on the grassy plain to catch a few hours' rest. He was tired, and the full belly made his weariness a need to be sated next. He closed his eyes. He listened to the Sylvan speaking as he waited for sweet sleep to take him.

"Must we sit and wait for this lout?" complained Rommaith.

Belusan's smooth, youthful, well-paced diction said, "We could strap him on his unicorn."

The suggestion was as absurd as it sounded. Glenia surprised him by not finding it funny.

Rommaith looked at him blankly. "You think that would work?"

Now Glenia smiled and shook her head so the gathering of her long green and ruddy pink leaves dashed back and forth. "No. Of course not, Rommaith."

"His voracious masticating echoes over the entire Plain of Sorka," said Belusan as he made a brushing sound with his hands. "It should likely draw every hungry mouth for fifteen leagues."

"It is impossible to imagine he was once Sylvan. I doubt he can be renewed, as the goddess implied,"

Glenia muttered in disgust. "But liable with him we are—and by divine citation. We are Sylvan and will endure. Think of this creature we guide as I do: an abused, discarded animal. It makes his ill manner easier to forgive."

The others nodded. Aieren was too spent to rise and engage, but her words bit into his soul. It was the truth, at its core. Morningsong had forgotten the Galean. He had become crude, even to his own distaste. He should have asked her about returning to being a Sylvan. It was his own fault. He was flawed.

Aieren drifted into fitful sleep. His dreams were filled with thoughts of impending danger—it was dark on the plain, and he smelled rats in the weeds— as Aieren's senses as a Sylvan were restored in the dreamworld. Some things, when you dreamed, were just the way you wanted them. He could smell the rats more than he could hear them, and he became acutely alert when they approached the circle of unaware Sylvan. He tried to rouse them, set them to alarm. But they scoffed at him, telling him he was unreasonable, going back to singing silly songs that brought out their fairy laughs—high pitched and quite annoying to anyone not Sylvan. He used to love that laughter, but now it evoked only deep resentment.

Some things, when you dreamed, were never the way you wanted them.

Crude javelins used by kvalid rained down on the singing Sylvan, piercing all three with multiple wounds. They fell, gasping, to the ground—Belusan's eyes were open and lifeless, and Rommaith rolled in painful anger, thrashing like a wounded beast.

Glenia reached out to him, her big, pleading eyes coaxing him, "Aieren…come..."

Her lips were so close he could feel her breath on his cheek. He had to save her, but how?

It was such a distant voice. He wanted to rise and help, but he was slow and weak, unable to move. Glenia was struck in the head by a stone ax. Blood gushed from her as her body fell lifeless, dead, on top of him.

Rommaith, bleeding from many wounds, knocked Glenia unceremoniously aside and kicked Aieren hard in the ribs. "Get up or I'll leave you to die—I won't carry you!"

CHAPTER 9

Rommaith Glè-luath

Aieren looked dazed even as his eyes opened from sleep.

"Get up—we need to go now!" said Rommaith, standing over him, his great reddish-brown mane draping into his face as he leaned over to get the useless Galean up. He hoisted Aieren to his feet with one great powerful arm, forcing the last of Aieren's sleep to leave him.

"Let's get to moving. There are kvalid prowling the grass here, everywhere," said Belusan with smooth precision, sweeping his hands over to emphasize and halting at each point to signal out the locations where nothing was obvious.

Aieren moved to his unicorn, who still shimmered with blue and red dust. The Sylvan each leaped gracefully in a single, unified motion to the backs of their unicorns, and they were off at a magically augmented gallop.

Aieren's quick mount and departure seemed clumsy by Rommaith and the other Sylvan's standards, but in truth, he was swift and smooth. Rommaith noted the stars as he led the trio behind him—they had turned north instead of west. Good. They would make for the northern side of the plains and avoid the home of the kvalid, the Rotte Hojle.

Aieren gained on them; he was learning to push his mount faster than the others had been moving. He was close to Glenia—who seemed to be trailing, almost waiting for him—and he called out to her. But Rommaith knew they were moving too fast to converse. He kept up the pace until they reached a safe distance from the kvalid javelins. They then slowed.

"Why have we turned north? This will take us to Toradh Dunne, won't it?" Aieren seemed to have a concern.

"We have come too close to Rotte Hojle. There are kvalid everywhere. Their fine noses must have picked up on your carnivorous activity back there—they would have overwhelmed us if we had stayed much longer." Rommaith had scouted and was sure that there were more than two hundred lurking in the tall grasses around them.

Aieren said, "Hardly my fault." He gestured to Rommaith. "He's the one leading us. Admit it, you got too close to the Rotte Hojle."

"It was your odor of charred meat that brought them upon us, Galean. Nothing else. Had it been us without you, we would not have needed to stop. We would have passed without notice. That is the Sylvan way." Rommaith would not let this forest outcast lay any of the Sylvan to blame. It was the Galean's deficiencies that created their problems.

"But Toradh Dunne?" Aieren questioned. "Even I know the icy danger that sleeps in that lake."

Rommaith knew too well what he meant.

The lake to the north held a cold menace itself. He had not forgotten the Vannfllott. Those frost giants of the cold waters would be a far more treacherous enemy than the rat-faced kvalid. That lake was where those faithless giants hid. Ishard, their king, still commanded the depths. How close did they dare go?

"Worry about the Destiny Stone, Galean. I know the best path to the Dwarrow ruins."

"It would not be wise to get too close." Aieren insisted on making his point.

Now it was Glenia who took up with the Galean. She glared at him with a fierce annoyance. "Do not think us fools. We go and you follow," she spat, devoid of any shred of respect.

Aieren looked abashed. Rommaith had never heard Glenia do anything but coddle the outcast. He kept his face straight, but inside, he nodded to her with respect.

"Morningsong told us we need to be in the Dwarrow ruins as fast as we may," Rommaith said. "We will go the way I show you."

Then Aieren told them, "I can feel the tug of the Destiny Stone. It is calling me almost due west."

Rommaith came to a halt along with the young Sylvan. He moved his unicorn around to be very close to Aieren. He leaned over, towering and intending to intimidate the Galean. "Good." That was all. "Let us move. Time is vital, and by the light of Morningsong, I will not waste another moment on this."

Glenia's face dropped. There was astonishment in her eyes. "You can?"

Aieren nodded to her. "Yes, I can." But then her face resigned, almost letting a smile slip out. "Good," was all she said. "That is well to know, Galean."

"Aieren," Aieren said to them. "My name is Aieren."

Riding through the cool night was swift work. No more signs of the kvalid showed as they sped away from the nesting hole. The air seemed fresher the farther north they drew. It felt good against his skin. Rommaith had not been out of the Daoine Maithe for…more than twenty years. He thought, fondly, that was too long. He did much traveling in his youth. He did not range too far, even then. But he had crossed the Plains of Sorka to the desert and had skirted just outside of Dwarrow lands. Tisroc those lands were called. He realized he was smiling as he rode. It was a spectacular freedom.

The Galean seemed able to keep this pace. Through the night and on into the day they went on the tireless unicorns. They stopped once again for the Galean to rest and feed. It was a delay Rommaith did not like, but they needed the Galean. He listened to conversations Aieren struck up with Glenia. She seemed willing to make light talk with him. Rommaith would grunt when he was addressed with some Galean frivolity. He smirked inwardly at Belusan, who ignored the golden fool entirely.

Rested and fed, Aieren was somewhat renewed. They continued again that evening and into another starry night. Through the night and on into the day they went. Always north.

"Let us stop a moment," Belusan spoke as he pulled astride Rommaith. He brought the unicorns harmoniously to a slow pace and finally a halt.

To the north in front of them were the sharp white peaks jutting like frosty daggers into the cloud layer of the skies over them. Soft, white, and pristine. No threat loomed in those clouds. The grass was tall all over the Plains of Sorka. But here they gave way a little, not reaching their height of more than a single meter. But they were as thick as a bramble patch. Lush and green, this grass differed. It was soft, and the blades were not sharp as much of the grass to the south. Rommaith knew how to navigate the sharp blades they had passed to get here. The unicorns, too, had magic to keep the blades away from themselves and their riders.

Rommaith looked around, uncomfortable, his bark-skin fidgeting with rising.

"What is it?" Belusan was urgent, his light-brown eyes open with alarm.

"We need to move. This is no place to rest," Rommaith warned them.

Then he heard it. A clicking noise, coming from all around them. Belusan's unicorn hopped into the air with a cry, blue dust billowing from an apparent wound on its leg. All at once, the unicorns hopped and moved, the riders struggling to avoid being thrown. Blue sparkles burst from various wounds.

There it was, in the brush—bluish-white, bulbous insects with large glowing thoraxes, crawling upon short, spider-like legs. They had been hidden in the grass, being no bigger than a tomcat. Their bites were ripping into the unicorns.

"*Cranne!*" yelled Rommaith.

There had to be ten around them, and more could be heard farther off. Cranne fed off blue magic to live— that would explain the locale of the insects. The nearby lake was full of creatures forged by blue magic. Even the lake itself held enough for them to survive. But four unicorns were a veritable feast.

Moving their wrists in short flicking motions, both Glenia and Belusan began flinging small wisps of fire from their fingers, burning the creatures and driving them away. Rommaith unsheathed his scian and began making carefully measured, sweeping gestures into the voracious creatures. He wanted to slice away enough of them to move out of danger. Aieren had his kindjal out, too, and slashed the head off of one—blue mist sprayed into the air, and the bug fell into dust. The melee did not last long, but all the unicorns sustained bites from the attack. Blue leakage spilled out of their many wounds.

Rommaith had them turned to the west, riding with controlled speed away from the other cranne. The wounds on the unicorns continued to spill, and their energies notably decreased. Once he felt they had traveled a safe distance, he brought them to a halt. Then they dismounted, and Glenia and Belusan tended to the wounded unicorns. They spoke in soft Sylvan tongues, evoking magic in an effort to heal the creatures and soothe their unrest. The unicorns settled, one by one, to lie on the grass.

Rommaith stalked around, patrolling. He needed to be sure they were safe. It was his responsibility. He was so overly concerned about the lake and avoiding frost giants, he forgot about the possibility of cranne. This was his mistake. He kicked angrily at the grass.

The grass probably held more danger, and it could come without notice. Aieren went to Glenia, who was tending the unicorn he had ridden. She looked back, and Rommaith thought he saw tears in her eyes.

"I cannot call forth healing. It is like the magic isn't there. It's just gone." She was shaken. "I can't feel it."

Belusan approached, looking very concerned. "I, too, cannot. This is wrong. This cannot be so. I fear the unicorns are doomed without our ability to heal." Belusan seemed lost—hopeless.

Rommaith let a rare soft moment come, putting a comforting hand on Belusan's shoulder. "Be still, young southerner. This has happened to me, as well. It is the decline of the Daoine Maithe. Magic fades with it. Mine was never strong like yours"—he tilted his head toward Glenia—"or hers, but I find it present less and less often."

Bitter was the laugh spilling from Aieren's mouth. The Sylvan all blazed hard looks at him, especially the younger two.

"It comes for us all," Aieren said almost in a sneer. "You cannot feel the magic because *the magic isn't there!*" The last words came in a hate-filled growl of despair. "Rommaith speaks true. This is the effect of the trees receding in the Daoine Maithe."

Aieren paused, his chin out to challenge and attack. But they listened in silent, fearful disbelief.

"I was as you are now," he continued, "a mighty Sylvan with strong magic, but it left me. Slowly at first. Simple things, like not calling fire. Then, more often and more serious. It continued until I could no longer feel the calling of the forest. I fear you are becoming as I am. Do you not hear the wrath in my voice every time I speak? I yearn for the feel of the forest. My life's blood has been drained from my body. I am a shell of my former self. *This* is why we need to bring the Destiny Stone to Galee. It is a chance to return our grace. We are all Sylvan. Do not let my gold-sullied pallor deceive you—it will be yours, one day, unless we succeed."

Rommaith did not like to hear it, but the Galean was right. The younger two did not know. They would resist until they felt it more strongly. It was just the way young children of Morningsong were. Full of life and hope and love of the wood and its magic. He was well past that.

"If you have answers, Galean, I would hear them now." Rommaith was sincere. He did not expect a solution.

"Yes, what do you bring other than bad omens and polluted speech?" Belusan was in no mood for more.

"Aieren, please," he said more softly. "My name is Aieren."

"Aieren," said Glenia, "is there a way?"

Aieren smiled at the small pleasure of hearing his name. "You all know the way. Morningsong told us. It is through the Destiny Stone. We can use it to restore the Daoine Maithe. But we must be urgent. Our unicorns are dying. The Dwarrow have the lead on us to get the Destiny Stone. We must get there first."

"Can you ride more today?" Glenia's voice held concern for him.

"Yes. I will not rest until we have the Destiny Stone in our hands."

Rommaith set his resolve into action. "Then let us be gone while we still have the gift of the goddess to speed our trip. It is not too long, due west. We can make it to Krath if the unicorns last and luck stays with us before the Sun greets a new day."

They rose and got the unicorns up. Although hurt, they kept their energy and spirits high. Less playful but as eager as ever to bear their riders to their destination.

Glenia stood in the center, her hands in the air, and cried aloud, clear as a chime, "Renew, sweet children of the fae." She let her tears dry in the sudden breeze, and light purple flew from her hands to the unicorns. She laughed aloud. "My magic! It has returned."

The magic swirled and gathered around the wounds on the unicorns, feeding strength to the mounts. But it had been too long, and their wounds were too great to heal completely. They could not be fully renewed. They would not be saved.

"It is good you have touched the magic again, Glenia." Belusan had a look of hidden pain he tried to smile through for her.

She joined them, mounting up. "There was little power to draw from. It will not last—let's ride."

They flew into the night as fast as ever. Glenia seemed less concerned, now that she had found some magic again.

On the horizon ahead, the sharp peaks of the Silfr Mountains where the Dwarrow lands existed slowly grew larger. Rommaith now had begun to drift south from their westerly course.

More and more, the unicorns began to shimmer and fade into translucence, losing their opaque quality. They were dying. Rommaith began to be concerned. The unicorns would not make it all the way there. He hoped Glenia would be able to try again and heal them, but she said her magic was gone once more. Glenia was the most gifted at healing magically. Belusan fared no better. The mystic infection of the cranne bites was terminally spreading.

Rommaith was no healer. He was a warrior. He hated being useless, but his magical skill would be pointless even if he felt the power in him. He was as void as they were.

Finally, they could see the southernmost spur of the mountains, jutting into the road along the range's edge. The road turned north into the gorge and up the mountains—Krath was not far now. Almost as if they knew, the unicorns gasped one after the other in short order. Blue and red dust spilled into the air, dissipating as the unicorns fell into a death as beautiful as their existence—more of a magical dispersal than a true death. They were creatures of magic, and they returned to the pure magic of their making.

Glenia fell to her knees at the sight of such a terrible fate for Morningsong's beautiful creations. She wept openly. Her shoulders shook. Aieren went to her and put his arm over her shoulder to comfort her. She pushed him off and went back to her grief. Aieren started to reach for her again, but the blade of a fhalá nipped a speck of blood under his chin.

"Leave her, Galean," Belusan warned. He was hot with protective anger. "She does not need you to touch her."

Aieren's look was one only offering sympathy. He held his arms out and hands open. "What can I do?" His voice shook, choking on empathy.

"Walk away." Rommaith was back to his gruff tones. The Galean had thought to be too close. He needed to make sure that he remembered his place, a Galean. "You offer nothing we need now."

Aieren stepped off to himself.

Rommaith was ready to go on, but he understood the young Sylvan's attachment to the conjured unicorns. For him, they had served their purpose. He walked nearby, flexing his hands tight until the snapping of wood sounded, then releasing them. Then he did it again and again.

They would be on foot from here out. None of them had the skill of the goddess—there would be no more summoning of unicorns. They were walking to Krath.

Glenia finally rose. Her face was stolid. "Rommaith, let us leave this place." Her voice matched her mood.

"It is not as far as it might have been." Rommaith winced at his own words. That wasn't what he meant.

Belusan fell in beside Glenia, and Aieren followed at an isolated distance.

They hiked off very swiftly. Rays of the Sun glinted over the crest of the mountains. Rommaith was pleased to see they were closer than he thought. Sometimes he misjudged things from so long ago.

When they approached the ruins of Krath, their sharp ears became aware of much chittering within the broken town. He knew the noise. Kvalid, and many of them. Rommaith wordlessly signaled for them to wait as he moved off to scout out the noises.

He slipped away, closing in on the town. There was a broken wall of mud and stone all around the ruins. He approached the wall, staying low. Peering over, he saw there were several scores of kvalid moving around. Something had them excited. He saw a few larger ones gathered in the center of a fire pit. Tralkvalid. They were far more fearsome than the kvalid.

Rommaith moved away from the wall and scouted into the pines on the western side of the ruins. There, he sensed something in the air that was out of place in the sparse pines. He kept hidden as soon as he heard them, relieved that the trees still spoke to him as they always had. His was almost never the raw form of magic like that wielded by Belusan or Glenia, but he was one with the forest—even this forest, who spoke with an accent thick as resin. These pines were strange and bitter on the tongue, but they were trees, nonetheless. Dwarrow. These might be the ones Morningsong had warned were already pursuing the Destiny Stone.

CHAPTER 10

Sylvan Magic

Aieren had taken the time while Rommaith was doing his reconnaissance to eat, and he was still asleep when Rommaith returned to relate his findings.

"Among the ruins themselves are about two hundred kvalid," Rommaith said with a bitterness on his tongue. He snarled with distaste. "There were also a few tralkvalid, their bigger cousins. I counted four of them. It is best if they can be avoided."

Belusan pitched in. "With our magic failing when we seem to need it most, I agree."

Rommaith was clenching his hands again, and Belusan noticed. "There is more, isn't there?"

"Yes." A creaking of wood bending came from his clenched fists. He released the pressure. "There is a small encampment of Dwarrow."

Belusan's eyes went wide. "Is it them?" Rommaith knew what he meant.

"What's this?" Glenia came over, rustling her pink-blushed leaves back from her face. "Dwarrow?"

Rommaith gave her a curt nod and looked back at Belusan. "Maybe so. They number fifty, and one is as tall as our Galean over there. But he's twice as thick. I've never seen one that big."

Belusan sucked in his breath and stepped back, turning in a full circle.

Glenia crossed her slender ash-gray arms and screwed up her face. "Big as Aieren? Impossible."

"It could be though," Belusan said, tapping his head in thought, "he could be a small giant and no Dwarrow at all."

Glenia now gave Belusan the same skeptical look.

"These Dwarrow could be very difficult—especially in the mountains," Rommaith told them. "Some of them know secret hidden causeways and traps. If we go under the mountain, we must be especially wary. They are not for our forest eyes to see or detect."

"With the way our luck has run since we began, we will find ourselves underground."

Rommaith froze at the thought. He did not like going underground. That was something for roots and moles and Dwarrow. That was no place for a Sylvan.

Both of the young Sylvan looked confident. He decided now was the best time to tell them the worst of it.

"They have a Gulprąst with them." He watched their reactions.

Belusan's head slowly leaned at an angle. "You sure you saw a Gulprąst, Rommaith?"

Glenia was silent and straight faced. Her hand came up over her mouth as it slowly began to form the word.

These Dwarrow were dangerous. Having a Gulprąst changed the dynamic. *These Dwarrow could use magic!* Despite being only yellow magic, a talented Gulprąst would be a fearsome enemy. This was no ordinary Dwarrow company.

"We should move quickly into the ruins and avoid this formidable group."

Glenia checked her arrows and bow, then began taking an inventory of the knives stashed everywhere around her body. Belusan was doing the same. Rommaith was ready when he noticed Aieren sleeping without a care in the world. "What about him?"

"Can we just…leave him there?" Belusan looked very insistent, almost happy with the idea.

Glenia had finished and shook her head, scolding the two males. "You know we need him. He would be slain by the kvalid or worse if we left him, anyway." She pointed accusingly at them both. "How would that weigh on you when Morningsong asked where her chosen one had gone?"

They both started laughing and trying to stifle the noise before it attracted attention. It woke Aieren out of his slumber, and he stretched, seeing them readying to go somewhere. "Are we leaving?"

Rommaith dismissed his question. "We can ignore the Dwarrow if we go off to the west. They would be too strong for us to tangle with, especially with a Gulprąst. I am not sure which way we should go from here. The last hint the goddess gave us was these ruins, but now we are here."

Having come to his feet, Aieren approached them. "We need to go into the mountainside over there." He pointed past the kvalid that lounged near the entrance.

Rommaith didn't want to listen, but Aieren was likely right. They were there for the artifact the goddess had told them about—they had no choice but to listen to him.

They moved up to the wall where Rommaith had scouted earlier. Aieren led them along it until they saw a breach. Looking past, they could see the rise of the mountain wall and a dark opening. That was the one place Rommaith did not want to go. Fighting kvalid and tralkvalid was one thing. He would rather face near-certain death of fighting the Dwarrow with their giant and Gulprąst than go in that accursed hole.

It was unknown what waited for them in the dark.

"In there." Aieren indicated the mountain's entrance. Of course it would be under the mountain. All of them turned at the creaking of wood. Rommaith unclenched his hands and took a breath.

"We can take out the six kvalid on guard at the gate," Rommaith said.

Belusan smiled with amusement and tapped into pure blue magic, then brushed the air, drawing his fingers across both Glenia and Rommaith, then finally himself. "Mirrors," he spoke. Blue shimmered through the air around them, forming into six perfect replications of each of the three Sylvan.

Chuckling out loud, Rommaith uttered, "Well done, Belusan, very well indeed."

As the others prepared their bows and chose targets in the ruins, Aieren inquired, "What about me?"

"Enduring one of you is quite enough." Belusan laughed openly.

"Stay with us and you will be out of sight," Glenia said. Her mischievous smile probably didn't make him feel any better.

"Arrows!" Rommaith told the others. Belusan and Glenia nocked their bows. "Now!"

Their bows twanged, shooting three arrows apiece—six kvalid crumpled to the ground. Their skins folded and became rigid as tree bark. Forward they leaped, all twenty-one of them moving in crossing pathways with coordinated fluidity, making it hard to ascertain their true number, the duplications masterfully disguised. The graceful Sylvan—with their clumsy golden mongrel in tow—were through the gate in an instant. No further guards were apparent as they spilled into the mountainside entrance.

It was darker in the cavern, but all of them had just as keen a sight in the dark as they did in full sunlight. Aieren, too—Morningsong's influence at work. Nothing about the cavern hinted at Dwarrow work. It was a natural hollow. Apart from the entrance, there were two egresses into the mountain. One seemed like a naturally formed cave; the other was of fine Dwarrow crafting. Rommaith, needing to know which way, looked to Aieren. The smug Galean smirked back at the Sylvan, who were all looking at him now for direction. Rommaith was getting tired of carrying the Galean. It was time for him to do his part, and every time, he behaved as if they owed him something for his contribution.

"Are you guarding a secret?" Rommaith asked. His voice was more gruff than usual. Impatience overtook him. "Which way?" he growled.

Ignoring him with the hubris of the goddess herself, Aieren stepped with poised confidence through the masonry archway.

Of course the overproud mongrel knew the way. None of the Sylvan had the touch of Morningsong upon them. Rommaith hoped it was the pull of the Destiny Stone and not some Galean game that could lead to all their deaths. Once they had entered the mountain, they were at his mercy. Rommaith hated the mountain.

He sent a silent prayer to Morningsong for guidance, then let the blind lead the way.

PART

Three

CHAPTER 11

Aieren's Choice

Aieren's choice brought them into a long stone hall strewn with broken doors—three on each side. Belusan had let the illusions of their doppelgangers fade away, leaving just the four of them, as before. They heard kvalid scratching and chittering somewhere inside—and by the sounds of rapid movement, the kvalid had also heard them.

Kvalid burst into the hall from different doors, then halted at the sight of the four well-armed forest dwellers. The kvalid just stood there, excitedly chittering to each other, the moment after clearing the doorways. Four more filed out from the last door on the left, three from the opposite door on the right. It seemed the reinforcements were enough for them to resume their antagonistic posture.

Belusan pulled his fhalá free, and they glinted at their sharp edges. Glenia tugged Aieren back, letting the two Sylvan males spread to fill the space between them and the kvalid. He began to pull away from her. Did she really think he was unable to fight? She whispered, breath cool as the woods, in his ear, "We would only be in their way."

More chittering followed, filled with excited apprehension, as they moved forward, javelins poised for an attack. Rommaith also unsheathed his two long fhalá knives before anyone else could move—the tight quarters made the fhalá a veteran's choice over his scian.

Aieren relaxed, although grudgingly. He understood the close quarters. She was probably right. He had only his hunting knife or his kindjal, and both would do him little good in this melee. He chose to draw his kindjal— just in case they got through. More than likely a naïve mistake, but he felt better with the heavy slicer in his hands. Glenia had her bow in her hands and an arrow already nocked.

Aieren looked back to see Rommaith already moving with embellished deftness. Belusan stepped a hair behind the big warrior but stayed close. Glenia had released one of her arrows and was reaching for another. A kvalid in the rear fell forward, Glenia's black shaft through its right eye all the way up to the fletching.

Rommaith stridently waded into the kvalid, the fhalá flashing their cruel, shiny death. Using size and a bullish assault to intimidate his foes, his straight steel swept through the air effortlessly. He made a clean, bloody sweep through the closest kvalid's neck. Then, leaning in hard, he gutted the second with the other single-edged blade. It was split from belly to chin, and its entrails spilled forward. Most Sylvans were adept with fhalá, bloodletting knives, but Rommaith proved to be their master. Belusan had moved to make his way into the fray, but Rommaith took up most of the hall.

In the time that had passed, Glenia had managed to stick two more of the rats with arrows and was still reaching for another. Aieren was feeling anxious, being forced into the role of spectator while the Sylvan all fought. Rommaith dispatched another, knocking aside the victim's javelin and striking in a rapid frenzy of slicing gore that spewed out a rain of kvalid blood on the walls and ceiling. There was nothing for Aieren to do.

He moved, and Glenia pushed him back to where he was. "Stay!" she said with force. "Unless you want an arrow in your back." She had to stop her missile strikes to get him out of her way. Then he was drawn back to the action before them.

A great yawp echoed from the room on their immediate left, and a tralkvalid lumbered through the door. The melee hesitated as the combatants all held their breath, either awaiting help or assessing the new threat. It was small for a tralkvalid; Rommaith's head was just shy of its shoulder. Aieren saw Rommaith smile up at his next target. The Galean's blood rose, the tension in the room boiled over. He was hoping Rommaith's grin meant the tralkvalid would only be sport for Rommaith, as he took on a wild battle lust uncharacteristic of a Sylvan. Only one who had begun to lose the grace of Morningsong could revel in such slaughtering.

Belusan stepped back and changed weapons—dropping his fhalá, nocking his bow, and sending two arrows at once into the chest of the large, fanged beast. They penetrated its wiry, pelted scales, but only seemed to anger it. Bringing its attention on the smaller Sylvan, it shoved Rommaith aside with the swat of its arm, then charged Belusan with an arrow-fueled fury. It bowled him over and fell upon him, its gaping maw searching to find his neck. Belusan's quickness allowed him to keep his throat away, but biting snaps still managed to snip the padded spaulder deep enough, drawing blood. Belusan's bow had been knocked out of his hands with the thunderous force of the charge. He couldn't draw his fhalá—they were on the floor—and the crushing weight had him pinned.

Aieren drew on the rush, his blood pumped like a hammer, and he moved forward and swept his kindjal across the back of the beast's neck—the sharp, heavy blade sliced clean and true. The tralkvalid's head tilted and fell straight over Belusan's wounded shoulder. Seeing their larger cousin so easily dispatched, the rats' fevered assault broke, and they looked to flee.

In a frenzied move, Rommaith caught two with a single sweep, reaching across their back sides as they attempted to escape. Both fell, and Glenia finished the last kvalid with a quickly released arrow into an ear, dropping it in a furry heap.

All around them lay carnage—the group of slain rats on the stone floor and their headless leader. No Sylvan casualties, but Belusan's shoulder was leaking blood. He grunted in pain before trying to rise from the floor.

"You have a wound," Glenia said, quite surprised, while she made sure the kvalid were dead with pokes from both hands with a couple of her many knives.

"It bit me." Belusan stood and kicked the head of the dead tralkvalid. He pulled the torn padding aside and examined the wound on his shoulder. "It's only a small scratch."

"It could get worse if you don't let me take a moment with it." She wiped off the knives before holstering each one. Aieren counted four—or was it five knives? She put them away so fast, he could not be sure.

"That was mine, you know. I could have saved you the trouble of that bite." Rommaith smiled at Belusan with fellowship. Then, changing mood like the turning of a new page, he glared at Aieren, frothing with the last tinges of bloodlust on his tongue. "And if *you* step in front of my prey again, Galean, you may take its place."

Aieren was taken aback. Was there nothing he could do to get even a shred of respect from this arrogant warrior? "I saved his life, Rommaith." It came out more like a weak plea than the proclamation rebuttal he had intended.

He was met with a stern frown and the palm of Rommaith's hand waving him off. "Be quiet, Galean," he said. "We are still not alone here."

Then he gestured back the way they came. Aieren heard it too. There was a commotion toward the mountain's entrance, then laughter—a harsh, mocking laughter.

"I hear the coarse breathing of those bearded louts," whispered Belusan.

Rommaith nodded with a sly grin that made his face bigger. "I will go in first and—"

"No!" Glenia hushed them. "We are not here for that, Rommaith. Aieren, where to?"

He was glad for Glenia and her cool head. Rommaith was still in the grip of his fever. Aieren asked quietly, "Are they following us?"

Belusan grabbed him by his shoulder sleeves and used an annoyed tone usually reserved for small, disobedient children. "Treasure seekers. It is what they do."

"And drink to excess," added Glenia.

"And fight," finished Rommaith, still sporting an anxious grin.

"Last thing we need is to bother with their reliable selfishness. It plagues all stone dwellers." Belusan shook him, looking at Aieren impatiently. "Well? Is this the way?" Belusan pointed to the last door on the right.

Aieren burned with embarrassment. It could have been either way—both had the same feel. But he'd be damned to let the Sylvan be right on this account too. He pulled free of Belusan's grip. Reclaiming a shred of dignity, he brushed at his wrinkled tunic, deliberately, making these haughty Sylvan wait. Then he answered by stepping into the corridor on the left, hiding a smile.

He could feel the annoyed looks they shot his way. He gathered fleeting pleasure from stifling them. Still, he had to convince himself he had won. Won at what, though? Nothing, he resolved and bit his lip. He continued and noticed that the path began to slope down.

Where it began its descent, the fine stonework ended and the walls became rough-hewn, cavern-like. He could feel the Destiny Stone, even in the bowels of the mountains.

"It looks like the Dwarrow never finished their work here. Much of this place feels as if the Dwarrow were rushed during its making," Glenia remarked as she followed at the rear.

Downward it delved, deeper into the mountain, farther from trees and living things. More and more discomforting, making the Sylvan especially edgy— Aieren did not like it either, but the effects on him seemed to weigh less heavily. The path went on for some distance, turning slightly one way and then the next. Ever downward they traveled, along the long shaft.

"I cannot hear the stone dwellers anymore," Glenia said very softly, after a time. "There are only our quiet footfalls. We are alone here."

"We and that golden-skinned beast," Belusan added. Then he sniped, "Must you breathe like oxen at hard labor?"

Aieren ignored him, still concerned about the Dwarrow. Either they weren't following the Sylvan, or they took the other path, to the right. Either was fine with him, as long as he wouldn't have to deal with them. "Stubborn as stone" and "greedily self-serving" were the axioms they were known for, and Aieren wanted none of it.

Then they reached the end of the cave. It spilled into a large room with no exit, the ceiling several meters high, like it had been hollowed out. The deep-grooved walls were not Dwarrow workmanship—they went this way and that, over each other, in arbitrary directions. It was almost like hundreds upon hundreds of claws had raked away at the mountain until the cavern was formed. Cold and unnatural as Christiemay's creatures, perverting blue magic—but far worse. It had Aieren feeling restless. He did not like being where the Sun or the moon could not penetrate under the ground. Under trees would be fine; that was natural. But this…this was not good.

He looked back at the Sylvan; they wordlessly scanned the room and moved their mouths, forming unspeakable distaste. Their guarded behavior screamed revulsion at the subterranean irreverence.

No light had been in the previous corridors. This cave was different. There, in the center of the room— floating over a round, waist-high dais of black, polished stone—hovered a fist-sized jewel. It gave off flickering light from its many facets—blue and yellow, for the most part, but occasionally a bit of red reflected and winked from its center.

The Destiny Stone.

CHAPTER 12

Runeweaver

Aieren and the Sylvan looked around the room, expecting to find some form of guardian. It could have been anything in this cold, distasteful setting. They took care, moving ahead slowly as a doe, watching with suspicious study. Perhaps a fiendish Dwarrow mechanism lay in wait? But they did not see anything that protected the Destiny Stone. No devices. No creatures. No magic, either.

Wary, the Sylvan slowly moved about the room, testing every crease of rock with extreme care. Caution governed their every turn. Morningsong said to be careful—the Destiny Stone was guarded. But there was nothing. In the end, they determined that she must have been wrong. Nothing was guarding the Stone.

Aieren lost track of the Sylvan as he gazed upon the Destiny Stone. It was a stunning creation. He saw the beauty of the gods themselves, their power glinting in the facets. Without taking a step, he came closer— just by his thoughts and his attention, he felt closer. It looked to be just out of his grasp. It became clearer, his will and mind very close to the Destiny Stone, gazing with incredulous wonder.

Aieren no longer took any notice of the others rummaging around, seeking some danger. He bathed in the Destiny Stone's glow, feeling the power it held, pressing him. It was like being forced underwater, unable to breathe—he gasped, and he breathed in its pure beauty. How fabulous. All he had to do was reach out and grasp it.

He thought he could touch the gods themselves through the Destiny Stone—they had created it, after all, poured their very own essence into it. What power it must hold. The power of not one, but *all* the gods. He sensed the yellow first, friendly and warm. Bruss and Jikseon. Tallow magic—then a touch of hot energy, edges of red, from both Jikseon and Morningsong. Yes, then the cool blue, flowing around the others like a protection. It had to be Christiemay, and of course Morningsong. No presence of the mad god, Noshid— he had been cast out to the land farther from the Sun, isolated from the other gods forever. It was pure and good, and Aieren felt its innocence wash over him. Here it was, within reach. All he had to do…

The Destiny Stone itself called to him:

Aieren…Galean…come.

He was decreed by Morningsong, his creator, to gather and bring it back to Galee and restore the glory of the Daoine Maithe. That thought stirred in his mind. He wanted to go to the Destiny Stone and take it now to get out of this cold tomb. But still the Destiny Stone held him fast. He wanted it, craved it. He looked at its pristine beauty, unflawed, perfection.

If he could just take the step forward and gather it, he would be whole once more. He would be Sylvan. It was everything he desired. But the Destiny Stone would not allow him any sort of advance—until, suddenly, its power pulled him. He was sliding, not just toward the Destiny Stone, but his mind, his thoughts drawn irresistibly into the Stone.

"*Aieren*, what are you doing?" He distantly heard Glenia cry out. "Get the Stone. Let us be gone."

Aieren came back to himself, like waking from a trance. He was slowly reaching for the Destiny Stone— yes, the Stone. He must have it!

His hand touched the Stone, and blue power filled him. The sweet renewal slapped his being with ecstasy—he felt whole. His grace fully returned. He was Sylvan again—not the crude Galean he had been for so many decades. Raw, pure, cleansing blue power. Reliable, refreshing yellow power. Tinges of wild, uncontrollable red power swirled around with freedom and chaos. Power of Morningsong. Power of Jikseon. Power of Bruss.

And still, something stood in the way of him feeling the whole of the Destiny Stone. A simple, yet complex thread made a barrier he could not pass. The power of Christiemay. Pure blue force, acting like a guardian to the Destiny Stone, but held within the Stone itself. It gently but firmly held him at bay, prodding and searching his being. And then, as if recognizing who he was and what he was there for, it expelled him, casting him away with a wall of solid blue force like the wind of a cyclone. Struck with the force, he fell back, knocking into Belusan and sending them both sprawling to the floor.

Aieren looked to see his restored body, expecting to be the fine red-maple Sylvan he had been before. But he was unchanged. He felt the sensation of restoration bleed away like water in an open drain. Anguish at the cruel tease hammered his mind and beat at his bruised will.

"Why?" he croaked and sank to his knees in front of the dais.

"What happened?" he heard Glenia ask, sounding very far away. His head was filled with a cloudy mist left by the evacuation of blue magic, confounding his ability to focus.

"Why?" he cried again, letting forth the anger. He felt a growing hatred emanating from somewhere amid the plinth. He tried to shake off the stunning effects of the Destiny Stone, a blue fog like the dew of cold, coastal mornings.

Now anxiety swept in, growing like a bad nightmare, an oppressive and unknown malice around him.

"*Glenia! Rommaith!*" yelled Belusan, pointing past Aieren's hand.

Aieren saw just beyond his shaking hand. There on the floor lay the Destiny Stone. He had touched the Destiny Stone, he realized—then, suddenly, he knew. He became urgently aware that he had triggered something terrible by touching the Destiny Stone.

Rommaith drew out his scian, his head swiveling to take in the room. "Up with you now, Galean! Your foolish carelessness has sprung the trap!"

A hissing sound—as if the air in the cavern was being drawn out—slithered within the space. From the dais came black tendrils, forming into a swirl at its surface. Rising from the shadows towered a being of absolute void. Its tattered robes hardly covered its decayed body. Patches of rotted skin draped loosely over its bleak-boned, skeletal frame. A full three meters tall it stood, reaching the cave's ceiling. A charcoal-black hood, tattered from an untold age of decaying fibers, partially veiled the unraveling cartonnage that scarcely hid its hideous face. It spewed out a dust-parched hiss that filled the room. The creature drew in an audible gasp, its first breath in perhaps centuries. The deep hollow filled with the ominous sound of death.

Its voice was thin, as the air itself, words slithering out with purloined breath.

"Woodlings, it is not for you. Your goddess has no sanction. The Destiny Stone is mine alone. It has been so for centuries. So, it must remain."

It began a gesture in the air as if writing. Black power formed where the bone finger etched, leaving the beginning constructs of an ancient red-and-black rune of fetid magic, unclean and forbidding, suspended in the air.

"A runeweaver," Belusan whispered under his breath, fear-filled recognition marking his every intonation.

Aieren remembered learning of runeweavers from stories. "But there are none," said Aieren with incredulity. "Not really. They are only legends."

But here he saw one with his own eyes—a terrifying lich, more than just a story. More than the fearsome look of the face of eternal death. It weighed upon him with the will of final reckoning. A nameless fear clawed at him. He needed to run, to escape, but he was paralyzed.

Glenia let loose like a cannon, launching a ball of fire to consume the shadowy guardian. A fireball such as that should easily immolate half a score of beings—but an expanding darkness surrounding the lich hungrily consumed her red magic. Her fire assault dissipated, fading and flickering out—useless. Unimpeded, the lich never even acknowledged her attack.

"It's true. A runeweaver." Glenia's face was pale as a young ash, her voice stricken. Despair quailed in her voice, and she whispered, but all could hear—every sound carried in this accursed cavity. "We should flee."

The lich finished its charcoal-black rune, and blood-red embers glowed through its heart. It sent the rune into a slow glide with the smoothest, indifferent gesture of long-emaciated fingertips. The rune sailed forward. In the same moment, the Sylvan now moved as if time had slowed them. The rune slipped to the stone floor underneath Glenia's feet, and the rock shone in lighted blackness, keeping the shape of the completed rune. Glenia shrieked like a trapped animal, the look of death gazing through her soul. She sank to her knees and wailed out hopeless despair.

Aieren somehow knew by her empty look that she was unable to leave the rune. He had once suffered the violation she was facing—she had been severed from magic. He saw her sweating in a rabid panic. Half her essence was taken from her. Her resistance was stifled and replaced with empty despondency, and the dark lich had already forgotten her. Aieren looked on in frozen silence while the ghastly runeweaver crafted a second deadly sign in the air.

Rommaith was in action, his scian out, closing with intent. Belusan had leaped to his feet and launched a pair of arrows at the arcane corpse. But the Sylvan moved slowly, and the black-thatched arrows passed through the lich's tattered robes and its wretched body harmlessly, without the slightest hint of effect. They hit the wall, clattering to the cavern floor.

It finished the second rune, thrusting it Aieren's way. It came toward him slowly. He watched, unable to move. Then it slid under him, and its irresistible pull dragged him down to the floor—he collapsed to his knees. Gripped by the rune's power, he remained immobilized, just inches away from the Destiny Stone.

He desired to touch it. To take it. But he could not muster enough will even to move his fingers, much less his whole arm. It was beyond reach. The ashen seal of the rune bound him.

Rommaith made a series of incredibly slow slashes at the tattered, wizened wraith with his scian. It harmlessly swept through the creature, which was seemingly made of air. The lich began work on a third rune. Each stroke of the scian was slower and slower. Rommaith flexed his empty sword hand and moved his shoulder as if trying to warm it from a winter's frozen chill. Then he made a few more strikes with his left hand before he dropped the scian altogether, clattering it to the floor. He shivered and stumbled to the side, losing balance, looking numbly at the lich but still hosting a seething rage behind helpless eyes.

Finishing its third rune, the lich sent the sigil to bind the stunned warrior. Only Belusan was free, the others trapped and devoid of magic. Belusan drew on pure blue magic and sent forth a torrent of air, blowing the unfinished fourth rune into a black spray of smoke, which quickly dissipated into a harmless nothingness. The lich stopped and turned to slowly look at Belusan. It gave off an air of offended surprise.

The cold, aerated chill of its voice broke the silence.

> *"You, Sylvan, dare to challenge me?
> You cannot defile death with the mere
> illusionary magic of your fae goddess. Your
> magic is a small trickster lie, trivial at*

best. I will deal with you in a more...
traditional manner."

Producing a long black sword from beneath the swirl of decayed robes, it waved it reproachfully. The heavy blade was etched with cold runes of power that flickered with red along its length.

The lich moved, and in hardly a blink, it was on Belusan. Its half-hidden face twisted in what could only be spite-filled rage. The lich struck out its blade with blinding speed. Defending, Belusan somehow parried with his fhalá, an amazingly quick stroke. Smoke sizzled off the weapons where they met, the lich's sword biting into the Sylvan's fhalá, leaving a molten scar. The strength of the blow carried Belusan back—only his deftness allowed him to stay afoot. The other Sylvan could only watch, powerless, as Belusan fought—completely outmatched.

A light blazed up, bright as the Sun itself, filling the cavern. Blinded, the Sylvan could only feel the loathing fear emanating from the lich lift away, and their hearts were raised with hope. Boisterous cries behind the light lasted only a few moments before fading, then the lich raised a shrieking wail that chilled their bones. Finally, the lich dissolved into a black cloud that shot down the hall, dragging its cold voice and dread with it. The runes faded, and the Sylvan were freed. Aieren slowly dragged himself to sitting.

Belusan's body shivered with the frosty chill of the black blade delivered through his own weapon. Aieren and the Sylvan were all too shaken to stand. Released, Glenia was first to recover, and she went to Belusan first, shakily using red healing magic to remedy some of the effects lingering from the encounter. Rommaith rubbed his arm, which suffered from the same icy effects. She went to Rommaith next. By the time she had gotten to Aieren, he was on his hands and knees, looking down at the cold stone floor. His eyes were still adjusting from the burning flash.

A new sort of dread filled Aieren. It wasn't the feeling of oppression and stifling evil that attacked him from within. It wasn't the mere presence of the runeweaver. He felt a sense of total loss. He had been whole again, and then had it ripped away in an instant. He was so empty. He could fall over and give up his life.

Aieren's voice was filled with loss and defeat as he poured out the words like spilling sand, "The Destiny Stone, it is gone."

Four

CHAPTER 13

The Right Decision

"Wy Jikseon, I did," Diwolde Stonescraper finally managed to get out after the echo of his own laughter faded.

"Light of Jikseon." It was the soft and calm invocation of Mevindh-Gulbard. An enchanted light emanating from the Gulprąst slowly illuminated the room. On the floor at Bolfath's feet was the severed head of the unfortunate first kvalid through the entranceway. He had lopped it off before Diwolde Stonescraper had slammed the rock door shut.

"One fer the Dwarrow with two axes," said Grambol Doomsayer, "an' one fer the Stonescraper knowin' his rocks." He laughed out loud, but his mirth was quelled with a harsh fit of coughing. Somehow, old Grambol Doomsayer always sounded like he scooted the edges of sanity when he laughed.

"That lot won't bother us with the front door shut," said Othro with heavy breathing brought on by battle.

"Aye, Othro," said Haggersath in agreement. "'Tis always good ta have the likes of a Grýttr when goin' underground." He was very glad to have Diwolde Stonescraper along. He was perhaps the greatest Grýttr living. Their path led under the mountain, and Grýttr were more at home here than anywhere else.

Grambol Doomsayer nodded and gulped a bit of the peat spirit that he kept in his goat-belly flask. He offered it up to Haggersath, who grinned and refused the spirits.

He wanted a clear head. The thoughts of the Sylvan coming in here weighed upon his mind. Why would those tree lovers go underground? It seemed unnatural. "Go an' have yerself another fer the Gulpr**a**st. Celebrate that he be makin' it light in here so's we kin see."

With the entrance closed off, the Dwarrow had no more concern about the kvalid outside. Haggersath looked over the cave in the new light. The open cavern of the entranceway was rough-hewn work. This was not done with care. It was hastily made.

Haggersath considered the options. They had to go further into the mountains now. This unfinished cave branched into two egresses. On the left was a mason-worked passage. To the right was an undeveloped cavern that had an air of foul stench to it. He put it to his troop to see if they might have some insight he missed.

"Any ideas from you louts?" Haggersath raised a bushy brow as he paused for suggestions. He stood there, flicking his thick forefinger back and forth over the worn leather-wrapped handle of his hatchet.

Silence.

He looked at Grölle, who returned an impassive gaze and began to shuffle uneasily. Moving to Mevindh-Gulbard, who stroked his beard with a warm smile on his face. Next, Diwolde Stonescraper, who was examining the rock of the portal he had just closed. His last hopes were dashed at Grambol Doomsayer. He was the whole reason for being here. His grin traced the image of lunacy, dripping a bit of peat spirit off the side of his toothy leer.

Silence.

Haggersath shook his head in reserved disappointment. No help from any of them. Even Grambol Doomsayer held only a blank stare in return.

"Why'd I bother with any of ya? Grambol, you old coot, choose one. What way is the treasure ya raved on about, eh?"

Grambol Doomsayer scratched at his wild gray beard, eyes rolling about in deep consideration. At last, he looked tentatively to the right, indicating the rough cave with a shaky hand. "They both be foul. This be a musty reek. It be different than the other one." He nodded to the left. "That one just looks all wrong ta me. Somethin' down there, methinks. But, ta speak true, Giftgiver, I cannot be sure where the treasure sits." He shrugged helplessly and took one more swig. "But they both have a nose I'd rather not sample."

Haggersath nodded. This was not what he wanted to hear. A musty smell and a wrong feeling. Being sometimes imprecise came with being a Doomsayer, but the drink was not always helpful, and the old Dwarrow's mind could get addled. He was now forced to make a decision between odor and feeling.

"All right then. Move out, lads. We be goin' ta the right." He looked to the senior Rock-Biter. "Grölle, lead on with yer ferskeyttr." He looked to where Avalanche was curled around his master's feet, licking the blood off his boots. "Othro, you follow at the rear with Bolfath. The rest of you are with me."

The Dwarrow filed into the cave, weapons ready. Grölle and his three Rock-Biters leading the way. Diwolde Stonescraper and Mevindh-Gulbard, with the light that moved with him, were more spread out.

Haggersath was paired off with Grambol Doomsayer. Bolfath had to come alone; there was no room with his bulk for another. Last was the ferskeyttr, missing the casualty, watching the rear of the group.

Haggersath could not see the entire expanse of the cave with the unnatural light the Gulpraşt provided, but it was apparent the room they ended up in was quite extensive, probably used as a storage holding. Maybe the armory, or even a barracks at the time Krath thrived as a trading outpost. Haggersath had the company spread out and explore. Some of the Rock-Biters found partial skeletal remains—most were kvalid, which meant they died sometime after the fall of Krath. There were Dwarrow remains too; those had been on the floor for the better part of the century and were severely degraded, almost unrecognizable.

A terrible stench had risen since they entered the room. No, Haggersath thought, that couldn't be true. It couldn't have just appeared—he must not have noticed it at first. Or maybe being in the room had made it more apparent now, pegging his senses. But the others were also sniffing and looking. The stench in the room was becoming unbearable—even to the Dwarrow nose, which was accustomed to funky cheeses and overly fermented food and drink (not to mention their own putrid feet and breath). It was wretched, this odor—like a composting of decayed flesh and steaming, lice-riddled manure.

To their light-headed bemoaning soon came the worst news: There was no exit and no other attached rooms. There had been a room on the right as they first came in, but it was totally closed off with collapsed stone.

"There's nothing here, Haggersath. No hidden ways. Strange though." Diwolde coughed from the refuse-filled air. "There be etched erosion all over the rock, but this hadn't been used for quite a long time. It be a strange thing, the way the stone is worn. I'd be wantin' ta examine it closer if it didn't stink like Jarlsalt's sour belchin' in here."

Haggersath said, "Best time to head the other way. You were sure this was worth a Dwarrow's minute, eh, Doomsayer?"

"By my beard, I'm sure. I also be sure there be nothin' in here ta make us stay. As I told ya b'fore. I be likin' the other way," Grambol Doomsayer answered, holding his nose and squinting.

That was the opposite of what he'd said. Haggersath looked at Grambol as if he'd broken an oath but let it go and called out to the captain leading his company. "Grölle, I've seen enough here. Let's go back the way we came."

Reversing at Grölle's signal, the company turned to head back and then out. But the Dwarrow in the lead now found their boots sliding, and Othro's ferskeyttr of Rock-Biters at the rear began suddenly slipping; both lost their footing and fell. When they tried to rise, their boots slipped again, unable to gain any purchase. The floor was slippery and sticky, quite unlike before. Avalanche had leaped to stand on Othro's shoulders, tail out straight, alarmed.

"What in the…AHHHH!!!" yelled one of the fallen Rock-Biters.

Mevindh-Gulbard stepped forward onto the muck-covered stone surface, bringing light with him. The slickness that covered the floor slid back as he moved— it would not touch him or his light. There, before them on the floor, was a mottled gray spill that glistened like oil but with a moldy texture. It covered the exit way and extended to the fallen rocks of the other room. The entire area was slick and sticky and mottled.

It was the source of the awful reek.

The two Dwarrow that were caught in the mess were partially covered with the slimy mold and were crying out in pain, struggling to right themselves— but the sludge was so slick they fell back, still unable to get to their feet. Each time they tried to escape, they only became more enveloped, more captured. It moved, making an effort to pull them back down into the muck. It would enclose them entirely if they stayed without rescue. A slight sizzling wisp of steam began to rise off them. Diwolde Stonescraper ran to the edge, careful not to step on the oozy mold, and tossed a length of rope to the ensnared Rock-Biters.

"Don' just stand there! Get over there an' pull!" roared Haggersath as he rushed to assist. Bolfath grabbed the rope, and more Rock-Biters joined in.

"That's right, me boys," Haggersath roared intently as they pulled together. "Just a bit more."

Slowly and none too gracefully, they pulled the two out until they stood on sturdy stone once more. Where it had made contact with the gray sludge, their skin was blistered and burned as if acid had bathed them. Steam came off the hardened steel, bits of muck still corroding their armor. They pulled and scraped at small patches of the stuff still clinging to them. As pieces dropped off, they slid back, rejoining the slimy mass.

A quick but acute observation revealed that there was no mistaking it—the gray mass was alive, and it was creeping toward them. Whether working as a collective or a single sentient being, whether intelligent or simply driven to feed, *this thing was alive!* It had overcome its fear of the Gulprąst's light and moved in such a way that there was no access to the exit except over it.

Some of the Rock-Biters assisted their wounded brothers who were having difficulties walking with acid-scorched feet. Mevindh-Gulbard was busy with the wounded, working the healing power through yellow magic. Gathering in the middle of the room, the Dwarrow slowly gave ground to the advancing gray mold.

"This be made of the stuff of its victims. I kin see parts of some dead kvalid floatin' about within its bloated form. It hasn't fully ingested them," Diwolde Stonescraper spoke his thoughts out loud. "Looks like it feeds well, hidin' here in these cold, wet catacombs. Almost like it be made fer jus' that task." He looked around, searching. "I be thinkin' we use fire ta clear mold off stone before we mortar them. Mebee it won't like fire too much."

One of the Rock-Biters took a flint from his pack and clipped it against his hatchet. Sparks flew into the bedroll he had stowed. He offered up the smoking cloth to Diwolde Stonescraper. "Ya owe me a new bedroll," the Rock-Biter told the Stonescraper with a brown-bearded grin, missing two front teeth.

Using it to light his own bedroll, Diwolde answered, "Now we be even, Oyleivur."

Oyleivur barked a laugh in return. "Burn the bastard. Then we'll be truly even."

Diwolde worked the smoldering cloth until he had a controlled flame. Waving fire at the mold, one in each hand, he seared the gray mass, bringing forth a gagging steam. It hissed and fumed and bubbled in a smoking, bilious retreat.

"Ha! That's the way it is, ya gray, moldy bastard. Get another fire, we got the thing on the run!" Grambol Doomsayer gleefully called out with a cackle.

The smoke flooding the room was stifling. Acrid clouds given off by the scorched mold stuck in their throats like trying to swallow threads of rusty steel, choking the Dwarrow.

"Push it away from the entrance," directed Haggersath through fits of coughing that made him almost incomprehensible. "We gotta get out, now!"

In united precision, Diwolde and the middle ferskeyttr of two Rock-Biters seared a safe path through to the exit. Plumes of venomous smoke rose furiously. When the retreating creature finally gave the exit up, the Dwarrow rushed out, piling over one another through the exit. They left the smoke-filled cave; the moldy collective seemed hesitant to follow, but nevertheless creeped ever so slowly back toward the doorway.

In the next room, they stopped, coughing and hacking to catch their breath.

"Gulprąst!" Haggersath called to Mevindh-Gulbard. "Do there be a way fer you ta…?"

"I can, Giftgiver, an' I will!" Mevindh-Gulbard stepped to the door, bringing out a vial from inside his vestments and spilling a small trail of oil across the exit floor in a thin, unbroken line. He mumbled something in a hoarse, undefined whisper as he worked. For a moment, the spilled oil flickered a dull yellow. He smiled calmly at Haggersath. "It will not follow us."

The gagging steam was held back too. Relieved, Haggersath bellowed, "All right, ye laggards. Get to movin'—this way."

He stepped off on the heels of Bolfath, who had read his mind and had already moved to the left corridor, leading the way. Always the protector, Bolfath would clear the way for Haggersath. The company went into the masonry work passage.

CHAPTER 14

The Greater Risk

Twelve Dwarrow stumbled their way into the hall.

Diwolde Stonescraper mentioned, "Now this be shoddy craftin'. Nothin' but hurried work." He sounded genuinely ashamed of the Dwarrow who made it. He scooped up a couple of pebbles from the floor and began shuffling them in his hand as he gazed at the walls, slightly shaking his dull, bronze-bearded head.

Haggersath did not share such an interest in masonry. He was more about crafting. He was the Giftgiver. As Haggersath came into the room with Mevindh-Gulbard's light, he saw the carnage of many kvalid bodies.

Diwolde Stonescraper was too busy studying the walls with detail and care. He could do this and still move quickly, showing no vested interest in the recently slain kvalid bodies strewn about. There were perhaps ten kvalid and a tralkvalid that had lost a battle—a recent battle, their blood still wet on the floor.

"Looks like those tree lovers did some fine handiwork here." Bolfath sounded impressed, unconsciously flexing his great shoulders. He wore that grin he would get when bloodletting was about.

Haggersath laughed and said, "It's a nice piece of work; saved us the bother." He was glad. Though his lads liked brawls, he knew it often came at a cost. Having these rats disposed of without raising a hammer was…efficient.

"Never had a use for these rats," Grambol Doomsayer said. "Fer once, I kin see the damn woodlings put to good use. But their strange magic still makes me feel uneasy."

Grölle came back to Haggersath after a short time conferring with the Rock-Biters. "All of the rooms be empty, prolly former dwellings. Looks like the kvalid been using them fer a while. The last one on the left leads on into the mountain. 'Tis the only one that goes somewhere. If the Doomsayer kin sense the treasure along that path, then that be the way ta go."

"Grambol, come here," said Haggersath.

The old Dwarrow came over, pulling at his beard like he wanted to remove it. "Aye, Haggersath?" Grambol

Doomsayer said, his mind somewhere else—likely thinking about his next bout with the harsh liquor.

"Bring yer addled mind ta the here an' now. I need yer skills." Haggersath worked with measured patience. The old Dwarrow couldn't help how he was. Age and the forces of being touched by Jikseon left him abnormal. "Speak ta me, Doomsayer. What do you know?"

Scrunching up his ruddy brown face shining with a tinge of red from the spirits—his few centuries of tight wrinkles folding up—Grambol Doomsayer let out his breath. "Yeah, it be closer. I kin feel somethin' getting stronger." Then he looked startled, even afraid. "Ohhhh, but there's something wrong down there. It be a blight of…" He stopped and looked at Haggersath. "Methinks this be a bad omen. Oh no. We best not be goin' that way. That way be…death."

"I agree with the Doomsayer. I sense it just through that hole," Mevindh-Gulbard put in. "There is something illicit down there. It feels—*wrong*."

"It be true!" Diwolde put in. "I kin feel it in the rock of the mountain. Even it be uneasy."

"Is that the way fer sure?" Haggersath asked Grambol Doomsayer.

Grambol Doomsayer helplessly frowned and nodded yes. "Aye. It be."

"*Bah!* What's this talk of fear and feelings?" scoffed Bolfath. "The Doomsayer says it be that way. Me an' me axes need some work. That Sylvan scum cheated me out o' me ax play. You! An' you! " he said, not to be deterred, at Grölle and Othro. "Bring yer rabble an' follow me. Earn yer keep. It's time we had some fun."

With that, he made for the last room on the left with Grölle and Othro leading, two gleeful ferskeyttr following them, itching for a fight. All the strange happenings had betrayed them the satisfaction of an honest battle, what with creeping molds that burned flesh and iron alike. Or the Stonescraper slamming shut crafty hidden doorways, cutting off the battle before it could begin. Or, worst of all, those filthy Sylvan thieves stealing their kills with unclean magic arrows. It was time for a glorious melee, one that was a real fight, raising the soul and spilling hot blood. It was time, but Haggersath lingered on his Haseti's wary warnings.

The hastily worked masonry finally ended. Now, the corridor became an unfinished passage that delved deeper into the mountain. Diwolde Stonescraper alone could tell they were headed northwest, to the heart of the western Silfr Mountains. The path went on for a long time, hardly changing direction but always going down. At last, there seemed to be an end ahead—and a commotion beyond, further in front of them. They could hear what sounded like Sylvan cries, and a shriek of horrified distress.

The Dwarrow did not take pleasure or even snicker at the apparent Sylvan plight. They had no love for tree folk, never had, but the abject fear in the air was more than just Sylvan terror. A dread hung thick—pendulous, striking a sudden fear into their hearts. Something of true evil lay ahead, and its power was indomitable.

Even Bolfath hung back from peering through the doorway. Haggersath took all his brevity and piled it against the dread. He inched closer to take a look. The others held back their faces, which were pulled into looks of fright—or, in some cases, pressed to a wall or the floor, seeking an impossible escape. The force of dread emanating was crushing, overwhelming.

Haggersath witnessed the Sylvan plight. They were being held at bay by a decrepit image of darkness who heralded death and reeked decay. It floated on air, gliding toward a slender Sylvan who was calling up some sort of magic with arcane movements. Two other Sylvan appeared to be helpless, on their knees—a slight, small Sylvan howled in fear-filled panic while the other was grim and large, and defiantly silent. Their movements were hindered. Perhaps it was the ashen rune under their knees that paralyzed them—they glowed slightly, eerily, with foul magic.

The third Sylvan was cursing and facing off with the lich, empty-handed. And the lich itself just stood there, silent. A great blade was drawn out by the floating evil, with runes that flickered and danced and a glint dark as blood. The third Sylvan faced his death as if he welcomed it, or knew it was an inevitable fact he was loath to resist.

Grambol Doomsayer had come around the corner, somehow overcoming the fear that gripped the rest, and tapped Haggersath's spauldered shoulder, whispering in his ear, "That, that be the treasure!" He gleamed with naked greed, never giving notice to anything else.

Haggersath followed the outstretched finger, gnarled with age, to the other end of the room, where a golden-skinned Man was held by another ashen rune. Perhaps it was not a Man—Haggersath wasn't sure what he was, but he was sure that he didn't care. What was sitting in front of the rune-bound figure, just out of their arms' reach, was what caught the Giftgiver's eye. It was a flickering, fist-sized jewel. He looked back at a greedily smiling Grambol Doomsayer. "That be a prize fit fer Jikseon," he said with hushed words.

"Aye," the old coot whispered, his greed flooding over his fear, nodding lustily at Haggersath.

"Aye," Haggersath answered, feeling his own greed overtake a trembling that no longer held sway over him.

All treasure came at a risk. He knew this to be true. The greater the treasure, the greater the risk—it just was. This treasure required the most risk he reasoned he had ever taken. But with it in sight, the oppressive evil was only a tingling memory, quite unimportant.

"Haggersath..." The Gulpraşt had his eyes closed, his voice quiet with notable strain. Veins in his temples were throbbing with visible pulsation. "We cannot stand against this being. He is of the Sun itself, an offspring of the black taint upon its face. It is like no power I have known. It is a runeweaver."

CHAPTER 15

Jikseon's Chosen

Haggersath gave the gravity of Gulprąst's plea no concern. The treasure they sought was there for the taking. Diwolde Stonescraper was talking, but he did not hear him, either. His focus on the glittering jewel before him had his lust enthralled, gripping him.

Diwolde Stonescraper slapped him on his chest, bringing his attention back. Diwolde Stonescraper was pointing to something only his experienced eyes could see. "We could make for the passage on the other side of the dais there. Do ya see it?" Greed twinkled in his eyes.

Squinting, the others looked on, finding nothing. Only Diwolde Stonescraper, a Grýttr, seemed to see what he spoke of. Confused nods and head shaking brought him astonishment. "Ya be a blind stone-headed bunch o' Dwarrow." He stopped shuffling the pebbles in his hand and absently tucked them into his pouch.

Rubbing his forehead in annoyed dismay, he said, "It's plain as the beards under your fat, stinkin' noses. Can ya not see it?" His frustration reached a fervent hiss. "I'm embarrassed ta call ye Dwarrow. Follow me. If we be quick, we might slip through unnoticed."

"Aye," agreed Haggersath, finally snapping out of the hazy funk. "You Rock-Biters help those with foot ailments to move fast. I don't want to lose any more of you." Turning to Mevindh-Gulbard, he asked, "Can you create a distraction to get us through?"

He looked incredulously at Haggersath, as if he was told to move the mountains aside. His arm raised toward the melee.

Pulling the Gulpraŝt's beard, Haggersath brought him closer to his face. "Listen! We are here for that gemstone." Haggersath gestured wildly with eager fury. "Find a way, if ya gotta call on Jikseon hisself."

"As you wish, Giftgiver," he relented with reservation. Then his eyes grew wide, and he went pale. "It be too late. The runeweaver sensed me. We are caught."

Mevindh-Gulbard closed his eyes as he drew on pure yellow power, feeding off whatever Jikseon would gift him. A flash of golden light blazing like the Sun came into the room itself and lit the cavern. Such a flash of intensity came that it seemed to stun not only the Sylvan but also hold the lich. Unaffected were the Dwarrow, and they were able to see as if it were daylight. The Gulprąst had tempered the yellow wrath of Jikseon to their benefit; his whole body shook as the flash was maintained. Sweat poured off his brow, and his veins bulged out of his skin. Dwarrow moved and rushed forward, with Diwolde Stonescraper leading the way to the hidden door. He swept a pattern on the wall, causing the door to appear and open.

Haggersath scooped up the gem in his rough-palmed hand as he ran, but it tugged him with a great weight and slowed him down short of the open door. This gemstone, this treasure, gripped him and held him fast. Haggersath's gait stalled with the weight of the mountains, slowly bringing him to a halt.

Haggersath could feel the gemstone as it reached out to him, filling his being—warming, comforting yellow magic of Jikseon. It soothed him. He was safe. Why run? Such wondrous power bound him in swaddled magic.

But there, on the edges of the yellow, just a bit of red. It was hot and enticing. He could sense something else. Something foreign to his being, cool and clear but untouchable. He knew it was blue power, but it kept a distance and did not touch him. It was held back from him.

Then, Jikseon—his own patron deity, creator of the Dwarrow—slid out of the red, bathed in yellow. He looked like any Dwarrow one might meet in the common walks of life. Nothing stood out as unique. He was not tall or short. He was not in any way special. But Haggersath knew him. Then, Jikseon spoke:

"Hail, Haggersath."

His voice rumbled like rocks crashing down a mountainside.

> *"At last, our time has come. The world is in great peril. In your hand, you hold the Destiny Stone, which I have created to save the Dwarrow from demise. In it you will find my own power. Wield it for all Dwarrow. I choose you.*

> *"Restore the might of the Horned Towers and claim your rightful place from the Bornholm, for those of Strongmedjie have lost their way and betrayed their own kin. Upon the forges of Konungr, use the Stone, and you, Haggersath Giftgiver, shall craft gifts of greater renown than even those*

Giftgivers of old. Distribute them, as your name declares, to raise the Dwarrow.

"Be wary though—other gods and their vassals will come to know that the Destiny Stone is in your fist. Each of the gods has designs to thwart you for their own kind. Be stingy of those who are not of the Horne. They are not your allies, no matter their bearing."

"Haggersath!" Haggersath heard in the depths—very far away. "Giftgiver!" An echo. No closer.

"Go now. The runeweaver even now recovers from the Gulprạst's power. It fades. Morningsong's children are here, and they will perceive you have what they desire. They will pursue you relentlessly. But be most aware of the spies of Noshid, for his hand is deceitful and it has been laid upon your shoulder, even now."

Haggersath came back to the scene of the cave with a snap. Bolfath had picked him up and was carrying him with one hand just as a mother cat might carry a kitten to where the others had dropped through a trap door in the floor. Dropping Haggersath none too gently, he followed, and Diwolde Stonescraper signed on the stone wall with the same gesture he used at the other entrance, closing the secret way and hopefully sealing the runeweaver (and the Sylvan) out.

They heard a shriek of pure vileness mixed with death-filled anguish, a shriek that left them face down on the stone for a moment. Fury of the runeweaver failing to guard the Destiny Stone. Haggersath felt it like cold ice penetrating every bone in his body. He could not see. There was no light. The Dwarrow were all speaking at once in the confusion of total darkness.

"Gulprąst," called out Diwolde Stonescraper, "bring us light. We need to see Haggersath. Something be wrong with him." But there was no reply, and no light came.

Haggersath could only listen as the Dwarrow fumbled in the dark, unable to see without the magic of Mevindh-Gulbard. After finding one of their flints to light a makeshift torch, light flickered up, and Haggersath could see them all around him looking concerned. The damn fools, he was fine. He tried to tell them as much, but he found that his voice was lost and all he could make was a garbled gurgle, which amplified their worry.

He felt the sweaty bulk that could only be Bolfath as he moved closer to Haggersath, seeming to sit on the floor. He nearly stumbled over another body onto Haggersath as he did.

Once the torch began to flicker up enough, the light shone, revealing their situation. Haggersath was aghast at what he saw. Mevindh-Gulbard was lying next to him and did not move. His eyes were open, staring blankly, his pale face pallid and gaunt. They were sunken sockets, deeply ringed and black. Haggersath touched the Gulprąst and drew back his hand. Icy cold, like death had taken his being.

Grambol Doomsayer crawled over him, looking into his blank eyes. After a relieved gulp of air, he clarified, "Bless me beard. Me sleeve moved at his breath. He be alive."

"Make haste, then—there be no time ta malinger here," insisted Diwolde Stonescraper. "That thing, whatever it was, didn't seem none too pleased we came along and took its pretty bauble."

Haggersath found his voice, although weak and creaky. "He be right. That runeweaver be lookin' fer us now." Following the gaze of the entire troop, Haggersath looked at his tightly clenched fist. In it he held a gem of remarkable beauty that shimmered unworldly in the flickering torchlight.

Haggersath shook off the cobwebs clogging his head. He wanted to keep it close, but it made him think outside his own mind. The way the Destiny Stone made him behave called him to question if he should hold it himself, but Jikseon had said a spy was close. Who could he trust? Bolfath, he could trust with his life—but Bolfath had a mind for fighting, not for keeping. He'd likely lose it out of carelessness. Grambol Doomsayer always reliably kept the treasure—yes, Grambol should hold it. But he needed to make sure the old Doomsayer never touched it directly, or he too might suffer the effects.

He told Grambol Doomsayer, "That shiny bauble be the will of Jikseon. Take it an' put it away fer safekeeping. But whatever ye do, don' touch—"

Too late. Grambol Doomsayer's fingers had ensnared the gemstone. He looked blankly at Haggersath, tucking it into the leather bag at his waist where he kept the most valuable of their findings.

"Ya din't feel nothing?" Haggersath was confused.

"Eh?" Grambol Doomsayer looked at him. "Feels like riches. What else should it feel like?"

"Well, don't that beat all." Haggersath mulled over the nonfeasance. "I'd rather ye didn't touch it. It is not just a pretty ornament...you truly didn't feel nothing?"

"I mean, it be nice an' all. Maybe I do feel like a king!" Grambol Doomsayer laughed. Haggersath let it go.

"This way." Diwolde Stonescraper headed down the tunnel quickly under their cloth-and-oil torchlight. "It seems to be takin' us back under the outpost proper."

Haggersath staggered to his feet to follow in the middle of the group. Bolfath was too tall, even bent over—he had to scramble on all fours, heaving Mevindh-Gulbard onto his back as he went. He slowed them to a snail's pace.

"I'm not goin' ta crawl like a beast all the way home, ya know," he grunted.

Laughing, Grölle sniped, "I knew ya was a beast in a battle, Bolfath. I jus' didn't know that creepin' around like one was yer habit."

Most of the company got a good chuckle. Dwarrow could find humor at the strangest of times.

As they went on, Haggersath pondered how Grambol Doomsayer seemed unaffected when he touched the Destiny Stone. He also wondered about the message. Jikseon had given him specific instructions. Haggersath was to make gifts for those leaders and captains of the Dwarrow he would select. A symbol of office, and in varied strengths and dominions of magic. They would wield great power. Ha! Imagine the Towers of the Horne greater than ever, once more the crowning achievement of the Silfr Mountains. He would cow those overproud Bornholm back to their places—Jikseon assured it. It was not just petty revenge on his part. It was a divine command of Jikseon.

Grambol Doomsayer would know where the master armorer of the Horne had kept the manuals. He and Diwolde Stonescraper could rekindle the mighty forges, and Haggersath and his Haseti would pave the way for the Horne to be revived. He was near giddy with the thought.

It was the warnings that Jikseon levied that tugged at his mind next. He did not bear much concern of danger from those Sylvan. Sure, they held magic, but so did the Dwarrow. Well, they would once the Gulprąst woke. The real worry was the idea of a spy faithful to Noshid. No Dwarrow would carry allegiance to the god of the Gnomôk over their own kind—even the western Dwarrow would never break that code. He trusted his party, even Jarlsalt and his ilk, to stay true to Jikseon. But a spy was bad news—as was having a runeweaver on their tails. He hoped the tunnels would have enough yellow and red magic to keep that lich away. What were liches, really? Where did they come from? They had no god of reference he knew of. The Gulprąst said something about the Sun and taint, but he could not follow it all. It would need to wait until Mevindh-Gulbard was back to his quiet, brooding self.

There was more to worry about—Jikseon had said all the gods would pursue it. He had only spoken of two. What of Bruss and the southerners, the race of Man? No word was given. And then there was that ice-queen goddess, Christiemay. Her mystery was a hidden shroud of devilry no Dwarrow had knowledge of. She could never be trusted with her cold secrecy and devious ways. Perhaps even Jikseon did not know.

It was a mystery, and he would find answers soon enough—it was he and the Dwarrow who held the Destiny Stone. He had a full company of warriors, four ferskeyttr of Rock-Biters, and his Haseti. Within his troop was the most fearsome Dwarrow warrior living, Bolfath. Nothing and no one had ever stood toe to toe with the bodyguard and lived to tell the tale. They were set with all the tools they'd need to win. The Destiny Stone was theirs.

CHAPTER 16

A Single Casualty

"Here it is," Diwolde Stonescraper said, finally pleased by his finding. "I don' know what manner Dwarrow made this end of the tunnel—their work be closer ta brewers than masons. There be no defense or hidden door. We be lucky no rats found their way in here."

Diwolde Stonescraper popped open the top of the tunnel, and the dim light of the last rays of the day greeted Haggersath, brightening the cramped passage. He followed Diwolde Stonescraper as they crept out of the low tunnel one by one. Diwolde Stonescraper was right again. They had come out in the middle of Krath outside the mountains.

Looking about, Haggersath could see the broken rubble of the town's buildings. Much was overgrown with clusters of short grasses browning at the edges.

The multitude of kvalid tracks running everywhere throughout the dirt pathways told the story of endless plunder. Those rats infested everything. Worse, their refuse left a distinct fetor. If left to spread, they would turn the whole of Thear into their own Rotte Hojle.

There was no sign of Jarlsalt. "Find that son of a Bornholm," Haggersath said to no one in particular. "He should be done clearing out those mangy rats."

Haggersath calmed his voice and gazed over at the Gulprąst, who Bolfath had laid on the grass. He did not move, and the pallor had not returned. Haggersath gulped back his worry and found his hand at his neck touching the gorget with the Alexandrite stone that told all who would see it that he was the Giftgiver of the Horned Towers. He needed Mevindh-Gulbard. Perhaps just some more rest. Looking at Bolfath, he said sadly, "We kin rest here till we get the Gulprąst back on his boots."

The two ferskeyttr of Rock-Biters spread out, one with Grölle and the other led by Othro, proudly escorted by his winter fox. Grambol Doomsayer was about to go with them, but Haggersath held out his arm.

"Not you, Doomsayer. You stay close to me and that beast with two axes so as ya don' get lost. You go with them, Diwolde."

Grambol Doomsayer had the Destiny Stone in his pouch, and the safest place was near Bolfath. They stayed watchful; there might be rats about, and who knows if that runeweaver had followed them. It might be able to pick up the "scent" of the Stone. Haggersath whispered a plea to Jikseon for luck—he wasn't sure why he'd done that. It wasn't his way, praying to gods and all.

Before long, the rapid movement of hurried short steps could only mean one thing, Jarlsalt approached, broadcasting his sly smile. It slipped from his face as he noticed Mevindh-Gulbard lying prone.

"What in the name of Jikseon happen' to him?" Jarlsalt said, rattling off like a blacksmith's hammer, more demanding than questioning. "Tell me at least ya got the loot that loony old bastard said was in that mountain there."

Grambol Doomsayer laughed to himself in between bites of the small pickled fish he was making a snack of. Haggersath looked up from his fallen friend to meet the swarthy Dwarrow's beady eyes. "Aye…we got it," he began slowly. "An' we cannot tell what be wrong with the Gulprąst. He's not moved since we got the Destiny Stone."

"Destiny Stone?" Jarlsalt said. "What do ya mean?"

Haggersath sighed. He supposed he should tell Jarlsalt some of it. But the parts from Jikseon, he would keep some of that to himself. Tugging with two fingers at the annoying Giftgiver gorget at his neck, he said, "That be the treasure. It be a pretty gemstone."

Surprise washed a ripple over Jarlsalt's face as he nodded, his smile flickering back. "Well, we kin rest here fer now. Me an' me boys—we cleared out them nasty rats and sent them a runnin' all the way back to Rotte Hojle. We whipped 'em good." He held his head proudly.

"At least that be some good news. We'll give the Gulpr̨ast some time to recover...mehopes it not be long." Haggersath let himself begin to relax. "Did we lose anybody in yer cleansin' of this place?"

"We be fine. Minor wounds." Haggersath smiled at hearing more good news. But then Jarlsalt said, "There was a strange accident though." He was almost smiling, like he was stuffing his mirth from the punchline of a joke.

"Accident?" What was this that had Jarlsalt bursting out laughing? "Why this be funny ta ya? Tell me, Captain Jarlsalt. What kind of accident be a joke ta ya?"

"Well, in the fightin' we did up near the rocks by the mountain, Nater caught a rock when swinin' his hammer an' the chip flew an' cut Melmir across his arm." Haggersath was still waiting for whatever was funny. "Y'know Melmir don't like to wear long mail on his arms. He be proud of the thick muscle an' thinks it be better ta show the enemy his strength." Haggersath had no idea what he was talking about. He did not know Melmir—must be a western Dwarrow out of Strongmedjie. Jarlsalt paused, looking at Haggersath, waiting for something, a reaction.

"I don't know no Melmir," Haggersath said, showing his boredom with the story. But he did remember seeing a Dwarrow with no mail sleeves and oversized arms. That had to be him.

"I remember him," Grambol Doomsayer said without invitation to comment. "He has the biggest arms I ever did see."

"Bah. Lookie here," said Bolfath as he stood, flexing his arms. "He be nothin'. Bolfath has the biggest arms."

Haggersath had to agree, and with Grambol Doomsayer nodding and washing his fish snack down with a nip of spirit, it was unanimous.

Jarlsalt only glowered at the interruptions and went on. "Well, the rock chip struck Melmir in the arm." He waited. Haggersath saw no reason to make this relevant to anything. It must have shown on his face because Jarlsalt let out an exasperated gasp. He held his hands out like he was offering something. "He be chipped!"

"Chipped," repeated Haggersath and Diwolde Stonescraper, who was just returning.

"Aye," acknowledged the greasy captain. "He left ta go back ta Strongmedjie. There was no stopping him."

"But fer him ta be chipped, the stone must have been mangeesum ore. Nothin' else will stir the blood," Diwolde Stonescraper said.

Haggersath knew this was true. Chipping only occurred when a sharp piece of mangeesum ore cut a male Dwarrow deep enough to draw blood. It triggered the need to find a female and match with her.

Jarlsalt was laughing now at his story's conclusion. He gasped out, saying, "He won't be back anytime soon. There be no females in our party, so he must go back ta Strongmedjie."

Haggersath had never been chipped, but he had seen it happen to Dwarrow. It was very uncommon, but it did happen. Once chipped, the male Dwarrow had to find the rock that cut him and take it to a female. The drive was so strong that nothing else would matter until he found a female to accept the bloodied chip from him. He did not know how long the chip would be "fertile" with the blood, but he had heard it was temporary. Failing to mate sometimes made the chipped male hopelessly insane.

So Melmir was the only casualty. *Luck of Jikseon to him,* Haggersath thought. He felt a weariness come on, but Jarlsalt was not going to let him find a moment's rest.

"Show me the artifact Grambol Doomsayer raved about. It better be worthy of the loss of our Gulprąst," ordered Jarlsalt at the small Dwarrow contingent.

Haggersath stood full up, losing the fatigue. "Ye ferget yerself, commander. This isn't Strongmedjie, where yer patriarch holds sway. The only lot you command here is the warhammers and Rock-Biters ya brought with you. I am Haggersath Giftgiver of the Horned Towers—not some toad out of your father's court. And here, I command *you*!"

After initially backing away, surprised by Haggersath's rage, Jarlsalt let a half-hidden sneer slip across his sharply angular face. "Of course, master Giftgiver, I meant no affront." His tenor moved from insincere platitude to a hate-filled hiss. "But do not forget who I am. I will see this thing we paid a price for, and I will see it now."

Haggersath frowned, glowering in resentment. He told Grambol Doomsayer, unfolding his tongue from the bitter taste, "Show him the Stone, Doomsayer."

Grambol Doomsayer reached in his pack and drew out the Stone of Destiny, holding it out high for all to see. It glittered and twinkled with the radiance of the Sun hidden inside the glorious crystal—its color shifting, indistinguishable.

Jarlsalt's mouth hung open at the spectacle, working wordlessly. "Well," he finally said, "that be a sight."

Haggersath saw the Destiny Stone draw Jarlsalt in, captivating his attention. He stepped closer in mindless wonder, as if the Destiny Stone called to him. Haggersath looked around the gathered Dwarrow. None of the others reacted as Jarlsalt did. It was just a pretty gemstone of remarkable size to them. But Jarlsalt was—mesmerized.

"That's enough, Doomsayer. Put the Stone away," said Haggersath. *Odd,* he thought. Only Jarlsalt. Not Grambol Doomsayer. Not the others around them. Only Jarlsalt—and himself. He did not feel Jikseon's call, but nonetheless, he felt the presence of the Destiny Stone. He could tell where it was, and had an idea of how close it was. No other Dwarrow reacted that way. He shelved his concern but did not forget it.

Jarlsalt started as if he'd been slapped when Grambol Doomsayer stowed the Destiny Stone from his eager view, back safely in his pack.

Haggersath leaned over to Grambol Doomsayer's ear. "I don' want ta see that thing again unless I be tellin' ya ta expose it. Ever!" His eyebrows raised to accent his severity.

Grambol Doomsayer met his eyes with his own placid, rheumy stare. "Aye."

Haggersath turned away without seeing the burning glance Jarlsalt shot at his back.

The rest of the Dwarrow had returned during the exchange and were getting ready to settle down in a camp. After flushing out the rats, many warriors had gone hunting. Being excellent hunters, they had scrounged up enough grouse and duck to feed them all for a week.

They converted comfortably into a boisterous Dwarrow camp. Forgetting the day's work and recent dangers were simple matters to achieve. Rock-Biters and regular soldiers sat around fires, trading tall tales of their recent exploits while sharing Siolvarin ale and grouse stew. Evening came on, and the last rays of the Sun withdrew behind the frosty peaks of the Silfr Mountains.

Haggersath picked at his stew, taking a piece of sweet potato with soft grouse in small bites, chewing well. The grouse was particularly gamey and must have lived off too many peppercorns. Onion and vinegar shared the duty to cut the lean gaminess, but it was the glistening, clear layer of melted duck fat over the top of the stew that made the dish really filling. Dwarrow knew their food, not just their drink. Grambol Doomsayer had directed a small team of Dwarrow in cooking the stew and preparing the duck meat into hard jerky for later on the road. Haggersath felt relaxed and smiled deeply.

After they all had time to eat and rest, Haggersath met his Haseti, Jarlsalt included. Haggersath needed to watch him and see if he might be the one, the spy. Only Mevindh-Gulbard was not in attendance.

Haggersath brought their excited chatting down as he waved his hands to shush them. "This Stone we have acquired, 'tis more than just some pretty trinket to be sold off or laid at the feet of the Bornholm." This got an immediate frown from Jarlsalt. "When I held the Stone, it spoke to me."

Murmurs and shifting around the fire belayed questions of sane talk. Most notably from Diwolde Stonescraper and Jarlsalt. *Hmm,* Haggersath thought, *he Stonescraper, a spy? Naw, couldn't be.*

"Better if I be sayin'," Haggersath corrected, noticing the skepticism, "the Stone allowed Jikseon hisself to speak to me through it. I cannot say how, but he did."

"Har!" burst out Jarlsalt, violently shaking his head. "An' what did our patron god have to discuss with the great Giftgiver of the Horned Towers? Did he tell ya ta go there and make them ruined turrets rise ta meet the sky?" Ridicule bit every word. He broke off laughing, and the rest smiled with mild amusement—until they saw that Haggersath was not amused. Then they cut off, one after another, to silence.

"I don' fault yer doubt, captain. I kin hardly believe it meself. But it be true, an' he spoke of a mission he bestowed upon this company of ours to take the Stone to do just that."

Jarlsalt rose to his feet to protest but instead looked off in the dark beyond the campfires. "What in the name o' Jikseon..." he said, his jaw dropping like he'd seen a ghost.

A crescendoing hiss built, closing in toward them, bringing a feeling of oppressive fear that riveted them to the spot. They all stood, facing the way of the commotion, but none made a move, even as Dwarrow cries of surprise carried in the night. A blackness out of the void of the distance glided through the ranks, spilling Dwarrow to the side as a longship might part the water on the sea.

The runeweaver from under the mountain was advancing toward their fire. Black runes with icy, pale blue cores were orbiting slowly around its shabby robes, emitting smoky, snakelike coils that wiggled and tossed the Dwarrow as it came on.

*"I claim the Destiny Stone. You cannot
stand against me—look to your priest."*

The voice was ice on a windy night, quivering with
unworldly breath.

"I bring you death!"

Jarlsalt and most of the warriors and Rock-Biters cast
themselves down on their faces. Diwolde Stonescraper
and Grambol Doomsayer looked on with horror,
pilfering their expressions—they were immobilized.
Haggersath could only look, but Bolfath did move, and
he stepped in front of Haggersath with an ax in each
hand, snarling with fear-driven rage. He would defend
Haggersath. Nothing short of death could stop him.

Before the runeweaver reached Haggersath's Haseti,
a cloaked, hooded, Man-sized figure leaped in front
of Bolfath, slashing with a long bihänder that glowed
with the true power of blue magic. Faster than mortally
possible, the lich shifted its ethereal body, phasing out
to avoid the stroke—but its advance was curtailed, and
its intent broken. The hooded figure brought the sword
back around with two hands on the grip, and it met the
icy black blade of the lich with a grinding crack like
ancient glacial ice. The lich's runed black sword flashed
with glints of blue.

There came off the cloaked figure's hand a blast of blue magic that was sopped up by the black sword. It bought time for the cloaked swordsman to attack with speed to match the lich. The figure was a picture of fury as it drove the runeweaver back—away their furious battle raged out into the night. In a flash of white-hot blue light—with the unearthly wail of the runeweaver— they were gone. Except for the Dwarrow coming back to agitated furor, the night was undisturbed and quiet around them.

Left in a disarray of confusion, the Dwarrow gathered their camp together. It was chaos. It took time for the fear and sickness to leave them this time, without the influence or protection provided by the Gulprąst.

When Jarlsalt was finally back to himself, he turned to Haggersath and yelled, "Didja know that thing be huntin' us, master bloody Giftgiver? What the fuck do we be doin' fightin' a thing like that?"

Haggersath slowly let a smile spread across his face. And he chuckled. Then a full-on belly laugh.

"Are ye daft? Didja lose yer mind?" Jarlsalt let his fear and rage boil into red-faced yelling, spit flying off in all directions.

Grölle arrived and interrupted, delivering his report to Jarlsalt in front of Haggersath, assessing their damage—perfect timing. His report allowed Jarlsalt some time to regain composure and Haggersath time to stop laughing. A few soldiers suffered from a paralyzing touch the lich delivered, Grölle said, but it was all localized, and they could travel again now.

"What in the halls of Strongmedjie was that thing?" While he'd calmed down closer to normal, Jarlsalt still held a demanding tone, expecting immediate answers.

"That be the guardian of the Destiny Stone from under the mountain," answered Haggersath. "An' as ye said yerself, we got no business fightin' a thing like that. If we know what be best fer us, we better be getting somewhere safer until we got the Gulprąst back on his feet."

"Ahhh, beggin' yer pardon, Haggersath," Grambol Doomsayer said, cutting in. Haggersath raised an eyebrow. "I don't think that be the same runeweaver as we saw below. That one had a longer, thinner blade, an' his magic was a perversion of blue, not red."

The Dwarrow exchanged queried looks among themselves. Those who saw the one in the tunnels nodded in agreement.

"Ya mean we got two o' them things after our hides, then?" Haggersath breathed through his teeth, letting a whistle sing out, stunned as new fear rocked him. More than one runeweaver. That would not be good. Hopefully his addlebrained Doomsayer hadn't overimbibed in spirits. "We'll keep a watch, Doomsayer. You an' me and Bolfath will leave with the Sun. Get yer lads rest, captain," he said to Grölle. "Methinks you'll be needin' it."

They started to leave the fire, Jarlsalt noticeably agitated. He looked sidelong at Haggersath as he was leaving, shaking his head in drastic disapproval. Haggersath knew the prickly captain was put off by going around him to give Grölle the order while he stood there.

"Captain Jarlsalt." Haggersath stopped him in his tracks. "You personally lead the watch tonight; I need your expertise patrolling the perimeter. Use warriors. I need the Rock-Biters fresh in the morning."

Jarlsalt growled back at him, "Yah, I hear you. Better concern yerself 'bout that other one too. Not just dead things. Methinks the Man with the blue bihänder be just as much a problem."

Then he stomped off into the darkness, leaving just one more concern at Haggersath's feet.

As Haggersath headed to sleep, he thought that perhaps the cropped-beard captain was right. Who was that who stood toe to toe with the runeweaver? He must garner a great power to be able to drive the lich away. Haggersath drifted into dreams fraught with bony fingers sneaking grabs at the Destiny Stone. His homecoming might not be all meat and mead and polished stone. His fitful night would end all too soon.

Diwolde Stonescraper spent the morning with two Dwarrow possessing a trickle of engineering skill. The three of them were searching Krath for pathways under the mountains. Finding the correct one could save days or even weeks of travel to their destination. This part of the Silfr Mountains was heavily interlaced with the burrowing habits of the Dwarrow. Centuries of Dwarrow inhabitation meant delving under and around and through the mountains. They were successful in finding half a score of hidden and not-so-hidden ways leading hither and thither, but it required Diwolde Stonescrarper's extensive Grýttr knowledge to identify the one they hoped to find. It was mid-morning when he approached Haggersath with the news.

"Hail, Haggersath!" Diwolde Stonescraper began, "I found two choices fer ya ta consider. We have one that goes directly to the Horned Towers. There be another—faster, too—it takes us to Strongmedjie in but a day sooner."

"The Towers?!" questioned a shocked Jarlsalt, overhearing the report. He came rushing over in an odd sort of waddle that he sometimes did when angered. "There be no reason to go there. It's a dead city."

"We go to the Towers, all right. It's what Jikseon declared," Haggersath said with genuine joy in his words and a pleased twinkle in his eye.

"Beggin' yer pardon, Haggersath, but the Bornholm decreed ya's ta return with the treasure, whatever it may be—yer precious little Stone included. Nobody here believes yer fairy tale that Jikseon talked ta ya," admonished Jarlsalt. "The sooner we get it safe from them two runeweavers—which, by yer own declarin', be chasin' it—the better fer us all. If ye hadn't noticed, we be vulnerable when it comes, an' we cannot touch it. Yer Gulprąst is our only magic, and he's not likely to stand up ta help anytime soon." Jarlsalt paused. "Captain Grölle, get yer boys together. We leave as soon as yer ready."

"Ya make good sense, captain," Haggersath commended with a slap on the back. "Let's be off then."

He smirked, seeing Jarlsalt throw his waterskin to the dirt in a fury as the company entered the tunnels leading to the Towers of the Horne.

CHAPTER 17

Gulpra̧st

Mevindh-Gulbard felt himself being torn from his own body. Yellow power blazed through him—it was the only thing stopping the black smoky mist from consuming him. All around him was impenetrably shrouded in darkness. Two forces drawn of the Sun battled with the familiarity of ages. The beaming yellow energies emanating as raw power were without limit. Slowly, by incremental progression founded through a concentration of evil, black power eroded his amber energies away. Instinctively Mevindh-Gulbard knew if it breached the resistance he clung to, and snuffed the light out, he would be consumed and his body left an empty husk. He could never match the black magic of a runeweaver. Jikseon did not grant a Gulpra̧st the essence of that kind of power.

Knowledge in the circles of Gulprạsts was scant when considering runeweavers. Scarcely were they mentioned even in older references. More often, myth and hearsay were gathered into legends or forgotten tales deeply drawn from ages long gone—they were mostly false truths and of little real use. He did know that runeweavers were creatures neither living nor dead, but both, that were born of an undefined evil. Stories told of no purpose or allegiance they held to. Theirs were tales of terror and death. They craved nothing, served nothing. Only death. Only fear. Terrible, indescribable terror. Death came with every story or account.

Black was the color of their magic. It came from no god, as the colors did. It was said to be drawn from the blemishes on the Sun, and these runeweavers—if the rumors spoke true—possessed a limitless power in rune magic. *Limitless* power.

He could feel it pressing him, crushing him. A blackness consuming the light Jikseon granted. He held on to a point of light the size of a pea against the dark onslaught. Mevindh-Gulbard knew his burst of power in the room had faded—it was only an extended flash. He could not maintain such a flow of yellow magic, such a great unleashing for any length of time. It was not to be granted to a mere Gulprạst. But he did so, and it was.

But all that power came at a cost. Now the cost was due to pay. His burst was gone, and only a shell of tallow magic remained. The runeweaver came to him with evil energies of black needing no runes to operate.

The lich brought to bear its focused will upon him, crushing his upstart sorcery as if it were a wad of paper in its fetid hand. Mevindh-Gulbard's magic yielded, withered and faded, now wan and flaxen, a last pitiful effort to preserve his spirit. He should have perished, but he did not. The force behind the black power hesitated as if distracted. He was no longer the focus of the runeweaver's will.

All at once, it was gone. He felt his spirit slide back toward his body—but there was no body to go to; it was not there. Nothing. He was isolated and weak. He had to rejoin with his corporeal self. The runeweaver had split him apart, shattering him, and now he was spliced in half.

In his fractured state, he was eternally tumbling and diminishing at the same time, and he could not right himself. This much was clear: He needed to find his body and become whole again or perish.

CHAPTER 18

Games

Travel under the Silfr Mountains was slow going. While the injured Rock-Biters had moved well after receiving limited mending from the Gulprąst, Mevindh-Gulbard himself had to be carried. The Gulprąst never got the chance to finish their healing before he was struck down.

Under the mountains, the passage was far more developed than the cramped tunnels under Krath. This was a hyljaleid, a sort of Dwarrow highway under the Silfr Mountains. Dwarrow had constructed a great network of tunnels, some wide enough to draw two fully loaded wagons astride. This tunnel was large and well constructed. It was a main part of the hyljaleid and had seen much use in its day.

Craggy cave walls covered the expanse up the sides and over the top of the hyljaleid. The rock and clay mixed with grays hinted at purple and brown that grew to a burnt orange. A steady drip drizzled down the walls in some places. In others, it came from above and splattered a drop here and there. Haggersath wiped his face dry from the rusty water. A healthy dose of iron gave it a taste of the mountain's blood.

"Four days now, Stonescraper," he said to Diwolde Stonescraper, who strode energetically beside him.

"Yes." Diwolde Stonescraper was breathless with excitement even now. "It be a wonder ta be here. What skill and cunning." Rock always brought Diwolde Stonescraper to a fever, but he was a Grýttr, and he saw that which other Dwarrow only glanced over with casual unawareness.

"Bah! How many more days?" Haggersath wiped another drop from his face with an exaggerated annoyance. He was anxious to reach the Towers at the other end of the tunnels.

"Hard to be sure." Diwolde Stonescraper looked around like a child discovering his first rainbow. "It has been decades since I be travelin' through the hyljaleid. If I had ta guess…" He looked at Haggersath and realized he was fully expected to make that guess. "Less than a week and more than a day."

Haggersath gave a stifled grunt of disapproving acknowledgement. That would have to be acceptable.

So far, the small band of Dwarrow had been pleased to be in a place crafted by their ancestors. Still, he worried about the pithy mix of east and west Dwarrow. It had remained amicable...so far.

The Dwarrow warmed their nights with fire and spirits. The preserved duck they had hunted was a simple but celebrated fare. At night meals, they cooked the duck with onions and fat little white beans into a stew. Grambol Doomsayer had found some lichen on the cavern walls that he scraped loose with general culinary enthusiasm. Gleefully giggling, he added it to the pot—garnering frowns from those who saw him, Haggersath included. But he had to admit, it made the stew quite delicious.

Haggersath knew that, more often than not, Grambol Doomsayer imbibed in Vallhah and enjoyed its hot burn on the tongue and strong pull on the mind. Haggersath and the great majority of others relished instead their Siolvarin ale. Although both were still plentiful, their journey had an unknown length to go. He hoped they would not run dry before they could get more.

By the fourth night, Haggersath noticed an odd development at the fireside: Jarlsalt carousing with Grambol Doomsayer. At first, they appeared at uncomfortable odds. But each night, Jarlsalt joined him—and each night, they shared a drink, and their banter warmed up. The unlikely melding of a new friendship grew into bawdy comradery by the fifth night.

Placing himself just close enough to hear, Haggersath took to eavesdropping on their talk tonight. He really didn't have to try, since Grambol Doomsayer was well into his cups and far louder than necessary. Jarlsalt had to speak loudly to be heard over the other Dwarrow, but he was clearly trying to keep his talk more restrained.

"How long to the Towers?" Jarlsalt probed the bleary-eyed Doomsayer. "I'm hopin' the Giftgiver don' tarry too long in that place. There be nothin' left but empty ghosts of the past there. Y'no we seen enough of ghosts these days fer any lifetime."

"Got that right," Grambol Doomsayer said, "them's ain't my kinda company. The farther we stay from the likes of them, the better for us all." He investigated his flask. "Now this—this be my kind of spirit." He guffawed loudly.

Jarlsalt joined with a feigned chortle. "Do there be a way under the mountains away from the Horned Towers?" Grambol Doomsayer looked confused at that, but Jarlsalt went on in more detail. "Y'no something, a path under the mountains an' direct to the Strongmedjie? We need ta be headin' home soon. The path the Giftgiver be takin', it be folly."

"Aye, there be that," Grambol Doomsayer said with a crackle back at him. "These mountains all be connected. But ya kin ne'er be sure what ways be still open an' what ways be closed. We have used them little in recent times. It be so long ago that I trudged those ways. I remember a great highway from the Horne to Strongmedjie. Sometimes the ways are closed because the mountain isself shifted. Sometimes it's more—"

"Yes, yes, I know," Jarlsalt interrupted with drunken impatience—or was it feigned as well? "But can ya show me the way? I'm longing to get back sometime after he finishes his gift makin' business."

Grambol Doomsayer took a long draw and spat with a choke at the fire before him, sputtering. He took a moment to recover. The whole time Haggersath saw Jarlsalt pounding on the Doomsayer's back, laughing at him.

"Wrong way?" Jarlsalt gave an inflated laugh.

Grambol Doomsayer wiped the wetness from his beard, smiling, almost squeezing it out like it was an old dishrag. Then he looked at Jarlsalt. "It can be done. But that be the realm of a Grýttr like the Stonescraper o'er there." Then he gestured at Diwolde Stonescraper, who was snoring like a bear in winter. He tapped his near-empty Vallhah bag. "Got anything ta pass the cold night on?"

"Har, ya old coot, I always have the good stuff with me—not like that stodgy, piss-bearded fool leading this lot." He produced a leather bag nearly full of liquor and passed it to the greedy-eyed Grambol Doomsayer.

Haggersath took offense to that—albeit, in silence. So, the captain planned to abscond to Strongmedjie as soon as he could. He would probably take the Rock-Biters and warriors with him. What would the Bornholm say to his 16th son when he came home empty-handed with nothing but news of rebuilding the Towers?

And of course, a huge gemstone.

Jarlsalt told the drunken listener, "Have at it. We be makin' the most of this futile expedition."

Grambol Doomsayer took an impressive swig, swallowed, and gave Jarlsalt a huge smile filled with large, brown-tinged teeth, one adorned with some gold. "Ya ain't half bad fer one of them Bornholm sorts."

They laughed and carried on and would do so well into the night. But Haggersath had heard enough, and he slipped back into the shadows to sit alone, near Bolfath, who lay sound asleep. For a big oaf, he slept remarkably quietly. Haggersath lay to rest with the concern of Jarlsalt's divided duties and obvious loyalty to Strongmedjie in his mind. Could he be the spy? He hoped so. If it was one of his Haseti...he would not think of that. Sleep came, despite the worry.

Haggersath took careful notice of the newfound friendship as they continued down the road to the Towers.

As they walked, Diwolde Stonescraper shared some of the more basic knowledge of stone working and crafting, rich with centuries-old expertise. He spoke with four Dwarrow he thought showed some potential, and these warriors followed him around the halls nightly, denoting him as their stone teacher. They were picking up some foundation of rock and stone— perhaps one might go on to become skilled in the ways of masonry. He was likely wasting his time, though.

Any Dwarrow could make a bridge or tunnel a mountain, but to know the ways of the hyljaleid and use them with precision, that was reserved for a true Grýttr. Diwolde Stonescraper knew where to look. He knew how to activate and operate the magic of the pathways. He understood their workings like no other living Dwarrow. He was the greatest Grýttr still living. He knew this and knew to hold these secrets to himself. But teaching passed the time and eased his stress, and so he continued on.

Even Bolfath found a way to escape stress. It was best to keep clear of the mountainous bodyguard as he sharpened his blades or practiced maneuvers in a deadly dance of axes. Many of the Rock-Biters showed interest when they dared, and Bolfath would relent, offering to spar, laughing with his deep voice that reverberated fully in the underground.

Some would spar—only the bravest. Never once did they even touch him. They walked away with deliberate red badges where Bolfath had let his ax nip just enough to reward the challenger with a reminder of his prominence. They would wear the nick as a badge of courage, proof they had sparred with the giant Dwarrow. Other times they might see Bolfath in deep brooding and steered clear of the solemn hulk, lest they find his ax bite deeper. Once, when a Rock-Biter failed to keep his temper and almost lost his head, Haggersath had to bring his own hammer in to stop the spar himself. No matter his state of rage or darkness, Bolfath always yielded to Haggersath with ingrained loyalty. His dedication was singular.

The rest of the company spent time telling tall tales or gambling with a set of seven preserved ibex testes. They played a game with loose rules that often fluxed this way or that. Of course this prompted heated, but friendly, arguments. These encounters were the meat of

Dwarrow bonding. Wagers lost or won mattered little, as the bluster and confrontations were the real goal of the game.

In one circle, Haggersath noticed particularly active Dwarrow. He stepped closer to see what prompted the noise. Othro was standing and waving a hand in the air. Avalanche lounged lazily away, eyes closed in peaceful rest. Another older Dwarrow stood by him in the middle, prodding him to take his turn at their game. Othro dug deep as he sucked in air and cleared his throat to prepare to spit. He leaned way back and let loose as he slung his body forward, head leading the way, and launched a congealed phlegm nearly three and a half meters.

He was met with cheers and laughter by the group. Some patted him on the back for his impressive ability. All the while the older Dwarrow was waving in the air to quiet the bluster as if nothing of note had happened. "No, no. That be a fine shot, me lad. A fine shot." He looked amused. "But, ya don't be spittin' against jus' any Dwarrow. Now it be my turn. An' ya all should be knowin' Curlie can spit like no other."

He drew in a great breath and let out growling howl, like an angry goat might. Then he cast out a stream of spit. It flew up and straight all the way to the hyljaleid wall, nine or more meters away.

Half the Dwarrow let loose laughter and cheers. Many met them with groans. Haggersath laughed quietly to himself, then called out to them, "That be a spit fer the ages there, Curlie. Ya be a wonder of the Dwarrow world." That brought more cheers from the whole lot of them.

Haggersath stepped away, resuming his quiet thoughts. He differed from his race in this respect. Scratching his beard and looking away, he chuckled at their foolishness. This was healthy behavior, he knew, and good spirits would arise from it—but personally, fireside storytelling was much more to his liking. Besides, as the leader, he steered clear, allowing the Dwarrow room to relax.

And at night, he got his fireside stories. On one occasion, Captain Grölle was giving a recount.

"We was surrounded by them Gnomôk filth, only me an' me four mates. That be before I became a Rock-Biter." Grölle went on in squally animation, "Me sword shined with the black blood of their kind, its ragged teeth baring death to their brutish faces."

Just then, Bolfath—who never participated much more than a rowdy listener, and never as the storyteller—joined them.

CHAPTER 19

Ice Giant

Bolfath's arrival caused a commotion, with some of the onlookers shifting about nervously, disturbed by his looming presence. Even Nater stopped combing his straight brown beard with the bone comb he had carved. He listened, showing interest in the story as Grölle hesitated. Bolfath gestured for him to continue.

"B-but they came anyhows," Grölle stammered back into the story. "They came at our left. We can handle what the likes of those filth had. But on the right, they had with them a few garm. You may know them, some call 'em inferno bitches."

This got the Dwarrow's attention. Haggersath knew of garm; he had encountered them before. Garm were pets the Gnomôk sometimes used for war in the same way Men used dogs. Mangy and thin, to the point of looking underfed, garm had the unpleasant ability to spit fire. It was acidic and burned well past the flames being extinguished. Their fire was said to be excruciatingly painful. "Inferno bitches" were a name that suited them just fine.

"They leaped upon us—flames in their howls. I took the first, me hammer dead center of her chest. It snapped with a crack, an' she belched the fetid fire right outa 'er body as I fell back. It burned like a hundred torches scorchin' me but good." Grölle pulled up his left sleeve, exposing permanently scarred, angry pink flesh. No hair grew up the grotesque, marred skin. He looked around, catching Bolfath's eye.

Haggersath smiled, looked down at his feet to hide it. The good captain sought Bolfath's approval. *Very good*, he thought.

The campfire leaned into the story, ears pricked— Grölle had them now. He looked confident, no more hesitation. "Smashing as I fell, me hammer broke shin and ankle, shattering their bones, leaving three o' the closest Gnomôk rolling on the dirt. I pushed the dead hound offa me. 'Twas easy for me to make short work of those I'd left on the dirt. I could see me mates cut up a bit, but the Gnomôk and their bitches lay there, broken and bleedin', smoke still steamin' offa them dogs."

"Har!" Bolfath belly laughed and slapped his enormous thigh. "Yer boys and you had a time with a few of them little desert pukes and their puppy dogs?"

"They was fire-spitting inferno bitches," Grölle insisted, waving his scarred arm high and looking sideways at Bolfath.

Then, support came from an unexpected source. "Gnomôk can be a real problem, 'specially when they got the numbers," piped in Jarlsalt, sipping his Vallhah next to Grambol at the fire.

"I kin see they'd be a problem fer you, ya little shit," Bolfath replied, "but I got more faith in the mettle of a war hammer borne by any Rock-Biter than the likes of a skulking snit like you."

The entire fireside broke into a raucous, uncontrolled laughter. Jarlsalt's face flushed into a blackish garnet of hatred-filled shame. He sputtered under the noise of their mocking. "Y-You!" he finally managed to get out. "I-I'll…"

Bolfath towered over him, at least twice his size in any direction, smiling with open amusement flavored with just enough taunting humiliation to bait the smaller Dwarrow. Jarlsalt shook in front of Haggersath's immense bodyguard but did not stand down. Fury betrayed his wisdom.

Haggersath froze. He did not need the death of the 16th son at the hands of his bodyguard over an insult.

"Don't be a stupid Gnomôk, ya fool," advised Grölle as the mirth quelled down.

But Jarlsalt did not relent. Haggersath began to rise. He would not let this go too far. He began to take in a draft of ale to steady his hand.

"Ya'd have no chance," pitched in Grambol Doomsayer. He struggled to speak, biting down chortling convulsions. Then with a sputtering spew of liquor and taunt, he let loose. "He's got two axes!"

The whole of the camp within earshot burst into a deafening roar. Dwarrow were rolling on the floor uncontrolled. Bolfath broke his seriousness and grinned through a chuckle. Even Haggersath had to stifle a bark, forcing ale to spray through his nose.

Jarlsalt shook, his temper exploding, but took the better choice. He bared his teeth and then turned and stomped off into the darkness, leaving his satchel of Vallhah and the shambles of his dignity at the fire's foot.

Once the bombastic yowling began to slacken, Bolfath returned to sit, beginning a new tale.

"'Tis a good thing he be gone. What I tell you now, he ne'er had the belly fer," Bolfath began. "Ye think that flamin' puppy dogs and some desert fucks be fearsome?

If so, ye better follow that gutless Bornholm 'princeling' away from here."

Bolfath let disdain roll especially thick off his tongue as he derided Jarlsalt's empty title.

"Har," the bodyguard roared out suddenly, making the listeners jump to attention at his words. "The frost that brings cold like the core of the Silfr Mountains' heart is the cold I be talkin' about. That be the cold ya kin find a league north of the shores of them frigid waters they call Toradh Dunne." He saw their eyes open in surprise. "Yeah, it be so. I have been there, all the way to the foot of Bargveoor Dodher."

He paused, looking at their eyes to measure their spirit while he unknowingly flexed his shoulders tight, increasing his bulk. Haggersath had never been there. Very few had. That was the heart of Christiemay's realm—nothing lived in those cold mountains. Nothing but danger. In that region, Jikseon was only gossip on the icy wind, balmier climates only a rumor. He knew Bolfath had traveled north of the ruins of the Horne but never that far east. And never that far north.

"I had just come of age. Me uncle sent me ta seek out me mother. Ahh, it was a fine journey, it was—that is, until me boots touched Bargveoor Dodher. All at once, the ice froze me toes. It gripped me ta the bones. Har! A lesser Dwarrow would still be there, frozen as a statue.

It was a strange thing, but me, it didn't stop. No, not me. It was…welcome ta me, familiar, like something me guts had craved that they had ta drink in. I made me way up the frigid slope—ice, solid from me nose ta me stingin' eyes, and beard its own glacier. It was beyond jus' cold—I mean it went to the core of me. Me own bones had become hard ice. But I was not numb. I was strengthened by the shiver of the slopes."

Haggersath had never heard this one before. Some of the listeners quaked, feeling the chill in the story. He could not blame them. The cavern grew darker with the frosty edge of the tale.

"The closer I got to the top, the more the clouds darkened. Snow began fallin', increasing with thickness. It hit me skin like a swarm of angry wasps, welting me face. But I trudged on. I laughed; the pain was welcome. Soon alls I could see was white whippin' by me eyes. The tempest was unnatural-like."

He paused to take a drink of ale, then set the cup down, smiling. Every Dwarrow had gathered and hung on his words. Haggersath waited as the great Dwarrow wiped his mouth with his forearm and back of the hand.

"I could hear the wind itself—first whispering at me, then howling in a distance, then upon me all at once." He paused to look at Haggersath and winked. "The wind demanded,

'Are you lost, child o' Jikseon? What manner of Dwarrow seeks his death upon the sacred face of the Bargveoor Dodher?'"

Bolfath shook his head at the ground. Then, with a wild-eyed stare, he stood, spreading his arms in a huge wingspan above. "A shadow loomed before me, tall as any pine ya saw out by Krath. She came closer ta me so I could see her." He saw their surprised faces and nodded at them. "That be right—she!" He smiled and let it sink in, then took another drink and wiped. "An' she wore shaggy skins o' beasts only seen in that far north. She had a long blonde mustache twisted together with silver baubles. Her hair be long an' yellow—braided too. So many uneven braids. She was a radiant beauty herself. Her face red an' brown from years of icy blasts snappin' at her skin. I was afeared, if that be believed. But there was somthin' about her that kept me locked in place.

"At her side crept up a Trō-lekær, a great, dirty, white beast looking very much like a bear. But

also lookin' jus' as much like it weren't no bear. It was big as a house. It opened its sharp-toothed maw and bellowed out a thunderin' roar. Now that forced me ta gasp in the frosted air—an' its rotten breath gagged me."

Another pause. Another drink. This time he continued without the wipe and let the extra ale drip off his beard and mustache like the slaver of the beast. In the flicker of the flame, it had its effect.

"At that moment, the great bearish monster leaped, toppling me under it. Its hot breath, fetid of rotten meat, blasting in me face. It drew back to strike. I was pinned under the weight of a hill—unable to move."

Bolfath stopped for a moment, fraught with emotion, to wipe his brow. His captive listeners hung on the last word. He reached for a sack of Vallhah, waving to a nearby Rock-Biter. He seemed to want something stronger than ale before he could continue.

"Ríkrr, give him the sack so's he'll get on with it," Haggersath told the Rock-Biter, waking him from the entrancement of the story. Ríkrr handed Bolfath the sack and sat back in his place. Bolfath drank and lowered his head, tossing the sack back to Ríkrr. He gulped and looked on in a fond reminiscence, his face relaxed, seeing the scene far off near the cave wall.

"Go on, Bolfath. What next?" Ríkrr encouraged with excitement.

After a very heavy sigh, Bolfath did go on. His voice was low, serious, and solemn. "The beast closed its mouth on me face. I was ready fer death then and there—but it wasn't yet to be so fer me. Not yet. Not by this huge bear. The damn beast licked me face like I was some blasted kind o' icicle! It stayed on me, panting like a long-lost puppy—a puppy the size of a small house. I heard a deep roar of laughter behind the Trō-lekær from the braided giant.

"'Har, little Dwarrow, ye must be of Stromurjotonn blood or ye'd be splayed a red stain on the snow,' she boomed in a voice rolling of thunder. 'Tell me who yer pater an' mater be? Yer kind be the only answer yer not dead.'

"I had no breath to answer with, and the creature's weight didn't allow me ta take another breath. She turn'd angry now and bellowed like clouds, ready to rip forth with lightning at me from their blackness.

"'I am not built with the patience of Dýrr, me pet. I'll lop off yer ugly head fer fun, even if

she seems to be soft on yas.'

"She stepped forward, looking down with death in her eyes—but I wer'nt afeared. Then her look softened some. I think she could see me blue face beggin' fer air."

"'Get you offa him, Dýrr. The little lad cannot breathe—how's he gonna answer me?'

"Dýrr crept offa me all sad, like the giant had taken her favorite toy away. I drew in me breath, and then another, rasping to find me voice. It came with a fit of coughing. 'Me father be Sokjar.' I coughed more. 'Sokjar o' The Horned Towers. An' me mother I cannot remember!'

"Her face shifted to a frightening smile baring broken, worn, fearsome teeth.

"'Sokjar, eh?' Her smile grew. 'Then you must be Bolfath?!' Her voice sang like a stinging winter's breeze. 'Bolfath, me lad—you've come home to me. I be Anisjorgg, yer mater.'

"She swept me up in her huge arms, a proud mother—an' full grown, I was still a babe in her arms."

Bolfath looked down and then about the Dwarrow, who were exchanging puzzled looks, unsure what to do, what to say. Should they applaud? Should they cheer? Tears were running down his rough face—never had any of the company seen Bolfath weep before. But he was smiling, too, creating an eerie look that made them very uncomfortable.

Haggersath held his breath. He would step in and tell a joke, or a fighting story, or…

Suddenly Bolfath burst out a full-hearted belly laugh, bringing more cautious, quizzical looks. "Aye, cannot you enjoy a happy telling? Do ya yearn only fer bloodletting and battle? Ya stinkin' barbarians. Ya got no heart," Bolfath scolded good-heartedly.

Such jovial levity was another shock when delivered by the brutish Dwarrow. At first confused, his audience finally came around to understanding. They joined in, reveling alongside his mirth, clapping him heartily on his great back and lauding adulations upon him for the touching story.

The chuckling continued to sound for some time in Haggersath's ears. So that was Bolfath's mother. Made perfect sense. They all knew he was at least partially giant, but he was half Stromurjotonn. No wonder he was so loyal and so violent. They were not to be trifled with. Once they committed their word, it was bond.

"But how did yer father mate with a giant?" said Nater. He had stopped combing his brown beard. "It not be possible. We be made by getting chipped and findin' a female ta take the chip. After that it's women's business how they come back with a full-grown Dwarrow in a few days."

Bolfath looked quizzical for a moment. "She did explain ta me how they met. But I be tellin' enough to you louts fer one night. It is a love story that needs a good full night ta tell." Bolfath sat down and leaned back, hands clasped behind his neck. He smiled, looking pleased with himself and content as if he had just lopped off the head of a tralkvalid.

Nater joined the others in disappointed groans. He put the bone comb away and looked for a skin of Vallhah. The gathering was the last one not sleeping, and it quickly tailed off toward slumber.

The next day, they were moving at a good clip. Last night's stories kept morale high. It was good to hear the crew blowing off steam. He could have used some of that himself, but the charge laid upon his head by Jikseon weighed heavy on him.

It had always been his family's destiny to make and discharge the gifts of office and wealth for the Dwarrow. The last century, though, had relegated his responsibility to a station of useless formality, where the gifts were either of no real charge or they were just not given out at all.

But now...now Jikseon's command and the Destiny Stone brought in meaning. He was to create and give great gifts he might fabricate—gifts of real power. What power might a trinket contain when forged with the power of the Destiny Stone? His was the skill of mounting gemstones in a setting. He knew many forms to place gems. Now he would place gems, and during the socketing, they would be imbibed with magic.

He bore the skill passed down in secret from one Giftgiver to the next—hah, some secret. He knew the craft did no actual difference than any other Silfrsmith. Forming trusilver might be an art, but did the ringing tone of the hammer really impart threads of magic, as his ancestors claimed? There was no evidence of the gifts bearing any honest magic. Those that came before had minor magical characteristics, if any at all. He still had one in his possession. It was given to him when he worked in the mines for the western Dwarrow by his uncle. It was supposed to gift fertility. Ha! That be a laugh. He had no sons, and none were likely to happen soon. Of late, the gifts that were given had no ability. They were symbols of authority or office, nothing more.

But now he had the Destiny Stone, and he felt Jikseon's power when he held it. He could sense other powers too. Something was there—something almost alive that moved to block him, keeping him at bay—but he could feel it within the Destiny Stone when he held it.

"Har, by me beard, there it is." Haggersath could hear the voice of Diwolde Stonescraper. Light broke through the hyljaleid as the door opened, and the Dwarrow rushed through without care or caution. Haggersath was no different—the urgency to see the Towers of the Horne pulled his caution away. Dwarrow cries of excitement changed as their eyes adjusted to the light.

"Gnomôk!" Grölle shouted. "Form up. Form up! Ferskeyttrs, on me now."

CHAPTER 20

Gnomôk

S teel rang on steel, and the throats of the Gnomôk let forth squawks of fury. Fifteen or twenty were spilling out from the many buildings, anxious to assault the Dwarrow. Axes flashing and hammers sweeping, the Dwarrow pounded the enemy's thin armor, Dwarrow fury causing the Gnomôk to falter as the ocean breaks against a mountain.

Grölle had swiftly and effectively formed three ferskeyttr across the front. They vanquished any momentum the Gnomôk had managed to gather. Steadfast as stone, Grölle and the eight Rock-Biters with him made a shield for the rest of the company to exit the mountain in good order.

"Har! There be the desert scum," barked out Jarlsalt. "You, last two ferskeyttr, form on me, Rock-Biters."

More Dwarrow poured out of the hyljaleid. Jarlsalt left a dozen warriors with Haggersath as a guard and sent twenty more around the left of Grölle's line. With the last eight, Jarlsalt motioned them around the far right. The Dwarrow had the numbers and the steel.

Numbers, of course, spoke for themselves, but steel was another matter. Dwarrow armor was finely crafted with few weaknesses or opportunities for weapons to do damage, while remaining light and maneuverable. It was not impenetrable, but it would turn a wood-shafted spear or an angled swipe of a sword, and was far, far better than the poorly made Gnomôk mail—immeasurably so.

Dwarrow were accustomed to fighting large melees, which were common in all-out war. Soldiers worked in sets of pairs, ensuring that one always had the defense, while the other attacked. They changed roles with signals based on the Dwarrow on offense, or on the changing state of their situation.

Rock-Biters had learned a more complex system that worked with these quad formations called ferskeyttr. The Dwarrow would rotate with smooth fluidity at will, directed by the one most forward. A ferskeyttr was a most deadly force, even alone against long odds. But it was against larger opponents when it was most effective. Since Dwarrow were usually the smallest people on a field of combat, this was a disadvantage a ferskeyttr reversed into a distinct advantage. Another feature was the ability to condense the ferskeyttr. Taking losses was always a possibility, so ferskeyttr were designed to be able to operate in twos or threes as well—albeit with less efficiency. When enough casualties occurred, ferskeyttr could combine with another depleted formation to form full units without losing quality. They could make the seamless transition even in the midst of battle. Thus, it was the most effective fighting formation anywhere in Thear.

And so, it was no surprise that cutting through the Gnomôk was easy for the Dwarrow. Unorganized, the Gnomôk did not realize that the Dwarrow outnumbered them; they stood no chance. Haggersath never got into the fray, and Bolfath lamented a mere two Gnomôk heads to his credit. No Dwarrow casualties had occurred. Just a few minor cuts that were shrugged off as earned badges.

Four of the Gnomôk escaped, limping into the hazy distance. Grölle had made the initial battle lines. Jarlsalt had whipped up an elaborate plan of attack, but the battle was over almost as fast as it began. Jarlsalt never even got his company fully deployed.

"Four escaped, you say?" Jarlsalt snarled at his captain. "If there are others, they will be alerted. Yer mistake lets me down, Captain Grölle." He waved a gesture at Haggersath. "Ya've let the eastern princeling down too." He said the last with a scoffing snort. "Better bow at his lordly feet and beg forgiveness."

His point was well taken, no matter the taste of its delivery. Haggersath turned from the belligerent captain and his subordinate. How many Gnomôk were here in the Towers of the Horne? It was a valid point, something Jarlsalt rarely had. Haggersath groaned quietly to himself. If only Mevindh-Gulbard wasn't incapacitated. He could have brought those four to bay. But now—now they would alert whoever else was here.

"Captain Jarlsalt," Haggersath called out. "Have yer boys move out an' clear a way to the north and east. This blasted haze be makin' it hard ta see. But I do think the Towers of the Horne be that way. That is if me memory serves me right proper."

"Aye, Giftgiver," Jarlsalt replied and reformed his company into a battle formation of four ferskeyttr of Rock-Biters and sixteen pairs of soldiers. They advanced as Haggersath had directed. In addition, Haggersath watched Jarlsalt detach four pairs of soldiers out to the perimeters to scout the other areas. With a smirking smile and an affirming nod, Haggersath thought, *Good*. He may not like the 16th son, but he had to respect his occasional grasp of military efficiency. The oily-bearded captain was not without his uses.

He followed the main body down the knobby graveled road between the old city huts. Most were in poor repair, much like the roadway, which had suffered from serious neglect. Painful memories welled up in Haggersath's heart from times well past. This road seemed familiar, as did most of those that intersected it, though it was all worn away to broken destitution.

Up ahead now, the company had halted. Jarlsalt waited with his small force of Dwarrow at the base of the shadow of a tall building. Haggersath hadn't noticed it until this very moment. The Giftgiver and his Haseti stopped, looking at the building before them.

Jarlsalt reported, "We found not hair nor hide of them sand dwellers in any direction. But methinks they may be watchin' us."

Haggersath never took his eyes off the building in front of him.

For-ungr, meaning Warning Tower, stood tall and strong before them. It had stood centuries and endured war and strife, yet unlike the huts along the way, it had little to no wear. It did not seem special to the unskilled eye, this first Tower of the Horne, but the Dwarrow understood the elegance and precision in the fine masonwork. Stones crafted to fit so ideally that mortar was unnecessary. A little bit of red magic worked in its place to make the Towers nearly indestructible. There was not a crafted building in Thear that had the strength of the Horned Towers.

It sat near the base of the mountain—not up against it, but out in front with walls running down either side back to the mountain. It was a lone sentinel stretching skyward. Stairs flanked on either side of the front gate, wide enough for two ferskeyttr to walk abreast up the twelve squat stone steps. They met at their pinnacle in the middle on a landing in front of the iron gate. The gate had not fared as well as the stone and was a twisted and broken ruin. It had once been the guardian doorway to the three-meter-tall portcullis, the Tower's entrance.

The Tower was no wider than a hundred steps from end to end in a perfect square. It rose fifty meters up and was flat at the top with slits for crossbows to fire from in defense. Each of the top corners had tattered leather canopies like peaked tents as cover for the rounded parapets that jutted out from the corner. Those parapets were echoed in design along the Tower's vertical corners, leaving no sharp edges down the lengths. Stylings of shields, and mountains, and crossed hammer and maul adorned For-ungr. It was the southern tower, closest to the roadway, and provided the Dwarrow's first alert of danger approaching.

And danger was flitting about now, like angry bees in a disturbed hive. Gnomôk buzzed as they came out of For-ungr, crowding one another as they flooded down the stairs on both sides—rapids from a river's spring runoff.

"Ahh, there they be." The greasy-faced captain smiled and dashed a quick look to Haggersath. "I told ya they be here."

Skirting carefully along the cover of the outer hovels, Jarlsalt deployed his company for battle. It seemed that the Tower was held by a minimum of fifty Gnomôk. They came all disarrayed, announcing their confusion with unpreparedness.

At once, Haggersath nodded to Jarlsalt and whispered out a quiet command, "Trap them on the stair, swiftly."

Jarlsalt slapped the helmet of the leaders of two ferskeyttr and tapped the mail of two more with his fat-tipped short sword. Haggersath noticed the overproud captain used the tip of the weapon. Of course, Jarlsalt wouldn't use the haft, afraid he might chip the gaudy, plum-sized ruby set in the base of the pommel. It was a ridiculous ornament on a weapon of war, more suited for a ceremonial weapon in a fine court. But then again, Jarlsalt was a ridiculous princeling.

Four ferskeyttr advanced, two at each stair entrance. They pressed into the soft Gnomôk turmoil, bottling them up quickly. They kept on without taking heed of their weakness—maybe more than fifty, but who was really counting? The Rock-Biters would let one slip through every so often, but the dozen warriors that had assembled behind the Rock-Biters in a ring easily collected the isolated Gnomôk.

Haggersath and his Haseti stayed back with the remaining Dwarrow. Jarlsalt barked out here and there, demonstrating his belief that they needed his direction. Haggersath observed that it actually interfered with the subordinates' effectiveness. Grambol Doomsayer and Diwolde Stonescraper superficially watched without much interest. Bolfath quietly stamped back and forth, itching to get in the mix but knowing his duty was near Haggersath. Captain Grölle had been left in command of the reserve this time near the Haseti, and Mevindh-Gulbard remained in his cold, deep sleep.

Gnomôk pouring out of the For-ungr were having no success—they were being slain or sent scattering back into their own ranks. Those that stood were swept under by swirling warhammers and the stamp of armored Dwarrow foot. Quickly, the Gnomôk gave way. It was a slaughter; numbers meant nothing.

Jarlsalt finally stepped forward to the stair's center. "Advance on the For-ungr!" he commanded the two lead ferskeyttr.

They moved like a sliding juggernaut up the stairs on both sides. But the area they vacated left no one between the slain in front of the Tower stairs and the Haseti. With a sudden movement, one of the "slain" Gnomôk sat up and blew its curved battle horn. A dozen of the Gnomôk that had been thought to be casualties leaped to their feet and charged the Haseti.

Haggersath was caught off guard as two of the fiends seemed to have singled him out. They came fast. He reached for his hammer but felt a point poke hard into his shoulder. It went numb as the two Gnomôk took him to the ground. Their weight pressing down on him, he could not free his arm to get to his hammer. His other arm was in the grasp of the second Gnomôk. Panic made his breathing fast and short. He was pinned under them. He could not move. Their scaly, reptilian tan skin scraped against his wire beard. Their breath permeated his next inhale with a gagging combination of rotten eggs and ammonia.

His shoulder stung, and his arms couldn't move. He kicked his legs into the left one, and it squealed into his ear so loud it started ringing. The other one jumped up off him. He was able to smash the ear of the squealing one with his freed-up hand. It rolled off in pain. He rolled up onto his knees, drawing in deep breaths, finally free of their stifling breath. Pulling his hatchet from his belt, he swung his numb arm down on the neck of the Gnomôk, hoping he had enough strength to get it deep. It twisted upon impact and wrenched the hatchet from his grasp.

Rearing up with the hatchet still in the armor on its neck, I raised its short sword. Haggersath tried to get his body to move, but the Gnomôk's sword moved too fast. A gleam of red flashed before him, and the Gnomôk's sword was parried away.

Jarlsalt stepped in front of him and buried that fancy sword of his with the big ruby hilt deep into the assailant's neck and down through his chest. Haggersath tried to shake off the lethargy and get to his feet. He saw that they had all been slain. Bolfath was choking the life from one holding him in the air by his neck.

"Are—are we all whole an' hale?" Haggersath said, not really sounding all that well himself.

"Aye, we be," Diwolde Stonescraper answered for the Haseti. There were no disagreements. Haggersath looked at his right shoulder where the Gnomôk had stabbed him with the sword. No blood, only a slice into the armor. It had held up. Good. He nodded. Now that was something that never should have happened.

"Captain Jarlsalt, don't ye think that mebbe ya should keep a bit o' yer forces between me and my Haseti? Ya left a gap in the lines there." Haggersath was not really that upset. He just felt that it was too poor a basic decision for his commander to make.

Jarlsalt looked at him with a sour face. "I am the commander of the forces here; an' yer alive aren't ye?" He pivoted without waiting and moved to the stair where the Dwarrow were nearing the top from both sides.

Slow and steady, they met at the top landing and stopped. All the sounds of battle went silent. There were no more Gnomôk willing to deter their entrance to the Warning Tower.

Jarlsalt sent the soldiers into the Tower to begin clearing out For-ungr. He left the Rock-Biters on guard after doing the majority of the fighting. They had secured the Warning Tower. It was built for defense against such an invasion, and the Dwarrow's combat methods had been paramount in the minds of the builders. The Gnomôk failed to use these advantages.

Haggersath judged that the skirmish might have served as a warning to all the Gnomôk in the northern tower. It may have given them time to devise a prepared defense. Of course, Gnomôk were not Dwarrow, and their leaders were rarely formidable in strategy or tactics. Thus, it came to be that Haggersath and his band gained the Warning Tower without losing a single Dwarrow, and while slaying more than their total number of the hapless Gnomôk. Haggersath climbed the southern stairs with Diwolde Stonescraper and Grambol Doomsayer. His shoulder had moved from numbness now to a distant dull ache. Bolfath carried the Gulprąst, following behind.

The stench left by the slain Gnomôk made their noses crinkle. It was the kind of wake only the Dwarrow left. Shattered limbs that were angled all wrong. Sharp edges of bones breaking the skin. Only warhammers, mauls, and other impact weapons did this damage. The bodies were mangled and, in some areas, piled upon each other. But it was the stench of the blood and guts of the Gnomôk that was most offensive. That unmistakable odor of rotten eggs and ammonia.

"Makin' me ill, the bracken blood o' these filthy louts pollutin' the walls of these fine Towers." Diwolde Stonescraper kicked one of the bodies that was draped over the landing wall where it met the northern stair and watched it fall, slack, to the dirt below.

Gnomôk had a texture to their rather thin skin like that of a lizard. Some were nearly blonde as bleached desert sand, while others had the tone of a dull gray. Gnomôk were similar in height to Dwarrow, perhaps a little taller, at just over one and a half meters. Their builds varied but tended to be scrawny and thinner than other races. Sometimes their nails were black and nearly talon-like. They had oily, stringy hair, either black or brown. Big eyes were set too wide and little, and no lips made their smiles unnerving.

They entered the mangled gates and into the Warning Tower. It had rooms going off left and right with broken pine-and-tar doors hanging from twisted hinges.

"Those be the barracks and storerooms the Stonescraper mentioned." Diwolde Stonescraper gestured at them, not quite pointing.

At the far end, straight away, was the opposite gate. This iron was still intact but pushed open. It was worn and speckled with orange rust flakes, making it appear brittle.

"So much work ta do here," Diwolde Stonescraper grieved, his face downcast with worn care.

"Be glad, Stonescraper," Grambol Doomsayer said with a supportive grin, his cheeks a rosy red. "Ya gots no more of them desert scum stinking up yer pretty rocks." He offered his sack of Vallhah to Diwolde.

Diwolde Stonescraper brightened some at this. "Aye." Accepting the bag, he took a swig.

They exited For-ungr into a large, walled courtyard.

"This be the Dvaligbjarg," Diwolde Stonescraper said with pride, his arms akimbo as he spun around the great expanse of the open court. It was almost as if he was involved in its making.

"The Crag of Dvalig," Haggersath said with some wonder in his voice.

"Aye, Giftgiver. This be named fer the father of all Grýttr, Dvalig Stonementor." Diwolde Stonescraper spoke his name with a reverence Haggersath had never heard from the master craftsman. "An' he made all this." He drew a grand gesture, sweeping over all they saw.

It was a wonder to behold. To the south was a wall with staircases and parapets to walk along the rim, continuing until it reached the mountainside. There, it joined and went up the mountain steeply as a rock stair, carved with the exact precision expected of the eastern Dwarrow. It led to an opening that went straight into the mountainside.

Now he looked directly west at the great mountain, Himinodurr, Horne of the Sky. This was where the wall of the Crag of Dvalig met the Silfr Mountains. It was a tremendous peak, taller than any other within sight and wide at its base like no other. It was from the Himinodurr that the Kings' Tower was wrought.

In the north and somewhat to the west lay Kon-ungr, or Kings' Tower. Grand and majestic, it stood tall, commanding the eye of all who beheld her. It was far greater in both splendor and magnitude than its smaller sister, For-ungr.

"Kon-ungr...ahhh, how I have missed thee," Haggersath said with a caressing whisper.

It was a grand thing to see the majesty of the great Towers of the Horne for the first time. Those of the western Dwarrow and those too young to remember stood awestruck. Haggersath smiled, knowing that the Bornholm never allowed them to learn of the majesty and greatness of the eastern Dwarrow and their workings at their pinnacle.

Scaling more than 150 meters high, the Kings' Tower seemed to touch the sky. Ornate and opulent, Kon-ungr bore decor of Dwarrow kings, forge fires, and—of course—set gemstones. Carvings and sculptures crawled up the sides in stone that shone like silver. The Tower glinted in the Sun. The company took it all in with reverent amazement. Even Jarlsalt drew in breath at what he saw.

It was quiet. No more Gnomôk polluted the Towers of the Horne, and when Jarlsalt gave the all clear,

Haggersath and his Haseti headed off to the Kings' Tower. It was here where he could grant rest and refuge to the Gulprąst in hopes of a rapid recovery for the ailing priest. He would have Jarlsalt's Dwarrow occupy the Warning Tower. The rest of his Haseti would house in the Kings' Tower, where the forge and its manuals of finer smithing were kept.

He left Mevindh-Gulbard and Grambol Doomsayer in the lower hall where they could rest, but he could not. Not yet. He and the Stonescraper went directly to the smithy's library. Bolfath was dispatched to keep a watchful eye on the untrustworthy 16th son.

As they went into the mountain deeper, the halls and rooms began to show less evidence of looting and wanton destruction. Every room had been bereft of anything of value. Evidence of attempts to remove the gems mounted into the walls were everywhere. Broken daggers and tools had been used to try to pry out the riches, but nothing could be removed that was in the stone walls. Riches were left unpoached where thieves failed.

Haggersath and Diwolde Stonescraper arrived at the library, and they froze in the doorway, mouths agape.

"Travesty!" said Diwolde Stonescraper under his breath.

CHAPTER 21

Dwarrow Resolve

It was a wrecked mass of disaster. Scrolls and books strewn and tossed aside. Some were intentionally destroyed and torn to shreds. Hundreds—no, *thousands* of timeless references and manuals traipsed upon and shredded.

"So much of the lore of the Giftgiver of the Horne, lost," Haggersath said as his voice cracked, nearly a cry. "It be reprehensible!" He looked around, seeing carnage as horrific as anything he could remember. Slowly, he felt a creeping anger. They destroyed an irreplaceable legacy. He fumed at the ruined wealth of knowledge. His legacy of lore dashed as unwanted refuse.

Slowly, sadly, they moved into the room. Diwolde Stonescraper led the way in solemn silence. Haggersath had not noticed, but he must have grabbed a couple of pebbles off the floor. Diwolde Stonescraper was defusing agitation as he ground and shuffled the stones in his hand. Haggersath picked up one of the torn books—its back cover was missing. He fanned through it without paying attention to what it was, then dropped it. It was all senseless.

It took time, rummaging through the Kings' Tower for the manuals on making the gifts his fathers, grandfathers, and beyond were named for. Many ledgers and tombs were left bereft, only holding half of the original contents.

Great was the damage that had been done. Gnomôk had little respect for such things. The Dwarrow sifted through even that which lay torn and scattered on the finely tiled floor. The Gnomôk had spat and done worse upon the discarded pages with unchecked, inbred hate for the children of Jikseon and all their works. It was the base value the race of Noshid knew. It was how he created the Gnomôk. They were fed from creation with only hate and destruction.

The Dwarrow searched through the day, painstakingly, meticulously, until their metallic beards dragged on the dusty stone floor, scraping and scratching the stone. They were bent as though a thousand years pressed them to meld with the stone. At last, Haggersath halted.

"It be not here, Stonescraper." He dropped to the floor, exhausted, his legs forgetfully akimbo. This was beyond anything he could have envisioned. "We cannot make them. I dunno how. All this is for naught."

It was more than just failing to find the records of instruction. It was the accumulated weariness of the road and its troubles. The unyielding pull of fatigue tore Haggersath to hopelessness. Jikseon had chosen wrong. He could not do as he was bid by the patron deity.

"Methinks we better rest," Diwolde Stonescraper said, face slack and a glum tone on his lips. "It be here— it must be. But we will not find it today, Giftgiver. It be a field of scrawling we must search. With rest we may yet find the manuals we seek."

Haggersath could barely nod. "Aye. Mebbe tomorrow. Or the day after." He was beyond tired.

"I will think on this with the mind of a Grýttr instead of working like a book tender. This can be found by the likes of the Stonementor's thoughts."

He looked at Haggersath, but Haggersath did not want to move and waved Diwolde Stonescraper away. Diwolde Stonescraper left the room, pacing tiredly down the hall.

The Stonementor. Master of all Grýttr. Diwolde Stonescraper could think like the ancient first Grýttr. Haggersath did not bother to get up; he made a pillow of some books and fell fast asleep, right there on the library floor.

It was dark when Haggersath awoke. He did so with a start. Where was he? He remembered as he saw the stacked books he had used for a pillow. *Home*, he thought with a pleasant sarcasm. It was true, he had come home. But it was far from the home he remembered a century ago. He could make it his home again, but it would take more than his small fellowship to repair and rebuild. It would take years, even with the entire eastern Dwarrow population. That is even if he could get them to come. They were yoked, working in near serfdom for the Bornholm in Strongmedjie. It was quite doubtful he could get the Bornholm to "release" his indentured guests.

Haggersath looked for a lantern or candle. Then he remembered he had no flint. No way to light it if he found one. He got to his feet on sore muscles. His legs ached like he had climbed to the top of the Konungr. He took a careful, unsteady step, and the book he stepped on slipped out from under him. He dumped onto the papers spread upon the floor. Now here was a fine Dwarrow mess. He was so bloody tired. He made the wizened choice to crawl to the library exit. It was not far, but his knees shot with pain at every step. He fell back into slumber on the tome-littered floor.

The light of the morning brought his eyes into focus. Diwolde Stonescraper had arrived by mid-morning and woke Haggersath. The Stonescraper paced the library in thought, scratching his healthy brown bush of a beard.

"Methinks we be doin' this all wrong." He turned to face Haggersath, who was still a million leagues off, not fully awake. "No need fer you to search fer the scroll we seek, Giftgiver. In this, you'd be as useful as a Gnomôk. Leave me be, and I'll get yer answers. I be sure it is hidden by the Stonementor, and only a Grýttr might find such a thing of secrecy."

After a moment, Haggersath stood, shaking off some weariness. "Very well, Stonescraper. I can better make use of time an' get the forge ready ta use."

He stood and looked at himself, taking inventory of his body. His armor had a mark where the Gnomôk blade had caught him the day before. He pulled away the armor and peered at the bruise. It was nearly gone. He moved the shoulder, and it seemed to be back to normal. *Good*, thought Haggersath. Dwarrow did not suffer impact wounds for long. Their healing rate was the envy of all other races. He reached for the ox-horned helm. Leaving the room, Haggersath set out to find the forge. He'd need to put it in working order to pound out the metals for placing the gems once Diwolde Stonescraper solved the questions of the manual.

He marveled at the halls as he went, doing the best to remember the way there. Perfectly rectified stones of identical proportions lined the hall, each still finely ground to a satiny polish that displayed the natural beauty of the rock. There was no such artisan expertise anywhere in Strongmedjie. Compared to Kon-ungr, the halls of the Bornholm were slapped together by strict amateurs. He reached the rock-insulated iron doors to the forge. In this deep place of Himinodurr, the forge waited for him.

As did another horrific travesty. Dust and rust permeated the finest forge Thear had ever known, but Haggersath could see through the eyes of the Giftgivers before him. Those were fathers of might, who crafted with trusilver and gold and steel of unmatched caliber. They were hewn with age-sharpened proficiency likely lost in the dust and rust. The deep sorrow of this demise would shadow over the hearts of the Dwarrow.

Time had eroded the gleam of well-wrought metal that the forge was crafted of, but Haggersath knew it could be set right once again with a little Dwarrow oeuvre. Magic was ingrained in the making of the forge, yellow and most especially red powers.

Bringing in some of the warriors, he assigned tasks, schooling them where they lacked knowledge. They were Dwarrow, and hard, hardy work made them glad. Scraping and mending. Measuring and bending. Hammering and shaving. It was grim, sweaty work, yes, but that was the Dwarrow way. The hard toil would restore that which had a purpose defined in crafting—especially metal and stone. They were gifted craftsmen from the Giftgiver to the Rock-Biter to the base soldier. Each was able minded at their core in the role of erecting and invention.

It began as a low, forbidding song. It began by laying out a story of grim passion, a reflection of the Dwarrow and their purpose, then moved to a central theme. The halls echoed with their grim singing voices, their emotions of grueling work.

> *Ho! Be wary, villain.*
> *We come again.*
> *Cold stone,*
> *of stone but not stone,*
> *common Dwarrow,*
> *we claim back our house.*

> *Stand fast.*
> *Yeah! We make it over,*
> *tall and fast.*
> *We make the Towers over,*
> *We have the will; we have the way.*
> *We claim back our house.*

The song raised its notes from low and ominous to a steadily paced humming, with lead voices joining to carry a melody that was not happy but spoke of fulfilled hearts. The song spread, not just in the forge and the rooms down the hall but all through the Towers. Dwarrow song rang out like a gathering storm, shaking the Towers of the Horne with a Dwarrow chorus for the first time in at least a century. This was a nimbus of hope and future, a rekindling of pride and joy, a spirit of brotherhood for east and west alike.

Run, villain.
Giftgiver comes again.
Towers rise.
Dwarrow are of the stone.
We will not be swept away.
We claim back our house.

Towers, Strongmedjie,
we bring us back together.
Under the Himinodurr joined,
we are Dwarrow; we are stone.
Under the mountain,
we claim back our house.

Their song and their work both went with swift efficiency, sweeping away the flotsam and jetsam of the years. Refurbishment began to show throughout the Tower, time passing without notice. Hours into days, all working constantly—except Jarlsalt.

Jarlsalt was often missing, though this was unnoticed by most of the company. Haggersath had made inquiries, but none knew where the swarthy captain spent so much of his time. He was out of sight. Conspicuous in his vacancy. If they did know, they did not let Haggersath know. When Jarlsalt was present, he wore a putrid scowl and did not participate in song or merriment. He never took up shovel or trowel and merely barked an occasional order. Haggersath could only surmise that the 16th son's misery was due to his lack of support in rebuilding the Towers of the Horne. He was, after all, not pleased at the detour from Strongmedjie to be here.

It was Bolfath who spoke of the craven captain of the guard, "He be talkin' low an' quiet among the warriors. Rock-Biters too. When I ask, they tell me he talks of Strongmedjie an' how you be wrong to keep them here." Bolfath looked puzzled. "Fer some reason, I kin see Grölle don't be too kind ta hear that talk from the princeling. He be a westerner, but he be loyal ta ya, Haggersath."

Haggersath nodded at the news. It was what he thought. "Fine work, Bolfath." He could always count on his bodyguard. So, Jarlsalt was spreading evil with his time. Sowing the seeds of discontent that they had come to the Towers.

"I be meanin' ta ask ya, Haggersath..." Bolfath tapped Haggersath's shoulder and hesitated. He never asked for anything except a chance to kill. This was a curious thing.

"What be yer pleasure?" He smiled up at the huge Dwarrow.

"I be needin' ta go into the mountain, now that we be back. It be me nature ta take a walk an' stay fer a night or two." Bolfath looked almost nostalgic. Haggersath must have looked at him with doubt that forced him to elaborate. "I be wantin' ta go an' visit me mater. It has been a very long time…an'—"

"Say no more, me friend. Aye, ye've earned it. By all means, go." Haggersath had to grant it. They were in the Towers now, and he had plenty to guard him. "While ye be playin' in the snow, get some huntin' done an' bring back meat." Haggersath saw him give a massive grin as if he expected to be declined his request. Haggersath backed away with his hands out to ward off the bear hug Bolfath spread his arms to give him.

Regaining control of himself, Bolfath dropped his attempt at embrace and spoke. "As ye wish, Haggersath." He chuckled in amused cheerfulness, his smile reaching both mangled ears. He clapped Haggersath so hard on the shoulder he nearly went to the ground. Then he turned and went off to do his ode to the Silfr Mountains and see his mother.

In one way, at least, Haggersath was not so much different from the 16th son: He wore his disappointment plain upon his face. He was carrying the weight of the missing tome, and Diwolde Stonescraper's daily reports brought empty news. No scroll. No reference of the gift-making skills he sought.

But the forge kept up hope with him. It was ready for operation, and it was an impressive brute. Haggersath displayed the finished work to Diwolde Stonescraper with the pride of a father introducing his new son. Opening the baffles to allow the molten heat of the heart of Himinodurr to flood the forge fires, they lit it with a red-tinged flame, bringing the furnace to life. It quickly took hold as a living thing, flourishing with motion and heat. The smell of steel and more noble molten metals saturated the air—residual traces of an age ago.

But it was the breath of common iron that packed their flared nostrils and dragged memories from the grave of Dwarrow glory. It was invigorating and contagious. As if to cue into the scene, a rather red-faced Grambol Doomsayer jollily waddled into the room, hopping from one foot to the other, likely drunk yet again.

"Ho there, young Haggersath! Yer fires be kindled," he reveled sloppily.

"It has the tang of a proper forge." Haggersath smiled. "Ya have the look of heavy drink upon ya already, Doomsayer. An' the day be only as young as a fresh-born goat."

"It does be true, by har! But by Jikseon, the Towers be blessed, an' me beard grows long—it be here!" He shook his head full of joy.

What he said showed in his face. The Towers of the Horne had been beneficial for all the Dwarrow in his band. They all thrived well and good. Only Haggersath and Jarlsalt showed tension or concern. Jarlsalt was probably still angry at seeing his westerners rejoicing in the success they were having in making some restorations with the Towers. Not only were the Towers being repaired and slowly returning to a livable space, but the fellowship of grim productivity—of being Dwarrow—thrived.

CHAPTER 22

Mangeesum and Gems

Despite the surface successes, Haggersath was stymied in his quest to do as Jikseon had bid. Soon it would have been a fortnight, and all his efforts had not yielded a single shred of evidence of where the answer to ring-making lay. Diwolde Stonescraper approached with defeat in his cast-down eyes, and Haggersath knew there was nothing for him.

Grambol Doomsayer looked back and forth at them both. "Yer faces be as long as Jikseon's own beard. How kin that be so, when all here be right an' good?" He was baffled.

"We cannot find the lore we came here for," Diwolde Stonescraper said, despair trailing in his voice. His arms sagged. Haggersath had never seen him this way. He seemed defeated.

"It be so. Makin' the Towers was only part of Jikseon's command," Haggersath said, both hands resting inside the gorget at his neck, pulling it with uncharacteristic frustration. A flare from the softly fired forge licked up in answer to his grief.

Grambol Doomsayer shook his head. He looked different when his hand pressed his stocking cap back to expose his baldness. "No, no, Haggersath Giftgiver," he croaked out, laughter almost spelling ridicule in his tone. He shook his whole body with his head in denial. Haggersath hoped he wasn't about to go into another mad frenzy.

Haggersath did not like being mocked. Even with his tremendous patience for the old Doomsayer, he would not take humiliation in front of the other Dwarrow. It was not fitting.

"Be wary of your amusements, Grambol Doomsayer. I love thee truly, but yer out of bounds."

"Hoho heeee!" ole Grambol Doomsayer rambled with glee. "It be here. It do be here. *Look!* Look around, and ye kin see it."

"What have ye found, Doomsayer?" Haggersath said. He did not think the old Dwarrow was offering anything related, and annoyance registered within him as he flicked a finger across his nose with curt sneering. Diwolde Stonescraper, however, looked around with curious interest. Haggersath knew deep down that the Doomsayer was rarely wrong—except when he passed the line with his drink. It was just frustration clouding his judgement.

Gathering and pressing aside his emotions, Haggersath asked the imbalanced sage, "Are ye too drunk again, you lout? Speak to me, an' not in yer ramblin' riddles. I want it plain, or by Jikseon, I'll…"

"Yes, yes, Giftgiver, as ye wish, of course." He sobered up just a touch. "It's here. Bring the fires of the forge to full bear. I remember the yarn of me father. 'Tis not a manual or script of sorts ye seek, but the will of Jikseon—wrought of rock and stone." His eyes twinkled as he finished, looking as if he'd solved and answered the question.

Pulling at his gorget so hard his neck ached to avoid choking the life out of Grambol Doomsayer, Haggersath raged at him, "Didn't I be speakin' clear to ya, looney Dwarrow? Yer words be riddles an' don't mean fuck ta anyone here. Put yer useless mind in yer words and talk plain, or I'll pound you so yas sleep a week!"

Grambol Doomsayer's eyes went wide as he backpedaled two steps, as if avoiding a strike that was not there. He was fearful of the temperament and anger fuming from Haggersath. Grambol Doomsayer cast his eyes down, looking hurt—but desperate to avoid the aforementioned beating. "A moment, Lord of the Horne, a moment so's I kin make plain my meaning." He took a tentative breath and slowed his excitement, the glee of liquor departing. He scrunched up his face, causing deep lines like those in a rock's crevice. All was silent except the soft rumble of the forge humming in the room. He, too, was silent. The damn Doomsayer could find a gem in a maze of mountains, but he couldn't speak a word of intelligent communication. The effort was almost comical, watching the range of emotion with every thought sliding over Grambol Doomsayer's craggy face.

Calming, Haggersath tapped his foot absently, losing tension. Grambol Doomsayer looked around, crazy-eyed, hither and thither, as if seeking an exit to run to. He moved around the room, looking closely at the walls and floors. He had taken out a few of those small pickled fish from his pouch and began absent-mindedly nibbling on them as he moved and thought.

Haggersath's rage began to build again. "Have ya finally lost yer wits? Did the drink split yer head?" He was going to strike the Doomsayer. By Jikseon's beard, why did the Doomsayer have to drink so much? He began to turn away. It was the only way he could avoid...and then.

"Aye," said Diwolde Stonescraper quietly, as if waking. "Aaaayyyyye!" he said louder, the excitement shining through as he spoke. "Yer a marvel, Grambol, ya ole trickster. Ye be right." He looked at Haggersath, astonished, as if smacked between the eyes with a smith's mallet. "Curse me fer a fool. Me Grýttr pride left me thinkin' all wrong."

Diwolde Stonescraper joined Grambol Doomsayer, moving to the forge fire itself. "There it be. Look, Haggersath, the fires reveal the lore we seek."

It was there. Faint at first, but as the fires built heat into the stone, it was a tome, the ledger of the Giftgivers. It had been placed upon the rock of the forge and hidden by red magic until the heat of the forge revealed it. Haggersath took to the stone and gazed at the charred enclave made with the hand of his forefathers, distinctly in the style unique to the craftsmen of the Towers. This was the book that held the secrets of making the gifts of the Dwarrow. On the cover, it read:

*The uses of Mangeesum and the ledger of the
Giftgivers of the Horne.*

Haggersath went to the ledger and reached for it. He wanted to grab it in case it might slip away. He touched it and lifted it. Heavy, but not as heavy as the stone it seemed to be at first. In his hands, it became a volume of curled and bunched papers, loosely bound together with leather ties. It was old but not fragile. He briefly began leafing through it. He was eager to see what it held. But he knew it would take time to find what he wanted.

"'Tis a treasure as great as the Destiny Stone," Diwolde Stonescraper said with truehearted reverence. He moved to Haggersath's side and gazed at the pages as Haggersath ranged through them. He was careful not to touch the ledger. "Ohh, this be very good indeed. The Towers will once more be the heart of the Silfr Mountains."

Haggersath chuckled and smiled at Diwolde Stonescraper. "Aye. This be true." He stopped at a page that seemed to stick out. He did not remember it doing that before. He went to tuck it back in, but the words caught his eye.

There was a small section, hardly a paragraph, that made little sense. Reading it was short work, as it was very few lines, but the words held a deep but hidden meaning. Each its own instruction in full.

"Oh, this be a fine pile of gibberish to rival yer own, Doomsayer," Haggersath grumbled out. "Supposin' we glean a clue of meanin' from another damn riddle. Did the smithies of old have so much time on their hands that they just could not speak as plainly as the mountains?"

Haggersath's complaints were empty. He knew that it was important to protect the lore of Giftgivers through the centuries, but by Jikseon's beard, he was tired of thinking through all the trickery.

"Tell me true, Doomsayer, how long fer ya ta sort out the meanin' of the words here?" He turned the ledger toward Grambol Doomsayer and held it for him to assess. "Can ya read this?"

Grambol Doomsayer looked with a cackle at his leader. "'Tis as plain as yer yellow beard. There be no secret." He read them as he would a children's poem:

Trusilver to searing fires tame red magic.
Trusilver imbeds ice of blue magic.
Trusilver calls to the power of yellow magic
through the Destiny Stone by Jikseon's
Giftgiver.
The mountain of the Towers shall rise again.

Fire flew from Haggersath's brow as his will was kindled. This was it! Diwolde Stonescraper looked on, astonished, and Grambol Doomsayer muttered to himself and faded into the shadows near a wall, seeing the elder Giftgivers in the face of his master.

As kings, they were, in the days of the Towers of the Horne. Haggersath looked no less than a king. With determination on his face, he knew. It was all clear. He would make these greatest of gifts.

The pages that followed had the detailed instructions. At long last, Haggersath knew what to do. He had answers in his hands. He understood how to begin. He needed trusilver. He knew there was only one ore that yielded trusilver. Mangeesum. There were some risks for Dwarrow to seek Mangeesum, but the price was, in this case, overshadowed.

Smiling, Haggersath spoke in a commanding voice, "This speaks of a making that must be with the Stone. It is time for the gifts to be fashioned. Find me mangeesum and bring gems. Any gems, and bring them hither. Let us begin."

CHAPTER 23

Hammer and Anvil

ll the Dwarrow moved to gather and prepare.
Haggersath was impressed at the way the
Dwarrow worked together. Warriors of
Strongmedjie seamlessly falling into step with the
brother peer of the Towers. It was a camaraderie that
surpassed the rifts of the past. Haggersath was proud
of the troop. One mindset bent on the single goal of
success. He could not remember a time when he felt so
energized, so loved.

It was time to forge. Haggersath was able to
understand the instructions in the ledger as if he had
written them himself. The Dwarrow gathered to him
gems and mangeesum ore. Little there was of the blue-
veined ore, but there was no time to venture to the
Desert of Cinders where it could be found or delve into
the mountainside where it lay waiting—and besides,

they had enough. Haggersath opened the tool chests and drew from them the tools of the Giftgivers.

Curlie and Nater were bringing in great loads of charcoal and dumping them on the floor of the forge near the furnace. Their faces and clothing were covered in blackened soot from breaking down the charcoal into smaller pieces to be able to stoke a greater heat for the smelting process. They were smiling and in good spirits even though Haggersath had never seen Nater without his hair and beard neatly combed by one of his hand-carved bone combs before. They went back for another load.

All the while, Mallonsmythe, a Dwarrow with masterful metallurgy skill, was charging the furnace to smelting temperature. Sweat rolled off his red face, bathed in the glowing orange. His copper beard added an infernal glow that almost gave the impression of madness when coupled with his strained intensity. He directed two other Dwarrow—Haggersath did not know their names. They cast in gray coal along with some iron shreds, raising the temperature and charging the furnace to smelting temperatures. Mallonsmythe had spent two days making gray coal to superheat the furnace.

"Is it ready fer the mangeesum, Mallonsmythe?" Haggersath said. He was so anxious to begin. He knew the furnace was close. He was bursting with the knowledge of the ledger. He could not wait.

"Aye, but lemme take a few more minutes. Then we will be ready," Mallonsmythe said, wiping a sweaty arm across his copper-headed brow. It really did nothing more than smudge the ash onto his face.

While he waited, Haggersath went to the dry, worn wooden table. It was warped from the constant heat of the room. He examined the molds placed there by Diwolde Stonescraper sometime earlier. Two molds of five mountings that would house the gems. They would be the source of the power in the gifts. It would be the combination of a gem set in the trusilver, as were the gifts of old. But with the use of the Destiny Stone, that power was untested. The magic they might possess would not be known until it was used.

He looked over the differing shapes and varied sizes. The gems were also on the table. Large precious gemstones. Haggersath was examining the differing cuts made on the stones. Expertly precise work. "Very good," he said aloud. He was surprised to hear an answer.

"I agree, if I say so meself." Haggersath looked up to see a balding older Dwarrow with crinkles in the corners of his eyes nodding in agreement. His big square teeth made his smile take up too much of his face, but it was the gleam in his eyes, like gemstones of cobalt blue, that steered the attention away from the smile.

"Bijur." Haggersath knew the Dwarrow to know his gemstones. He had done the cutting. If he knew his Dwarrow, and he did, Bijur was likely the finder of these spectacular specimens too. He had an innate ability to know where they would be found in rock or mountain. "These be fit fer Jikseon hisself. Very well done."

"Anything, Giftgiver. I be proud ta be part of yer divine work here." He rocked his head, never once diminishing the massive smile. Haggersath picked up a ruby. It was a smooth oval with a single flat cut upon its top. It should have not glinted like it did with the circumference of the edge being a rounded smooth border, but it did as if it was multifaceted. Astounding work.

"My Lord Haggersath," Mallonsmythe said, calling to him. "The forge be charged. It be ready fer ya."

"Aye, me lads. We begin the work of Jikseon. This be the work ta begin the rebirth of the Towers of the Horne. The Dwarrow will flourish, and all others will come ta know that we be the chosen ta make Thear a land of wealth an' prosperity."

The room thundered with cheers, and then Othro pumped one bellows, while another Dwarrow he had seen but did not know, a youngster, pumped the other. Haggersath noticed that Avalanche, Othro's white fox, was nowhere to be seen. But it made sense. The heat would be too much for the little girl.

Mallonsmythe began to feed in some of the mangeesum. He made sure that Curlie did not add charcoal too fast. Haggersath understood that the balance of charcoal to mangeesum must be maintained to break down the ore into trusilver. Too much and the metal became a mineral-rich stone, too little and the trusilver would be tainted. But the magic was the release of trusilver from the mangeesum. That was the moment Haggersath would imbue the powers as he placed the gemstones.

Mangeesum ore held a certain reverence— *mangeesum!* It was ignored or discarded by the brash Gnomôk—they called it useless rock that polluted the deserts of their homeland, the Desert of Cinders. But here among the Dwarrow, it was prized. Often, it was requisite in crafting finer artifacts. Its singular properties of magical bonding were principal.

Work began on the blue-veined ore with furnace heat. It reached a point where the rock cracked open and spit cobalt sparks the size of a fist in random directions around the room. Dwarrow danced around to avoid being struck by the flickering showers. Intently and without notice, Haggersath pulled the orange, glowing heated ore rocks one at a time from the furnace with pointed crucible tongs and hammered at the rock until it split and broke, showering more blue sparks.

"By Jikseon's beard," the young Dwarrow on the bellows cried out, slapping away a spark that had caught him full on, actually melting a part of his iron black beard.

"Get yer hands back on that bellows. Don't ya step away—a little blue light won' hurt ya none," Haggersath said, commanding him. He resumed his work on the bellows, pumping. Haggersath felt the heat too. It was gloriously hot. Sweat flowed like he was melting.

Dark smoke belched forth as the temperature reached vulcanization and the black slag melted away. Charred sludge drained off as his enlisted assistants shoveled at the sludge, goading it to the shoot. It pooled below, remaining sticky and steaming. Smithies of Strongmedjie would discard the slag, but not Haggersath. He knew its uses, knew it had value.

Mangeesum transformed into a pale molten metal of silvery gold, with the blue veins released and hovering magically within and around the purified metal. It was a beautiful sight. Many of the gathered Dwarrow gasped in delighted wonder, having never before seen pure, smelted mangeesum. Trusilver, it was fully transformed. When it was added to other metals, they became enhanced. Gold became more lustrous. Iron, harder. Tin, more flexible. Lead, heavier. Mercury... well, Haggersath and never tried that one. With that metal's temperament, though, it might be best left alone.

"The molds, Bijur, bring the molds over." He came with them, placing them upon the stone workbench at Haggersath's right hand. The forge roared with sentient glee as Haggersath moved the molten trusilver, now purged of any impurities, into the crucibles to prepare pouring the precious metal into the molds.

Grambol Doomsayer brought over the imprinting mallet to stamp the individual mountings after the trusilver began to hold shape. Haggersath took the small engraving stones and chose the seal he needed to shape the mounting. None were alike. He hammered the imprint and shapes onto the first mold, making five different settings. He did the same on the second mold. Ten perfect mountings of trusilver.

Hot work brought back a low, resolute song of trudging pride but at a low, melodic hum. No words, just the hum of many Dwarrow voices deep in their work. Indeed, the Dwarrow believed the song was part of the process of proper forging. Their mood infused the metals drawn from the mountains.

Just before he was to add the gemstones to their specific mountings, Haggersath was in distant thought. He said out loud, "Grambol Doomsayer! It be time. Bring me that pretty little rock yer holdin'. Bring the Destiny Stone. I need it here."

Grambol Doomsayer, wide-eyed at the process, pulled forth the twinkling Destiny Stone and laid it on the flat of an anvil near Haggersath. He stepped away, as if the forge might reach out and burn him. His face was raining sweat, as was Haggersath's.

Haggersath took up the Destiny Stone in both hands. "Now lads, bring me that blue slag left at the bottom of the forge there. Put it in a spare crucible and leave it here on the stone bench." He began to stir it, and bright blue sparks spritely popped up over the edge. *Not too fast*, he thought to himself. *Careful!* He caught himself as he stared into the bench materials all gathered for the final stage, smiling greedily with anticipation.

He lifted the crucible with the tongs and spilled a slow stream of droplets over the mounting sockets of the ten molded mountings, still a golden hot. Slowly, the metals met. They swirled together, grudgingly mixing. Haggersath took up the Destiny Stone in his hands, and from it a pale tallow glow, barely noticeable, covered them much like gloves. A faint tingle of golden magic.

They felt no heat from the nearby fire. He lowered his hands and the Destiny Stone, just enough to touch the forming alloy. It did not burn his hands as it should have.

At the touch, the Destiny Stone gripped him, pulling his mind into its depths. There were entities within each, looking at him. He was stripped bare, his soul exposed in their prying gazes. A reproachful blue stare with fiery eyes pierced him through his very being, hissing chilling words:

> *"Unclean miscreant, depart—you are not welcome here!"*

He pulled his will away from her disdainful regard, meeting a hot, angry, distorted face. Hate seethed through him with pyretic intensity. She was a goddess, the Sylvan goddess. She did not want him here.

> *"Come closer, rock lover. I will bring your eternal immolation!"*

Haggersath wanted out of the gem, but another caught him before he could leave. She was cool but not cold, unlike him in every way—but calm and pleasant.

> *"Do not depart, Giftgiver. They await you. Go to them."*

This was not Morningsong. She was calm and fair, but there was a hidden danger to her. Christiemay.

With her simple dismissive gesture, his mind was swept to a place of safety. It was comfortable and without oppression. Here, finally, he sensed Jikseon, along with another, which had to be Bruss, the god of Man.

Jikseon grabbed his thoughts and turned them this way and that, performing smithy work far beyond mortal ideas. His god became as one with him, directing his movements. He worked Haggersath's hands, and they moved with intent and drew out power from the Destiny Stone. He was deft, and with Jikseon working his mind and body, Haggersath understood all crafting—so easy, why of course. He doused the mold and turned out the mountings to work upon the stone bench.

His jeweler's hammer rang with the force of a mountainside crumbling, but it touched the gems softly, caressing them with the power inside the Stone. Swaths of yellow magic surrounded the forge, diving into the gems. Blazing red sparks burst into red flames then swallowed themselves, flying off the stone, imbedding in the gemstones as he mounted them. The force of the hammer toppled some mountings to hit the stone floor, leaving blackened scars where they landed.

Haggersath knew the power of Jikseon had been reinforced by pure, pale, flaxen magic. The other being must have been Bruss. Bruss worked only the purest yellow power, never tainted by the unpredictability of blue or the intensity of red. The race of Man, Bruss's people, had always been the closest ally the Dwarrow knew—yet distant all the same.

Haggersath felt as if he would get swept into the cabochon himself in the golden deluge that the forging fostered, but a pure blue blade sliced his nose away from the power in the Stone. Haggersath was suddenly cut from all power. Jikseon was gone. He saw Bruss no more.

"Enough!" cried the rage of Christiemay, whose benign friendly face was no more. Blue as a Silfr Mountain glacier, her stare wilted Haggersath. *"You assume too much, Giftgiver. All is not for you alone— nor for only your kind. There be others with need. Now—begone!"*

With that, she motioned a push, and Haggersath was blown back in a wash of cerulean force. It threw him to the stone floor of the forge. He had been cast out of the Stone.

Faintly, he heard Grambol Doomsayer yelling as if he were drowning, choking, "Curse upon ye, Dokkur Dvergur!"

Haggersath lay there unseeing, stunned until arms pulled him to his feet. "Up now, Giftgiver. Yer mischief be done here."

He didn't answer. He could not place the voice. His head was so cloudy, unable to focus, to think clearly. They dragged him away, his blurry vision incapable of making out all of the room's commotion.

But things slowly came into view. He must have been delusional. It was Jarlsalt's band of soldiers. They were dragging him away from the forge. They filled the room—so many, some Rock-Biters too. He could not see what was happening. Then he saw Jarlsalt's snarling face coming close to his own, blood spattered across his swarthy skin.

"I tried ta tell ya, but ya foolish pride be yer problem. It won' be mine no more." Jarlsalt spat as he raged in Haggersath's face.

Jarlsalt raised his sword, flashing its gaudy ruby gem, high, and the flat came down so hard Haggersath saw a flash of white. He thought, with the echo in his mind of Grambol's words, he had heard, "Aye, curse ye indeed, Dokkur Dvergur."

Then there was nothing.

CHAPTER 24

Witness

How long? His thoughts would not…connect. He was dead. Tumbling through nothing. Nowhere to go. No needs. No wants. No emotion. The world around him had long since gone from thought or sight. There was no world. Alone. Had he done as he claimed he would during his lifetime? Was his life full and complete now that the end had come? Did he give enough or take too much? He could not fathom the concept of time. It seemed long—but then again, was it? How could such a thing be measured? There were no points to reference. There was only now. What was accomplished? Did it matter? There were no answers. Only questions leading to more questions. His thoughts were all awry. Nothing made sense. Nothing.

It had finally come after so very long. Death.

He opened up to receive that final passage, to join the Dwarrow fathers of old. Hrajaar awaits those Dwarrow that fall in battle. He waited for it—then, it came. A distant call. At first like a memory of something long forgotten. It drew him, bringing him closer—Hrajaar awaits. It had the warmth of waking to see the morning Sun only just peeking its first rays after a long night swallowed in an icy mountain blizzard. How long? Did it matter?

A darkness that was nothing now swirled with light, making a scene that fought his chaos. His mind tangled, unable to see, but now it was breaking into a vision. That which called him manifested itself into song.

Proper sounds droning on in unison, voiced by worthy Dwarrow. Some distant past, joined with those of the moment, together in a relentless, driving, deep bass chorus. It molded, shaping a work song teemed with swelling pride. It was good. It was welcome. It soothed him, and slowly, he felt renewed. The lights formed into distinct scenes.

Scenes of Dwarrow. They sang, familiar faces rebuilding and refinishing structures. He saw so many working with heart in their song, voices booming in their chests as they went. Ah! Such camaraderie. It was always the Dwarrow way.

Then he felt a twinge of broken harmony. An unrelated melody, heaped in discord with the song. It drew him in to see. There, among those who built and toiled for the common good, were seeds of evil, grim and angry. Some were speaking malcontent with hidden scowls under their beards. Plotting in secret, remaining concealed—but their souls and intentions lay bare for him to know.

They moved through the settlement, recruiting other gruff faces who joined them. Some seemed willing, others—holding in loyalty—refused. When their evil had spread and was full grown, it called in its supporters. They were led to a tall building—he knew the building, the Kon-ungr, in the Towers of the Horne. His memory was returning. His recognition was seeping back. Evil was led by the swarthy face of the most untrustworthy of sorts. Jarlsalt? His mind went racing. *Jarlsalt!* Into the Kings' Tower they went, weapons in hand and malice on their breath.

He followed with ever more urgency as he became more aware of the events unfolding around him. He saw more vividly. He heard more distinctly. He began to piece the confused spectacle into a comprehensible picture. He knew these Dwarrow. Hushed collusion in whispers stepped out of the droning and clipped at the ears of the evil conspiracy. He strained to focus his mind, gathering in the plot.

He began to count, take an inventory. In total there were twenty-two. No, twenty-five—ahh! Blast, this was impossible. He could not do a simple task of…again he drifted. There! He singled out the one in the center. He was a befouled darkness in the unremarkable sea of the others. Something tainted set him apart.

This dark Dwarrow set about directing the others, and they spread in purposeful, efficient movements. They had surrounded the central hall in which the forge was pluming out its own rage, full tilt, belching forth heat and smoke. He could not feel the heat, but in a way, he could "see" it. The dark Dwarrow's coalition outnumbered those in the forge better than three to one. Weapons out, they slunk forward until they were ready to strike.

In the great hall, the forge thrived. He knew the Dwarrow at the anvil, hammering and honing his work to life, his face alive with passion. Haggersath Giftgiver. The yellow-bearded smith was in a focus, totally resolute on the golden settings cast into molds before him. Eight assisting onlookers watched, glassy-eyed, entranced by the making of the trusilver mountings.

But it was the hot flare of the fist-sized gemstone held by Haggersath that dragged at his core. He could feel the power in the gemstone. Yellow power cascaded freely from the gem into the work before the hammering blacksmith. Hot, blue, bombastic sparks of magic shot out from the work. Red and blue magic was far less disciplined than their mundane golden cousin. Some magic found refuge in the gemstone being mounted in the trusilver, while some expended its energy with showy outbursts in the air—they landed and extinguished on the rock floor. Most, however, became drawn back into the gem only to resurface again. A cycle of magic. It was a wondrously beautiful thing to see. But during the spectacle, out of the gem burst a sudden sparkling wave of blue force, bowling over the Dwarrow in the room and sending Haggersath crashing hard to the floor, sprawled, stunned.

That was when the assailants struck. The Dwarrow in the forge never stood a chance. Jarlsalt's forces entered the room with hammers and blades ready for use. When they fell upon the lot of the surprised workers, they were slaughtered like in a butchery. He tried to call their names, he tried to warn them, but no sound came to his lips.

Haggersath did not rise from the blast; his beard was scorched, and he lay, lolling on the floor. Jarlsalt led the attackers, but he was not killing. He was looking, searching—for something. He made his way purposefully once he spied the Destiny Stone, that large gemstone that emitted the burst that had knocked the forge crew off their feet. Jarlsalt snatched up the Stone in his hands with a covetousness driven by cold ice in his greedy grasp.

"Jarlsalt! I'll have that," roared a grizzled old Dwarrow coming from behind the bellows, startling the insurgent commander out of his fixation. Grambol Doomsayer reached for the Destiny Stone as he approached, face intent with a determined odium.

Jarlsalt swatted away the gnarled hand. "Bah, ye drunken dotard. Off with ya before I lift yer head from yer shoulders."

But Grambol Doomsayer persisted. "That do not belong in yer filthy hands, betrayer." He reached over a leathery hand, clutching the Destiny Stone with Jarlsalt contesting for custody. They wrestled over the Destiny Stone, but the younger commander overpowered him and pulled it from Grambol Doomsayer's tight grasp. He was breathing heavily from the exertion.

"What do ya be doin'? Look at what you've done, boy!" He spread his arms at the scene of blood in the forge—a room of murders. Jarlsalt showed no remorse, but instead smiled.

Around the forge, it was a slaughter. The unprepared Dwarrow had been equipped for forging and were mostly unarmed, busy working without armor in the immense heat of the forge. Jarlsalt's force was fully armed and wearing their travel armor. It was a kin slaying, the worst of tragedies. Those in the forge met their fates with bloody evil. Some victims were western, some were eastern, but those of Jarlsalt's murderers were all westerners and all loyal to the 16th son of the Bornholm.

Then, without further provocation, Jarlsalt unsheathed his knife, its wicked blade flashing red in the light of the forge fires. His grin held a malice born of a baleful will. Malintent dripped from Jarlsalt's oily beard, glinting in the hot, sweaty light.

Grambol Doomsayer held his gaze, the ages of his long life heavy upon him. "What do ya be doin', Jarlsalt? Yer own kin!" Grambol Doomsayer said, heavy loss flowing with a hurt dismay.

"Doin'? Can ye not see yerself, ya batty bygone?" Jarlsalt flashed his dirk in a sweeping strike—Grambol Doomsayer drew away, dodging. The blade whiffed through his long, wiry beard. A few stray strands caught and were shaved away. Wispy gray hairs floated like lost souls down to the rectified stone foundation.

"Gimme the Destiny Stone and ye can go. I won't bother ye." Grambol Doomsayer stretched out a hand to receive the artifact.

In a flash of crimson, Jarlsalt's dirk raised and sank to the hilt into Grambol Doomsayer's collar, where it met the neck. His eyes went wide as blood spurted. Grambol Doomsayer's heart raced to send his life's blood, thick and hot—it sprayed over Jarlsalt and made the floor slick.

Wild-eyed, Jarlsalt held a mad glee as he dragged the dirk free, making way for the gushing river of blood to leave Grambol Doomsayer's failing body.

"I was tired of yer talk. Now look at ya. Think ya kin see the future now? Never had me fooled. I knew ye was false, a showman fer the ages, eh?" he growled close to Grambol Doomsayer's face. "Tell me, Doomsayer, did ya see this comin'? Methinks ya didn't."

Jarlsalt laughed in his face, blowing spittle off his raging mouth. Slowly, Grambol Doomsayer slid to the stone floor, his arms waving randomly about, reaching to retrieve his ebbing life back.

"A curse upon ye, Dokkur Dvergur!" gurgled Grambol Doomsayer weakly. "Your life will be bitter indeed, your truth I will take to Hrajaar with me. They will know ye fer who ye be."

Witnessing the kin slaying was too much to bear. But he could not cry out. He had no corporeal body. He was a voiceless wraith, watching a scene he could not influence or change. Yet now he focused and could maintain consistent thought.

Jarlsalt stood over the old Doomsayer; he was as good as dead. With a satisfied nod paired with a congratulatory smirk, he turned away and went directly to the mounted gems in their molds, toppling the pendants from them. He seized them, then fell back, screaming and dropping the hot pendants. They tumbled, spilling off in all directions around the forge. Agitated to painful anger, he scraped the ones off that had seared into the flesh of his hand.

He abandoned his attempt to pilfer the half-forged pendants and instead turned to his soldiers, raging with agony-driven frustration.

"Slay them all," he barked to the soldiers. "Save Haggersath Giftgiver. He is mine, an' me father will want him alive—an' *reasonably* unharmed." He glinted a smile off one side of his bloodied mouth. Swiftly, they dispatched any who might have still lived in the room.

Jarlsalt went over to the dazed Haggersath, who was held up by Dwarrow on either side. "I tried ta tell ya, but ya foolish pride be yer problem. It won' be mine no more." Jarlsalt spat in Haggersath's face. He slammed the flat of his sword across Haggersath's head. The yellow-bearded Giftgiver went limp in the soldiers' grasp.

Their sanguineous work completed, they left the room, dragging Haggersath with them. He wished to continue to witness and follow them, but he found he could not. His spirit was at its end. Without the body to reclaim life…

A pulling came, drawing him away. It overcame his intense need to follow the murderous thieves. He was drawn backward, away from the crimes that had taken place in the forge. He fought to stay and follow Jarlsalt, but the yellow swath of power that drew him was irresistible. It towed him down into darkness. Nothing to see, no sound reached him, and it swallowed him up, and he began to drown. He felt his essence winking out as a yellow light approached him, covering him, consuming him.

He took a deep, ragged breath, and his eyes opened slowly, dry and stinging from weeks of preserved slumber. Hoarse words whispered, wry as the wind of the Silfr Mountains in deep winter. "Dokkur Dvergur… Jarlsalt…murder!"

He saw a grinning hope from the Dwarrow soldier in attendance. Running from the room, the soldier yelled, "The Gulprąst! He's back! Mevindh-Gulbard has awoken."

CHAPTER 25

Only Seven?

Bolfath's fury was expected, but it was not the time for such things. No matter what was said or how he levied logic in Bolfath's direction, Mevindh-Gulbard could not get through his single-minded persistence. He would take Jarlsalt's skin for his own when he rescued the abducted Haggersath. Mevindh-Gulbard tried to enlist Diwolde Stonescraper, but the talent of a Grýttr was not parallel to the conciliations of a Gulprąst. He fared no better at holding off the blustering wrath of Bolfath, who was stomping with furious intent.

"Bah! We be wastin' our time ditherin' here. That mound of bear crap be makin' his way to his daddy on the other side o' the mountain," Bolfath sputtered, raging at all of them, and no one. "If he gets there before we can get our axes 'cross his scrawny neck, that wannabe kingshit'll get the Bornholm ta save his pup's greasy head."

"We must tend to those who fell in his treachery," explained Mevindh-Gulbard. "We cannot leave their souls to be wanderin' and haunt the Towers. That'd be irreverent."

He had to calm the big bodyguard down. They needed to be swift, yes, but also wise. Who knows what other preparations Jarlsalt had done in devising his terrible plot?

Tearing furiously at his beard and swatting at the air, Bolfath argued back, "Settle that matter when we get back. Leave it fer the Giftgiver ta handle then. If we don' act now, he might be dead before we can get ta him. I'll take that slinkin' snake's head back ta the Bornholm and lob it at his feet fer him ta gaze upon. 'Here be yer 15th son,' I'll say ta him."

"16th," corrected Diwolde. "And—"

"What manner of Dwarrow gives a…?!" sputtered Bolfath. "15th son, 16th son…60th son!! He'll be a *dead* son by the close of the day! All I need be the two ferskeyttr here. I'll take 'em an' go get the wretched goat fucker!"

Mevindh-Gulbard was still exhausted from his astral split. It had been scarcely an hour since he felt strong enough to stand. He had returned from the brink of death; he needed rest and time to recover. But he also knew it was best to channel the bodyguard's rage. He could see now that he would never stifle it. Only then could he find rest to heal and recover properly.

Until then, he had to be strong and offer reason in this storm of running emotion. "You ferget your duty, Bolfath. None here can dispute yer loyalty to the Giftgiver." He purposefully paced out his most mellow voice. "Take one ferskeyttr with you and leave one for us—as you can see, I am not yet able to protect anyone. I need time to regain strength. But before ye go, give these Dwarrow their due. They caused you no affront. Loyal were the Dwarrow who lost their lives in the forge." Mevindh-Gulbard paused and then began again with a stronger voice, the force of yellow magic behind him. Nobody noticed the hint of yellow glow that came off his lips. "Grambol Doomsayer was more than just an old fortune teller. He was the last of an age who remembered the height of the Dwarrow in their glory. Do not dilute the importance of the Doomsayer or his service to the Dwarrow—to *Haggersath* in particular."

He slouched, exhaustion setting in hard. He had to be careful. His condition was more serious than he thought.

"Aye, Gulprąst. Ye are right, as always," Bolfath haltingly admitted. A rationale settled over his demeanor as he nodded first to Mevindh-Gulbard and then to Diwolde Stonescraper. "I will take time. But I be not waitin' fer the skies ta bring the moon. I leave before the Sun does."

Then the great warrior turned, and he headed off to speak in his own way to the recently slain. Mevindh-Gulbard felt his last reserve of strength fail. His knees buckled; Diwolde Stonescraper caught him. He sagged, leaning upon the sturdy, squat frame of Diwolde Stonescraper.

"Grölle!" Diwolde Stonescraper called out to the Rock-Biter. "Help the Gulprąst to a bed. He be needen' rest."

Grölle turned his head, face hidden from expression by his bushy beard. Mevindh-Gulbard wondered if, by Jikseon, Grölle had the most impressive beard any Dwarrow could wish for.

"Yer ferskeyttr stays with us," Diwolde Stonescraper continued. "Bolfath be takin' Orm's troop with him into the mountain."

Grölle caught another Dwarrow to help him, and together they brought Mevindh-Gulbard to his room to rest. He reached out, grabbing the sleeve of the Rock-Biter captain.

"Bring me the socketed gemstones that be scattered about in the forge." He had to stop and take several wheezing half breaths before continuing. "There should be ten." Again, weakness demanded a pause. Blast that lich for severing his spirit. Even this was too much effort. "Tell no one what you do." He slunk back to the bed. Breathing took real effort. "An' Captain Grölle…" He had more to say, but he moved his lips like a silent prayer and not a sound came out.

"Aye, Gulprąst," he answered. "I'll do as ye bid. Rest well. We will be needin' ye, an' too soon, methinks."

He faintly heard Grölle leaving as the black void of sleep took him completely.

He woke to deep gray clouds rumbling ominous despair. That morning, tears of the Silfr Mountains had begun their weeping with a rhythmic patter. A fitting day Jikseon had made for these fine fallen to follow their way to Hrajaar.

Mevindh-Gulbard was feeling much better after his rest. How long he lay, he could not be sure. He wondered if Bolfath had left, letting impatient rage lead his heart, or if he cooled his stubborn head. Sitting up, he looked around the room. It was time to see what preparations the Dwarrow had done for the pyres to send those lost to Hrajaar. He stood on steady legs. That was good. He was recovered well enough for now.

Much of the work had been prepared, and the somber tone carried itself deeper with the mood of mountains reaching into the marrow of the Horned Towers. Mevindh-Gulbard shuffled along and replied to quiet, grim greetings of Dwarrow he encountered along the way. Most of the time he was quiet and responded with an unsmiling tilt of his pale, straw-tufted head.

He was correct in assuming where Diwolde Stonescraper would be in the early hours—he found the Stonescraper sitting on a large boulder that served well as a chair. He was shuffling some pebbles in his hand in thought and staring at the splendid panorama of the Silfr Mountains against the Towers of the Horne.

Diwolde Stonescraper smiled up at him, his breakfast partially eaten in front of him. He was a strange Dwarrow, not eating his softened duck separate from the bread that had been baked that morn, in the traditional manner. Diwolde Stonescraper had placed the duck inside the bread, which he split so he could eat it with a single hand. Mevindh-Gulbard watched as he swiped the einkorn berry bread into a pot of cold duck fat, which had bits of minced apple and clove in it. Diwolde Stonescraper would then take a bite off the end with the fat and chew with epic delight.

"Ya should try this, Gulprąst," he offered enthusiastically. "I have some more bread an' duck right here." Diwolde Stonescraper gestured to the wooden platter setting on a boulder next to him.

He was hungry. Healing and rest were hard work, especially when your spirit had been ripped away from your body. Grateful, he accepted and sat upon the boulder on the other side.

"Many thanks, Stonescraper. I be famished."

He watched as Diwolde Stonescraper took the bread and cut a long slit down the side. With the same knife, he slathered the opening with a thick layer of spiced apple duck fat. He then slapped a piece of the duck—boiled soft, and still steaming from the pot—in the middle. He handed the strange meal to Mevindh-Gulbard with a beaming smile.

"That'll make ya better than all the rest ye kin get in a week."

The odd thing dripped clear grease out the back of the split loaf. It smelled good, like pepper-spiced roasted duck, with a smokiness, too. He thought, *It didn't kill the Stonescraper*, so he took a bite. It hit him with all the flavors at once. Spicy pepper, rich smoky duck, sweet-salty fat melted to creamy goodness. All this, a meal complete, and neatly packaged in nutty einkorn berry bread.

Diwolde Stonescraper stared at him expectantly, his eyebrows bouncing over his gaze like hummingbird wings. It was good—his mouth was too full to answer. This was...exceptional!

"Yeah, I know. It be hard ta speak when it be this good."

He nodded as he affirmed the Gulprąst's reaction.

After getting a few bites in, he chased the food down with a drought of water. "What do ya call this thing ya made here?" he asked Diwolde Stonescraper, moving in for another bite.

"I call it strammagen." His grin returned. "Easy ta eat, an' better than most."

"Strammagen," echoed Mevindh-Gulbard. It was simple. That was an old tongue that meant hand-to-mouth. He smiled at the simplicity of it all and took another bite.

Diwolde Stonescraper's face returned to the cool seriousness that seemed to plague the Towers since the kin slaying. His mood became all business. "Bolfath left last evening with the Sun."

That wasn't really a surprise. "Did he take Grölle's ferskeyttr with him?"

"Naw, he's a good lad. He took Orm and his three Rock-Biters and set off in a hurry after that swarthy villain. He took Fjolmodr too—he be one of the eastern boys. Mebee ya remember the lad. He be one of the

Dwarrow I began studyin' up in the ways of hyljaleid on the road here."

Diwolde Stonescraper paused to take his last bite of strammagen. He did not wait more than a quick chew or two before relating more.

"Fjolmodr has a lot yet ta learn, but he learned enough to navigate under this mountain. It was the most traveled of all the hyljaleid in days gone, as it lay between the Towers of the Horne and Strongmedjie." Diwolde Stonescraper finished talking, his mouth so full that he was dropping clumps of greasy bread.

Mevindh-Gulbard knew these tunnels from times before—he was old enough to have traveled them many times. They were unlike any other tunnels under the Silfr Mountains. This was a broad avenue, large enough for heavy traffic and well represented for easy passage. Perhaps after facilitating the funerals, they could catch up. It was possible. Hardly likely, though. Knowing Bolfath and his drive, he might outpace his escort and come upon Jarlsalt's troop alone. Those two score western scoundrels would be hard-pressed to survive Bolfath.

Diwolde Stonescraper brought him out of deep thought. "It was the strangest thing I saw," he started with candid musing. "Before the rock of the hyljaleid closed, I saw blue shimmers. I dunno, like ghosts. Or mebbe I din't see nothin'."

Mevindh-Gulbard finished his last bite and was about to answer when he noticed the brown-bearded Rock-Biter standing off away from them. He was trying so hard to look inconspicuous, but he was far from subtle. It was plain that he was waiting. It was Grölle. What was he doing?

"He waitin' fer you?" Diwolde Stonescraper gave an uncharacteristic smirk. When Mevindh-Gulbard just looked with exhausted bewilderment at him, Diwolde Stonescraper chuckled, shaking his head. "Methinks he is."

"Me?" the Gulprąst answered, confused. Why was Grölle needing him?

"He be askin' if ya had been awake fer the last four hours. I think he be wantin' ta give ya those mounted gemstones he gathered up from the forge floor." Diwolde Stonescraper stifled back his amusement. "That one don't be good fer keepin' secrets, Mevindh-Gulbard. Ye must have been truly tired if ye asked him that. But he's a good one ta get things done. An' he be trustworthy too."

Mevindh-Gulbard felt a flush of heat come up in embarrassed thought. Of course, he shouldn't keep secrets from Haggersath's Haseti. That is, even if he could—and it appeared he could not.

"Ahh, that do be it, Stonescraper, that do be it." He got up and approached the unusually twitchy Grölle.

Grölle looked this way and that, shuffling around nervously, belying any hope of clandestine privacy.

"I got 'em," he said in a hoarse whisper, reaching into a small, hideously bright yellow leather pouch. "There be only seven. I did not find the other three."

He looked left and right quickly to verify their privacy, and his shaking hands spilled the mounted gemstones—some into Mevindh-Gulbard's waiting hand, others onto the dirt, rolling this way and that. Yet others dropped back into the bag.

"Blast me beard!" Grölle said with a complaining apology. "I be not built fer this kind o' work."

"I do believe you are correct in that, Captain Grölle. I count three in me hand, three more in the dirt, an' methinks one more is back in yer discreetly bright yellow pouch."

Grölle looked at him as if overworked with worry. "Me apologies, Gulprąst. I be no spy or agent. War and fightin' is me pride." He bent over and nabbed up the gemstones, handing them to Mevindh-Gulbard.

"May I have the bag?" Mevindh-Gulbard asked, plain-faced.

Grölle somehow looked even more sheepish and daintily handed it over with a half smile. Sweat rained down his red face like he'd been pushing ore carts out of a mine all morning long. "If ye be done with me, I'd be getting ready fer the funeral."

Mevindh-Gulbard dismissed the captain. It seemed to him that he would be the one to oversee the Towers of the Horne in Haggersath's absence. Even Diwolde Stonescraper was deferring to his judgment. He would do it, of course.

His thoughts returned to Bolfath's chase. Even outnumbered five or six to one, there wasn't a question that he could wade through Jarlsalt's small force and recover Haggersath and the Destiny Stone. But that was only if they could catch them. He despised the thought of Dwarrow slaying other Dwarrow, especially travel companions. It was beyond repugnant. This was all on the head of that betrayal and the horrible crime the Dokkur Dvergur had committed.

Admittedly, Strongmedjie and the Horned Towers had always been friendly rivals—perhaps more rivals than friends, even in the best of times. But never outright enemies. Now, it was the saddest of times.

The shimmering blue ghosts Diwolde Stonescraper mentioned were of particular interest...Mevindh-Gulbard harnessed a thought. It was not the first time something blue had been around the Destiny Stone. But he tucked it away and thought nothing more of it. Dwarrow did not sit well with blue magic, even benign blue magic. Often, it was helpful—but it came with an exacting price at heavy expense, and usually at the most inopportune time. Best not to be indebted to it.

CHAPTER 26

Doomsayer

The funeral barge was well stocked with dried grasses and broken pine stems fit for fuel and pyre kindling. Grambol Doomsayer and eight Dwarrow had been laid in their places and were ready for their passage to Hrajaar. After lighting the pyre, they would drift down the River Undan until the flames and river took their bodies. A Dwarrow's celebration of their death in battle was greatly honored.

Mevindh-Gulbard arrived, looking over the scene. He understood the honor, and that their deaths stood in the highest regard. But death was still death, and its finality meant that Jikseon must claim back his children. Only death in battle guaranteed passage to Hrajaar. Even after a good life, if a Dwarrow died old or through accident, he or she must stand in judgment before Jikseon. Perhaps they would be granted Hrajaar, and perhaps they would be returned to the stone of Thear. He was a fair but stern god, just like mountain and steel.

This river, the River Undan, sprouted in a fall some forty meters high off the northern spine of the Himiniodurr. It dropped and splashed along the jagged mountain wall, through several jutting columns of rock until it settled to run its course. It fed the cool frosted lake called Toradh Dunne many leagues off to the east, as did all the interior rivers of the Silfr Mountains. Dwarrow lore proclaimed the water carried pure blue magic with it, imbued by the goddess Christiemay's protection. Mevindh-Gulbard knew much of her protection—an unpredictable conundrum of blessing and curse. Something best avoided.

But in the case of the river, at least while in the Horne, it seemed a blessing alone. Perhaps there was still a cost to manifest, and its toll would be devastating. Some traditions held their way through the danger. To be sure, the Dwarrow would light the funeral pyre before the barge left the Tower of the Horne. While in the Towers, Jikseon held sway and would ensure passage for their comrades to Hrajaar.

Mevindh-Gulbard, Diwolde Stonescraper, Grölle, and the three Rock-Biters of his ferskeyttr were the only living Dwarrow left in the Towers. Fate spelled that the glory of the Towers of the Horne may have faded to dust for the last time. The wicker on the funeral barge was lit, and the ferskeyttr as a unit pushed off their dead. It caught quickly and burned with hot yellow fury as if Jikseon himself mourned the passing of these nine Dwarrow.

It was the Gulprąst's duty to speak on these occasions. He was proud to do it. He would honor their loss as best he could.

"Grambol Doomsayer was perhaps the oldest living Dwarrow, east or west," he began, at a methodical pace and in his best, resonant voice. "None alive had commanded his knowledge of the thoughts of Jikseon. Having a mind that a god spoke through—not directly, but in suggestion or inspiration—made the Doomsayer somewhat touched. We saw his erratic behaviors and unconventional chatter. He talked through clouds of divine inception—and through the fog of heavy drink, as well."

This brought fond chuckles and nodding from the others, pleasant smiles flickering from face to face.

"Ahh, that be true, so true," Grölle related out loud, fighting tears with reminiscent sniggers.

"He was a lovable loon, to be sure," another of the Rock-Biters added in.

Mevindh-Gulbard waited a moment for the Dwarrow to finish. It was a good and respectful gesture to give them time to recollect and speak out their grief and love for those fallen in a Dwarrow funeral. When silence came, he continued.

"But the knowledge he shared brought us here. He shared, and wealth followed. There will be no other bearing such a gift as his. Doomsayers were always uncommon, but Grambol Doomsayer was the last." He paused, looking to see if there was mention. But they were silent. "We send him to the Hrajaar with eight Dwarrow who were cruelly murdered at his side."

Now he took the time to speak their names out loud, each clear and separate—for those here, and for Jikseon to receive them.

"Othro. Led his ferskeyttr well and as fine a warrior as any ye might have seen."

The others murmured, "Yeah," and, "Fine warrior."

"Bijur. Had a way of findin' gems in any manner of dig." Just nods of agreement.

"Nater. Didn't know much more 'bout him other than he combed his beard all the time."

At this, one of the Rock-Biters said, "He made this comb fer me." He held it up for all to see like a trophy. "It be carved of a peak deer antler. Methinks it should go with him."

"Aye, Vékell, put it in his hand on the barge," Grölle told him.

Mevindh-Gulbard proceeded while Vekell brought forth the elaborately carved comb and placed it in Nater's hand.

"Mallonsmythe. A fine smithy. They say he was expert in bronze castin'."

Another Dwarrow verified, "That he was."

"Cürlle. By Jikseon, he could snort an' spit like he was a goat."

Laughs came from the retinue. So it went with Gottié, Gerthur, and Aenur.

Then he closed with, "Eternal shall be their praise."

Without warning, the fires suddenly climbed, and blue wisps came off the tips of the pyre. They then descended, extending into the flame until the blaze was a brilliant cobalt. Mevindh-Gulbard had never before seen this extreme of an azure display. From the looks of the others' faces, neither had they.

The water of the river bubbled beneath the barge, fuming with blue steam as if feeding the fire itself. A smoke of bright blue formed into an image of a slight woman with a cold beauty that pierced their hearts. She was chill and blue as pristine ice in consummate purity, a frigid beauty both fearsome and disarming. She was something benign but altogether radiant and dangerous, genial and reserved. She spoke soft words like a trickling brook touched by the icy tongue of the Undan River.

> *"Tarry not here, sons of Jikseon. You and the foul runeweavers may be fighting over the Destiny Stone, but it does not belong to you or them. It belongs to me and me alone. I allow others to use it as I will. Your Giftgiver is in more danger than the mere Dokkur Dvergur you pursue. Noshid would destroy that which is your salvation. Make haste—his minions, they are here."*

The blue image flashed out in a flare of azure fire consuming the barge. It was gone in a wisp of smoke, all its occupants taken. There was nothing left on the river.

Clattering noises of armor brought the Dwarrow back to focus.

"Gnomôk at the gates," declared Grölle. He rushed to gather his weapons. "To arms, to arms! Ferskeyttr, form on me."

Mevindh-Gulbard saw their numbers. It was impossible to manage with only one ferskeyttr. "To the mountainside. Stonescraper, get us inside the mountains. We need to take the fastest way to Strongmedjie. Grölle, with me. There be no fight for us here, today."

"Aye, Gulprąst, already startin' on it." Diwolde Stonescraper motioned for them to move into the Kings' Tower. "We can get what we need in the Kon-ungr. It was stowed b'fore. I was expectin' ta chase that razor-bearded fuck soon as ya said so."

Good, thought Mevindh-Gulbard. "All right, lads, let's get after the Giftgiver." He ran down the hall amid the others. They gathered their bags and weapons, and in mere moments they were ready for travel.

They dashed through the Kings' Tower. Something drove the Gnomôk hot after them. It wasn't in their makeup to move with this kind of controlled intensity. They seemed to have a mind of where to go without knowing the exact location of the Dwarrow. Something was steering their pursuit.

Diwolde Stonescraper stopped at the blank stone and moved his hand over the rock. It glowed fiery orange, forming a large outline that slid open. "This way, lads."

They shuffled through the opening, and Diwolde Stonescraper motioned his hands along the stone as if tickling its surface. Smoothly, the rock door closed before the first Gnomôk turned the corner.

CHAPTER 27

Bolfath

The Sun had been about to set when Bolfath and Orm's ferskeyttr were setting off through the mountain. Diwolde Stonescraper chose Fjolmodr to be their guide. Was the Grýttr afraid he'd get lost? His parental concern was overly cautious. Well, that is the same thing the Gulprąst would have done, had he not been resting. Bolfath accepted the help. He did need somebody to open the doors. That was as good a reason as any to take Fjolmodr along. Just so long as he knew his place and stayed out of Bolfath's way when the time came to kill.

Bolfath did not wait for the rock to slide closed. He sped down the wide path at a sprint. It was more than difficult for the ferskeyttr to keep up with him, and soon Orm was calling out to an empty passage for him to slacken his pace. He stopped and turned to look, but the others were too far back to be seen. It didn't matter. He wouldn't need them for Jarlsalt.

He sped off down the well-traveled avenue that served the Dwarrow as their primary trade route between their two great strongholds. Light cascaded from some opening above and was amplified by crystals, shaped and formed in the walls of the hyljaleid to reflect an expanded illumination. It showed only mild wear; the grandeur of the work done in this Dwarrow edifice was an unequaled building feat. Bolfath had been running for what seemed like hours. He had lost all traces of Orm's ferskeyttr.

He paused for a moment to catch his breath. It was not something he let the other Dwarrow know, but even he grew weary if the exertion was intense. While resting, he took in the spectacle of the work crafted during the peak of the Dwarrow kingdoms and felt the presence of the spirit of the creators. Clean straight lines of passage with running cornices of Dwarrow faces watching his travel along the hyljaleid. The decades upon decades, even possibly centuries, of heavy traffic left no mark on the solid stone floor.

Mighty square columns, wrought of a stone brought in, supported the tall passage every hundred steps or so. They were cut with straight striations of vertical striping coupled at the top and bottom with parabolic scrollwork.

Their sweat and toil left a distinct fingerprint upon their workings. For a moment or so, it seemed as if he were not alone. But there was no one ahead of him, and no sign of Orm's troop behind.

Setting his ice giant's will in his step, he began to run once more, but then something snagged his feet and tangled them. There, he thought he saw just a shimmering glimpse of blue—he was propelled headlong into the cobbled floor. Dazed, he wiped the blood out of his eyes; it was streaming from his cut forehead.

"Blast me beard," he wheezed out.

He went to stand but felt himself flung into a wall and then another, and the next, as if he were but a child's doll. There was no one there, no one grabbing him. Warm blood oozed from his head into his beard. He felt battered but got to hands and knees.

"By Jikseon," he said with ragged pain thick and present. "Sylvan magic!"

Through clouded vision, he made out three—no, *four* shapes, all Sylvan. Violet ropes of crackling magic wrapped him up, and he couldn't move. He hated blue and red magic, especially combined. He was raised away from the wall and discourteously slammed with the strength to rival a frost giant to the cavern floor.

The world went black.

PART

Eight

CHAPTER 28

Of Wood and Stone

"Let us leave this accursed place. It drains the essence of Sylvan life from our very skins," Rommaith said, as if the walls of rock were responsible for the injuries they suffered. "Even with the runeweaver gone, the air hangs with uninvited malice."

"You feel it too, then," Glenia said, echoing as she hastened a healing upon Rommaith. Her fingers showed a faint red glow. "That won't be much, but it should help some."

She went over to Belusan and did the same. "We are blessed by Morningsong to have survived. One does not suffer an attack of a runeweaver and live to tell of it. At least not that I have ever heard."

Belusan shakily followed Rommaith, who already started back the way they had come. The two

Sylvan moved without speed, and Belusan's gait was clumsily uneven. Glenia must have noticed, as she lent him a shoulder to assist. Then Glenia stopped and looked over her shoulder, apparently just remembering.

"Let us go, Galean. We have what we came for." With Belusan leaning heavy upon her, she returned her attention to helping him. Again, she called out, without looking Aieren's way this time, "You can rest when we are safe."

They had almost forgotten him. Aieren the Galean, an afterthought. Worse than that—a burden. He was laid at their feet by the goddess and was made their charge. They had no choice but to escort him. His part in this quest was paramount. But they despised him. That was always in the forefront. But he had failed. He did not do his part. They could not be pleased with him.

Aieren was still blinking with disbelief. No Destiny Stone. All of them were nearly slain by the wretched runeweaver, and they had nothing to show for it. Did the lich have it? Did it flee to hide it somewhere else? Aieren had no answers, and only knew that *he* did not have the Destiny Stone. He did feel it—it was not too far. But he could not focus enough to determine exactly which way. It was so easy before. He had the

Destiny Stone in his hands. But it was gone. His role was simple. He…

The anguish overcame him, and he leaned on the cave wall, vomiting. It did not purge his guilt. No wonder he was a hated outcast. He wasn't worthy of respect. A total failure.

As Aieren numbly followed the Sylvan, he tried to reach out and locate the Destiny Stone again, but he was more fatigued than he realized. He could barely sense anything there. It was moving. Every time he tried, it was farther away.

He needed rest. Seeing the state of the three marred, dispirited Sylvan in front of him, he was sure they would need time to recover too. He would search again, but not yet, no.

He recalled that wail, that bone-jarring howl the runeweaver emitted as it swept off. It was abrupt in a way that seemed to carry final anger and despair. It was as fearsome in memory as it was when he witnessed it in person. He shivered so hard he stumbled to his knees, just catching himself. He couldn't even walk uninjured—he was so clumsy. He had to rest. Then he would locate the Destiny Stone.

The entrance to the cavern was sealed shut. Kvalid bodies lay slain on the floor, along with a single

Dwarrow. Aieren did not remember this carnage, but events were jumbled. His mind screamed for sleep.

"The rock-dwellers came in behind us," Rommaith said, spitting as if it made him retch to talk of them.

It came to Aieren then. Was it possible that those bearded louts nabbed up the Destiny Stone while that flash of magic blinded them?

No. They could not touch such an artifact of worth. He had felt the unstoppable power contained in the Destiny Stone. More likely the lich had stolen off with it.

"We seem to be trapped in this cave, whether we like it or not," said Glenia. She made the resignation clear that they were not getting out this way. "That is, unless one of you knows how to open this door."

The following silence was its own answer. Glenia began nervously picking at her skin as it began to bark then faded back to normal. A flake of bark fell here and there as she worked it like a scab itchy from healing.

"Dwarrow keep their secrets from even their own kin. There is nothing we children of the wood might know of," Belusan said with strained effort. He carefully sat himself on the rock floor with a helping grasp from Rommaith. "I suspect we may need to explore the other rooms for an exit."

Glenia shook her leafy head. The ruddy pink foliage slapped back and forth like the wind had taken them.

"My magic is dampened in here," she lamented. "The walls must carry some Dwarrow perversion of magic to blunt my healing ability. I am sorry."

"It will have to do. Let us recover for now." Belusan looked at Aieren and added, "Aieren, bring out the Destiny Stone and let us see if there might be a way to use it to aid us. It may hold a key to opening these Dwarrow locks."

Aieren was paralyzed. His fear ran through every part of his being, electrifying him. The feeling buzzed in his head. He shook at the asking, as if Belusan's voice was a crack of thunder. This was a request he could not do. It was the last thing he wanted to hear. He stared at Belusan, horrified at the response they would have, then whispered out in a breath so dry it barely hissed past his lips, "I-I don't have the Stone."

Rommaith began chuckling morbidly. "Of course. How could I be surprised?"

Belusan repeated, "Aieren—the Stone? It was the only thing you needed to do back there."

Shame and fear were battling for dominance inside him. He tried to speak clearly, but it came out stuttering, as if dragging his voice from the abyss. "N-no Stone. I don't have it. It just was there, and then it wasn't."

Suddenly Rommaith stood up and reared on him menacingly, flexing his big hands. His voice was pitiless and held a quiet threat. "It wasn't there? What were you doing, Galean?" Rommaith drew in breaths as his rage built and face took on that of a gnarled old oak.

Glenia slapped the wall with her open hand. "Sit down, Rommaith." Her face carried a rage of another kind. She shook her head of ruddy pink leaves, making a rustling noise.

But the big warrior came forward in two long steps and loomed over Aieren with anger flooding his every movement. The creaking as his hands clenched sounded like branches of a tree snapping.

Belusan let his chin drop as he shook his head. "You do not fail to disappoint in every way, Galean. So, this was all for naught."

As one, the Sylvan looked at him in disbelief. He knew they saw him grab the Destiny Stone. All of them saw. But now, nothing. Failure. Again!

"No," Aieren whispered. "I don't have it. I do not know where it has gone."

Dismayed, Glenia said, as her despair dragged her to the floor next to Belusan, "Why? Aieren, why?"

"I don't know," Aieren conceded, struggling to get the words out, to make sense of what happened. "I was reaching for it. Then, after that flash, it was just gone." He was feeling even more useless than before. His head dropped, chin against his chest. Self-pity overwhelmed him. "There is no more. I just don't know."

Rommaith had a different response. The first blow connected hard, coming across his head, above the temple, sending flashes of light and dark through his sight. There should have been pain, but he was numb already. Aieren went reeling backward and into the rough, uneven cavern wall. He touched his head and drew back a bloodied hand hardly visible through clouded vision. A hot flash of blood broke loose and streamed into his mouth, a copper taste. The second fist came in slow motion. He watched it slowly come in, and blackness hit as it pummeled his head against the wall, where it rattled between Rommaith's fist and the rock. He slid to the floor just in time to feel Rommaith's knee slamming into his unprotected gut. Aieren gasped out a muffled grunt. He lay there, limp and bleeding, on the stone floor. It was cool and felt good. He saw only blackness but could hear them around the room. A failure. He deserved no less.

"Rommaith, stop!" said Glenia. "*Rommaith!*" This time it halted Rommaith.

Aieren braced for the next blow to land. It never came. Aieren opened his eyes with a lazy need to see. Rommaith had frozen, seething, over Aieren. He didn't strike Aieren, but he did not step away, either.

Belusan stood up and half-heartedly pulled the fuming Rommaith away from Aieren. "We need him still, Rommaith. Do not break the Galean so far that he is unable to locate the Destiny Stone."

Belusan must have reached the logic in Rommaith's head. The big Sylvan relaxed his stance. His face, however, remained in a permanent state of fury.

"We have been quested by the goddess of the wood, and he is the only one of us who can find the Destiny Stone," Belusan reasoned with him.

"He deserves more," Rommaith said matter-of-factly. Looking at Aieren, he left him with a promise: "It will come, Galean. You will not live past our quest."

Glenia started to go over to Aieren, but Rommaith reached out and gripped her shoulder. His hand rested gently but held her with an iron force. He slowly moved his head side to side in a convincing no. "Leave him to remember the error of his ways."

She relented after a moment, moving away. Aieren struggled slowly, painfully, into a sitting position where Rommaith had left him, bleeding and bruised. Rommaith was right. He deserved more. He was lucky. Ha! Left with bruised pride and the only thing broken was skin. Sickly, detestable, golden skin.

Time passed without reference. The Sylvan mission had stalled. They relied on natural healing, which had to happen over days. Attempts at "false healing" through dampened red magic with blue enhancement assisted very little in their recovery. Over this time, Belusan seemed to darken in spirit as he began to lose faith that escaping the cavern was possible. His despair bled through, and Aieren saw the Sylvan decline. Being cut off from magic, over enough time, would be deadly.

Sylvan needed to draw upon red and blue magic from the Sun for sustenance. Aieren was a different case. He was Galean and did not have the ability (or need) to supplement food and water with blue and red magic in the way of the Sylvan. He gave a wry smile to himself. So, being Galean had one miserable benefit. In their current state, they had enough food for him to outlast them. Glenia stole moments away when the others were not looking to heal him, but he saw the cost it was taking on her. Her cheeks had lost the sapling, youthful smoothness and were sunken with folded lines. A single crack had split into a tiny lesion under her left eye. Her eyes themselves looked dry, and the gray had begun to yellow at the outer lids.

"Glenia," he said quietly so only she might hear, as she kneeled to begin. "I am well enough," he lied. "Save your healing for a better time. In here you are fading, yet I remain strong. Do not trouble with me further."

She looked him over carefully, then smiled—just a hint. Her eyes, gray as a storm coming in, pierced him. Even in her deteriorating condition, she was quite beautiful. "I will save it for a greater need. We may be here a long while."

Then she stood and moved over to see to Belusan. Glenia spent most of her time with the slender Sylvan. They seemed to have a rapport that dated back to childhood. Best of friends, Aieren observed. They spoke in quiet familiarity. It made sense that they found some comfort in each other while in this dismal trap.

Aieren decided to ask, "Belusan, are you and Glenia...?" He hesitated. It was a very personal question. Perhaps he overstepped, but their expressions as they looked his way seemed more mildly amused than affronted. "Are you both...?" This was so hard. What had he started? His face felt flushed with embarrassment.

Belusan said, smiling with a chuckle, "We are not kindling for each other, if that is your question."

Glenia covered her mouth with a hand, giggling. "No, we are closest friends," she said in conclusion. Her laughter rocked her some.

"We have known each other from sprout to tree," Belusan said with a nostalgic happiness flooding his face. Glenia mirrored the glow with her own mirthful glance that made her leafy hair even brighter pink. It was the first time Aieren thought that Belusan was actually talking to him.

"You are both from the south of the Daoine Maithe. Are your families there?" Aieren was curious. He wanted to keep the pleasantries going. Perhaps he could forge some lasting relation to make their quest less hostile.

"My family is very extensive," Belusan answered. "Chestnuts thrive in the south, and I have a very many hundred relatives. We serve the Daoine Maithe patrolling the borders to keep the outsiders away." He paused, brushing at his thigh with one hand. "That is what we were doing when we first found you. We were removing the ogrekaru. They have no business in the Daoine Maithe."

Despite the Sylvan's disdain for him, Aieren quite liked Belusan. Belusan was fair and operated on reason. He was also the Sylvan who was suffering the most and deteriorating the fastest in this cavern. His would be the first death in here, unless Glenia spent her last life force to keep him alive.

"What about you, Glenia? Is your family large too? Do you have an obligation such as Belusan?" Aieren really wanted to know more now. Before he just thought it might ease their relationship, but now he began to see them more personally.

She seemed shy to speak about herself. She twisted her limbs up and moved around where she sat before answering. "Oh no. I am not so important. We elders do not kindle as often as those frisky chestnuts do." She passed a coy look Belusan's way, and he laughed with Sylvan gaiety that lit the room. "I was traveling with my good friend Belusan to keep him company and find some adventure away from the quiet of the Mulńntirna Ban-dia, where we are from."

Aieren thought she was not telling everything. He wanted to know more about her. He prodded on. "What do you do there when you aren't frolicking for adventure with Belusan?"

"Me?" She seemed surprised at more inquiry. She drew her knees up and wrapped her arms around them in reminiscent thought. "I am a healer. Most of the elders in the south find healing a soothing and rewarding task." She suddenly looked distant and sad. "It crushes me that I cannot do what I am best at here under this tomb that we are left to."

Aieren regretted it immediately. He did not mean to bring any pain to her. He just wanted to know her. He looked for a way to change the conversation back to a more pleasant feeling. "What of you, Rommaith? How did you come to be with these two?"

He glared at Aieren. "Do not include me in your banter, Galean. I harbor no favor for you. Had I made my decision, you would be dead at my own hands."

Aieren felt fear creep over him. This oaken Sylvan would never be more than a suspended hate. He decided to be quiet. The cloud of animosity and distance pushed its way back into the room.

Rommaith spent his time brooding and sleeping. At any other time, he was casting harsh glances at Aieren, never hiding his disgust for the Galean. He was the loner. Big and brutal. Aieren did not feel the same about Rommaith as he did toward Belusan. He could do without the violent threats, especially since Rommaith had proven that they could take form and be a reality in a flash of unpredictable anger.

Then there was Glenia. She was kind to him. Yes, she treated him as less than Sylvan, but that was what he was. Her pinkish leaves looked soft, and they fell in a cascade that made her a pleasant sight—especially in this dismal place otherwise devoid of hope and life. It would be her or Belusan that would die first. The other would quickly follow. That would leave him alone with Rommaith. He shuddered at the thought. Rommaith would be free to do his vengeance. He withdrew even further into his corner and avoided looking at Rommaith.

Rommaith had explored the extent of the caverns. There was nothing but small rooms off the way they had gone before. Those and the cavern they had fought in. But in that cave Rommaith said there was no exit.

The other way was a large room that Rommaith said held only decay and death. He told them that a living mold of a most vile nature dwelled there. He said once they expired it might come for them all, but it seemed loath to leave the safety of its abode and likely would be of no bother yet while they lived.

Belusan would often inquire of Aieren, "Can you feel the Stone now, Galean?" But Aieren was despondent—he could not feel anything. His regular replies of "no" or averted silence continued to spiral their hopes of success. He wished Belusan would stop asking.

The inquiries put Aieren's thoughts into despair. He needed the Destiny Stone. At that moment when he held it in his hand, he was Sylvan again. He could not forget that elation, that feeling of magic once more washing over him and filling the void of his emptiness. It had to be found. It was the will of Morningsong, yes—but he desired his Sylvan grace back too. He tried locating the Destiny Stone many times. It felt near, but also far. He could not tell the others; it was useless, as it would not serve to ease their suffering. He bore the knowledge alone.

Aieren was grateful for the comforts Glenia gave him. She seemed to care that he survived and suffered as little as possible. After he told her not to use her magic on him, instead of healing, she would dress his wounds with cloth, in the way of the Man. She was skilled and gentle and soothing. Aieren's physical wounds were minor and simple. His spiritual ailments were much deeper and more complex. She did not realize how her small attention to him, distant and standoffish as it was, kept him with a faint hope. Hope of what, he could not say. Survival, he supposed—or maybe something more. His thoughts of her softened his heart. He felt she would defend him if the others forsook him. At least, as long as she could.

Time spent in frustrated stagnation did nothing to improve Sylvan disdain for Aieren's obvious contrasts. His health was just beginning to be compromised; theirs was far more deteriorated. The lack of food and artificially conjured water was not sustainable for him forever, but it was sufficient for now; the lack of magic penetration, however, was already showing in their haggard faces. Aieren's hope was waning. He was unsure of the passage of time, but they had to have been stuck there for days, maybe weeks. Like prisoners in isolated darkness, they lost their sense of time. It was always just now.

He had resigned that they would die there. But even as hope slid to nonexistence, it came back in a glimmer. The rock door slid open.

CHAPTER 29

Ice Serpents

Rommaith was the only one of them able to get to his feet. The others slowly tried to rise. In front of the surprised prisoners stood a Dwarrow, looking just as surprised as they were. He stood very short even for one of his kind, and his ruddy brown beard reached down to an impressively bulbous gut. His smiling red cheeks were full of pleasant surprise. Belusan noticed a faint blue shimmer around the unarmed Dwarrow.

"Bless me beard, har! Now tell me true, what do four of yer kind doin' hidin' in the rockpile?" the nutbrown-haired Dwarrow mused out loud.

Belusan was immediately on guard. This Dwarrow had magic, blue magic. This was horribly out of place. Dwarrow never used blue magic! It was not within the realm of Jikseon's powers. He stepped forward to place himself between the Dwarrow and Glenia, who seemed to be unaware of the abnormality. She was not as gifted at blue magic as he was. Perhaps she could not detect it. It was only a trickle of power.

Glenia recovered her voice, speaking first. "We were caught in here unaware, trapped without the knowledge needed to open the mountain. We are glad and grateful to you, son of Jikseon, for opening the door." The peaks in her voice soared with a generous melody. "How the smile of Morningsong must shine upon us, that one such as you come to these ruins in our time of need."

He grinned at her, showing a gold tooth. "It be not unusual fer a Dwarrow ta be wanderin'...."

Belusan saw the blue magic was an illusion. The tricky Dwarrow or whatever he really was. He fed a wave of blue magic over the mousy Dwarrow; the blue shimmered and sparkled as it swept over their rosy-cheeked savior with silver pops and flashes. The illusion of a Dwarrow fell away from the figure, and before them stood a tall, lean, and powerful lord of Men.

Glenia leaped back with a yelp she tried to muffle. Belusan knew she did not see the telltale flickers of blue magic that he had discerned; but he had, knowing a Dwarrow, seemingly kind on the face of it, was intentionally deceiving them.

The Sylvan were all on their feet in an instant. Rommaith pulled out his scian, and Belusan fingered his twin Fhalá. Glenia recovered, stringing her bow and reaching for an arrow. Belusan was not surprised that the Galean only shuddered backward from the unexpected. Then Aieren just stood there, watching with empty interest.

This Man before them was unlike others of his kind. His skin glistened with silvery blue magic, he was taller than most Men, and there was a sort of grace about him. Sylvan, yet not Sylvan. As his true form was revealed, Belusan saw he wore a flowing blue-gray cape, which was hooded and well worn, and the haft of a long elaborately crafted hilt belonging to the bihänder was strapped across his back. It was tipped with a light blue sapphire the size of a walnut. His hair was long and white, streaked with jet black and unnatural silver. His face was worn with care like it carried a heavy burden, but he did not look old, nor did he look young. He appeared to be both all at once.

He let out a laugh. "Well met, Belusan Qûmhachdach." He winked at him. "I should have known you'd see through my illusion." His voice was precise but clean as a winter mountain stream. He pulled back his hood. Gleaming brighter than the most brilliant star in the night sky, a bright silver-blue sapphire was set in the center of his forehead.

Now Belusan was more than suspicious; he was on full alert. His body was tensed, ready to draw both fhalá for close action. "Who are you to know my name? Name yourself, trickster," Belusan laid out his question with open suspicion. "Why do you disguise yourself as a Dwarrow?"

The stranger did not move or react. He was calm and kept his pleasant look. "Forgive my little ruse." He gave a slight nod. "It was meant to put you at ease. I see now the folly in my choice." The silvery Man's voice crackled in unison with the metallic energies that sizzled off the sapphire in his brow. "I am called Crúimthier. I am of the Silroh."

"A Silroh?" Belusan did not believe it. There were no more Silroh. None except the wizard in the south. But this was not him. That one was known to be old, and besides, he was half a world away. Gasps from Glenia and Aieren showed that they felt the same surprise.

"There are no more Silroh," Aieren said, to Belusan's surprise.

"Except the wizard in the south," Glenia said. She had not relaxed her bow with an arrow nocked.

"Yes, and he is Cúrolum, and he wears a jade, a jewel as green as the Daoine Maithe in its zenith, upon his brow," replied Crúimthier. "He is a very good friend of mine."

"But you wear a sapphire. I do not care about the difference in your jewels. Why has one of the Silroh come here?" Belusan's strained voice was growing uneasy. "Silroh are not known to be trustworthy friends of the Daoine Maithe."

"Our lore tells us the Silroh were taken by Christiemay and locked in glaciers to pay for their treachery," Glenia said. She did not give him a chance to answer Belusan's question.

Belusan gave a sidelong look at her. She needed to let him do the questioning. But he dared not take his eyes from Crúimthier—all of them watched him with curious suspicion, except Aieren.

"A price paid for centuries, yes. I was one of those. We all were—except Cúrolum, of course," Crúimthier admitted. "But now a penance of action is due. The time for reflection has served, and I am brought forth to do that which is appointed to me by Christiemay. Just as you, Aieren, have been tasked by Morningsong. Much is in motion. The gods are making their play against the essence that fuels corruption of power—the blackness that befouls the Sun. Our paths have been laid out, and ours are aligned at this juncture, as *we* should be. That is why I am here now."

There was a silence as the Sylvan measured his words. How did he know so much about them and their quest from Morningsong? Belusan wondered what he meant by "aligned at this juncture." So, this Silroh claimed to be an ally—for the moment, anyway. Rommaith had slowly begun to work his way to the side of the Silroh. He crept so very slowly.

"You have tarried long enough; your maladies will heal swiftly now that the mountain no longer hinders your magic." Crúimthier looked them over as if assessing their condition. "The Dwarrow have lost the lead they once held for Jikseon, and Noshid now holds the Destiny Stone. That is an ill-fated turn we cannot allow. But all is not lost. Reckless is his greed, and he will blunder endlessly. His servants are loyal but operate in blind darkness. Make haste—the Race to Destiny careens toward its finish. One of us must win. Thear will suffer a terrible fate if Noshid succeeds."

"Not so fast, Silroh of the frozen goddess. Why would a servant of Christiemay concern themselves with us?" asked Glenia. It was exactly what Belusan was going to ask. He smiled inwardly, but he would add more to the question.

"Your goddess has always shown an indifference to the Sylvan. Even as the Daoine Maithe began failing and our race began to fade, we have never seen any aid or missive from your lady. Yours seems to be the path of a servant of Noshid. It smells of his vengeance with your urgency." Belusan said this with no emotion. He wanted a direct answer. In case their suspicion was correct.

"Be at peace, Glenia Fìor-ghlan, I bear no ill to you or your kin. In your time of restitution under this mountain, you have lost ground. The Dwarrow have used the Destiny Stone already, but they do not yet know the way to open its power completely. Your time draws nigh." He turned to Aieren. "You, Aieren of Galee, will save the Daoine Maithe. You need to make haste. I will provide such that no other might be able. Behold!"

Crúimthier raised a hand to the clear blue above, and cerulean magic stemmed skyward. Belusan was about to demand answers to their questions. Rommaith was already nearly around the back side. He slowly began to slide a fhalá from its sheath.

"Wait!" cried Aieren. "Look." He pointed in the direction Crúimthier's magic had been sent.

They came from the north and east, where the power of Christiemay held no rival. Silver glints in the distance grew in size and grace as they drew closer. Not quite dragons—small silver worms they were, four meters long and fast on flight. Lean with slender short wings and long, snakelike bodies. Almost like silver ice, their skins glittered. White frost hissed out their breath like a cold north wind.

"Ice serpents." Glenia gasped in admiration and wonder. "These are truly creatures of Christiemay." Glenia was smiling like she had received a gift long awaited for. Even Rommaith had lost his dour mood for combat and was moved to look about like a joyous child. Aieren stood stupefied. He had never seen ice serpents before.

Belusan was impressed. These were as wild as the wind. Ice serpents were nobody's servant, save Christiemay. Crúimthier was as he said. No servant of Noshid could master a feat such as this. They were glorious to see.

They were extremely rare, creatures of storied legend. One would only find them in the deepest of Christiemay's mountains, and they were shy of other creatures even there.

"They will bear you to the Towers of the Horne and no further," said Crúimthier. "The Dwarrow are betrayed by their own kin—embattled among themselves, as you might find the children of Jikseon from time to time. But this treachery is beyond mere argument, and the hand of Noshid is at its root. I cannot say if the words of Noshid or the taint of the blackness stretching forth its fetid tendrils will reach for the Destiny Stone next. It is not on its foreseen path. Those deceived by Noshid flee with it in the tunnels to Strongmedjie. Do not let the Destiny Stone reach that destination, or your beloved forest may lose the chance to see glory once more."

Belusan had no choice but to trust the silver-tongued Silroh. Aieren had no choice but to follow him. Two Ice serpents floated in the air before them. Their slow undulations made them almost seem to ride the air like gently moving water. It was strange that they kept buoyant, floating without wings.

They were immaculate, appearing as if made of glass crystal, with flat scales that culled up at the tail end. They flexed and moved with each breath the serpents took. Icy blue and then sometimes white, almost a silver. The foot-sized scales covered their entire length.

Belusan was entranced by their hypnotic movement and beauty. Glenia and Rommaith seemed dazzled. Even Aieren was drawn in by their elegant, cold presence.

With a chuckle at their expense, Crúimthier said, "Just straddle their backs and lie flat on them. But hold on tightly. They will bear you but are not fond of doing it."

Belusan was first to move, and he put his leg over the serpent's length, then leaned forward to lie upon its back, wrapping his arms around the body. They did not come close to touching, but he felt he had a good enough grip. The first thing he noticed was how icy cold the serpent's body was. It was like embracing ice.

He saw that Aieren had done the same on the other one. Belusan held out a hand to Glenia, beckoning her to climb on with him. Much to his surprise, Aieren did the same, calling her name. She looked at Belusan and then Aieren, then back to Belusan. He saw she was going to come to him, but then Rommaith told her, "You go ride with the Galean. I'll have no part in being close to him unless I'm killing him." Glenia gave Belusan a helpless look and went to ride behind Aieren.

Rommaith mounted behind him and leaned forward, hugging him with his powerful arms.

"Take care to let me breathe. It doesn't need to be so tight," Belusan told him.

The ice serpents moved with a sudden smoothness and launched skyward.

"Fare well, my friends. Be steady and be swift," Crúimthier called out after them. "Swift" was a deficient word to describe how they moved. The ice serpents flew like lightning.

Belusan was frozen. His fingers should hurt, but they had lost their feeling. Frigid, icy wind whistled past, a frost that was only found in the deepest winters. A cold chill that should not exist on such a day as this one—clear and full of warming Sun—emanated from the silver-scaled bodies of these ice serpents. They were the essence of an endless winter.

Sylvan legend told of ice serpents crashing with bright flashes surging through electric fury that danced during the storms over those peaks. It was those violent winter storms that gave life to new aerial serpents. Belusan could believe it.

Riding them wasn't pleasant. Their contempt at having to bear stifling, base creatures of lesser gods upon their slender backs showed in the frenzied hurry in which they made to shorten the trip.

Belusan saw that the others looked somewhat frosty in their uneasy traverses too. He smiled openly at Rommaith, who shook with cold and perhaps even fear. Rommaith never showed fear. This was a rare occasion indeed.

Aieren seemed to be bearing the cold without much discomfort. Belusan did not like the way Glenia clung to the Galean as they flew over snowcapped mountains northward.

Belusan held no favor for Aieren, but he was trying to be reasonable. They had a common goal, so he hid his hatred with diplomacy in mind. Belusan was a typical Sylvan—proud, rational, and as full of magic as the day he stepped into the world from the core of the Daoine

Maithe. He had not been touched by the fading of the Daoine Maithe. At least not until this venture they had set forth on. He did not want to become as Aieren was. He began to feel empathy for the Galean, until he saw Aieren take one of his arms free of the serpent and place it over Glenia's, which was around Aieren's waist. Belusan felt a hint of jealousy swimming around in his mind. Why was he so affected? He had no claim on her, and besides, Aieren was no threat. He was no Sylvan.

Just then, the ice serpent bearing Glenia swept up directly in front of him, catching his eye. Fair Glenia, how she looked, the cold wind sending frosty wisps off the tips of her autumnal, pale red, leafy hair like iced dew on long grasses in the wind. She carried a grace of elegance. Her recovery had come quickly, and she did not look as she did under the mountain. She glanced at him, a happy, almost fetching look, and he froze, a shiver running through him as her gaze met his eyes. They were always kind.

She smiled and laughed out loud. "Belusan, they are wonderful," she sent him through magic. He smiled back at her; he could not help himself. The jealousy slipped away without a trace. "Wonderful, but too cold, I'm frozen," he sent back to her. She seemed to reach to Aieren and clasp his hand, but he thought the cold might be playing with him. He turned his eyes downward, scanning the lands sweeping past below.

Glenia had been his closest friend ever since they were saplings. Somehow, it gave him an energizing tickle in his chest, almost a strange form of pride. Like she had chosen him over the others to play a childhood game. He could not shake the look she had given him. But he knew there was more. It burned like a warm ache in his chest.

All at once—the daydream broken, the feeling left him—he realized they had landed. Bellowing a frosted, very audible exhale, the ice serpent under him snorted and wiggled obviously in a rush for him to dismount.

A cloud-like steam came off the scaly skin of the ice serpents and a layer of it froze making them *very* slick. There was nothing graceful in the way they slipped off, ejected from the frosted backs of the serpents. He and Rommaith nearly tumbled to the ground. Somehow, Glenia managed to slip off without difficulty, but Aieren was left with his golden face in the dirt. Belusan cast a dark look at the serpent who seemed pleasantly liberated of its burden.

They were in the crumbled hamlet not far from a pair of Dwarrow towers that looked to be carved right out of the side of a massive mountain. They looked around, taking in their surroundings.

"Looks like we aren't done with mountains yet," Rommaith said with annoyance, grimacing darkly at the prospect. "With luck tending the way it has been, we'll be under them before long." He began clenching his fists as he always did when stressed.

"From what the Silroh told us," said Belusan, "I think these are the Horned Towers. If they are, then we should find not Dwarrow here, but instead Gnomôk. Let us be wary as we go." He knew that the Horned Towers had long ago been overthrown through the pettiness of Dwarrow greed-born strife. These did look like how he had heard the Towers described.

Aieren pointed at the mountain nearby. "I am aware of the Destiny Stone once more. It is in that mountain, or near it." He started off in that direction, and appeared to be expecting the Sylvan to follow.

"Galean, did you hear what Belusan said?" Aieren stopped and turned to see what Rommaith was talking about. "You better wait for us unless you feel like fighting packs of Gnomôk alone."

Just then, with a flash of speeding silver frost, the ice serpents took to the skies and faded swiftly into the skyline in the same instant it took them to launch. Glenia giggled girlishly, all smiles, like she tended to get whenever magical creatures were around her. "That was …just…grand," she gushed.

"Well. Let's go, Rommaith," Glenia said once they were out of sight. "*He* is the guide; *we* are the escort."

"Right she is." Belusan smiled. He would not spoil her mood, and besides, she *was* right. He took a step behind her as they followed Aieren, who led them off to the west—toward the biggest mountain. They went through the hamlet, not encountering any Gnomôk. Then, with surprise, Belusan heard it. He was sure of it, but it made no sense.

He heard Dwarrow voices.

CHAPTER 30

Under the Mountain

Glenia's pure joy at the ride of the ice serpents was quickly brought back to the problem at hand.

"Fool. Can you not hear my messages? Are you so mundane that—" Belusan said, hissing audible enough for even Glenia to hear. Belusan had warned them all. He had sent messages to all of them that Dwarrow were very near, bidding them to stop for a moment.

Glenia believed that Aieren could not hear messaging sent by Belusan or any other Sylvan, so she cut him off with a soft clap on his shoulder. "Of course he can't," she said, admonishing Belusan. "He is fully Galean. Your messages only reach Sylvan ears."

Belusan rolled his eyes up into his head. "He just makes everything arduous."

They spied on the Dwarrow at the base of the mountain. There were ten or eleven of them.

"They are the same ones we saw in the woods before," whispered an excited Rommaith. "See the big one? And look there, a Gulprạst."

Belusan nodded in agreement. Then he asked Aieren, "Do they have the Stone? Can you tell?"

Aieren relaxed and took on an appearance of meditation. His face flinched and twitched near his eyes. He looked to be struggling within himself. He opened and closed his dark brown eyes slowly, but then his awareness of his locale returned, and he focused on where he was.

"It was here, but in the mountains. The sensation is very faint. It has eluded me at the end there," Aieren said. Then he looked at Glenia. "I seem to have lost track of the time. It felt like I was gone searching for a sense of the Destiny Stone for half the day."

That was interesting. He was strange to begin with. She had never known—never met a Galean before Aieren. She found herself unusually intrigued. She loved a good puzzle to solve, and he was becoming something to solve. "But those Dwarrow do not have the Destiny Stone?"

"No. Not them. It is further on. It has passed deep into the mountain."

Rommaith pounded his thighs with clenched fists and growled at Aieren. "Into the mountain?" His breathy retort was a loathsome one. Belusan put a hand on his great shoulder and motioned with his other hand to quiet. "Again, you steer us under the mountains?" He raised his clenched fist as if to strike Aieren.

"Rommaith!" Glenia sent an urgent message to the big warrior. She started moving to interpose herself between them. His temper was too much for her. Sometimes she thought those Sylvan from Aìte Longotahce were too proud, always short of patience with others. Even with her and Belusan, he seemed like a fuse ready to be lit.

Rommaith turned away and stomped, shooting fast breaths from his nostrils, calming his ever-present temper. The fit lasted only a moment and was gone. He turned to face them, calm again.

Aieren let his tension go, and he smiled at Glenia. "Keep that beast away from me."

Now why did he do that? Was he trying to rekindle Rommaith to rage? She started to send him a message and stopped. He could not hear magic. Belusan was right. This whole dynamic was frustrating. She did not return the smile and instead said, "Do not smile at me, Galean. I would let him pummel you for sending us back under a mountain, if we did not need you whole and hale."

She must have had a serious glare. He went expressionless at her redress. Not even a flicker of a smile crossed his face. In fact, not a hint of friendliness at all. He was as cold as the snow-capped mountain they were about to enter. Fine with her. She did not need his attention. But somehow, she felt a little ashamed that she had spoken the words. She resolved to herself that they were necessary, and she was being foolish. She was, after all, young, only about 120 years old. Elder Sylvan, like her, had a lifespan of as much as 600 years.

Aieren shifted his gaze from Glenia and turned to Belusan. "Perhaps we can skirt around the edge there and…"

Belusan ignored him. He was already working on some magic. "Let us vanish unnoticed, into the mountain."

Glenia saw what he was doing. He pulled on pure blue magic for illusion. It was very similar to the mirroring effect he had used days ago when they went into the mountain before. She joined him, pouring her efforts his way to enhance his magic with her own limited access to the blue magic. Together they created the illusion that Aieren and the Sylvan were invisible. Only a faint, bluish glimmer would shimmer in and out, phasing at unpredictable moments. They would be able to see each other normally but all other eyes would see nothing. All eyes except those watching with intent scrutiny. Those might detect the shimmering blue that could not be hidden. But to most, they would be nearly invisible.

They moved in and saw five of the Dwarrow going into the cave, while another six stayed behind. Aieren rushed forward into the mountain, and the Sylvan followed. They passed the Dwarrow who lingered at the entrance, arguing about something.

The cavern pathway was unmistakably of Dwarrow crafting. Mason-worked walls and natural light filtered through some kind of engineered crystal from above, defying nature and unsettling the Sylvan and Aieren. They moved with graceful speed past the Dwarrow party—that is, except for the huge Dwarrow with two great axes strapped across his broad back. He looked to have giant's blood in him. The big Dwarrow took off at a driven pace the others would never achieve.

Aieren tried to wave to the Sylvan to follow that one that ran ahead. Perhaps it was the Destiny Stone that drove his anxious pace. They followed him in silence, passing the Dwarrow escort for the lone big one, for more than an hour, losing sight and sound of the remaining Dwarrow who lagged behind. The Sylvan were able to stay with the big Dwarrow, but Aieren could not keep pace and fell back, huffing and puffing.

Suddenly, as if realizing he outpaced the others, the half giant stopped in his tracks. It wasn't long before Aieren caught up. Belusan messaged her and Rommaith to wait for Aieren. They stopped, waiting and watching. The Sylvan drew crisp, quiet breaths, fresh and ready to continue. Glenia and the other Sylvan were once again reminded that Aieren was merely Galean. She was wary of the danger that Aieren's heavy breathing had given them away. But the big Dwarrow had a loud, laborious breathing of his own. They would not be detected for his weakness.

Just as the Dwarrow began to resume his run, Rommaith slammed into him from behind while Belusan sent violet ropes, entangling the big Dwarrow's feet and dropping him hard to the cobbled floor. To her surprise, he hefted himself up and rose with an angry face. He looked around, unseeing. Both Rommaith and Belusan were no longer hidden. Glenia thought to use red magic to attack the Dwarrow more directly. Her fire could make short work of a single Dwarrow, no matter how big he was.

But Belusan showed restraint and skill using his blended red-blue magic to sling the ensnared target into the walls and floor repeatedly, leaving him to lie bleeding. In the exertion, his concealing enchantment had to be aborted—they were all now fully visible. Incredibly, the bloody form in front of them began to rise yet again, streams of blood dribbling off the beaten body. He stood, seeing them for the first time. Through a bloody face, he smiled. Rommaith let out an exasperated sigh and drew his scian.

Glenia reached over to stay his hand. Belusan had the right idea. They did not need to kill him. "Let us not slay the oaf," she pressed in a whisper. "Belusan—again, and with real effort this time."

Belusan responded as the Dwarrow gained his full stature, fumbling toward the twin axes strapped across his broad back. Thick ropes of deep violet snared his limbs, pinning him to the wall. With all the transcendent will he could muster, Belusan flung the captive with heroic force to the cavern floor. This time, he did not move again.

Aieren had just recovered enough breath to be focused, and he drew his kindjal, advancing on the motionless hulk.

"Do not use your weapon on him, Aieren," Glenia said. "We will manage him with magic. You should stay clear."

Rommaith sniggered at him with satirical disapproval, commenting sidelong, "We are rescued, fellow woodlings. The ferocious princeling is ready to shield us poor Sylvan from danger." He sheathed his scian.

Belusan let forth a weary smile and chuckled a laugh that made Aieren frown. Glenia smiled too. Aieren looked silly, but she felt for him a little. He was always a source of humor or ridicule or disappointment. *It must be hard,* she thought. *Yet he goes on. He bears it.* That made her nod unconsciously to him with a warm smile. She did not share their contempt. She never had as directly as the others did. But she began to see him as a person. Aieren returned a sheepish hint of a smile and sheathed his weapon.

"Aieren, get the Destiny Stone, and let us be off from these accursed Dwarrow halls," she said to him. "I am tired of the rock and need to feel the bounty of life in the woods once more."

Aieren looked at her and then dashed skeptical looks to the others, only very briefly at Rommaith, and gulped to gather his reply. His breathing nearly normal, he ran his hand through his dark blond hair. Without taking a look to check, he said, "He doesn't possess the Destiny Stone. It is still further ahead." He tried to carry off sharp indignation, but he just sounded hollow. So, it was clear that *none* of those Dwarrow held the

Destiny Stone and that it was off into the mountain, now a way ahead of them.

"Ahead?" Rommaith said in surprise. "This wasn't the only one. You're telling me there is more of this rabble?" Then he smiled. He didn't like Dwarrow at all. He probably wanted to test their mettle against his own. A warrior and their ego. Glenia would never fully understand this sentiment.

"There must be more Dwarrow ahead. I do not believe he was in flight, but rather that he was in pursuit," suggested Glenia, realizing their mistake.

"Glenia is correct. It is the only way things make sense," Aieren supported. "It is up ahead. How far though, I cannot say."

"Go," Rommaith said as a command. With those words, he started off with renewed speed. Aieren tried to stay with them, struggling visibly, pushing to keep pace.

They raced on to the Destiny Stone.

PART

Nine

CHAPTER 31

Escape

Jarlsalt felt the hot pursuit of Haggersath's loyalists like the sweat running down the back of his neck. His small troop of Dwarrow had fled at an anxiously hurried pace into the hyljaleid. It was the inevitable pursuit of the two ferskeyttr, led by that damn turncoat Grölle. They would pursue, yes, but they numbered less than ten. His small group could handle ten. Grölle's boys would be hard-pressed to catch them. Their lead and their pace should be enough to keep them off until Jarlsalt could reach the safety of his father's halls.

It was the inflated lord of the Horne's Haseti that gave him cause for feeling unsettled. They would have the fury to make a hot pursuit, and they had a Gulprąst with them—a good one. His magic was something they could not counter. At least, not until they reached Strongmedjie.

Then again, he thought, he did have the Destiny Stone. But it did nothing except glitter, like any other gem. There did not seem to be an inkling of magic anywhere in the Stone. He looked at his burned palms. The left's angry red flesh burned with the imprint of two settings and partial of a third he had grasped in the forge. He unwittingly received these brands when, without thinking, he grabbed the searing-hot mold, fully intending to commandeer them. Idiot! Of course, the blasted thing was hot. They had only been forged moments before. Two had stuck to his hand, and in a panic from the burning, he peeled them out of his skin with uncontrollably shaking hands. They fell, rolling to the floor. He had tried to snatch them up but could only gather one successfully. Why did his hands shake like a lifelong drunkard's at the worst of times?

No matter. He had one of them. Did it have magic he could use? Maybe, but he had no time to stop and find out now. He continued puffing along.

Then his mind fixed on the thought that terrified him most: Bolfath. That giant-sized bodyguard was tireless and far faster than they were. If Bolfath caught them, Jarlsalt would be a dead Dwarrow.

"Faster, blast you all, faster," he called out the useless order. He knew they would not be increasing their pace. It was as fast as they could reasonably go. They would all die—not one of their party was likely to survive Bolfath's berserker rage.…

He shook it off. Best to put it out of mind. He picked up his pace slightly and found he was trickling toward the lead. His guts swirled, and bitter bile kept his breath hot. He felt like vomiting.

For a group numbering roughly thirty including one hostage, they made respectable progress, but they could go no faster than the prisoner. Haggersath would stall and delay them at every turn, and even began limping until kicked. Jarlsalt's soldiers were happy to correct his behavior with fists and kicks and other creative methods to motivate the overproud Giftgiver. When he fell down and refused to rise, they began to drag him by his feet with a noosed rope.

Western Dwarrow were tired of his passive haughtiness. His line would end with him. The Towers of the Horne had been dead longer than most of those from Strongmedjie had been alive. This upstart who tried to rekindle that rival society needed to know his place, and these were just the Dwarrow to remind Haggersath what was what. Haggersath obviously struggled to keep up, and it looked like the constant abuse levied upon him by his dissolute captors was causing him distress. Good. Jarlsalt smiled inwardly.

It had been at least two days traveling under the mountain when Fjolmodr, one of the soldiers loyal to Jarlsalt who had trained with the Stonescraper in the ways of the hyljaleid, told him, "Captain, we be close now—very close ta the gates of Strongmedjie."

"Har, that be the way, me boys!" Jarlsalt had a grin so big as to split his own face. They would make it. Those fools following were too far behind. There had been no sign of Bolfath, nor any other Dwarrow, for that matter. "Faster now. We don' want ta give them eastern bastards a chance ta catch us."

He knew they were safe from any of the Horne pursuers—but Bolfath held some concern, still. He knew his chase would be relentless. So, he pressed them hard. His legacy depended on it. And, well, their lives also. Jarlsalt was ready to bring the Destiny Stone before his father. With Haggersath a disgraced and traitorous prisoner, Jarlsalt would be a celebrated hero of the Strongmedjie. There would be no reason for him— Jarlsalt, 16th son of the Bornholm—not to be favored as a 1st son and be placed next in line to become the next Bornholm. Tickled by the thought, Jarlsalt let out a lecherous giggle that he believed no one heard. He was so close to—

He was snapped back to the moment by whizzing arrows and Dwarrow calling to battle formations.

Jarlsalt brought his scarred hand up to his face. "What in Jikseon's blasted beard of steel!" Blood. He felt no pain, but the blood was apparent. Just a trace. He was barely grazed. The warrior right next to him fell forward with a grunt. Dabbing and looking at his maligned hands, he thought, by Jikseon, that was close. Too close. *But arrows?* The easterners had no arrows....

Chaos erupted around him. Two of his soldiers had been hit, already, one mortally...by a fletched shaft that bore the unmistakable black feathering of the Daoine Maithe. He began to panic. This could only be—

"Sylvan!" he said, calling his Dwarrow to battle.

Then he saw one. A bluish light flickered around a Sylvan warrior of unusual size. He moved through Dwarrow soldiers with a flashing blade, parrying axe blows with blurring speed and precise strikes that found the hairline creases in their travel armor. He was big, but it wasn't Bolfath. He was exceptionally dangerous in his own right.

Then another. She was a female Sylvan with ruddy leaves clutching a long forest bow, searching for something through the developing melee. She was flanked by yet another Sylvan pulling and motioning his hands in the despicable way of those woodland sorcerers, apparently wielding some form of magic. Bah! Jarlsalt spat out the bile that bit at the back of his throat. Forest magic was foul and unnatural. This Sylvan's doing was at the root of some perversion of the natural order of things.

But there was another, a fourth, and he was unlike any Sylvan Jarlsalt had ever seen. He looked almost Mannish, with smooth skin bearing a golden hue. Moving deftly, not seeking a fight, he was following the big Sylvan warrior and searching those Dwarrow left in his wake of death.

This golden-skinned one then stopped and drew out a curved blade with a fat tip that rounded back on itself sharply to form a barb. He looked straight at Jarlsalt with piercing eyes that flared with recognition and awareness—he knew!

A chill ran through Jarlsalt's body as the golden Sylvan singled him out with the tip of his sword and shouted, "Rommaith, it is he; that one bears the Destiny Stone!"

The big warrior's eyes followed the tip of the directing blade as he turned all his fury and attention Jarlsalt's way. Jarlsalt felt his knees melt. Outright panic set in, and beads of sweat became a salty rain from his brow, blinding his eyes with stinging moisture. His breath caught in his throat and made his tongue hang out. They would be on him in moments.

Parrying mauls and hammers, and ramming shields, all of them—three Sylvan and the golden warrior—bent their efforts toward Jarlsalt. The archer had discarded her bow and moved in graceful leaps over the Dwarrow heads. Bhardald's ferskeyttr stepped forward to protect him and caught the leaping archer with a pair of shields. That took her off balance and sent her sailing back the way she came, flailing in the air.

Jarlsalt was at a fever pitch in fear. His body surged, feeding him with a panic that blocked all reason. He turned this way and that. What to do? He knew they would be on him in seconds.

Then he heard it over the din. "We be here, Captain Jarlsalt, over here," called out Fjolmodr. "The door ta Strongmedjie!"

Already scurrying through the door were the soldiers and their prisoner, Haggersath. Jarlsalt turned and fled. His legs twiddled in short steps so fast he waddled like a duck but triple the speed. He covered the short distance so fast he surprised himself, expecting every second that the big Sylvan might cut him down from behind. Fjolmodr motioned him through with an excited smile, split by the sweaty worry he tried to hide. Jarlsalt turned as soon as he was through the door to see the situation behind him. Dwarrow poured through with the Sylvan coming fast—too fast. The big one was upon them. He would clear the door before they all could get through.

Fjolmodr called out to Bhardald, who was holding a rearguard action. "Bhardald, bring yer lads through! We have—"

"Close the door, you fool," cut in Jarlsalt in a fear-laden high pitch.

Fjolmodr looked at him aghast, seeing that most of the Dwarrow were still in the passage. Jarlsalt did not need those in the passage any longer; they had done all they could for him.

"They will be trapped with those Sylvan scum," Fjolmodr said, pleading with disbelief.

"Close it! Close it! Close it! Close it, you rock-headed son o' goat dung heap!" Jarlsalt was shrieking with maniacal madness leaping from his crazed, reddened face. Did the idiot understand him? He added one more, as if it made a difference: *"Close it!"*

Fjolmodr's face went slack. The big Sylvan was nearly upon them. His commands unheeded, Jarlsalt drew his short sword, the great ruby in the hilt flashing red like the eye of death staring in their faces. He would gut the idiot.

"Close it, or I'll run ya through," Jarlsalt said, with his eyes bulging at the gaping Dwarrow.

"Aye, captain," Fjolmodr answered, urgency becoming his new priority. He followed the order with a quick swipe of his hand, and the stone slid swiftly closed.

But not before the big Sylvan warrior slipped through.

Rommaith's great chest heaved gasps of air as his wild-eyed look scanned the Dwarrow arrayed in front of him. He towered over the gathered Dwarrow. His scian dripped Dwarrow blood.

Fixing on Jarlsalt, he let forth a smile and offered, "Surrender the Destiny Stone to me and save the lives of your rock brothers. I will not hurt them." Rommaith had all the confidence of one who believed he held the advantage. "I might let you live too. Might." He accentuated the last word. Jarlsalt did not believe him.

Jarlsalt had eight Dwarrow who stood between him and Rommaith, along with their prisoner, Haggersath. Rommaith's presence and even his size appeared diminished with the door closed behind him. The blue magic that had brought a sense of unnatural intimidation had been cut away. Reduced into just a warrior, he now, somehow, seemed…manageable.

Jarlsalt smiled back that sickly sly grin he used when he needed to look deviously menacing. "Defend me, brothers. That be an order from yer captain."

It was reasonable to believe eight of them might defeat him, but he could get a lucky stroke in, and that was Jarlsalt's only concern. Jarlsalt fidgeted around. In his pouch, his hands clutched hard on the Destiny Stone and tickled at the loose gemstone in the trusilver setting, the gift Haggersath had been making. What might they be able to do? But he would not surrender them to this tree lover. "No. I will not surrender."

Another voice closed in behind Jarlsalt's ragged party. "Methinks it be you who could be spared, if ye jus' drop that bloody weapon in yer hand and come peacefully with us." Nearly twenty well-armed guards of the Bornholm filtered in, continuing for some distance behind them. "Unless ya think ya can fight a full battalion of Strongmedjie's finest. That'd be what I be likened ta see, ya tree fucker."

The Sylvan looked over his predicament. After a moment, his face resigned and his scian clattered on the stone floor. His shoulders slumped in submission, but his eyes blazed in defiance. "All right, son of Jikseon. But I will see the Bornholm."

"Har!" Jarlsalt no longer felt uneasy. Things had turned his way, and he would bring both his enemies in chains to his father. "You be seeing the Bornholm all right. Take him to the holding, lads." Then, referring to Haggersath, Jarlsalt said, "An' take this traitorous so-called Lord of the Horne too."

The other voice cut in with command, surging past Jarlsalt's words. "You don' be givin' no orders here, 16th son."

It was Captain Skökull, the 3rd son of the 38th Bornholm. Not him. Anyone but him, the overbearing favorite son of Strongmedjie.

"You'll be seeing the Bornholm yerself," Skökull informed him. "But aye, take that woodlander to the holdings. The rest need be patched up to be ready when the Bornholm summons them."

This just wasn't fair. Skökull was always taking the glory, always stealing from the other sons of the Bornholm. Jarlsalt spewed contempt and sputtered in silent venting—but he still held the Destiny Stone. That, at least, the greedy captain could not take credit for. He would not relinquish anything he did not have to.

"Aye, Captain Skökull," he answered. "As ye command, brother."

CHAPTER 32

Twelve to One

ieren saw Rommaith barrel through the opening just as the rock door rolled shut. For a moment, the melee slacked off as the Sylvan realized they had been cut off from their most formidable warrior. Their friend had been isolated. Maybe not Aieren's friend, but certainly Glenia and Belusan's comrade. Aieren felt an immediate relief—he never liked the warrior—but his guilt flushed when he saw Glenia's face stricken with loss. He was immediately ashamed of his selfish emotions. Then he noticed the fight drain out of the Dwarrow remaining. A look of abandonment, betrayal. Then a growing rage.

"Now we be trapped with these woodlanders fer sure," a red-faced Rock-Biter growled, spittle flying around his fiery red beard.

Aieren waited, hoping the fight would defuse. The Destiny Stone had passed through the door, after all, and it was shut.

For the moment, the Dwarrow's hatred and fury were suspended. Aieren tried to think. He knew he had to say something, but what? His mind was a clouded blur. He searched for words that never formed. As he mouthed his missing words, the Dwarrow weighed the situation and considered their options. This red-bearded, red-faced fury looked around him and saw a few more than a dozen soldiers, two of them severely wounded. The ill-tempered Dwarrow gathered a resolute determination in his bloodshot eyes seeing only two Sylvan and the golden mongrel in front of him, but what most probably had changed his mood was that the deadliest Sylvan warrior was gone, sealed off.

"Damn," Aieren whispered under his breath. He knew their decision. It would be twelve to one.

The fire-bearded rock dweller struck with his battle worn hammer, the force and weight of it passing through Aieren's guard and making a jagged arc for his shoulder. The stone dwellers' eyes narrowed, and aggression filled their brows as they raised their weapons, slid off one after another. The battle resumed as if it had never stopped, as if nothing had changed.

Aieren had just barely parried the first strike at him with a flash of his kindjal. The second caught the warhammer by the wide, flat side. Despite the numbing jar that shot down his arm all the way to his shoulder, Aieren leaned closer. He leveraged it over and stepped toward the fire-beard. He pressed, expecting to push the Dwarrow to the floor. It was like pushing a mountain. The Dwarrow was far heavier than he expected. He used his fading momentum and pushed with everything he could muster. The Dwarrow merely stepped back to keep balance. That was all his greatest effort accomplished.

More than half of the Dwarrow closed on him. Where were the others? He glanced around. Belusan remained somewhat in the shadows, wielding blue magic. Glenia was also at a distance as an archer. Aieren faced them all—alone!

A Dwarrow sporting a massive pimpled nose, inflamed as if from endless drink, swung his mining pick up in a strike meant to catch Aieren under his chin. But it only found air, as Aieren's kindjal slapped the very end of the pick downward. Aieren peeled the blade down so sharply that it slid down the shaft and severed the Dwarrow's thumb. He screamed and released the pick. Blood splattered over Aieren's hand and arm. He took a deep breath. Effectively disarmed, the Dwarrow dove to the floor. Aieren saw him reaching for the pick with his uninjured hand. One heaving breath at a time, he calmed himself. He kicked the pick away, clattering on the stone floor, and skittering it into a sea of stunted legs. Some stepped on it as it slid and they lost footing, falling. Like a fat little lizard, the profoundly nosed Dwarrow crawled after it.

Fire-beard's eyes lit on Aieren, and he hammered away, seeing his chance, with several fast, awkward strikes. Aieren caught the first, and his arm was getting heavy. It was already numb, these Dwarrow hit with a strength he never imagined. By the time the last one slammed, he was reeling backward. His arm was dead. But the haft of the hammer was right at the tip of his kindjal. Right where the hooked tip had caught it. With a nifty move of the hooked end of his blade, he pulled and twisted. The hammer came free of the Dwarrow's grip and went flying past his head, disarming the surprised fire-beard.

Aieren was still surrounded. He was out of breath; his last energy was being spent just standing there. The Dwarrow had not closed. But their eyes made it understood. They were coming for him. In the shadows, Belusan had called a blue glow to his hands. Aieren smiled, expecting to feel a rush of rejuvenation or sudden strength from the magic the Sylvan was conjuring. It didn't come. Aieren felt no different. There came no enhancement like that he had bestowed upon

Rommaith. Looking at Belusan, he saw Belusan looking at Glenia. Just then, they vanished in a blue shimmer, both of them.

"No!" Aieren said. The emptiness of abandonment closed in, like the Dwarrow, from all sides. *No!* He screamed inside his head. He was stunned. Alone. They had left him to die. Light flickered with blackness as the mailed fist cuffed him across the face. He stepped back, trying to maintain balance. From behind, another pelted him hard in the ribs. He felt a snap. Staggering in a new direction, he was disoriented. He had to gain his footing. He winced at the pain, trying to draw in a breath. It hurt to breathe. He had broken ribs.

Another blow. This time a hammer slammed into his leg. It made alarms of pain go through his body as he collapsed to one knee. There were too many. He could not fight. He tried to stand, but his muscles refused to move. His leg burned where the hammer smashed him. It was not broken, but it would not work. It could not bear his weight. He swam with pain, only loosely aware of the Dwarrow all around him. A Dwarrow fist cuffed him in the ribs, with another quickly after. That damned fire-beard. Aieren groaned and bent over, stepping back to find his breath.

Glenia called out in the Sylvan tongue, "We cannot leave him to die here." He heard her.

"We can do no more here without the scian of Rommaith," said Belusan with cold indifference. "I will not die in this lifeless hall of dust, soiled by these curs. Look, he is dead already."

Aieren thought he saw a faint shimmer of an outline of Glenia. Her face was sad with empathy at his plight; Belusan's was cold with disappointment. Then, they faded from sight, invisible.

"Lookie here, woodlander or what manner of creature ye be." A skimpy-bearded Dwarrow stood before him brandishing two hatchets. "I got somethin' fer ya."

Skimpy-beard's hatchet telegraphed its broad swing, coming for his neck in an overly long arc. Aieren would not die. No. He could not give up. He let out all his air and bent to the floor, ribs screaming with the pressure crunching up on him. With both hands on his kindjal, he came up, taking in a painful deep breath and bringing the round, heavy tip all the way from crotch to chin, slicing open the skimpy-beard. Hot blood gushed over him, and the Dwarrow fell back dead.

Dropping the point of his suddenly very heavy kindjal to the floor and propping himself upon it, he gasped in ragged breaths. They came short and fast, each one stabbing him with pain. Dwarrow blood had the strangest odor. It smelled of wet mud on the hottest of summer days. He was sipping in shallow, short gulps of air. He could not take a deep breath. His broken ribs would not allow it.

A hammer blow came crashing down on his right shoulder that didn't hurt. It was only pressure on him. His hand opened, and in slow motion, he watched as his kindjal fell to the stone floor, just out of reach. Something had pulled his attention to his shoulder. He was dimly aware, like in a slowly moving dream. There, deep in his shoulder, the pick was lodged. He felt no pain. None. Just a hot swell and dull, steady pressure all over his body.

He had small scratches everywhere. Near misses that could have incapacitated him or ended him. He must have given off a fearsome appearance, as the Dwarrow did not all come. There were so many of them, too many, yet they did not all come.

But he was far from safe. Aieren watched as the fire-beard wrenched the pick loose, jolting him back and forth like a rag doll. He then moved behind him, mouthing words Aieren could no longer hear. It was all silent. Only the clamor of battle filled Aieren's ears. It changed to a steady noise of deafening ringing penetrating his head, an unbearable roaring barrage of silent dissonance. He wanted it to stop. Flashes of the fire-beard delivering a great strike flickered as he watched, head turned, and the pick descended. Slowly it came. He saw it. He knew, somehow, he had to move. It came. Closer. Closer. It bit deep through his shoulder, breaking bones as it went, slamming into rib after rib. Each one jolting him to his core with painless pressure bearing through him. Aieren saw only white light now. He crumpled to the stone floor. He knew by the triumphant look in his adversaries' eyes that it was a fatal blow, and his life was leaving him as he fell.

"Nooo!" Glenia screamed. Pretty Glenia with her ruddy pink leaves and delicate ashen skin. At least she cared. He would smile, but he was too busy trying to find his breath. He gasped like a fish on the pier, caught and destined for its end.

The mission of Morningsong had failed. He had failed. The Sylvan would fade away and die out. He failed himself, his people. He had failed Glenia. He moaned slightly.

A noise came from down the hall. It was very far off, but it came fast and fearful: the growl of what sounded like a bear.

But before it arrived, Aieren slipped into the black silence of death. It was a welcome end to his misery-filled life.

At last, he thought. *At last.*

CHAPTER 33

Return to Strongmedjie

What sounded like a massive bear barreled down the hall and into the fray with a bellowing roar, freezing Jarlsalt's renegade Dwarrow in their tracks. With the speed of a charging rabid animal, Bolfath came crashing down on them, scattering the Dwarrow as a wolf among sheep. Some ran. Those who didn't found that their travel armor offered little protection from the strength of Bolfath's unforgiving axes. Three—no, four were opened like river fish, split and cleaned for the pan. He raged out in a bloodbath of spinning axes that eviscerated in all directions.

Bolfath let forth his fury upon Haggersath's forlorn abductors. His hate rained death among the former companions, releasing Bolfath's wrath at their heinous betrayal. He was fully a berserker, having reduced their number in half at the first onset. Only seven unscathed warriors remained unhurt after his first pass. They let their fear take them in all directions with nowhere to go, dropping their weapons. Try as they may, they could not flee. They were trapped to face their fates, and Bolfath was their judgment.

Up from the tunnel, more Dwarrow followed— more than a dozen, as Grölle and Orm each led their ferskeyttr. Mevindh-Gulbard quickly assessed the scene. Possibly three dozen Dwarrow were mutilated, dead, or dying on the stone floor, but not a one from his party. Bolfath was howling with bared teeth, showered in blood. He could not see if the bodyguard had sustained injury, drenched in sanguine dankness as he was. In the middle of the pile of vanquished bodies lay the golden warrior he had seen with the Sylvan before. He lay on his side, his back cut through the ribs vertically like a butchered pig.

His attention stayed on the fallen golden one. Something in him stirred. He knew this was important. He could not fathom why. But there was something. He was not Sylvan, nor Dwarrow. He was…strange to Mevindh-Gulbard. He needed to go to him and heal him. He did not know why he had to, but he knew he must. This kind of feeling had happened before to him. It was a rare thing. It was the hand of Jikseon that was steering him. He got close to the fallen warrior, still coaxed, then dropped to his knees and examined the destroyed rib cage. He could not be saved. This was asking too much. Even the yellow healing of Jikseon could not heal such total devastation and bring him back. Still, the light had not completely left the dying Galean's eyes.

Mevindh-Gulbard reached into his pouch. He did not know why—but when he took his hand out again, he saw he had a broach in his palm. It was a malachite, polished in a fat rounded teardrop. Almost square cut with many facets, it glinted in his hands. He took the Galean's hand and slipped it into the golden one's fist. Then, reaching back to the bag, he took another and placed it in his own left hand. It was a golden beryl, almost square cut with many facets as well.

He still did not know why he was doing this or how it would help, but he knew one thing for certain: He would try to heal this certain corpse. Pulling on yellow magic did not need effort. It came easily, now, and it came through the pendant in his hand with force pushing behind it. Once opened, it flowed—indeed, it *gushed* into him and into the pendant in the hand of the Galean. It was almost too much comfort, smothering contentment. Never had he felt such a true kinship with the yellow magic of Jikseon.

It soothed him, and the ribs of the Galean pulled themselves together and mended. He *would* heal this wretched figure torn asunder by pick and malice. Mevindh-Gulbard felt a keen air of satisfaction soothing him. He slowly, regretfully, let the power of Jikseon slide away and returned to the mundane world, finding time had stopped for long hours as he was flooded with magic of a god. The red-bearded Dwarrow of Jarlsalt's faction was waving his pick overhead; he had climbed up from mock death to take his just due.

"Ye have done yer last healin', Gulpraṣt!" he shot out, spraying his sour spittle in Mevindh-Gulbard's face.

Grölle's boot took fire-beard full in the face, crushing his nose bloody. "I be tired of yer mouth flappin', Hrœsinn," yelled Grölle back at him.

Hrœsinn, fire-beard, sent a weak pick swipe at Grölle, who blocked with his shield and used the edge of it to catch Hrœsinn in the throat and send him to the ground. His helm came off; Grölle neatly planted his warhammer, crushing the skull on the top of Hrœsinn's head.

Mevindh-Gulbard saw the Galean move at his knees, his eyes open.

"How?" was all his wisp of a voice croaked out.

He smiled down at the Galean. "Ahh, laddie, it was the will of Jikseon that ye be saved."

It was true. Mevindh-Gulbard, through the direct will of Jikseon, had saved the golden warrior. He helped the Galean to his feet. Gently and slowly, he stood. The wound had a thin white line for a scar—something to remember that today, the impossible happened. He could see it would take time for the Galean to fully recover.

"Go slow now. Ye have lived an' died an' lived again in the same day."

"Th-thank you," was all the Galean could muster as he leaned heavily on Mevindh-Gulbard. He knew time would be needed for the healing, and he handed the Galean a smooth, flat gray stone the size of a plum.

"This be a healing stone. Take it an' me healing will continue without me attention," Mevindh-Gulbard said.

Aieren accepted the stone weakly and fumbled to put it in his pouch. Mevindh-Gulbard silently approved. That would work. Holding it was more effective, but he did not think that in his present condition the Galean would retain anything more he had to say.

Bolfath came striding up with a blood-soaked smile, seeming like a child returning from winning at his favorite sport.

"Har, the blessing of Jikseon tastes finer than that Sylvan wine ya like ta be tippin' when ya think no one's watchin'." He laughed as he addressed the Gulprąst.

"Fine Dwarrow work you've done, Bolfath," Mevindh-Gulbard served up praise. He looked at the bloodbath spread throughout the hall. Not a single traitor was left standing. "I'll ask ye ta carry this Galean fer a bit. He cannot move about well himself. Those poor excuses fer Dwarrow seemed intent on killin' him. An' Jikseon drew me ta heal him. That be enough fer me to want to take him to Haggersath."

Bolfath frowned with dislike and let his terms be known. "I'll carry him fer ya, Gulprąst, but I'll be lettin' ya know that I'm gonna be the one who takes his head once yer done talkin' to it."

"If the Giftgiver wishes it. But take care ta protect him as if Jikseon hisself told ye to."

Bolfath hoisted the Galean up with ease. Mevindh-Gulbard was sure he could have carried him, but when he tried, the Galean put up a fuss, so he merely assisted him to walk.

Diwolde Stonescraper had gone over to the rock door and made some motions to open it. As the Dwarrow gathered themselves, flickers of blue went unnoticed through the passage like a flash of lightning. They were there, and then they were not. Mevindh-Gulbard noticed, but it was nothing he had time to bother with now.

Bolfath went first, helping the Galean without so much as a grunt. Then the two ferskeyttr passed through, many shaking their heads with disappointment. Their approach was whetted for battle after witnessing Bolfath's slaughter, but there were no enemies to fight. They carried on in lighthearted conversation, praising the complete brutality and uncanny war prowess with which Bolfath single-handedly dispatched a dozen well-trained warriors. Not one of the corpses was left whole. Mevindh-Gulbard silently thanked Jikseon that the giant bodyguard was their ally.

Through the corridor that split both right and left, they went left. It opened into a cavern once used for storage and travel supplies intended for journeys through the hyljaleid. It was now used for just waste storage and anything discarded and forgotten. In the room waited a soldier of rank flanked by four Strongmedjie guards in their pale blue and golden tabards, a golden four-pointed crown on the breast. They stood ready with short halberds poised at attention.

Another stepped forward. He was slender but wiry with an air of danger that harbored in his quick, darting eyes. Highly polished scale mail armor covered him without joints. It flexed and bent as he moved forward to greet them and included a braid of gold showing significant rank. His billowy black beard had long mustaches that draped halfway down his chest. He gave a sharp look at the arrivals, raising an eyebrow at Bolfath and the Galean. Mevindh-Gulbard could be sure that the commander also felt the air of confrontation that hung tight between the parties. He blew out at his mustaches, and they fluttered like the wind had caught them. Then he settled his gaze on Mevindh-Gulbard.

"Welcome home, Gulprąst," the officer announced. "I be Skökull, 3rd son of the 38th Bornholm and Captain of the Guard in Strongmedjie. The Bornholm himself sent us to escort ye to quarters already prepared for yer return. It be the wish of the Bornholm that ye be comfortable. He has great expectation of tributes ye have collected fer all Dwarrow in your questing." Skökull paused to look over the reaction to his welcome. Mevindh-Gulbard saw that he kept lingering on Bolfath—or was he curious about the Galean?

The captain of the guard continued his greeting. "The Bornholm also realizes there be no need to carry weapons here. Me lads will provide all the protection any friend of the Bornholm would need." He waited again. Nobody moved.

"We be keepin' our weapons because they be old friends, ones we know we can trust," answered Diwolde Stonescraper.

Bolfath smiled toothily, giving a fearsome appearance, all covered in blood. "Ahh, it be good ta see ya agin, ya little prick. If ye want me axes, I suggest ya come take them yerself."

"I offer that ye best leave them set over there." He sneered without disguising his dislike for the giant Dwarrow. He gestured to a place beside a pile of particularly offensive refuse. "That is, *if* we still be friends." Still no movement. "We do be friends, eh, Gulprąst?"

Skökull raised an eyebrow—he was unimpressed outwardly, but the fast-forming sweat on his brow told a differing story. Bolfath let the Galean slump to the floor, freeing his hands for bloodwork. Shifting uneasiness ran around the room like it was being chased.

"We'll be keeping our weapons, herald of the Bornholm," Mevindh-Gulbard intervened diplomatically. "An' we welcome the quarters ye offer. But first I wish to see the Giftgiver. He was taken by the captain of our guard, yer own brother who did kin slaughter in the Towers."

Skökull shook his head. "That may be so, but yer Giftgiver be charged with his own treasonous behavior by me brother, the 16th son of the Bornholm. The Bornholm will be holdin' an audience to determine what be what." His tone and face lightened with a duplicitous smile. "Har, me friends, in the by and by, I suggest that ye rest. Ye kin keep yer weapons, but be warned—drawing weapon on any Dwarrow of the Strongmedjie will be treated with the harshest authority."

"Understood. Ye be gracious hosts, Skökull, 3rd son of the Bornholm," Mevindh-Gulbard said flatly. He waved his hands at the anxious Dwarrow, calming their tense stances.

Skökull had his four guards follow the Gulprąst's party.

As they filtered through the city's hallways to the assigned lodgings, Diwolde Stonescraper came close and whispered to Mevindh-Gulbard, "Detained?! Haggersath be locked up on the lyin' words of that little snit? I'd flay the Dokkur Dvergur meself."

"Restraint be on yer tongue, Stonescraper—look past their petty words of kinship. We be not among friends here," he cautioned with just enough breath to be heard by only Diwolde Stonescraper. "These offspring of the Bornholm are ever present and loyal to Strongmedjie. They and their loyalists care nothing for those of the Towers."

"Aye, ye have that right. I shoulda knew better."

The tunnels leading from the door were all unfinished caverns. Their walls looked hastily burrowed, and in the fashion of shoddy western Dwarrow work, they never refined the caves. Mevindh-Gulbard wondered just how bad their situation was. Skökull allowed them to keep their weapons, so they were not prisoners...but the escort and manner in which he welcomed them was hardly as guests. His thoughts mused on Haggersath. Where had they stashed the Giftgiver? This would come to no good, and soon.

Finally, they arrived at the "lodgings," which had heavy, tarred doors set with a large pine bar across the outside door. Mevindh-Gulbard turned to Skökull with unmasked fire in his eyes.

"Do ya expect us to be caged in this way? Like common thieves? This be a prison cell—not guest accommodations."

As if on cue, several Strongmedjie ferskeyttr filtered into the bay behind Skökull's troop. Their leader was unmistakable; he was half a head taller than most Dwarrow. Thin as a rail and bald, he made up for the lack of hair on his head with an excessively long, wavy blond-gray beard. It swept the floor as his head moved around. He did not wear any armor. Instead— presenting the pious side of being a Gulprąst—he wore a white robe with golden trim. His chest bore the crest of the yellow priests, and at his side was slung a slender, purely decorative facsimile of a jeweled mace.

"Mevindh-Gulbard. My brother of Jikseon. You return to your kin with one dubious hand closed and the other poised with a war hammer. Where has your conviction fled to?"

"Osjalfradr, you sanction this mockery?" asked Mevindh-Gulbard. He already knew the answer, but he intended the fancied Gulprąst of Strongmedjie admit or recant the treatment.

"Aye, my old friend, I do. Ye best follow the orders of the good captain here, or things may not go so well fer ye."

Bolfath grew ominously restless, looking particularly dangerous. Posturing an aggressive stance, he pushed to the front of the group. He would have waded into the gathering forces opposing them, and it could have gone all awry. Mevindh-Gulbard touched his arm with a faint golden glow.

"Not now, Bolfath." He did not like to use calming magic on the bulky bodyguard, but without Haggersath here to heel him, it had become an occasional necessity.

Osjalfradr let a smile slide onto his face, more a sneer than anything else. He nodded. "Wise you are ta leash that one."

"That's right, Gulprąst." Skökull picked up on what happened and scoffed at him, his true colors revealed openly with the arrival of the elite units and their own Gulprąst. "Hold yer fuckin' dog back or we'll neuter him while ye watch. Now get in there and wait fer the Bornholm to summon ye."

He inclined his head to the tarred door that his guard had just unbarred. They swung it open, and it creaked under the strain of the heavy doors.

Fighting now would be pointless. If any lived, it would be only a few. It was better to wait until they could find Haggersath. He had to keep the peace and release hold of nagging inherent calls to resist. He was surprised that neither Osjalfradr nor Skökull demanded they be disarmed—a curious mistake? Mevindh-Gulbard led the Dwarrow, Bolfath at his side, through the door. He turned to see Skökull's soldiers grab the Galean, drawing him up, roughly.

"Not you, goldskin," Skökull growled.

"He is under my care, Captain Skökull. He is not well enough to travel without me."

"I will provide to his needs," Osjalfradr replied apathetically, "do not trouble yourself on his account."

Certainly, he would do quite the opposite, but there was little Mevindh-Gulbard could do. Even Bolfath could not fight off the entirety of the Bornholm's palace guard alone—but then again, he mused, maybe he could.

"Be glad I have provided a pleasant reunion. Now you should give no more thought to this golden-shad, deposed lord of the trees."

They shoved the last ones through the opening disrespectfully and slammed home the door with a boom that echoed enough to shake the mountain. Dropping the pine crossbar, they took the Galean with them, leaving two regular soldiers on guard. They also left Osjalfradr to keep Mevindh-Gulbard company, a yellow magic offset.

Osjalfradr was a Gulprąst much like Mevindh-Gulbard, and quite unlike him too. Mevindh-Gulbard remembered their retreats, learning at the hand of those favored by Jikseon—elders who never became Gulprąsts but knew and taught their ways. They were inseparable companions. After rising to their stations, though, Osjalfradr became closer to the ways of the Bornholm. Instead of advising his liege, he accommodated him in every direction he was commanded to. It was not the way of the Gulprąst to appease; it was his obligation to enlighten the path Jikseon taught, to live the way Jikseon had laid out for his children. But the Bornholm, fat and overproud, led his own way. He abandoned the Dwarrow he ruled over. Riches and fealty he demanded.

If not given freely with much adoration, then with severe cost and coerced devotion.

CHAPTER 34

Lhiannan-Shee

Having left the Dwarrow to wait in their holding cell, Aieren was marched down the hewn stone maze. He was weak. He tried to get his legs under him, but the Dwarrow dragged him rapidly, and he could not match their pace. His chest was on fire as he wheezed out each breath. It hurt the same as when his chest was laid open from the back by that fire-beard's sneak attack.

Why did the Dwarrow Gulprąst save him? He was reaching home, sliding into the eternity of the Daoine Maithe. He welcomed the end of strife, the end of a life of failure and disgrace—but could not get in. Try as he may, the way was blocked, and he was cast back into this wretched, broken body, this accursed body without grace. It was empty, none of the blessing of Morningsong. He was only mildly aware as they cast him into the door headfirst. His head cracked into wood as they used it to open the door, and dazed, he fell through the opening. "In here, tree climber," Skökull said with a laugh. "She will pick yer bones clean. Watch the show, boys. This one will be quick. He got no fight in him, this one. And she be hungry fer sure."

He lay, groaning and wallowing, in an ever-replenishing deluge of self-pity. Injured and finally, eternally, and completely broken, Aieren of Galee lay waiting for death on the cold stone floor. Appallingly dank, it reeked of something foul—not just in odor but of something malicious. Dwarrow crowded the window on the closed door, laughing and pushing as they watched, jostling each other for the best view.

It was a prison cell. Light was marginal, almost inhibited, despite the two tiny, barred windows. A chilly damp mustiness permeated the air. From the darkest corner, a murmur.

"Uhhmmm-hmmmmm, who comes into my stone house—*hmmmmm*?" The voice was like water falling over pebbles in a brook. Smooth and chilling. "Ahhhhhhh." A gasping exhale filled the cell with fresh scents of the forest floor—wet bark and dew-covered mushrooms, but mostly decaying wood. Very old wood. There, in the dark, something shifted. Aieren raised his head and strained to see into the mist.

From the shadow in the far part of the room, it stirred, rusty iron chains clinking, then slowly dragging across the floor as it came to him. A haze seemed to travel with it, but as it came closer, the mist receded, exposing the most beautiful Sylvan he ever imagined. Or was she Sylvan? Her hair was a cascade of autumn leaves, but wet and decayed and moldy instead of fresh fallen. They dripped a gelatinous slime of rot and decomposition like one might find in an old, dead forest. Her skin resembled bark but gave way in several areas to pest-riddled, rotting wood. Termites and beetles bored out from the gaps in her husk.

She offered a fetching smile, her eyes filled with lustful desire. Her scent tasted unmistakably thick with the spirit of the Daoine Maithe, greatest of forests. An old spirit of the first order. Aieren found, to his amazement, that he desired her with every memory that remained, every deep-seated Sylvan recollection. With barely a breath—part thought, part leaves in the wind—she beckoned him.

"Ahhhh, Galean, come to me. *I need you.* Some of the forest must still reside in your faded being. *I want it.*"

He began to move to her. He wanted to touch her, to feel her—she was everything he had lost. Her command was his absolute wish. He did not care that the room was littered with bones of her victims. It did not matter that she was brimming with decay and pestilence, deadly to all living things, especially those of the Daoine Maithe.

It did not even matter that he knew, deep inside, that she was a lhiannan-shee—a dryad siren. They were the parasites of the deep woods. They cleansed the Daoine Maithe, but they also went rogue and wrought irreverent death when their hunger overwhelmed them. She reached for him, and he fell into her deadly embrace. She met his lips in a death kiss to drain whatever grace of Sylvan power still lay within him. He surrendered to her, his will, his life essence, his all, and she drew as with a great thirst upon him.

Her eyes lost their lust and grew wide—was it fear? Blue magic crackled through the air and the lhiannan-shee was flung, shrieking, across the room, landing in a disheveled heap among her barrows. Her hair thrown in disarray—she looked up at him fiercely, as an animal cornered, her beauty diminished. Not completely gone, but it was no longer enhanced. She was ragged and reeked of lost years, of a fallen tree infested by withering parasites. They feasted upon her flesh, pardoned for their natural transgressions. Thin vapors of rotting stench poured out of her.

Speaking in the ancient tongue of the Sylvan, the true language of the Daoine Maithe, she said, "You are chosen by Morningsong. Her breath is upon your lips." Somehow, he understood her ancient tongue. She seemed in awe of him now, seeing who he really was for the very first time. "The emissary of the Lady Morningsong. Please, your grace, forgive me. I was only taking from your lordship to survive. I-I did not know. I have no ill will for the Sylvan, for I am of the Daoine Maithe at its core. I live by taking only. I know no other way." She kneeled in reverence at his feet, groveling, begging his pity. "P-please. I am your servant. Forgive me. I did not know."

Blinking and slipping from the dream state, Aieren looked at the lhiannan-shee and saw the pitiful being at his feet in a new light. She could not stop herself from stealing magic from Sylvan and fae alike. It was what a lhiannan-shee did to survive. Yet, just now, stop she had. She was pitiful and miserable. He saw she hated what she was, and yet was forced to be who she was—despite herself.

The two of them were not so different.

Aieren was moved. If he were Sylvan, she would be his subject and he her prince. If he had been Sylvan, she also would have drained him and left him hollow—*to die horribly empty!* But he was not Sylvan. Not anymore. He was Galean, and more than that, he was the chosen of Morningsong, her emissary. It saved his life.

And she, meanwhile, was a pitiful, starving wreck, laid away here in the cold-toned dungeons of the Silfr Mountains. Without the forest of the Daoine Maithe, she had only survived off the cruelty of the Dwarrow who tossed her whatever victims they found. Any creature of magic sufficed to grant survival. The scattered bones he could now clearly see were of all kinds of creatures. Most had no blue magic in their accused carcasses. They had fed her, but it was like surviving off spoiled meat or pestilent bread.

Her bark-like skin oozed sap like festering wounds. She would fade and die here eventually. Her beauty was marred and worn on her face—she must have used great energy to hide the hideousness she had become to seduce her victims into surrendering whatever magic their bodies possessed. It was a decline unto death.

"There is little I can offer, fair one." He spoke with great care in his voice. His concern for her spilled out with each word. "I understand your plight, but I too am imprisoned. I hold not sway over those who hold you captive. I, too, am their captive."

She did not move but looked up at him with near reverence and a hopeful smile. "My lord, you are touched by the goddess Morningsong. Do you not know yourself? I was put here not of the accord of those cold-hearted stone dwellers gaping at the doorway.

I have known since I was swept away at the behest of Morningsong that I needed to be here—for *you*. It is why I fought so hard to survive...this." She swept her hand around the room, her tone filling with scorn. "I crave the taste of clean blue magic. It is my delight, as a piece of perfect ripe fruit might be to you and your kin. Red is hot in the mouth—it can burn as I draw it in—and yellow tastes stale and used, soiled. Lacking essence and filled with emptiness. It leaves me quite unwell. But blue..." Her face changed, and she carried a thin smile as if relieved of a great burden. "Please, my lord, allow me to give you the gift I bear so I may make an end to the misery that my life has become."

Aieren knew she could not hurt him. She had tried that, but the aura from Morningsong made him safe from her ravishes. "As you wish, but first, what is your name? I wish to know who it is that has suffered so on my behalf."

"My lord is too kind," she offered up through fluttering lashes. She smiled at his mercy. "Once I was called Duilleog Deas. But I am merely a shadow of my woodland being now."

"Duilleog Deas—Pretty Leaf!" he said with delight. "Indeed, you are still. Rise, Pretty Leaf, and do as your divine errand commands. Your suffering here, I will try to deliver prominence for."

Duilleog Deas tore her own bark off her belly and held a piece as the sap ran like blood over the bark. She molded it with her delicate hands, displaying unbelievable strength as she crushed the bark of her skin together with heat and the pressure of an oak breaking rock and stone in the depths of the forest, where wood rules. When she finished pulling her hands away, she offered a coin-sized gem. It was orange and red, yellow and cobalt, silver and gold all at once, flickering and moving with living flames.

"I tribute the seed of the forest, the heart of a lhiannan-shee."

He took it. It was resinous hard, and yet soft and pliable as an overripe grape. It was hot with magic and life. Holding it curiously in his palm, he gazed upon her. He had not noticed while she formed the seed, but now he saw that it had aged her tremendously. She was now aged—ancient, in fact. Her bark had fractured all over, and there was no glow of optimistic future left in her bearing. Her autumnal leaves were rotting memories of what she was only moments before.

With a creaky bow, the old creature turned, enfeebled, and ambled slowly back to the corner of the room she had egressed from, quietly lying down to die. A gasp of musty air escaped her, and she was no more. The parasitic insects that had used her came to life and consumed her from the inside out in moments, leaving only a wet pile of sawdust where she once lay.

The fire opal in Aieren's hand slid into his skin, merging with his body. He felt the Daoine Maithe inside him. It gathered, full of fire and life. It was a living invigoration, a return of the feel of the wood. He was transformed inside. He could hear the sounds of the woods far off. His grace was somewhat restored, and he was fulfilled—he was closer to being Sylvan!

But it was different. His skin did not change; his appearance was completely untouched. He was more Sylvan than before, yes—but he was also Galean. He had become something *more* than Sylvan.

He sat to wait. The Dwarrow that had crowded the doorway had left, probably disappointed that the lhiannan-shee did not consume him for their entertainment. He was not offended as he might have been before. He was calm, understanding their behavior. Nothing to forgive. It was just their way. The scattered bones in the barrow were evidence.

Aieren smiled and waited, sitting in the room in complete contentment. They would be coming for him soon. He knew how he could get the Destiny Stone. He knew it was here. He would fulfill the quest Morningsong had placed upon him. The heart of the lhiannan-shee had given him awareness. It had given him peace. He would save the Daoine Maithe.

PART

Ten

CHAPTER 35

The 16th Son

I t was during the wait in his lavish quarters that Jarlsalt, 16th son of the 38th Bornholm, languished. Dust delicately floated about in streaming rays of sunlight, a distinct contrast from the heavy red velvet drapes, weighty with tasseled selvage. The walls showcased burgundy tapestries with silvery fields and ruby stones in the likeness of monotone peacocks lekking at their finest.

Why peacocks, he did not know. Ever since he could remember, he'd had an affinity for the colorful birds and their flawless pride. Never did they give heed to the disdainful chirping of other lesser birds, squawking about with their jealous jeering. They knew themselves and made their way uninhibited, imperious, perfect. He liked the bird, he thought with a hungry smile—and how he did like to eat them, roasted with green apples and hot white onions. Add fluffed potatoes and ale to rinse and he would be happy for days. Yes, he always did like peacocks.

He kicked his stockinged foot on the heavy red blankets under him. The bed was far too large. Dust sprayed up and caught the glint of Sun once more. He watched it fall. By the light of this day, he would see his father laud praise and salutation over his achievement in the name of the Bornholm and the Dwarrow of Strongmedjie. But Jarlsalt was antsy; it was taking far too long. How busy was the Bornholm, anyway? He had come through shadow and strife to bring the Bornholm a great prize—didn't that deserve priority?

His father would offer him a considerable reward for the power he proffered and cowed traitors he laid at his feet. He would be a hero to the people of Strongmedjie. In all likelihood, he, Jarlsalt, would be elevated past his brothers before him to reign over the kingdom at their father's passing! The Bornholm was, after all, named by its predecessor. There had been many a time over the centuries when the eldest son was not named to lead. The title was earned by merit—and, of course, bloodline.

Grimmr, 25th Bornholm, was named by his father, despite his being the 3rd son. He was a cruel tyrant, taking task with subjects. His spitefulness ran thick, causing great harm to the Dwarrow by simply entertaining his deranged mind for personal amusement. Even upon his death, he did not name any of his fourteen sons Bornholm, and instead opted with malice to name his venal nephew, Bryniolf, 1st son of his brother, Börjel. Börjel was the 1st son of the 24th Bornholm, so this move brought the line back to its original firstborns.

It was a mind-twisting mess that did not always work out well for the Dwarrow of Strongmedjie, but sometimes, just as things were darkest, they would right themselves. Rísmál, 11th son of the 11th Bornholm, Hrodvaldr, had been one of Strongmedjie's finest warrior generals. He brought riches and victory to Strongmedjie in the Sorkan wars of old, where the grassland rats had raided the border settlements into near total impoverishment. Jarlsalt felt a kinship with Rísmál. He believed his father was a wise Dwarrow who could conceive decisions upon successors beyond strict lineage. He would recognize what Jarlsalt brought to Strongmedjie: a gem of unthinkable value and immense magic infused by all the gods.

That self-righteous Mevindh-Gulbard seemed to think the magic belonged only to that pretender, Haggersath Giftgiver, but it was he, Jarlsalt, who possessed the artifact now. He brought out the Destiny

Stone, holding the massive gem in his hands, and gazed at it approvingly.

Yes, he was a good son—the best the Bornholm had. Surely his father would recognize this. His mind wandered into a daydream of his coronation.

He caught a glimpse of red deep in the Stone; it flashed and struck him with a jolt. He felt a deep scorn of—of…everything. He was more than they knew, and that brought a slow, throaty chuckle to his lips. Let his abusive older brothers chew on that ironic piece of leather.

CHAPTER 36

The Offenses of Mevindh-Gulbard

Haggersath had been kept alone in a small cell the size of an ore cart. No light. No room to move. He had been abused with kicks and fists for as long as his memory would allow, but he had to trim his thoughts past bodily aches to get beyond the mere days since his capture. They moved him along at an unbearable pace through the hyljaleid—that was where he woke from the knot on the head during the abduction. His head still ached. Cramped and stuffed into an impossible cell, his world was now limited. He should be able to think, to focus, but that was incredibly difficult. When traveling through the hyljaleid, he had challenged them passively, hindering speed wherever he could, hoping rescue could pluck him from the torment.

But the incessant battering had its weighty effects, and he did as his abusers bid just as often as he tried to resist.

No help had arrived in time for liberation.

There at the end of the tunnel, there occurred an attack on his oppressors. They were Sylvan. How odd. Those woodlanders were an uncommon sight in the Silfr Mountains. Less than uncommon, really—they were almost unheard of. In his lifetime, he had only seen one other, at a distance, on the road into Strongmedjie.

The Dwarrow, faithful to the lecherous Jarlsalt, dragged Haggersath away before the Sylvan could cause enough distraction for him to attempt an escape. No matter. Haggersath doubted he could have outrun a pursuer in his throttled condition.

Worst of the lot had been that fire-bearded lout, Hrœsinn. He represented the worst of Strongmedjie, and Jarlsalt had made this vicious fiend his jailor. It was he who doled out the most pummeling treatments. Even when Haggersath was doing his best, trying to run and meet their needs, Hrœsinn would strike Haggersath and laugh. That red-bearded fuck was just looking for reasons to be cruel.

But now Haggersath was alone in the tiny cell. Most or all his smithing crew were slain during his kidnapping, for the crime of merely being present. They were unarmed! They were a smithing team, not a well-fortified ferskeyttr. Cowards! He did not know what else had happened. Where was his Haseti? Surely, they had gone into pursuit. *Oh,* he thought. *Bolfath!* He would surely be hot on their tails. But Haggersath had seen no sight of him. Instead, there was an attack by a group of Sylvan. How odd.

The Sylvan had caused havoc with Jarlsalt's party and managed to make the oily Dokkur Dvergur panic. He was not sure—were these the same Sylvan from the tunnels beneath Krath? They had to be. How many Sylvan could be found in Tisroc, land of the Dwarrow? Those he saw there had been seeking the Destiny Stone, just as he was.

The Stone! He panicked, wanting to rummage through his bags—but he could barely move. He couldn't see anything, either. Where was it? The mounted gemstones. Those gifts he was making before all this! He growled in total frustration and helpless dismay. He had to get out of this cell. He needed answers.

As if on cue, he heard voices outside the small door. Keys clinked, and the door creaked open. The light blinded him, and he used his hand, caked with dry blood and sweat, to shield his eyes.

"Let's go. Out with ya," grumbled a Dwarrow. His eyes came to focus on the soldier who released him. No beard. By Jikseon, a female Dwarrow. She was dressed in the same armor and regalia, but she looked more slender, straighter and less round. Humph. He hadn't seen a female Dwarrow since before...he wasn't sure. It was unusual but really not all that rare, maybe one in a hundred or so came from the rock or mud as female. Some were soldiers. Their roles were not any different than males' roles. Unless they dealt with chipping, Dwarrow reproduction. That and no beards.

Haggersath let himself be led. He couldn't see, so he really had no other option. He was dragged along with them for some distance, hearing heavy footfalls and keys rattling by his escort's side. When she pulled on his arm, halting him, the keys clinked again—this time, the Dwarrow was searching for the one she needed. His eyes had adjusted to near normal, and he saw a tar-covered door with a crossbar and the lock, which she had opened.

"In ya go," came the female soldier's harsh voice, and she pushed Haggersath roughly through the open door.

He went to the floor with a stumble. His limbs were still stiff and weak from the tight box. With a loud bang, the cell door slammed shut like the sound of a gallows counterweight when the lever had been pulled, making him jump as if he had been kicked by

Hrœsinn yet again. He turned back to the cell and, as depleted as he was, found a smidgen of renewed energy. He managed a half smile when he realized he knew the faces of the throng of Dwarrow already held there.

"Tear me beard out! Stonescraper! Gulprąst! My Haseti!" He gathered them in great bear hugs. "Ahh, what a sight ye are!"

He nearly teared in two when something whisked him up in the air from behind, ripping him away from his team. He wheezed a gasp from a sudden sharp pain that starkly reminded him of the kicks to the ribs he recently experienced. They ached in sharp pangs, making breathing a chore for another time. A roaring voice in his ear laughing with joy let him know his assailant.

He gasped out in jagged breaths, finding little air to speak, "B-B-olfath, ya great oaf—I-I c-c-ant breathe." It was another moment, and he coughed, "P-p-put me down." Bolfath released the suffocating embrace, and Haggersath turned to see a toothy grin on a hairy face stained with enormous amounts of dried blood. He was never more beautiful.

"I be sorry, me lord, but—" Bolfath let loose a laughter that shook the halls. "You be livin' still!" Bolfath broke out, somewhere between crying and mirth.

Haggersath gathered most of his breath and then punched the big Dwarrow in the shoulder. "What in the name of…is all that?" he exclaimed, waving his hands at the well-browned spatter that decorated Bolfath from head to toe.

Bolfath gazed at himself as if realizing for the first time that he never cleaned off all the blood from battle. He gave an even bigger grin. "That be all that be left of some of yer enemies. We had…a little talk about how I be thinkin' things should be."

"I hope ya did a good dealin' with tha fire-bearded fuck, Hrœsinn," Haggersath said, still grinning back.

"Aye, he be nothin' but blood an' bones, now," Bolfath continued with a grin.

"'Tis a thing o' beauty, me boy." He rubbed his sore ribs. Then Haggersath turned to Diwolde Stonescraper and Mevindh-Gulbard once more, his face becoming more serious. "Tell me what has happened. I be needin' ta know what passed when I was prisoner."

They related the assault by Jarlsalt and his traitorous band. When the Gulprast told of Grambol Doomsayer's bid to reclaim the Destiny Stone and his heartless murder, Haggersath took the news with pained gravity. He turned away and walked to the cell wall. Ah, he did love the old coot. But to die in such a way. Grambol Doomsayer had sacrificed his ageless life to protect the

Destiny Stone—to protect *him*! He pounded his fist on the stone and let out an anguished wail. It wasn't right that Grambol Doomsayer, a Dwarrow of such distinction, had met such an ungainly end. His fury was short, but he would not forget. No.

Softly he said, "Ah, the old coot, his need fer drink made a mark of him fer that shifty cretin."

"That useless son of a Bornholm! An' he's got the Destiny Stone. Me thinks he trade to his father to try and gain favor," Diwolde Stonescraper added from behind him.

"'Twill do him no favor, methinks." Haggersath turned to face them and felt a hot flush on his face, knowing that his pain was visible. It should be. Crazy as a loon the old Doomsayer was, but he was as a father to him. "Seems the Stone knows who be sent by the gods an' who isn't. It has its own mind, so ta speak."

Bolfath offered, "Let me have him once we be free again."

"Aye, my friend, I'd let you have the honors. He'll regret his birth." Haggersath gave a knowing nod.

There was something dark in the traitor's nature. Everyone who spent time around him gleaned the feeling that he was up to something unsavory. It wasn't an evil, certainly not a true evil. It was more a motivation that self-served—something other races simply termed as "greed." Haggersath always tried to mitigate usefulness out of the felonious captain, assuming, at worst, that he was a spy. But he was wrong. The greed ran deep, and Jarlsalt's lust to fulfill it had caused many deaths, including that of Grambol Doomsayer, likely the oldest living Dwarrow until his untimely murder. This could not go unpunished, yet it was unlikely the Bornholm would castigate his 16th son for any betrayal of the likes of Haggersath Giftgiver.

"What became of the mounted gemstones, those mounted broaches? I didn't finish their work—they were only partly made when the attack came," Haggersath asked. Before anyone could answer, he continued, "It was a peculiar thing, the power in that Stone. I began ta use it, feelin' the different magics in the Destiny Stone. Most were just there, wary of me and untouchable. But others I could gather with me hands and use ta forge it to the gifts."

He stopped as a lost remembrance came to him like a new thought. It was so real he flinched at the memory. He recounted with a slow voice, "I felt a force blocking me in the Destiny Stone itself. There be something living inside. I dunno. Mebee it be part of the gods. Jikseon hisself spoke that I had work to do, but maybe it be more than just the mounting of gemstones ta make the gifts." Then Haggersath returned to dealing with what he knew he needed to do. "I didn't finish makin' them. They be only partway completed."

Where had they gone? He needed them back. He needed the Destiny Stone. "Mevindh-Gulbard, ye said that lyin' murderer burned hisself on the broaches I made, and they spilt on the forge floor. Didja find them and bring 'em here?"

Looking slightly abashed at his leader, Mevindh-Gulbard admitted, "I did. Captain Grölle went on me behalf ta gather them, an' he passed the gifts ta me." His lip curled downward on one side while nodding with regret. "I have only seven."

"Only seven?" Haggersath sucked in his breath. "Where be the others? The mold had spaces fer ten! We have more than half, then. But…" Haggersath stopped in his tracks. Now he wasn't sure how many he cast. Did he set all ten in their mountings? It was all so fuzzy. "Blast! Me mind was not me own while I made them. I cannot be sure."

Mevindh-Gulbard handed over the bright colored bag containing the forged broaches. Haggersath eagerly opened the drawstrings, fumbling a bit with his numb fingers. His thumbs were of even less use. He was still suffering from the tight prison cell. Looking in, he counted. Five. He shook the bag even though it was a clear view to them all and counted five—again. Raising his gaze, he was about to inquire from Mevindh-Gulbard if he meant five and not seven. This would create more questions.

"I…uhhmmm. I…" Mevindh-Gulbard looked askance at the master of the Horne. "I took one fer use in the hyljaleid." He looked unusually sheepish at Haggersath. "I needed it ta save lives." He held his hand up, showing the broach holding the golden beryl in his hand. He reached and held it out to Haggersath.

"No." Haggersath nodded. "That be good. Methinks ya should be wearin' one. It was me thought to bestow it upon ye. Consider it done. But when I be ready ta finish the work, I will be needin' it back. If ye be holdin' a gift of Haggersath Giftgiver, I want ya ta have its full power. Perhaps it can join yer other gems in yer Gulprąst's mace."

"As you wish, Haggersath," Mevindh-Gulbard replied. Still the Gulprąst seemed to wait, as if he had more to say.

Haggersath narrowed his eyes at the Gulprąst for perhaps the first time since he'd known him. "Ya know more, don't ya?"

Mevindh-Gulbard continued, regaining himself as he spoke. "I passed one to the golden-skinned creature that be travelin' with the Sylvan. He was severely wounded and near death when I fell upon him, and I could not save him without it. It had ta be so."

Haggersath's eyes grew wider. A gift of the Horne—given to a Sylvan?! This was not something he could let pass without consequence. It had been so long since a Giftgiver had given gifts. What was the punishment for this crime? He was never told. He did not know. He calmed his blood and heard Mevindh-Gulbard finish his telling.

"Something about him, I cannot say what—but Jikseon's hand guided me in this. He *had to be saved*." The Gulprąst looked anxiously at Haggersath, waiting for a decision. His face pleaded forgiveness with eyebrows raised and a look much like a common beggar on the street hoping for a lifesaving coin.

"Bah! It be not yours ta give, Jikseon or no. I will deal with your requital later." Haggersath then said, "We must have it back. It does not belong ta another race, no matter what strange creature he be." Hmm. Not Sylvan nor Man. Golden skin could not be Gnomôk. But there were other gifts missing. "And what of the others? That be seven ye should be having, when ya gave five ta me. Now I be questioning yer countin'." He raised an eyebrow at Mevindh-Guilbard.

"Aye, Haggersath Giftgiver, that be true. But I tell you, as Jikseon as me witness, I carry only five. We did not get there b'fore Jarlsalt and his lads had their chance first."

"A curse up his oily beard." Haggersath was in a fit. "I kin feel yer words be the answer. That traitor holds them other three." Haggersath paced, scratching his beard in thought. "Methinks I need that Destiny Stone back."

"That'll be a fine thing ta do," retorted Diwolde Stonescraper with a sharpness in his tone. "But that Dokkur Dvergur has it. We tried ta catch the murderin' thief afore he got here, but we had a debt to the fallen by his hand. Their final launch ta Hrajaar had ta be done."

"Aye, Stonescraper, ya done right. It will find a way into our hands once again, if Jikseon wills it." Haggersath stared off in the direction of the Towers as if he could see them from the prison cell. He had to get the gifts and the Destiny Stone again. Jikseon's will needed to be completed. Not finishing a task was never his way. This was different though. He was sent by his patron deity to make the Dwarrow mighty as they had been long ago.

Outside the door, guards were gathering. The door was unbarred, and it creaked open.

"All right, you Tower rabble—let's move. The Bornholm is ready fer the likes of you. He's particularly prickly today," the guard with no beard leading the escort said with an ominous chuckle. How many female Dwarrow were there in Strongmedjie? Or was it the same one? Bah! All of them females looked alike.

CHAPTER 37

Sylvan Thirst

Glenia and Belusan halted once they were through the rock doorway. They did not dare linger for more than an instant. They were hidden with an illusion created through Belusan's blue magic, but they were not truly invisible. The telltale shimmer of blue could be seen by those heedful or tending toward scrutiny. The shimmer would normally come and go at random, but here in the mountains of the Dwarrow, his magic was impeded, and the blue shimmer was almost ever-present. Most Dwarrow kept their concerns to drink and meat and things that appeased their boundless greed, but still, it was best the Sylvan did not test their luck. Things had not been trending in their direction lately, and being caught in the bowels of this forsaken pile of rock the Dwarrow called home with thousands of the uncouth ruffians might not play out in the scheme of Morningsong's plan.

The Dwarrow behind the rock door would follow shortly, but even if they were friendly, there was the question of that blood-varnished berserker. He had a grudge to settle with them and needed no other reason to slay them without regard. His bulky, raging fury gave Glenia a shiver. She had seen Rommaith at work, and he did what a warrior must. He did not seem to mind swinging his scian when he had to. That, she understood. Her arrows were just as deadly, and she shot them with inexpressive precision—when she had to. But there was a different look to the giant Dwarrow's demeanor. He relished spilling blood with a zeal that told her it was his greatest pleasure. After what they did to him in the halls of this stone oubliette, he would not treat them with leniency. She did not want to nurture the thought another moment.

The choice was simple: left or right. Whichever way led to Rommaith. It was on her to find him, since she was the leader of this expedition. Belusan was of a quick mind and held the greatest sway with magic, but he was a follower. He could never lead. Rommaith would like to have led, and in fact, she often let him feel he was leading. Let him make the small choices. But any decision of import, she held the final word. Of course, it went without saying that Aieren the Galean was not even considered to lead. He was not even Sylvan. Perhaps in the days before he lost his grace, he might have been a great leader of Sylvan, but not now. Sylvan would never follow a Galean—he may be destined to find the Destiny Stone, but that didn't mean he was the leader. He never could be so. Clearly, it was left for her to make this divine quest a success. She smiled. Yes, she would do it.

To the left, the air hung thick with the Dwarrow's bawdy stench. It was everywhere, but the right wafted a lesser pungency. Nothing signaled relief from the bowels of the mountain.

"This way," messaged Belusan.

That was dangerous, messaging while cloaked. He was already pressed with magical governance from the mountain. It was a depleting strain to operate any other magic while maintaining the cloak. What if it slipped? Her strength in blue magic was not enough to maintain or even make the illusion of invisibility. She had assisted him in creating it before, but all she could do in this was assist.

But Glenia kept the mood light and showed him confidence as she messaged back, "Agreed. It has a lighter feel to it. But let us speak in whispers and save our magic. We do not know the limits the mountain holds for us."

He nodded. She was good. She knew how to manage her friends, how to lead them while letting them think they were making all the decisions. She smiled at her own wiles and followed him.

It was unusual how magic seemed to fail when most needed, as of late. Maybe Aieren was right. Morningsong hinted that the fate of all Sylvan would be to fade and lose what made them special, what set them apart from the other races of Thear. To become a mere Galean— the dread of it. Never to touch the benedictions of the woodland realms again. Oh, such sadness to be left devoid, to live a life as mundane as those poor, empty Men. A life where life other than oneself was to be taken without thought or repute. Galean were nearly as coarse as Man. Such awfulness.

It was imperative that they retrieve the Destiny Stone. The fate of the Daione Maithe was vital to them all.

But what of Aieren, then? He was chosen by Morningsong to bring the full beauty back to the Daoine Maithe. She saw him as he lay dying, a pick hefted through his body. Tears sprouted in the corners of her eyes even now. That poor Galean had led a cursed life, even before he was cut down in failure of such a glorious appointment. She had seen the Dwarrow Gulprąst rush to his side. Could he heal such a wound as was dealt? Could he help the Galean survive? She knew she could not, and she was rather adept at healing. Her thoughts raged in unbridled confusion through her head as Belusan towed her along the hollows of the mountainside. She kept returning to the sight of Aieren collapsing from the fatal blow, and his eyes focused in her direction, almost as if he could see her through the cloaking. The light of his life dulling in those eyes, reflecting a sadness willowing into nothing. A life of failure. She fought back from replaying the scene, forcing her will away from the fate of the fallen Galean. Not the Galean. He had a name; he was not to be dismissed without recognition. Aieren. Poor Aieren.

How did she become indifferent? He was, after all, once a prince of the Sylvan. He may have once been handsome. Galean he was, though. They had no beauty and texture in a skin that reflected attractive wood. Their bodies, misshapen like waterskins stretched and full. He had once mentioned to her he was of the maple. They were always glorious, with long straight rows of noble bark, so full of character. What a glory he must have been as a Sylvan.

"Glenia!" hissed Belusan. "Stay with me. I cannot drag you this whole way. Are you injured?"

Coming out of her dream state, she stammered, "Uhh, n-no. No, I'm sorry." She was going to say more, but he stared at her with hot intensity. He was staring. She looked at him inquisitively. "What?" she said. He was under too much strain, trying to maintain the illusion.

"Be alert," was all he said. Then he looked in the direction he intended to continue. "We have company ahead."

The hallway opened into a large mining cavern where the walls glittered with deposits of fine precious metals and crystalline minerals. The entire cavern sparkled with reflective twinkles, like those celebrations in the Daoine Maithe where fairies of all sizes and types would gather and dazzle with magical sparks and smokes that bewitched throngs of Sylvan. Those were the very best of times. She felt herself grinning wide with wonder much the same way now. Even these two Sylvan had to admire the beauty of the natural state of the mountain's bounty. They stood a few meters into the great cavern, looking in awe.

Clinking in the distance were a dozen or so miners picking their way through the mountain, extracting the wealth with expert exactitude. There was a rhythm to the metallic clinks they made; their toil was steady and relentless. What a curious Dwarrow behavior, rock-making.

So, this was where metallurgy began, and it went on as it must have for hundreds of years. There was a time, Glenia thought, that the cavern must not have been so large. Interposed in the mining site, she could see others not working but watching. Dwarrow that seemed serious, wearing pale blue tabards with gold, four-pointed crowns upon their barrel chests. Warriors. Those guards, hatchets on their belts and halberds in their hands, stood at the exits and near workers, observing, patrolling. Now would be the worst time for Belusan's magic to fail.

There were half a dozen or so exits to choose from. This was one of those times Glenia would let Belusan lead. His choice was no worse than any other she could think of. Belusan took them directly to the largest opening. It looked to be a highway of sorts with a wide mouth, easily ten meters across and five high. Unlike the planned rock of most of the passageways here in Strongmedjie, this one was convex along the top and, to a lesser extent, on the sides. The masonry was finished in that this one had an air of fine attention to detail, while the others were less refined.

They swiftly moved through the opening, which bustled with traffic. Carts pulled by sweating, swarthy

Gnomôk slaves sluggishly ambled to and from the mining site. Their stench was repellant and unmistakably different from that of these stone dwellers. Dwarrow were bad enough, with their greed and crude tastes and bawdy behaviors, but Gnomôk were vile. From their inception through fire and malice, they lived to destroy. There was nothing that race did that made anything better. She heard Belusan sniff at the odor, and she held her breath. No passersby noticed. There was too much activity, and they were too far away.

They slipped through unnoticed, and the magic held. No one caught a hint of the blue shimmer that occasionally threatened to reveal them. It was the most unnerving downside of the glamour they were using. Further into the hall they passed, until the traffic subsided and Belusan pulled her around the corner from the main thoroughfare. Belusan stopped looking in Glenia's direction.

"I need a moment's respite from maintaining the veil. It is more draining in this rocky dwelling," he said outright with a soft whisper.

They found stored crates they could crouch behind for a break.

Belusan dropped to his knees the moment he lifted the illusion. His face was worn and strained like the bark of a young tree too long without water. Glenia took his face in her hands with concern.

"I-I'll be all right," he said in a weary whisper. He could not do this much longer without some water. She looked at her waterskin; empty. She needed to remedy this.

"Rest, Belusan. We can take some time here," Glenia comforted. "We need to decide what to do, though. Aieren may still live. I saw the Dwarrow Gulprąst—"

"The Galean?!" Belusan cut her off. "I don't care about some reckless, golden-skinned fool who had his grace stripped from him. We owe him nothing. We are worth more than a thousand of his kind. We are Sylvan!"

Glenia backed away, shocked at his unfeeling outburst. It was, she knew, the truth of how Galean were perceived. The way all other races were perceived. The way she, previously, saw them—but at this moment, she was changed. She did not think that way. Not anymore. All her short life she had felt the hubris of the Sylvan, but here and now, laid at her feet, she saw it exposed for the ethnocentric theme it perpetuated.

She scoured the storage room they were resting in, looking through the crates and boxes for water. Other races being equal to Sylvan was a thought foreign to them. She became hot in the face, aware of the scandalous ideas that popped up in her silly head. They were Sylvan, and they were the race of Morningsong. It was through his own fault that Aieren had lost his grace. Yes, yes. She was coming around now. He was Galean for reasons of his own doing. It was not her place to forgive his transgressions, those that brought about his own downfall.

Aha! A crate with small barrels of ale. Sylvan did not like the bitter taste of grain water that the Dwarrow gushed over, but it could suffice. She filled her waterskin and brought it over to Belusan. He made a face the moment the odor touched his nose. It wrinkled up.

"Really?" His voice squeaked. "There was nothing else?"

Glenia let loose a mischievous smile fit for a pixie and buried the giggle on her lips. Belusan looked even more miserable than before. He plugged his nose with his slender fingers and pulled frothy amber ale into his mouth. His eyes grew big, and he spluttered the contents out onto the floor, splattering everywhere over the crates. He only missed her by turning at the last moment. Glenia couldn't contain it a moment longer, and the laugh burst out. Between Belusan's coughing fit and her inability to stop laughing, they would inevitably be caught.

He raised a hand at her, attempting to hush her while gathering his own reflexes back to control. When he finally stopped, she was looking into her childhood friend's deep, light brown eyes. He wore the earnestness of the chestnut trees his skin mimicked. Ashen gray bark with deep-lined grooves leading straight to his soul was just below the thin veil. Just as she softened her heart, he smiled a gentile smile filled with wonder and teetering on vulnerability. It was that look again. The one earlier in these halls. Perhaps he might kiss her, as they did when they were kids. It would be nice, she thought. She wouldn't mind. He was—

"You try it," he said with a laugh, back to the youthful prankster she knew so well. The moment, if there even was one, broke into a shattered fancy. She wouldn't let him get the better of her. Oh no, he would not. She was about to try it when they froze. They heard Dwarrow voices approaching at a fast, uneven lope.

"I heard it. It be here, in the storage," a gruff stone dweller claimed, coming around the hall.

Recovering somewhat, Belusan leaped to his feet in a flash of blue magic, and the Sylvan duo shimmered and vanished.

He sent a hot message to her: "Forget the Galean; he is lost. We saw him die. Rommaith, we may still save. He is one of us."

Glenia understood. He was right about that. They would die if they remained here, one way or another. She and Belusan dashed around the opposite way the Dwarrow came to the stockroom. They headed back into the grand hall, taking up the same direction as before. Behind them, she heard frustrated complaints.

"Blast me beard, look at this mess. Some bastards gotten in ta the ale!"

She muffled a laugh. She and Belusan, close as brother and sister, ran. Yes, siblings—that was how it had always been. Belusan kissing her? He was just tired from the strain of the magic and lack of fresh forest water.

As they moved down the large gray hall, Dwarrow passed by them without notice. Belusan's magic was holding strong. He may have hated the ale, but it had done him some good. He was revitalized and moved with deft swiftness. A troop of eight guards with halberds and pale blue tabards with the now familiar golden trim passed by. She held her breath, but they took no notice at all. Good.

They sought to find Rommaith and looked in here and there as they went, but he would be hard to find in the Dwarrow maze. She knew that. So, why did she have concern for the Galean when Sylvan lives were in peril? True, Morningsong had said that Aieren was focal for the survival of the Daoine Maithe. But he was likely dead. Their final days should not be floundered in this rocky tomb searching for a dead Galean—it was not their way.

But his last moment of life slipped into her memory once more. She was torn. Whatever path they chose looked endless and hopeless.

"Belusan is right," she said to herself in an inaudible whisper. They would look for the big Sylvan warrior. They could do nothing for the Galean, who had probably perished by now.

This endless maze under the Silfr Mountains was unfamiliar, and she knew Belusan was no more at ease or adept underground than she. Belusan did not take many pauses to rest, and Glenia did not need any. Still, Glenia could see he was wearing down. The strain began showing again in his appearance, as the tips of his barkskin began to dry and split. His once idyllic face was worn with ages of concern that longed for the woods. He could not maintain their concealment indefinitely.

They found another room off to the side of the hall that was empty. It appeared to be a quarter of some sort. There was a cot in the corner with a ratty woolen blanket of red that was once gaudy, but now looked to be dull and stained with whatever Dwarrow spilled on blankets. There was a platter with cheeses—some pared recently, the others slightly moldy. A hock of dark brown bread, hard as a rock, sat forgotten next to the cheese. Upon the table was a dull cheese knife and a tall stone pitcher. Two mugs sat next to the blue pitcher.

Belusan let the veil drop again and ignored Glenia when she offered him the skin of ale. She knew he hated the stuff, but he was drying out. He went to the table and poured some of the contents into a mug and tentatively took a sniff. He looked at her, beaming a great smile that split a nip of bark painfully off his cheek.

"Ahh!" He flinched. Then he smiled, using reservation, less-exaggerated expressiveness. "It's water," he rang out with joy.

Glenia rushed over while Belusan drank deep and long without spilling a drop.

She waited patiently. She was thirsty, too, but he was doing the work of magic, and she would lead by waiting. Being a leader meant taking care of those around you first.

After he was satisfied, she took the pitcher and poured a half mug for herself. It was good. She felt it spread through her blood like fresh sap, invigorating her all over. She could have drunk more, but instead she poured out the terrible ale and topped off her waterbag.

Was it hours they sought for Rommaith, or days? They could not be sure. It went on, and Glenia was getting more and more confused. Down here under the mountain, each room looked much like the last. Stockpiles of endless pottery or armor or tools for everything from stonework to warcraft—it was endless. All these items of typical Dwarrow crafting, crated up and ready, waiting for something. War? Forgotten? It did not matter. It was all clutter, keeping their companion from them—and from rescue.

Other rooms had dried food of the stone dwellers and cask after cask of their awful, bitter ale. It was a lucky boon that they found fresh water stored very often. They kept their skins topped with water, and even being surrounded by stone, Belusan was getting better. His magic held strong, and the look of a healthy tree glowed on his skin once more. Even so, Glenia was losing hope. Were they going in circles, exploring the same rooms again and again?

She knew that Belusan was of like mind when, upon entering the next room, he said with exhaling relief, "Ah, at last."

She rushed in, expecting to find a rope-bound Rommaith sitting on the floor. But all she saw were rows of wooden bunks, short and stacked. Blankets were carelessly left on most of them, half hanging off or bundled like a ball. It was a barracks. By the size of it, it could house a hundred Dwarrow. Chests with locks in all shapes, but universally small, were haphazardly spaced around the bunks and walls. She suspected they would hold personal possessions important only to the owner. At least they could be sure they weren't repeating their search in a pointless circle.

There were several more of these barracks, and then the hallway split in five new directions. The four to the left were smaller—in use only by traveling peasants and soldiers, most likely. But the one on the right was larger. It was grand in size and looked to receive more care. This one. It had to be this one.

CHAPTER 38

Throne of the Bornholm

Traffic was light through the tunnel, but the Dwarrow passing through were either the now familiar guards or wealthy citizens. At the end of the tunnel, Glenia saw four elaborately dressed soldiers with ceremonial halberds. Those kinds of weapons were never to be used in combat; the frilly loops and curls that twisted at the tips and bases of the blades were entirely for show. Their armor was pale golden scale mail that convexed outward, looking like the feathers of an agitated pigeon. She suppressed a giggle at the ridiculous silliness of their garb.

Belusan again had read her mind and was already making his way down that hall. Glenia whispered a silent plea to Morningsong that the blue magic would be strong. They could not be discovered here. It would mean capture and probable execution. The Dwarrow would not treat them well and might find a flimsy excuse to murder them in the halls.

Luck and magic held along with Glenia's breath until they finally crossed into the great room past the massive doorway and gaudy guards. The room blustered with boisterous chatter of a hundred Dwarrow conversations. Glenia tapped Belusan, who had frozen in the middle of the grand vestibule. He followed her. She had to get them away from the center of it all. She searched for a place to hide. Carefully winding so they did not come too close to anyone, they moved with swift Sylvan nimbleness. She had selected the closest wall, which had pedestals with stone busts of Bornholm long gone in a row all along it. There they could hide and get a good view of the room.

Still careful to remain plastered close to the wall, they peered around the pedestal of a bust with a tight-bearded Dwarrow. The room was large. It was, however, not as great as the mining pit they had seen before. It was filled with an enormous gathering of dour and mirthful Dwarrow. They were caught up in an electrified mood. Something had them geared for entertainment, something of a more conspicuous spectacle.

Directly across from them, another score or so of Dwarrow busts ran the length of that wall. The gilded doors they had passed through were of all black iron with many harsh riveted bolts sunk into the strapping bands that striped the doors. Those doors had to be as tall as a full-grown elder. The ceilings were unfinished, with a cavern that had been gleaned of its stalactites and then forgotten. It was not smooth and reminded her of the warty skin of an ogrekaru. Scanning the room, Glenia was drawn to where many eyes were locked at the head of the assembly.

There, idled a large, rather fat Dwarrow. He sat on an ornate throne wrought of bright white metal that, despite its obvious neglect and age, shined. It could only be made of trusilver. It was molded with angry rams' heads tilted in differing directions, snorting visible steam; one stacked on top of each other along its front made up the arm rests, and a final rounded ram's head conveniently placed where hands could rest comfortably. The back rose four or five meters with a grooved, flat design, as if a thick gear had its teeth laid flat to streak upward. Above the hefty Dwarrow on the throne was a pair of crossed warhammers over his crowned head. The throne was too large for any single Dwarrow. It must have been made to hold the ego of the Bornholm instead of just the frame of the typical rock dweller. Fine rubies the size of a closed fist or even a mite larger glinted in the Sun's rays as they danced upon the glorious throne, suggesting a great king was seated there.

He was a large Dwarrow. Not overly muscled, yet powerful as any Dwarrow his size might be. His great belly burst out, and a long gray beard spilled down well past his belt, nearly to the floor. Upon his head sat a pale golden crown with four points, like the ones Glenia had seen on the tabards of the palace guards who traveled beneath the mountain. He drew a long draught, allowing some ale to spill off the sides of his bearded mouth and onto his finery without apparent awareness. There were telltale stains to expose that this was a common thing. He handed the carved pewter stoup to a young-looking stone dweller who barely could sprout a beard. Taking the mug, he retreated again. The throned Dwarrow gave off a loud belch that echoed in the hall; the crowd erupted in cheers and applause as if he had done something impressive. Glenia could feel her own nose curl in disgust. Oh, how she hated these uncouth louts.

He leaned back in his gilded chair with a satisfied exhale, wiping his face and beard with his sleeve. He watched the room with amused interest—she could almost hear his soft chuckle over the clamoring crowd. So, this crude, slovenly creature was the King of the Dwarrow in Strongmedjie, aggrandized by his kin throughout the lands of Thear. Here sat none other than the 38th Bornholm.

Glenia's eyes swept the chamber, taking in the spectacle of such a gathering. There were all variants of Dwarrow merrily engaged in petty conversation filling the perimeters of the cavern. Many wore armor or carried trade tools that easily could be used as weapons. And there were so many of them. A virtual forest of stone lovers.

Toward the front of the crowd, near the throne, Glenia saw the Gulprąst who had kneeled with that aura of yellow magic, as well as several familiar, haggard-looking companions looking tentative and somewhat indignant. Next to them was a grubby Dwarrow, sardonically glancing at the party near him and at other regions of the room. His posture was sure. He seemed to be making poor endeavors to be regal and instead looked isolated in an awkward state of misplaced hubris. She knew him too. He was the one that escaped when they caught them in the caves.

"There!" She sent an energized message to Belusan at the same moment her eyes perceived him. Towering over the guards that surrounded him, tethered in chains, stood the proud, indomitable figure of Rommaith. His chin was high and his presence defiant as an oak among brambled shrubs.

Rommaith looked their way briefly as he scanned the room. Belusan must have messaged him that they were there. He held a grim smile, and his eyes made knowing contact. Glenia saw that he was still in a fighting condition and would be able to move quickly once the situation presented itself. If Belusan wasn't too weary and her magic didn't leave them, she might be able to assist him enough to make their escape. But with all these Dwarrow watching, they would need a distraction.

"Be ready," Glenia sent to them both. Then she whispered to Belusan, "How can we do this?"

"We will need distractions," he said, as if he'd read her mind, "and a way to shed his chains. Maybe we can bring forth an illusion, then he can disappear right before their eyes."

She did not respond. Her magic was gone again! Of late, she had begun to struggle with consistent ability. She showed no other signs of fading away from the Daoine Maithe, but her magic leaving her often was an alarming sign alone. She kept feeling for it as the other two waited. She could remove the chains when it returned.

But before it did, she was helpless.

Eleven

CHAPTER 39

The 38th Bornholm

"**A**hem!" barked the 38th Bornholm at the crowd. "Shut yer yappin'!"

The crowd dropped out with barely a trickle of chatter until a hasty silence was achieved. Then, turning to his left, he spoke openly to his court advisor, Hugat Maela, whose silver-speckled beard swept the floor with the movements of his ancient head.

"What does this rabble need of the Bornholm? Tell me why I need bother with this gathering of black crows, hmmm?" He wiggled his sausage-thick fingers toward the groupings poised in front of his dais.

Hugat Maela licked his lips, looking far too important to be bothered by anyone or anything. His unnaturally tall and slender frame—for a Dwarrow—looked brittle as a first-year sapling. The long, pale, blue-and-gold robe draped over his shoulders (which were thin as a wire hanger) disguised his frail form ineffectively. With his deep, rich, and resinous voice, he responded to the Bornholm in a measured modulation that carried far into the room, further than one might expect from his frail appearance.

"Behold, Dwarrow of the Strongmedjie: Here comes before the Bornholm his 16th son, a treasure seeker, captain of the tireless quest to collect wealth upon the Strongmedjie, as charged by the Bornholm himself. He brings news of completing his trust. Amidst him, he brings the deposed Giftgiver formerly of the eastern ruins and his band of ruffians. Be they Dwarrow as well, and yet, *not* of the Strongmedjie, but of those now nameless, without a hall of their own, from east of the Silfr Mountains."

He paused to look and cast a tight, thin-lipped smile, false as a wolf's loyalty. He took an exaggerated breath.

"Also comes a being unbeknownst of origins who claims to venture from the barren lands once forested, but not repentant of the Sylvan ways. This being is claiming a mission of divine providence. And lastly comes this wretched beast of the accursed forests, in chains."

He raised his taut face up on his scant pole of a neck.

"Each of these interlopers is confounded in their own purgatory without the final guidance of your wisdom. Each arrives as a beggar in the night, hand stretched out to the hem of your royal regalia to await your judgment, oh great Bornholm of Strongmedjie."

The Bornholm sat unmoving. Waiting. Watching. A long, uncomfortable silence filled the room. Shifting and murmurs flitted about with shushing silencers. Stirring grew, and the impatience of the Dwarrow flared among the throng with obvious turmoil-plagued fuss. Still, the Bornholm did not move.

Hugat Maela, at the side of the Bornholm, held a passive, uninterested way about him. Steady as an ancient mountain. On the other side of the throne, the sparsely whiskered Dwarrow casting off a first appearance of not yet forty years still held the chalice handed to him by the Bornholm at the outset. He stood with slumped shoulders but bright eyes in anticipation of the next whim demanded of him. A closer look gave way to the truth in age of many more decades. Almost missed was the thick, well-armored Dwarrow looming with menace behind him. He was Borgar-hlid, bodyguard to the Bornholm.

Borgar-hlid was taller than any on the dais, except the ancient court advisor. His powerful frame stood as wide as any two Dwarrow in the kingdom. The curved haft of his famous maul, Malas (meaning great splatterer), reached just past his topknot. Borgar-hlid was the first in the line of bodyguards for the Bornholm who possessed the strength necessary to wield the weapon. Fearsome in motionless silence like a stone golem, he stood. His mouth was a straight line, no hint of emotion, his face nearly completely hidden by his bristling, dusky brown beard and his great ram-horned helm.

No one moved. Glenia watched, waiting for a chance to break the chains and gather Rommaith, then slip out of this lifeless rock the Dwarrow called home. Still, no one moved. She had to wait.

Then, the swarthy Dwarrow—the one bearing the permanent smirk and oiled, tight-cropped beard—stepped forward. "Great Bornholm…er, Father." He smiled sardonically, displaying a flourishing bow. "I return home, an' with great treasure. I, Jarlsalt, your 16th son, be thwarting a treason, an' I gather the culprit in chains. With me pleasure, I ask only—"

"What of it, Haggersath Giftgiver?" the Bornholm abruptly slashed through Jarlsalt's opening monologue. The Bornholm's voice carried deep and powerful over Jarlsalt, ignoring him as if he said nothing at all. His attention was on the yellow-bearded traveler in shabby rags.

Jarlsalt's face scrunched up. But he caught himself, seeming to remember that he was in front of the Bornholm. Still, he brazenly interjected with a pleading ploy, "Father—he be traitorous. By yer own laws, he cannot speak. His head should be mine fer the taking. He—"

"Silence!" bellowed the Bornholm. "I be speaking to the Giftgiver, not yer pampered ass, ya slimy fool. I be gettin' ta yer slinky self in good time. Now..." He paused and shifted in his chair to bring the weight of his full attention back to Haggersath. Brushing some lingering foam from his bushy mustaches and beard, he set forth, "I sent ye ta gather treasure ta build wealth of me kingdom. Fer the likes of the Strongmedjie. We have been kind ta you and yers of the Towers in the east, but ye owe me. I rule here, as in *all* Tisroc, east as well as west. Tell me what I want to know. Tell me, what did ye do fer me, hmm?"

Haggersath strode forward, still bloodied and worse for wear after his brief internment. His stance did not reveal any deference to a superior, but rather that of an equal. He offered a short, curt bow of respect that reinforced that stratum.

"'Tisn't as it appears. We did find treasure, aye. Great treasure, by the likes of it. 'Tis the Destiny Stone we discovered."

Glenia went rigid. The Destiny Stone. Her breathing was suddenly rapid. Belusan was looking at her, mouth open, aware now that this was where it went. The crowd in the room seemed clueless. They did not know what the Destiny Stone was. Upon the dais, the Bornholm and his entourage seemed just as ill-informed.

"We did this at terrible peril. We cast back the guardians of the Stone—runeweavers they be. Jikseon hisself came ta me an' spoke o' the destiny of all Dwarrow, and how it be linked to the Destiny Stone—not just yours of the Strongmedjie." Haggersath stopped, and Glenia saw his gaze meet that harsh glare the Bornholm had brought, along with a harumph of disbelief cast at the yellow-bearded Giftgiver's talk. With a slight nod hinting at understanding the Bornholm's meaning, Haggersath again spoke on. "Yeah, 'twas Jikseon, an' he charged me party ta make the gifts in the Horned Towers fer all Dwarrow." Again, he paused. It might have been the Bornholm raising his eyebrows, lolling his eyes, and leaning back against his silver throne. "Aye, that be right," Haggersath reinforced. "All Dwarrow," he said. "In case ye fergot, I kin tell ya: that be the Strongmedjie *and* the Horned Towers. Bornholm in the west an' Giftgivers in the east."

The Bornholm chuckled until the hall echoed his mocking chortle. Then he calmed and passed his hand out to the right. "*Boy!*" The skinny, scraggly-bearded Dwarrow passed the freshly filled stoup to his king. The Bornholm took it and drained the thing, spilling a cascade of wet ale foam down either side of his face to splatter on the front of his great, round belly.

"Jikseon spoke to you, eh?" He let forth another impressive belch, greater than the first. The feeble-minded Dwarrow who served his cup started to clap, but the Bornholm's face reared on him, and he shrank back, trying to disappear. "The failed Dwarrow of the Towers? On speakin' terms with me own god? And ye put yerself at an equal to me—the Bornholm." Disbelief rattled blatantly in the Bornholm's retorts. He dropped the empty stoup, which the idiot moved too slowly to take. It rattled, unnoticed by the Bornholm, and the cupbearer snuck under every gaze in the hall to scoop it up and step back.

"An' this…" He put his hand out to his left, and Hugat Maela produced from under his draped robes a fist-sized gemstone. He placed it carefully in the Bornholm's leathery sausage fingers. "This be the Stone of Destiny?"

He looked over the Stone, turning it and examining it in his grasp. He took a bleary-eyed, careful survey. He held it up to the light. It glittered.

Glenia gasped and whispered, reaching to Belusan's shoulder, "That is the Destiny Stone!" He shifted anxiously at her touch. They were both on pins and needles. Belusan nodded with an excited grin.

Even Rommaith looked in their direction once more. He looked quite satisfied. He could reach it when they made their move. But the magic was not in Glenia, and the drama continued to unfold before them. She guiltily remembered Aieren. What had become of him? He wasn't there. Alarm went through her. Was he dead and the Dwarrow healer failed him? It was an icy realization. His warmth she had felt holding on to him as they rode upon the back of the ice serpent flashed in her memory. She was missing him.

The Bornholm rubbed the Destiny Stone like he was expecting magic to sprout from one of its facets. He looked perplexed. "Speak to me, Jikseon. It is I, the 38th Bornholm, king of all Dwarrow. I summon ya here ta the Strongmedjie." He glanced at Haggersath around the Stone as he said the last part. He waited, holding the Destiny Stone aloft for all to see. Then he let his arm down and nodded with the truth of knowing on his ale-drenched lips. "There be no god in this. No magic either. 'Tis a fine piece o' glass, but there be no power here." He looked on harshly at Haggersath. Speaking plainly, as if he just tasted a commonly made ale, he added, "I am the Bornholm. I am no upstart pretender. I am not the beaten down, self-important shell of a Dwarrow that you be. Never forget that we are not equals."

Without breaking his fierce eye contact, he handed off the Destiny Stone to his youthful-looking, feebleminded cup bearer, who fumbled to take it; it fell with a clatter, tumbling into the middle of the floor. "Get back, ya fool of a 7th son!" he blasted the nerve-wracked youngster, who obediently scurried clumsily to recover only the stoup in his nervously shaking hands. Not another blink of attention was wasted by the Bornholm, and the Destiny Stone lay forgotten as he continued bearing down on Haggersath.

"Now—there be this little matter of making some gifts an' rebuildin' yer towers east o' me mountain. Did I not treat the likes of you an' yer kinfolk same as me own?" He nodded in answer for himself with solemn, manufactured hurt, thumping an open hand on his chest. "But my hospitality has been taken as weakness. I see that be so, now." He stopped and let his head drop to his chest in lamentation. Then he looked up at Haggersath. "Aye. All right. Ye brought this on yer own people's heads. I've no choice."

He began at a deliberate pace, with gravity. The entire room knew a judgment was being set upon the

Giftgiver. "I, 38th Bornholm, declare…" His voice rang out strong with royal proclamation. "…the Dwarrow of the east need make a lasting choice. Stay here an' claim allegiance ta the Strongmedjie, an' take the Bornholm as yer king. Forsake the ruins of the east, those crumblin' towers. Live as we do among us in peace and be me own vassals." He nodded in righteous resolve, his face alive with intensity, revealing a hidden acrimony.

"Or…ye can follow this yellow-bearded dreamer off to those decrepit ruins an' resume an outcast's life, ne'er to benefit o' the Strongmedjie, unless ye be thrall ta the Bornholm." His voice raised higher and louder; his face reddened with the strain. His anger he wore plain upon his face. Standing now, he continued, "No more will the Dwarrow of the west shield and feed those with their eyes and minds east o' the mountains. No more will ye be welcome as brothers at my gates. It has been skinned like an onion here today, yer layers of deceit and treachery and self-regard; ye wish ta be at those ruins. So be it! Ye have yer wishes. By the mornin' Sun of the morrow, all ye rabble make yer allegiance clear. If ye be here then, I'll know your loyalty be ta the Strongmedjie. If not—ye best be gone." Then he sat back into a lounging posture upon the throne.

Hugat Maela came to life from his statue pose as if suddenly awakened. "All who remain in the grand steadfastness of Strongmedjie by the rise of the next Sun shall be loyal or expelled." He rapped his staff on the floor twice to make it the law of the Bornholm, and it was done.

Haggersath did not bow, but instead nodded in understanding. A condescending smile played across one corner of his blood-caked mouth. He began to turn and leave, his retinue following.

"Lord Bornholm…" Jarlsalt pleaded with a strained disbelief. "Father…no imprisonment? He deserves execution, does he not?" The Bornholm did not look at him. "But he be released to do as he wishes—even under the shadow of banishment, this be an accommodation. This be not a retribution of a crime against yer own greatness." His voice rose, thronged with insistence. "*Father!* He be a traitorous lout! Ya cannot just…"

The Bornholm's head snapped directly to Jarlsalt with searing fire in his eyes. "Cannot…?!" bellowed the Bornholm, leaping dexterously to his feet in a sudden red-faced rage. "Cannot? Foolish boy! Ye dare to order the likes of me? Be silent!" Spittle leaped from his wet lips, leaving foamy slaver all around the corners of his bearded mouth. "Are you master of this hall that you might question me? You dare speak at me, the 38th Bornholm, as if ye be…Jikseon?" His flare and intensity melted Jarlsalt before him. All those gathered in the hall went silent, expecting the 16th son to drop dead in his gaze or perhaps be executed on the spot. But in deference to his habitual conduct, he surprisingly calmed down. "Aye, but ye have got a point."

The Bornholm almost sounded calm. Dangerously calm.

The Bornholm smiled sardonically and called, "Giftgiver." Haggersath stopped in his steps. "I be havin' one of those gifts ye jus' made. Fer me cost, an' me trouble, keepin' an' feedin' yer shabby herd o'er the years." Changing his tone to goodwilled humor, he poorly feigned a cheerful hubris. "An' because I be the Bornholm."

In a half turn, Haggersath's eyes rose to meet the Bornholm. "Yes," he said in a voice loud enough to reach through the large hall. The Bornholm nodded and smiled, and he slackened back to his gilded throne, hands neatly splayed over the curved ram heads. Not quite finished, Haggersath continued, "Yes, you be the Bornholm, and this be your kingdom here west o' the mountain. But I am Haggersath, *the Giftgiver*. I, an' only I, will determine what gift I give, and to who I give it." The Bornholm tightened his posture on his chair. "Ye stated us Dwarrow of the Horned Towers be yer cold associates at best and sworn enemies at yer pleasure. No. I will not yield as great a treasure made by me own hand, guided by the power of Jikseon. No, I refuse ya a gift. None an' nothing ta the likes of you."

The Bornholm raised a halting hand as Borgar-hlid started to move around the throne.

"Oh. Ya might be tempted ta try to take it—but I warn ye, even in the cold hostility of yer own stone halls, it will not come easy." Haggersath's Haseti gathered around him. They had weapons, and they were ready to fight.

Borgar-hlid halted, waiting for the Bornholm's thick fingers to close into a fist. The hand shook in the air, but it did not close.

Glenia saw the chance coming. This fight would be just the distraction they needed to get Rommaith and the Destiny Stone out of these lifeless mountain halls. Belusan smiled and nodded, ready to act. Across the room, Rommaith met eyes with her. Yes, they were ready. Poised, the three Sylvan waited on the coming clash.

After a long pause—in which the Bornholm's smile faded completely—he sat up, controlled in a hostile temperament. His mouth twitched with soundless aggravation. He mulled over the challenge Haggersath so boldly purported at him in his own hall. The Bornholm had to be aware of the power of a Gulprąst, no matter what a rudderless blowhard of a fool he appeared to be.

And that massive bodyguard with the twin axes may be a match for Borgar-hlid. That would be a battle to remember. Glenia had seen the kind of bloodbath that was written on those axes.

It was, to her surprise, Haggersath who broke the tense silence. "Ye be getting no gift of that sort from me. I take my leave ta the east. Good day to ya. May the Strongmedjie be well with ye."

The chance melted away too soon. An opportunity had slipped through their fingers. She slackened. Belusan remained tense. Rommaith did not glance at them. She would have to wait.

With that, Haggersath walked out with his full ragged entourage, Bolfath beaming with teeth from wall to wall, and Mevindh-Gulbard steady but watchful. She flinched as his eye stopped on her. He slowed as if recognizing their glamor. Did the blue flicker? she wondered. He saw them. She was sure. He looked back at Rommaith, then turned and, with a steady pace, went out the great doors.

Jarlsalt again stepped forward. "Great Bornholm, I be knowin' ya know yer business, but ye let them jus' leave like that?"

The Bornholm leaned back, rubbing his chin through the beard. He seemed to be considering what had just occurred.

"Father!" Jarlsalt yelled, exasperated.

The Bornholm sharply looked at Jarlsalt, drawn out of his dream state, his eyes narrowed with hidden wrath. He leveled his words with a cold, calm command. "Ye be dismissed, Captain Jarlsalt. I be done hearin' yer mouth." He flicked his hands as if brushing away breadcrumbs.

Now it was Jarlsalt who stood aghast at his father, mouth hanging open. But the Bornholm sat up again, and his voice took on the commanding sound of a thoroughly disappointed father.

"Did you not hear me, boy?" His voice was nearing a roar.

Heedless of growing peril, Jarlsalt's shoulders drooped. "I-I bring a traitor to you, in chains," he began in an incredulous stammer. "I bring an artifact of value beyond the riches of all Strongmedjie. I even bring this woodland fuck who be killin' our warriors—an' would have killed me if I'd be not a crafty captain of the Strongmedjie." He sounded so hurt. So injured.

"And? What of it?" A dangerous edge cut through the Bornholm's question. It should have righted the younger Dwarrow. Even Glenia knew further talk was treacherous.

But Jarlsalt pressed on. "Ye let that bastard Giftgiver walk out o' here with his band o' criminals free as can be." He waved to the door of the hall, flip-flopping his hand.

"Aye, that I did." The Bornholm waited like he was hanging on for just the right word; but Glenia saw it even if Jarlsalt did not. There was a harbored, growing rage. This was kindling for his coming bonfire, and Jarlsalt was foolishly stoking it.

"Ya tossed aside the Destiny Stone fer that simpleton of a 7th son ya use fer a cupbearer ta play with. It be no mere trinket o' glass. It have the power o' Jikseon inside it."

Leaning in toward the 16th son, the Bornholm coaxed, "Go on. I see ye be not fearful of yankin' on a storm giant's beard. Know that ye be on a perilous path. I be the thunder ya hear now and the storm. Well, it be comin' now." His anger poorly shielded by a smile bordering on insanity, he goaded the swarthy captain to an apparent trap.

Glenia found herself tensing. Something was going to happen. She was not sure what. She looked to see if Belusan was thinking the same thing. He was staring, engrossed in the powder keg before them. She was hoping, carefully waiting. Ready to move. Another opportunity, it seemed, had been set for their move.

"I cannot wait ta see what ye do with the Sylvan," Jarlsalt said, dripping with sarcasm. "I expect ya give him the Destiny Stone an' have a feast in his honor before sending him off ta the woods." Jarlsalt's father rose to his feet, no longer hiding his shaking rage. "Ye do me wrong, Father. Ye give me no reward fer me accomplishments as if I done nothin'. I deserve a reward fer—"

With a motion of his wrist, the Bornholm signaled for Borgar-hlid. The great bodyguard pushed past the foppish, simple 7th son, who dropped the king's stoup—it skidded across the throne room floor and into the unattended Destiny Stone, both sliding at the ricochet. Reaching above his head, Borgar-hlid gripped Malas, pulling it free as he advanced on the beleaguered 16th son, bloodlust filling his terrible face.

Glenia nodded. It was time. She received the word from Belusan, as did Rommaith: "Go!" was his magically sent message.

They began to run with the swiftness and skill of deer in a dense forest—only here, the trees were stone columns and Dwarrow. She used her red magic to melt away a link off each manacle, then Rommaith shook off the chains and made his move to where the Destiny Stone lay.

Borgar-hlid began swinging the maul in a circular arc with advancing momentum. Jarlsalt fell to his hands and knees in fear, quaking, shaking his head in denial. "No!" he cried, seeing his death coming.

Borgar-hlid made a wide swing, catching the back of Rommaith's right knee unexpectedly with the hammer side of the maul. It cracked and splintered bone like an oaken branch in a windstorm. Rommaith fell, crashing down on his shattered knee and caught himself before landing face to the stone floor. The downed Sylvan warrior howled as much from surprise as he did the pain of his shattered knee, postured on all fours on the floor.

Glenia felt as if the wind was taken from her. Belusan was ahead of her and pressed faster. They were both flashing blue magic. Her efforts with red left her exposed, visible, but the Dwarrow were watching the action in front of the throne.

Continuing the motion of the maul's unwavering path, Borgar-hlid followed through with a twist of Malas, using the precisely honed axe side of the maul. It bit hard, making a clean stroke through the neck, cleaving Rommaith's head from his body.

Rommaith's severed head rolled, spraying brown Sylvan blood, thick and sticky, across the audience and the hall floor. His large, decapitated body collapsed. The silence and the gasps of the onlookers was momentary.

Then, ear-shattering screams broke the horrified silence.

Glenia felt her uncloaked body go rigid, her mind still trying to comprehend the dread of what just happened. *Rommaith! Oh, what have they done to you? Great loyal warrior of the wood—why didn't we move faster? Why didn't we save you?*

Belusan stood still as tears ran freely upon his fine tree-bark face. He fell to his knees, soundlessly mouthing denial. Then, Glenia heard that horrible shriek of grief again, and realized it came from her own mouth.

Borgar-hlid stood in front of Jarlsalt, smiling at him through the blood spatter, leaning with his elbow on the great maul, Malas, to prop him up as casually as if they were here at a gala event. Glenia could hear the Dwarrow executioner and the Bornholm, but did not comprehend the words. *Oh, Rommaith! If only we…*

CHAPTER 40

Who am I?

The cheers of the crowd at the execution had become deafening. This was not at all what Jarlsalt had expected. Everything had gone wrong. His father had gone mad! He had done so much more than his father had asked of him. He had made him the most powerful person in Thear. He had exposed his most dangerous enemy. He had—

"Now then, 'captain glory seeker,'" the Bornholm quipped at Jarlsalt with threatening mirth. "I do believe that answers yer third question, eh?" Pausing, he watched. "Are you withering in front of me? Go on, scoundrel, twitch and sweat." He shifted from derision to a commanding fatherly speech. "Rise now, on yer feet. Tell me true, an ya best not hide or lie, like the coward ye be: What reward did yer greasy-bearded face think ya'd be gettin' from the Bornholm?"

Jarlsalt slowly and shakily got to his feet, looking like he could spill over at any moment. Borgar-hlid terrified him even more now than ever before. It looked like he was just waiting for the Bornholm to say the word. He touched his throat as if to check if he was still whole.

"Out with it, or by Jikseon, I'll be putting yer head on display fer lyin' to yer king." As if to reinforce the king's need for sincerity, Borgar-hlid tapped Malas on the stone floor, chipping the tile. The ringing noise echoing in the hall startled Jarlsalt, and he jumped.

Jarlsalt surveyed the blood splattered about the room in front of him. His terror peaked, knowing that his fate now teetered on the edge of a knife. He gathered courage—but it was not courage; it was fear; it was self-preservation. His mouth was sandpaper and his throat sawdust. He began at barely a croak, "I-I-thought that—"

"Speak up with yer voice, ya oily villain. Not a one of these proud folk in the hall kin hear yer pitiful mumblin'." This was Borgar-hlid. He must have been sure of Jarlsalt's fate to take the liberty of speaking. But the Bornholm said no more, waiting.

"I th-thought that I'd be named to b-be the 39th Bornholm." He did not even recognize his own voice. Its raspy, thin sound was foreign in his own throat.

The Bornholm broke into an uncontrollable fit of laughter. It shook his great body mercilessly. He slapped the rams' heads carved in the throne with a meaty palm. Much of the crowd joined in, slowly at first, then growing to fill the room with excessive mirth. It echoed the halls and the room with raucous laughter. Jarlsalt shrank into a tiny speck on the floor. Face on the flat, cold stone, he lay. He would not be the 39th Bornholm. He was nothing.

Then the Bornholm stood and passed his hand over the crowd, his face deadly serious. A silence moved like a blanket until the quiet breathed an exhalation of uneasy air.

He began to pace in front of the dais, hands cupped together behind his back. "Bornholm, eh?" The king nodded, his head looking down. "That would be something. It really would." He looked at Jarlsalt, whose face was slack on the floor, and stopped. "The 39th Bornholm. Huh." Then he began to pace once more. "No, that can never be." He spoke as if a weight was leaving his mind. He broke a smile like he might if he saw a child tasting bitter ale for the first time. "Up with ya. I'll not be havin' ya grovel like a snake."

Jarlsalt took his face off of the wet floor, saliva dripping off his pointed beard. "B-but—" Jarlsalt was cut off as the Bornholm leveled a scathing gaze at him.

"Never! Not you! *No!*" His roar shook the room.

"Father?!" He didn't understand. Why never? Why so final? With a squeak, he pleaded, almost pitifully forlorn, "Fath—"

He never finished the word. "Don't breathe that blasphemy! *I am not your father!*" the Bornholm growled out with rage, as if the word burned of bitter bile straight from the gall. Spittle flew as he blasted Jarlsalt with the words. Gasps and murmurs filled the room.

Jarlsalt must have heard wrong. He was so confused. Crushed. Was that true? Standing on shaky legs, he went to walk around Borgar-hlid, but the bodyguard pushed him roughly and shook his head that there would be no passage, and another try would likely be his end. Jarlsalt went to speak again. His hands up and fingers open as if to grasp the air.

"Not a word. Or by my beard, I be havin' Borgar-hlid spill yer head next to his." The Bornholm pointed to the Sylvan head not far from him. He slowed for a moment to wind his anger back some. "You are no son o' me rock," he continued. "You be the son of me sister who is gone to Jikseon last summer. I promised ta keep ya as me own fer her—but now I see that ye cannot escape yer own fate. Ye exist because of the bloodied hand of some befouled Gnomôk, from that blasted desert to the south. Yes, ya be half Dwarrow. Only half, boy. Ya kin never be a Bornholm, not even if every one of me sons did die and yer the only one left. Because, by Jikseon's bronzed beard, ya be half Gnomôk!"

The mirth of the crowd faded to loathsome surprise. Any Dwarrow near to him pulled away. Like a ripple from a stone tossed into a pond, the crowd drifted back. All, that is, except the straight-faced bodyguard of the Bornholm. He just stood there smiling with a deadly air, waiting for his chance. Waiting for the command. Jarlsalt himself felt a wave of self-doubt shoot through him.

He didn't believe it. It was a lie. It had to be a lie. Falling back to his knees, Jarlsalt couldn't talk if he dared. Not Dwarrow. Not his father. Not of the direct line of the Bornholm... *not* the 16th son—not a son at all. A son of a *Gnomôk*!

"I also didn't want to believe it. I had hoped fer ye, ta come out as Dwarrow," the Bornholm continued. "But it be now clear in yer doings—failures all, like yer father's kind. Yer true calling be yer father's work; ye be more Gnomôk than Dwarrow. In all fairness, I'd be wise ta let Borgar-hlid swipe yer head here an' now. But it'd be an insult ta the weapon of legend to be used on one as you.

"Go find yer father—if he be havin' ya. If not, still—ya belong with yer kind, not here. Be off south to the Desert of Cinders, I'd say. Do not wait fer the Sun ta set, or ya be findin' yer head apart from yer lecherous frame. Now go!"

"But fath—" He stopped short at the menacing glare formed in the Bornholm's eyes—a glare that, he knew too well, meant death. "What I be meanin', great Bornholm...who be me father?"

Not looking back, he spat out, "As I said, he be some slimy Gnomôk like yerself. Begone. Me patience with ye is at an end."

With a wave of dismissal, Jarlsalt was seized from behind by Dwarrow guards. He tripped as they pulled him away from the dais; he landed hard on a rock that drove the breath out of him. He grasped the rock and slipped it into his shirt at the belt just as the guards grabbed him under his arms.

"Let's go, ya nothing son o' no Bornholm." One of them laughed.

He didn't struggle or try to escape. He was in shock. He didn't even know who he was anymore. He was brought out through the doors. Where they were taking him, he didn't know. He didn't care. He had no father. His mother was dead. He had no legacy. He wasn't even a Dwarrow. He was—nothing.

The only solace in his whole life was that he held the Destiny Stone. He held it tight under his armor. It was warm. Not the cold empty glass the Bornholm had discarded. He felt fire in it. He felt comfort.

CHAPTER 41

Ashes and Dust

Glenia was still on the floor, having collapsed with terror-stricken grief. Her tears ran hot on her fair arbor skin. *Oh, Rommaith! We have failed you so.* She pounded the hall floor. The illusion of invisibility that Belusan had laid upon them had failed, and they were both fully exposed to the entire room. She didn't care. It was all for naught. They had failed utterly and so completely that nothing mattered.

Calls made for more blood died off at the rapping staff on the dais floor by Hugat Maela. Once more over the din of the hall, the voice of Hugat Maela rang out, clear and deep. "Oh great Bornholm, what of the golden-skinned stranger who awaits your sanction?"

"Bah, let him wait," the Bornholm growled back at him. "I have rid meself of a curse laid long upon me. Me belly is callin' me louder than some outlander." He began to make his way back to the chambers behind the throne with his bodyguard in tow.

Glenia looked up from her grieving. Did she hear correctly? Aieren, alive? She glanced at Belusan. He did not hear. He was caught too deep in his despair.

Hugat Maela asked once more, never rushing, "What of the Giftgiver? Shall I assign a team of Dwarrow chasers to gather your rightful gift?"

"No matter. I can deal with that self-righteous yellow-beard on the morrow." And with a swift move toward his private dwelling behind the throne, he disappeared from the hall. He could be heard bellowing at the 7th son, "Bring me roasted goat an' strong ale. Do it before I clout ya on that broken head o' yers."

Glenia kept replaying the murder in her mind. She was appalled by the Dwarrow's reaction—they seemed to relish the slaying with heartless cheers and supportive calls for more bloodshed. Glenia looked upon the wretched, uncouth behavior of the rock dwellers with a renewed hatred.

Belusan, his face torn in agony and fury, looked about ready to leap up and lash out in an amok frenzy.

Glenia grabbed his arm. "No, Belusan, don't. I cannot lose you too." He was still tense, but he slackened. "Belusan, be of sound mind. We are but two, and this place is a full room of enemies. Do not throw away our lives." He pulled, but she held him tight. "Aieren lives. We still have our divine task." He blinked at her.

He wavered upon her words and looked to see the hundreds of Dwarrow leaving. Only then did he relent. He tried to raise the veil again and make them invisible to the eye before the Dwarrow realized their presence. However, though he tried, they were still visible.

"What's wrong?" Glenia asked, seeing him look at his hands and arms like they belonged to somebody else.

He answered, soft but quick, "My magic is—gone. I couldn't even message you." He whispered as softly as his nervous rage allowed, "Glenia, I cannot touch the blue power, my magic has left me. Ah, this is a foul day in a foul place!"

She knew this feeling and understood his plight. She had found times when she could not touch the Daoine Maithe. They were few and rare, but they seemed to be coming much more often and for longer periods than before. It was especially unnerving the first few times.

But this had never happened to Belusan before. At least not that she could remember. Belusan was the strongest in magic of the three of them—and now only two of them. She gulped and shivered. The two of them that remained had set out with Aieren on this accursed quest. If even Belusan was losing touch with the Daoine Maithe, then they were all doomed to lose their essence of the wood even sooner than thought. She had not his skill to become nearly invisible, but she could mask them. She pulled on the blue magic, making a gray haze that blurred them. Stepping back into a corner made them quite undetectable, especially to non-Sylvan eyes, unless they were actively sought out. They hid in the misty veil by a bust of a very wide Bornholm of yesteryear.

By now, the Dwarrow were mostly done drifting out, still animated with amused, chattering recounts of the Bornholm's spectacle. They had been so caught up they never saw the pair of Sylvan in their midst. Slowly, the room reached a morose silence, a far cry from the erratic reactions to death and dismissals that had permeated the day thus far. Soon they were alone, and Glenia released their haze, bringing the Sylvan into full view. She rushed to the great, crumpled, headless warrior and bent over him. Belusan enfolded the severed head, bringing it to the body Glenia kneeled tearfully by.

Their grief spilled, gushing out unabated. Glenia wept on her knees while Belusan stood forlorn and cried behind her in his own, private way. He cradled the head, looking into lifeless eyes. Even through the tumult of anguish, Belusan remained vigilant. He placed the head near Rommaith. If caught, he and Glenia would doubtless share the same grisly fate. Glenia racked through her sobs, and Belusan embraced her closely. They wept together for a time.

Finally, she spoke out, still broken with sobs, "We c-can-cannot leave him h-here alone, in this lifeless tomb."

"He should rest in the forest, nothing less," Belusan replied, laden with concern and softness, quite unlike his stoic manner. "We must take him to the Daoine Maithe; but how?"

Glenia tried to pull at Rommaith's dead arm, but he was much heavier in death than he was when aerated with the spirit of life. She knew before she tried that it was a pointless task ruled by the heart. Even with the two of them, there was no chance to lift him for more than a few paces. In passing, he became as heavy and unwieldy as a great fallen oak—and just as out of place on the pitiless stone floor.

Finally admitting defeat, they both collapsed on the rock floor, mourning over their fallen brother. They could not move him. He would be forced to remain here, alone, in the bowels of these foul mountains.

"It's my fault," Glenia mumbled to herself through a fresh onset of dolorous, tearful blubbering. Her heart felt like it would break out of her chest. Never did she think any of them would die on this quest. She had always thought she was the wise one, the leader of this trio—but now the truth spat in her eye. She was not wise. No, and she was no leader, not at all. They were no longer a trio. Now they were a duo, a useless duo who could not even take Rommaith to a place of honor.

"It is beyond us, Glenia," Belusan leveled, heavy despair choking his every word. "We must leave him or share his fate. We cannot remain."

This only served to bring her sorrow to near breaking. "We should just leave him here?"

Her face was on fire. She wanted to hit him at the thought. She wanted to...*Oh, Rommaith! I have failed you.* But Belusan was right. She had to gather herself. Damn, he was always right. Leaving the great oaken warrior here was a fate they must accept.

Moving in the halls would be very difficult with Belusan's magic still missing. Her magic could not cover them without shadows to slither in and out of. A gray haze moving about the corridors was unnatural—they would be noticed. There was no telling when his magic might return. Sometimes it was less than an hour for her, but there had been times where days had passed before the ability to wield magic would return. It was occurring more often now, but this was the first instance for him where he seemed to understand that he too may suffer Aieren's fate. Glenia believed that it would only be a short time for his magic to resume.

He was taking the absence of it remarkably well. It had been a genuine tragedy that nearly crushed her the first few times it had happened to her. But other than the initial shock he had voiced, he made no show of bother. Rommaith had been like that as well.

Tears began anew. She had to stop thinking of him. She needed a clear head to get them out of here.

In the halls, they would be unable to hide. But lingering in this vast room was just as dangerous. There would be traffic. They were trapped. There was no way to escape, and no way to give Rommaith the honor he deserved.

"I cannot bring him to the forest," said a sudden voice from behind them, "but I may of sorts bring the forest to him."

Tension to spring into action fell away from the Sylvan before it had fully gathered. The voice startled them, but it did not strike fear or carry even a hint of malevolence in its melodic clarity. The golden-skinned being that arrived bore no threat.

"Aieren!" exclaimed Glenia. She started toward him to gather him in her arms, but she caught herself. She had felt a smile come, a smile that pushed her sorrow to a corner. "Aieren. How are you alive? I-I saw you slain. In the tunnel."

But it was Aieren. At least it seemed so. He had changed, somehow—no, it was Aieren. It was good to see him. She had almost forgotten him, thinking he was dead. He was tall and looked to be unhurt. Did that Gulprąst heal him so completely from that grievous death blow? She saw him carved open like a butchered stag.

Belusan was less enamored. "What are you babbling about, Galean? There are no forests here, unless you mean a forest of rock. One such as you cannot know our loss."

"You are quite correct, Belusan. Your loss is wholly Sylvan. I am Galean, and although I do respect life and mourn its losses, I do not share your deep hurt. But I do see the damage done to you both, and that levies terrible sorrow on my being. I am sorry this happened to Rommaith. He was a proud and fearsome warrior." His words were kind and soothing. "Rommaith belongs in the forest, yes. Let us bring the forest to him."

Belusan was looking at him like he had lost all wit. Glenia was struggling to make sense of what he was saying, just as confused. Bring the forest to him? What an impossible idyllic notion to spill upon them—especially now, with urgency needed and her and Belusan distractedly upset. Belusan looked upon him coolly, making this feel like a most unwelcome reunion after all.

"I will help, if you allow it." Aieren's voice rang with pleasing qualities, soothing again, like when he first arrived in this room.

Glenia gaped at Aieren, truly seeing him now for the first time. Something definitely had changed. He stood taller—not proud, but regal. His voice eased with the song of the forest itself. His dull, golden skin now almost shone. He had a presence of the woods upon him. Yes, that was it. Like the forest after a morning rain, the keen smell of fresh dew upon its leaves. He glowed with life. Life of the Daoine Maithe. She gasped to herself. What has happened to him?

"What would you do?" asked Glenia, her tears now dry on her bark-skin cheeks.

"I would bring the way of the forest to Rommaith and honor his sacrifice with the laurels he warrants." Aieren spoke as if his intention was a redundancy of the obvious. He walked to a table where some of the Dwarrow had been and picked up a pewter chalice still holding unfinished ale. "This will do to bring the power of water and metal. The grain in this is of the seeds of life. It will inspire the path of the woods."

He returned to Rommaith's corpse among the perplexed pair of Sylvan, then focused on the chalice. It began to glow slightly, and steam rose off the top. It wasn't as if it were hot, but rather cold—very cold. Oddly, the ale was boiling, tumultuously, in the cup. The strange black-and-green malachite gemstone mounted upon a trusilver setting he held in the other hand moved and flowed, looking liquid. No, not liquid. It looked alive. His own hand turned to a hot dark orange, almost brown.

Glenia stood, her mouth agape. That was a blend of red magic! Aieren was using red magic—how? Yes, there was a hint of blue, which they both used. Blending red and blue was useful. She could do it too. But this was more. This was mixed with a magic Glenia could not use. Was it yellow, maybe? But no Sylvan could touch yellow magic. Surely no Galean. Galean held no magic at all. Belusan relinquished his sour face, looking on in amazement. The Galean was working magic! Here was a disgraced former Sylvan whose magic was swept away, and yet…he was working magic.

The magic was difficult for the two onlookers to understand. As it went on, it became clear that there was a presence that had to be yellow. Yellow was the magic of more mundane creatures, useless in most ways—all Sylvan would agree on this. But to combine with red…

that was Dwarrow work. Even so, yellow was alien to blue magic. It was never, ever combined with blue. Yet here it was happening.

"Impossible!" The word dribbled out across Belusan's tree-bark lips.

Aieren poured the animated, cold liquid over Rommaith. Instead of running off the corpse, it spread over a wider area until the sheen of it covered most of his form. Then, all at once it soaked into the body, completely absorbed—gone without a trace. Rommaith's wooden skin dried rapidly, with the bark beginning to peel away. Moisture steamed off his remains, escaping with the smell of dead wood.

As the bark peeled away, it revealed a layer underneath that seemed to be wholly dried wood. It began to split as the steam subsided. Out from the cracks emerged beetles and ants, grubs and weevils. They came in unimaginable numbers—hordes, slithering and crawling over each other until they could no longer see any hint of the warrior's corpse. Nothing except the general shape of Rommaith. They feasted upon the dead wooden flesh in a frenzy, spewing dust in the air around their meal, clouding up and making a horrific vision.

"In the name of Morningsong, *what have you done?!*" exclaimed an alarmed Belusan without considering the danger yelling could bring. "Stop this madness, Galean."

Glenia was speechless at the capricious butchery. She saw it, but it didn't sink in. She just watched, mouth open, in what was becoming dread. It was only moments more that the cellulose carnage of degradation went on before it stilled. As the dust settled, only the metallic equipment Rommaith bore remained, empty on the stone floor. Empty except for bits of sawdust-like refuse discarded in the decomposition. No insect or worm remained. The smell of rotted wood filled the air, a musty odor, a reminder of the deepest old forests.

"He is ready now," Aieren said, flatly emotionless.

The Sylvan were incredulous.

"Ready?" shrilled out Belusan. "Ready for what?"

Before the Galean could answer him, Glenia gasped out, "Wh-why—Aieren?"

Rommaith had been dissolved, right before her eyes. It was *mortifying*. It was abysmal. It was unforgivable. She could not stop her hands from trembling from fear and aberrant disgust.

Aieren looked at her with childlike uncertainty. "What do you mean?"

With hate-infused intensity, Belusan approached Aieren. There was the sound of a cool scraping that could only be his fhalá sliding out for revenge. "I don't care why. You have befouled Rommaith with your tainted magics. I will make you pay for this, Galean; your blood will wash the stones!"

Aieren, surprised, backed away, reaching for his own scian. But his scabbard was that of a prisoner; it was empty. He ducked and spun with the lithe dexterity only Sylvan held, and Belusan pursued him. Aieren looked around and grabbed up a platter in one hand and the bone of some bovine beast from the roast. He used it to parry off Belusan's strike. The other fhalá glanced off the platter, knocking it out of Aieren's hand. Again, Belusan pressed on, attacking the bewildered Galean. Aieren worked defensively, parrying with the bone only. Chips flew as the bone twisted, greasy and slippery. Aieren made efforts to disarm the maddened Sylvan.

"Stop this!" Glenia's voice rang out over the flashing metal assault. This was madness. All of it. "Belusan! Aieren—stop!"

It was too late. She heard armored shuffling coming from the main corridor, and then Strongmedjie guards began to flow in to find the source of the commotion in the throne room. Axes bared, they closed on the embattled pair and Glenia. What should she do? There were a dozen of them. Maybe if Belusan had his magic, or if Rommaith—*oh, Rommaith, why?* They began to circle the trio. Dwarrow were always a little mistrustful of Sylvan magic—it was wise that they were. The ring was nearly closed around them.

"No, no, no!" Belusan snarled as he stopped his assault on Aieren. He made a motion, and then he and Glenia shimmered and faded from sight, leaving Aieren, chipped leg bone in hand, facing the half dozen Dwarrow to descend upon him. Belusan's magic had returned.

Glenia watched Aieren's plight as she and Belusan slipped with fluid dexterity around the surrounding Dwarrow. She sent to Belusan, "We need Aieren. We can't just leave him to the Dwarrow."

Belusan sent back, "We are done with him. Come, Glenia. We must go while magic works and that fool of a Galean provides a diversion."

"Well now," began one of the Dwarrow. "It seems yer pretty friends have left ya ta play with us. Drop that meat yer holdin' and ya won't meet yer faerie god today."

Aieren looked blankly at them, doomed, weaponless. Even had he been armed, twelve bearded stone dwellers itching for a fight was more than Aieren could handle. She was sure of that.

A different Dwarrow spoke up. She said, "Looks like he'd want ta feed us, Borgat. He be standin' there with a bone in his hands."

Slowly shaking his head, Aieren muttered out loud, "So be it—I tried." And he vanished into nothing. The bone dropped from empty air to the floor and bounced.

Aieren was gone. It wasn't a glamour like the one Belusan used. It was something else. He wasn't hidden—he was gone. Maybe truly invisible—or gone completely. But gone where?

Belusan tugged at her, and she sent to him, "Wait. Not yet. He's gone. But where?"

"Well, don' that beat the goat's arse," Borgat said. "Me skin be crawlin' with woodland magic here. I be needin' a spot of something stronger than ale. Ya with me, me hammers?" Putting their hammers up, they left the room, occasionally stopping to look over their shoulders.

"Be sure they don' be making no trap. Eyes on the walls, me soldiers. Watch fer 'em—they be tricky bitches, them folk be."

Glenia and Belusan had to move to the side, out of the doorway, to avoid the Dwarrow barreling out. They had to be sure no blue shimmers came to draw wayward hammer swipes from jumpy Dwarrow fearful of things they didn't understand.

After the hall cleared once more, Aieren popped back into view. He had never moved. He came over to the pile of Rommaith's dust and reverently kneeled. She heard him speak to Rommaith as if he were there.

He never liked Rommaith. And to be fair, Rommaith was brutal to the point of cruelty to Aieren. So, his manner came as a surprise to Glenia.

"I know you never thought much of me," Aieren said, "or understood the plight of becoming a Galean. It wasn't to be your fate. But I am now more than Galean. The forest is renewed within me. Galean and Sylvan must be as one if we are to survive. We are one, in truth. To be Galean, one must first have to be Sylvan. And all Sylvan, in time, will become Galean—if my divine quest for the Destiny Stone fails. Come, brother. I will bring you home." With that, Aieren ever so gently swept the wood dust remains into a small satchel he tied to his belt. He looked at Glenia, seeing her as if the glamour had failed. She saw the blue flickers and knew it exposed them.

"I can see you two. Let us depart." Aieren sped from the room. The two Sylvan were stunned, but followed, matching his onerous pace.

PART

Twelve

CHAPTER 42

Tragedy of the Bornholm

E invalde, the 1st son of the 37th Bornholm, was formidable and valiant like no Dwarrow had been in six hundred years. He was everything a Bornholm needed to be.

Then there was Swievalde, Einvalde's twin, born second. In battle, he was but a slightly lesser twin of Einvalde—yet he was, conversely, outright stupid and inherently callous. Hardly a fit to rule. Swievalde did what he could to hide his jealousy of Einvalde. He wished to be the better warrior. He wished to be the commander his father would put first. He wished he would be named when the time arrived, to be the 38th Bornholm. He was none of those. That was for Einvalde.

But neither Einvalde nor Swievalde were the first child born of the 37th Bornholm. That honor went to Feikinstafir, the daughter of Augabragd, 37th

Bornholm. First born of the mountain she was—but that did not matter. She wore no beard and could never be named the 38th Bornholm. This was a Dwarrow certitude since the day Jikseon had brought the first Dwarrow from the mountainside.

Feikinstafir was the first blight upon the Bornholm in all the long history of great Dwarrow. Never before had a chip from the Bornholm drawn a female Dwarrow from a clod of the land. It was destined to happen though. Scarcely one in a hundred that sprung from the tilling were lesser—were female. She was especially cursed. Because she was the daughter of the Bornholm, no Dwarrow in his right mind would dare approach her to present their stone chip when the moment struck them bloody. For a female Dwarrow to accept a chip, the male must be of a higher station or possess greater prowess than she. No male possessed more success in their craft than Feikinstafir did as a warrior, and none held a higher station than she, save her brothers and the Bornholm himself. She had no purpose.

Doomed to this bleak consequence, she immersed herself in the Gnomôk wars. Here she was very much accomplished. She was a better warrior than any of her brothers—except her brother Einvalde. At his side, she wreaked havoc upon the dusky fiends the desert spewed. Einvalde, who led the armies of the eastern

Dwarrow, imposed victory upon victory and drove the Gnomôk hordes before his army, fleeing deep into their desert lands.

In the heated core of the Desert of Cinders, where naught but empty sands the eye beheld, lay the smoking mountain, Saurr-modr. It was in this hideous home—the birthplace of all Gnomôk, that the companies of Feikinstafir and Swievalde followed Einvalde. They advanced so quickly that Einvalde outpaced his own ferskeyttr and was alone, without escort, carving a pathway through the retreating ranks of Gnomôk. But it was a trap. Feikinstafir saw the danger her older brother, in his urgent fury, had so rashly missed. There were a great many Gnomôk hidden in the crevices of the barren volcano. They came with renewed fury at the chance to slay the leader of the Dwarrow.

Threats within this sanctum went beyond just Gnomôk. She saw coming out of the rock walls in which they hid as part of the mountain, gifr. These fearsome creatures were more than twice the size of Gnomôk with boil-pocked skin seared by fire and flame. To look upon them one must believe they had climbed out of a pool of bubbling molten rock. Their skin was hard like volcanic stone, seemingly impossible to crack—and yet once cracked, their life would ooze out to their inevitable demise. None was like the other, as each had a random assortment of limbs—some two, others three or four. There had been seen yet more having just a single appendage; more uncommonly, five or more. Their configuration was as random as the god who made them: Noshid, god of the fires who was cast from the skies. The limbs were of a varied nature too. Often those limbs resembled tentacles or had odd bone structures, joints bending in random illogical directions rather than arms or legs. Hideous to behold.

It wasn't the gifr that caused Feikinstafir the climbing anxiety for her brother's predicament. No. It was a far more fearsome and much more infrequent creature: the svigalae, terrible fire lizards who wielded red magic at the blessing of Noshid. They preferred to stand upright on their hind legs and were the elite commanders of many Gnomôk battle units. They were never found off a battlefield, yet here one stood, a cornered commander of the destroyed Gnomôk army. Its tongue flicked in and out, dangling, accompanied by a hiss, expelling forth a sort of steam from its anguine maw.

Einvalde slew the Gnomôk in his path with a great fury, then launched at the svigalae, his maul deflected by its skillful parry. Flames danced upon its glaive as it swirled deftly in the air to strike the Dwarrow leader. Not squandering his heavy maul's inertia, he released his grip, allowing the maul to crack the stone-skinned gifr coming in from the side. Einvalde dropped and rolled backward under the legs of the slower gifr, then with his other hand, brought around the maul again, thunking with a loud *chink* on the igneous, rock-hard skin. More cracks split, and lava oozed freely out of the giant, stunned creature.

Feikinstafir was at a dead run up the rocky path in the blazing hot cavern. Her ferskeyttr was keeping the Gnomôk off of her, but they would not be able to slay the scoundrels fast enough to stay with her. The smell of sulfur combined with Gnomôk refuse accosted her. Far worse than rotting eggs and meat. She was still too far, and each breath became closer to trying to breathe lava.

Seeing opportunity, the svigalae struck its glaive home at the head of Einvalde, but he was agile and cunning. He ducked without looking as the glaive passed over his head, spitting its flame with frustration in its wake. Einvalde went to knock back the svigalae with the haft of his maul; as he did, the hardened lava-fist of a second gifr connected a glancing blow that sent the Dwarrow commander off balance. He stumbled past the fire lizard, parrying yet another swipe of the glaive like it was an afterthought.

Feikinstafir rushed forward, ordering her ferskeyttr to disengage and help her beset brother. Her troop had been touted as the finest elite combat unit in the army of

Strongmedjie. The team responded effectively, bowling over the Gnomôk on their way to reach the gifr that had nearly toppled Einvalde. She was almost there. Her legs slammed the rock like hammers, and her arms pulsed with her fury.

The gifr turned to face this new threat. Feikinstafir ignored the gifr and reached, straining and holding the head of her own maul out as far as she could. It caught a sliding swipe of the svigalae's glaive and kept it from delivering the death blow upon the 1st son. The tug on her maul pulled Feikinstafir off balance, and she went forward, falling. Any other Dwarrow holding the maul would have had it torn from their grip. But she held it tight. Undeterred, the svigalae turned the glaive over in its hands so fast it blurred, adjusting faster than thought to the interruption as if it never happened, and the glaive blade was once more coming at Einvalde. This time as a stab. Einvalde used both hands on his maul to deflect the blow, but it still sliced through armor on the outset of his arm. Feikinstafir let loose a kick to the svigalae's elbow, causing the lizard-like commander to fumble the grip on its glaive.

Her kick left her falling off balance. But it lessened the power of the glaive strike and the damage to her brother was rifted. She felt two heavy blows consecutively coming on her battle-armored back. The metallic clank of her armor bent, taking most of the brunt. She still let out a breathy grunt. The force caught her back in balance. She knew her attacker and let the force guide her into a great full-circle swing of her maul, this time by the handle. She missed the gifr behind her by a breadth of air. The weapon then whistled with a swoosh over the head of the svigalae. Her maul began to hum with greater and greater speed as she spun it in prodigious circles.

Swievalde and his ferskeyttr faced the larger contingent of Gnomôk along with a third gifr in their midst. They battled heedless of the danger Einvalde had placed himself into. Swievalde engaged the third gifr, smashing his axe downward, shattering its skin and opening a fissure along the crusty lava chest. Molten rock spilled in dollop-like globs, and the great creature crashed to its knees with a mortal wound. His ferskeyttr kept the Gnomôk back, whittling their numbers in exchange for flesh wounds.

Einvalde recovered, relieved of onslaught by the distractions his sister and her ferskeyttr provided. His maul cracked the reversed leg of the second gifr so deep it gushed super-heated lava, bringing down yet another of the volcanic beasts. Inside the cavern, the air had been stiflingly hot. But now with the release of the gifr's lava-like blood, it blazed with incinerating effect, each stroke bringing a blasting wave of swelter that compounded, making the cavern a veritable furnace. The Dwarrow suffered under the oppression with only sweat and dizzy heads, where other races of Thear might falter and die on the spot. Even the Gnomôk, used to the volcano and the surrounding desert, began to fail. The wounded expired, and many more were unable to stand.

But the gifr and their commander welcomed the ambiance of stepping into the Sun itself. The gifr moved more fluidly—but the lava had drained from two of them and spelled their fetid end. With the heat burning so intensely, their wounds did not heal, and the leaking magma consumed them where they lay, converting into the puddles of the lava of their origin.

Feikinstafir varied the orbit of her maul at the last second. She twisted with all her might to bring it straight into the midsection of the svigalae. It hit home, and scorching-hot flames burst from its body like blood from any other being. They sprayed out, missing both Feikinstafir and Einvalde. Even so, the gout of heat hit in a wave that forced them both back with concussive force. Feikinstafir was nearly floored again. By Jikseon, these fire lizards were trouble. Sweat rolled off her like she was placed in a smelting forge herself. She shook off the blow and the dizziness from the spinning that amplified the effects of the putrid air. She was shaken for a moment. But she steadied herself, and her head cleared. She had heard her brother grunting and yelling. He was fighting. He was unhurt. She raised her head, looking up.

Einvalde's maul had slew the last Gnomôk, and as it passed through, it struck a rock, sending chipped fragments in all directions. She saw one strike him, catching across the nose before landing on a dead Gnomôk nearby. He stopped with his face looking like he was realizing something new. An awareness or just a change—something in his being moved him. She saw no lust for battle left in him. He was just standing there, stunned. It was a wound that should have gone unnoticed by him. She thought it unremarkable.

A need suddenly gripped him as powerful as the thirst for battle, which she understood so well. But this was different. He did not seek a fight. He instead began frantically looking around like he was lost.

"Einvalde. What is it? Are you hurt?" Feikinstafir said in her command voice. He cast aside his maul, carelessly forgetting it, and began moving about the bodies of the fallen. "Where do it be?" He pulled at limbs of Gnomôk, turning bodies over in his search. He was sweating even more than she was. "I must! I must find it. It be me son."

It came upon her like ice water in the heat of the cavern. He had been chipped. Dwarrow males could not resist the need to find a willing female at the very moment they were chipped. They would seek tirelessly until they found a mate that would accept the bloodied stone. He looked feverishly for the chip.

Not just any chip; it had to be the one that clipped his nose. Heedless of the danger around him, Einvalde continued to search. He needed that stone shard, the one that slashed his nose and drew the blood that would become his son.

Her attention was pulled away from Einvalde. A coughing hiss of a snake brought her back. Feikinstafir saw the look of resignation upon the svigalae commander that understood its forces were doomed. It was using its glaive planted like a crutch on the stony floor to pull its broken, bleeding body up. Its head was shivering with resolution of its reckoning. Its fiery glaive lifted into the air, and it let out a hissing scream, a discordant chord of three clashing tones. Then it slammed the heel of the glaive to the floor, sending gushes of flaming torrents radiating out in all directions. Flesh was seared, heedless of whether it be Dwarrow or Gnomôk. The single remaining gifr began to soften, its vulcanized hide jellifying and collapsing onto the floor.

When the blazing torrent subsided, the commander leaned heavily upon its weapon. It looked to be an empty dull skin. It stood alone, propped up with all others dead or dying in the cavern. Slowly, it advanced, moving with broken animation to come upon the 1st son, who was still clasping a chip of stone in his armored fist. He lived still; his trusilver armor had resisted the heat protecting him from cooking alive.

Feikinstafir stirred, shakily trying to get to Einvalde as well. Through her tired eyes, singed free of lashes, she saw Swievalde getting to his feet. They had survived the desperate fire magic of the svigalae. But, amazingly, so did a bare few Gnomôk.

The commander stood over its victim, readying to finish him. Feikinstafir willed her burnt body to move her feet faster. Any contact with her skin caused needles of fire. She was the daughter of the Bornholm. She came, each step easier than the last, to aid her brother. Her hair was singed away, and blisters of burns plagued her exposed skin. Still, she came. She leaned forward and charged, a battle cry on her lips. *"For Strongmedjie!"* Her maul took the broken svigalae commander full force, crashing through its glaive, snapping the weapon's haft. The force of her maul carried through, crushing into its chest and shattering ribs, splattering smolderings of red flesh and blood dark as devil-mahogany. It collapsed in two pieces.

Consumed by his fever, Einvalde, the 1st son, seemed unaware of his surroundings. He only gazed in wonder at the chip in his fist as he started to rise. Feikinstafir reached out a hand to help her brother up.

But the axe of Swievalde took him in the gut, ripping his entrails out. Einvalde, the 1st son of the 37th Bornholm, fell to the ground, dying. His eyes looked in frothy abhorrence upon his brother—his slayer.

CHAPTER 43

The Curse of Einvalde

Feikinstafir nearly dropped her maul. She did not believe it. "Why? Swievalde, w-why?" Her knees became weak, and she fell where she stood, unable to comprehend the scene.

Swievalde met Einvalde's confounded, angry gaze with an equal enmity. "Ye meet a fitting end, brother. They will cheer yer name as hero, as they always have. Great warrior and 1st son." His face filled with hatred, and he spewed his jealousy in a spat on his dying twin. "You led well on the battlefield. Unequaled, they will claim. But ye will ne'er be the king. It is I, Swievalde, 2nd son, who will be the 38th Bornholm." Her brother's lip curled in triumphant contempt.

"Have you no couth?" Feikinstafir insisted, breathing hard, still on her knees. "I would slay you where you stand myself. But it is not for me to make this be right. Our father will know yer treachery, an' by Jikseon, he be havin' yer head. He was yer brother! An' ye slayed him like a goat ta be spit roasted fer yer dinner."

"Aye, I did. Don' act so quick, dear sister. Methinks, ya crave the seat of Strongmedjie yerself," he countered. "Yer cursed from yer birthin' ta be a bitch. There be no way fer a woman ta be Bornholm. The Dwarrow east or west would ne'er accept it."

Feikinstafir let her temper flare at this. "I lead the finest ferskeyttr in the entire army, brother. I could lead the Strongmedjie better than ye could." Her hand waved in his face, and she stood to face him. Taller, she glared down at him. He looked unmoved.

"Aye, that may be true. But the Bornholm is and always be a male. This cannot change any more than you can make it snow in this fire-breathin' cave." He pushed her hand out of her face. "But if ye keep quiet of what you've seen, and if you have a son, I'll pass on the legacy to him, an' after me—*he would become the 39th Bornholm,* ehh?" His smile was filled with deceit as the corners of his eyes twitched like warning beacons. He was right; she craved to rule the Strongmedjie. But even this offer was hopelessly flawed.

"Ya be a fool, Swievalde. No Dwarrow will offer me his chip. Our father would flay him in the throne room and hang 'im from the barbican. Me fate is sealed in this armor an' on this field. I be a warrior an' no nursemaid." She was true in her words, but there was something that tickled the back of her mind. Something she could not quite grasp.

"Look in me twin brother's fist. I saw his maul send a bit o' stone to his face in the din of battle." She remembered that, now. She plodded heavily over. She looked at the fist, which was indeed clenching a bloodied rock. "He be chipped!" she exclaimed. She had forgotten during all the battle and carnage.

This was fortunate indeed. He could make a son and keep the first of the line alive...but there were no female Dwarrow near this forsaken desert. She could bring it to Strongmedjie, but each day the seed would grow weaker. It was already dry from the infernal heat of the cavern. It was indeterminate how long dry blood would be virile. Eventually, the seed would die.

Swievalde smiled at her. His look was comforting, yet uncomfortable to see. Malice shone in his eye as his brows raised in empathy. "Ye be a female. Despite yer warlike tendencies, ye be female."

"No! By Jikseon, it be stealin'. He should give it freely, I cannot just pry it from his grasp. That be wrong. An' besides, he be me own brother. Fates would curdle the line, and the son o' Einvalde would be cursed fer all his days. No." She refuted his illicit plot.

"Bah! It be yer only way." He smiled with evil now hot on his breath. He pawed at her awkwardly as if to soothe her. She recoiled from his tainted touch.

She was about to cuff him and beat him bloody. She could do it. She was always stronger, faster, better. But there inside, the tingle, it stayed her hand. She wanted her son to rule if she could not. Einvalde was spent. She could not bring her brother back.

She halted, her face brightening somewhat as the darkness left her thoughts. "It could be so. But ye'd 'ave ta call him yer own son. The Bornholm would not question the likes of yer own offspring comin' home from war. If he be mine, only questions and trouble could come of it. An' he would not be in line at all after yer other fifteen sons. None but we two may be privy to the truth. That'd be proof enough fer our father an' ta hold ya ta yer promise."

A gurgling harsh voice brought them back to Einvalde, who was not yet dead. "Ya d-dastardly curs. Are ye such fools?" Einvalde spoke with blood in his mouth as he lay dying, "D-don't do it. It'll bring the wrath of Jikseon down on yer heads. He would never allow—"

Swievalde tapped his axe on his brother's helm. "Be silent. Yer time has passed." Looking at his sister, he raised an eyebrow and chuckled. "Ye got a demon in yer soul! Aye, I'll do it." He smiled a great toothy grin.

She reached down to where her first brother lay, a furious intensity raging through her. She leaned down and grasped the chip in his hand. But before she took the chipped stone, she demanded, "Swear it. Swear it now, and let us be done with it."

Swievalde, smirking, delivered an honest malice dancing across his face. "I swear it! Upon the mountains that Jikseon drew us, I swear it. Now, go an' get the next Bornholm before the blood be dry and yer birthin' be barren."

She tried to wrest the chip from Einvalde; he would not let it go. His fingers still held strength. She cuffed the older twin across his face, and the chip came loose in her hand. She looked still hesitant at the bloodied chip. Blue mangeesum ore shown at the corner in deep contrast to her brother's blood. She resolved; she only needed the chip with his blood on it from the event where it struck him. She did not need more. It would work.

"Ye be cursed. Both of ya. Yer rule as Bornholm, me brother, will falter. You will fail and fall in fire as I have here, betrayed by yer own kin. And you, me sister, yer son will be unlike you in all ways—may he bear the likeness of his father and ferget you. He will rue this day, and Jikseon will have revenge!" With that, Einvalde, 1st son of the 37th Bornholm, drew breath no more.

A shiver ran down Feikinstafir's spine. His words held venom, and she faltered. In battle, she was courageous beyond fearless. She was shaking the chipped stone around in her fist as she thought. This was wrong, and she knew it. But so was the limitation because she was female. She wanted this. It would be fine. Words of her dead brother were just noise that had already faded to nothing. She would have her son. She turned wordlessly to find a place in the desert, where softer terrain lay. When she exited the volcano, she saw the remains of the battle. The dead lay littered all around Saurr-modr. She was aware of the moaning of the dying and smoke from the fires nearby. It clouded her eyes to match the fog on her mind. Her brother's curse did bother her—but she was determined. She sought a place secluded from eyes where she might own a time of undisturbed privacy to make her son.

Walking with a purpose, she turned her thoughts off the terrain and carnage of the battlefield. She tried to push the death malediction of her brother out, but it lingered. A patch of sand over to her right beside a lava stone resembled an irregular sponge. It was perfect, she felt through the chip in her hand. That was the place. In truth, it was unremarkable. No different than the endless sand that stretched in every direction but north, where lay the outlines of the Silfr Mountains, home. But this was the spot, and no other would do.

She looked now at the bloodied stone, and focusing her will, she opened her cold, jaded heart to accept the stone as her child. She ran her thumb along the same jagged edge that she believed drew her brother's blood, now grown cool. It was razor sharp. She tucked the chip in her belt.

Even though she grew up thinking it would never be her place to draw forth a son, she knew how. A son? What if the blood of her brother was tainted? What if her son was deformed? Jikseon would not be so cruel. What about the curse of Einvalde?

She shook her head and let out a scream of frustration. Her despair released through the fear of it. "Have I not suffered enough? Do I not serve Jikseon through the Dwarrow of the Strongmedjie without personal desire? Let it be hale. Let him rule in my stead. I will ask no more of you." She looked down now and then began. She knew the way. It was what all Dwarrow females knew. Her proclivity for war and battle did not dissuade that innate knowledge. She kneeled down over the patch of sand that pulled at her and dug a well, fist deep in the sand. It was hot and soft against her fingers, but the heat was welcome. It felt pleasurable, like the heat of battle where she took life and dominated with power. Intoxicating and exciting. Her breathing increased, and sweat formed anew on her brow.

She pulled the chip out of her waistband. It had been just another chip of rock when she had taken it from her brother's dying hand, but now—now it was perfect. Its sharp edge made her mind swim with desire. She could smell the scent of strength in the blood, even dry as it was. It made her breath and heart quicken. This was thrilling. The hot scent of a heady male Dwarrow was more welcome than hot, roasted, bloody-rare lamb. She shook with the exhilaration. It was her brother's blood—*so wrong!* And yet, she had never felt anything so stimulating, so satisfying.

It was too late to stop—she would be sated! Her breath was now pounding in and out of her chest with a fever. Oh, she stoked the hot fire inside her. She took the chip and gashed her wrist deeply. It caused her to wince in pain for a moment, but the pain was good, pain she was used to coping with. Hers was a warrior's heart. Her head spun. She dropped the shard in the soil. Feikinstafir's excitement brought drooled spittle down the sides of her mouth; she watered the chip with it and then with her own blood until the sticky red ooze swathed it like a blanket, and there was a pool enough for it to drink deep and grow. She fell back, breathing in short, rasping quakes, moving her booted feet, kicking sand over the fertilized chip.

Once it was covered, she fell out of the lust of the event. She was returning to herself once more. She lay there in a sweat, her breath rippling out in chirps. Her mind adrift, she thought of nothing but happiness. Contentment. This was the only place she wanted to be right now. Nothing to do, she just lay and slowed her breathing, fulfilled.

Until Einvalde's words came back like a ghost. *"Yer son will be unlike you in all ways—may he bear the likeness of his father and ferget you."* She sat up, cupped her hands, and waited, cross-legged. Somewhere in her mind, a door closed. She had betrayed the brother she looked up to. She took from him against his will to make a son for her own designs. She had done grievous evil. Now she had a pact with her flawed brother. He would be the 38th Bornholm. All Strongmedjie would pay the price for her. No light or good was left in her. All came in darkness now, both in her mood and mind and feel of flesh. It flowed over her being as she sat. She waited in shadow for her son.

CHAPTER 44

Bad Blood

T he victors surveyed the battlefield, taking captives or slaying those that resisted. There was pilfering of the dead, even among the Dwarrow—their own brethren took what was of use only to the living. Cries were in the air; the pitiful wounded begging for help or an end to their agony mixed with the noises of pain and loss. Notice was taken of the bloodied female warrior sitting in somber brooding, never once looking at those who passed by. No one dared bother her. They knew her fearsome reputation. Doubtless they would rather live intact to see the next day than speak to her.

Swievalde exited the volcano—the only remaining survivor. His enemy, dead. His ferskeyttr, dead. His brother, dead. He glanced over to where his sister brooded, nodding inwardly that she had planted the seed of the Dwarrow, and a son would rise. He would be Einvalde's 1st and only son. But no one could know this. The scandal that Einvalde had given his chip to his sister was an affront to Jikseon. She would never betray her son's secret. Or her own.

Dwarrow paled at the thought of incest. Offspring between siblings with a single common parent would live with a curse of Jikseon on them. Sometimes it was noticeable, a physical deformation. Missing an ear or crooked legs. Very often it was a mentally inhibited characteristic. On occasion it was not as noticeable, manifesting as a very short life or uncanny bad luck. Smiling, he knew he would be able to use that deficiency against the illicit nephew. There was also another fact he kept from his sister that he was sure she did not know. The blood on the chip might not be all Einvalde's. He saw his brother wrench the chip from the skull of a dying Gnomôk. He chuckled, a spit filled with laughter. Oh, this was a good twist. What if the offspring was a half breed or female? He lit up as he built the worst case: a female half breed. No matter, Feikinstafir would lose out.

He knew when he made the promise that he had no intention of keeping it. But that was a problem to be dealt with in the far distant future. He had thirteen grown sons already and had chipped two more before leaving the fortress on the west side of the Silfr Mountains. One of these boys would make a fine Bornholm.

He would loathe to see a child of incest on the ram's head throne of Strongmedjie. Still, he would keep enough of the promise to appease her until the time came. He would name his nephew his own son, his 16th son, for now. He would never name the boy Bornholm. But that would be decades away, maybe more than a century before he had to name a Bornholm to follow him. He was more concerned with impressing his father, Augabragd, enough to be named the 38th Bornholm. One step at a time, he mused with a smile, then set off to the north, to Strongmedjie and home.

CHAPTER 45

Desert Flame

The moon rose full and red that evening. A black mist made stringy trails across its face, masking it and then slowly dropping away like a veil of pure evil. Feikinstafir looked on in bleak indifference. She knew the evil she and her brother had concocted that day. It ate at her. But life had dealt her an unfair fate, granting her a warrior's prowess and then callously relegating her to the role of a caregiver. A blasted female, inferior? She was not inferior. In every way, she had proven throughout her life she was superior. She knew she was the best Dwarrow to follow her father. Dwarrow were always set in their ways.

Tradition was ingrained—even in her own thinking. She used to feel like a heretic when she let the thought of her becoming Bornholm into her head. A defilement of law and righteousness. But she saw the weaknesses in

Swievalde. That was easy, for he was hopelessly flawed. Although Einvalde would be a fine Bornholm, he was not ideal. She was the best fit. Better than her father, even. But she knew it could never happen. It would be as it always was. A decision of the Bornholm based in unyielding stone-wrought tradition.

Maybe the fates weren't done chiding her yet. Nothing had yet come of her seeding the chip into the ground. And even if a child came of it, Jikseon would curse it—there had never been an exception for a child born of brother and sister. His rage would levy a terrible curse on her son. Especially when they had done it in such a despicably clandestine manner.

Her mind moved to continue its twisted path with thoughts that mocked Jikseon. She knew she was descending into falsehoods of evildoings, but she couldn't stop herself. Perhaps she could rule through her son. Ahh, but that would be unfulfilling. Her son would have the pride and fury of their line, of both her brother and her. He would never succumb to being a puppet.

Then it struck her.

A price through Jikseon for her betrayal. What if... *No!* She balked at the thought, knowing her wrongdoing might be weighted upon her son. Her child! What if Jikseon's reprisal extended her misfortune? What if she had made a *daughter!* That would be an irony worthy of a god.

She tortured herself through the night in this way, chasing evil thoughts and exploring all that could go wrong. It wrenched at her and tore her remaining virtues down one after another until she was empty.

She paced anxiously, unable to sleep. The Sun rose and set once more. Those wounded and left to die on the battlefield had done their due diligence. The silence of the desert permeated the heated air. She was alone during the night's moon—no longer red, but smoky black fingers held it akin to a claw all night long. The Sun rose and set once more. She noticed the passing of time less and less. He was taking longer to spring forth than any other she had known of. Was it possible their immoral coupling had yielded a bad seed? Did the fires of the chasm in the volcano burn the life from the seed placed on the chip? She clung to the thought that this might be Jikseon's curse.

No Dwarrow had yet been born of the blasted desert land. Dwarrow born of land not in the Silfr Mountains or Tisroc were always a bit touched or of compromised constitutions. She had defied Jikseon in two ways with this chip. The smile she wore now was fearsome. It bordered on insanity. In truth, she knew she was skirting the edge. If Jikseon left her without a son, she might take the fate of a death where she stood. It was welcome. Her life was empty, and now her soul was too.

Just before the next Sun, it came. First the hand stretching forth out of the loose dirt she had dug in the sand. She resisted the urge to help it. It must escape the earth on its own, lest it be too weak to make its own way through life. It pulled itself out of the grainy dirt. She looked carefully as it took in its first breath, and she saw the stubble of beard upon its chin. He looked upon her and knew his mother. He was whole, full grown, but young. A longing to live and love rushed back into her so rapidly she gasped, and she hugged him with fierce care, the kind only a mother could manifest. He allowed the embrace, then he squirmed to get loose. She was strong, but regretfully, she released the crushing arms with which she wrapped him.

Her smile glowed with her love, and she then began to dust him off. His skin was darker than any Dwarrow she had seen, and his features sharpened and shaped. Completing his growth took only minutes. In no way did he resemble her brother, the father who had been chipped. He smiled with mischief on his lips and carried with him the knowledge of his father and mother.

"Chok si minna?" he asked. Feikinstafir looked blankly at the foreign, harsh words he spoke with perfect clarity. That was no Dwarrow tongue of east or west. That was the harsh, guttural speaking of the Gnomôk.

Shock struck her, and she feared the gods had indeed brought their price upon her son. He was in truth *her son*, but he was not of pure blood. Somehow, someway, in the battle, the blood of a Gnomôk had caught the half of the stone she had seeded. The blood on the chip was *not* that of Einvalde, her brother. He was not the bloodline of the 1st son, Einvalde. This creature before her was a half breed—half Dwarrow, half terrible Gnomôk. Yet her heinous pact with her brother would make him Bornholm someday. His face looked confused. Then he said once more, in the language of the Dwarrow, the language of his mother, complete with a western accent, "Mother, who am I?"

She replied, naming him Jarlsalt. In the words in the dialect of Strongmedjie: desert flame. "You are my son. You are named Jarlsalt, 16th son of the Bornholm."

PART
Thirteen

CHAPTER 46

Flight South

Outside the fortress of Strongmedjie, word had spread of the Bornholm's proclamation and that the Giftgiver had come with newly forged gifts of trusilver and precious gems. Many Dwarrow had dwelled in the city as refugees after the demise of the Towers of the Horne, and they remembered the days before their flight. Now, new generations that had never seen the Towers, hearing of them only from relatives who had once thrived there, were bright with the wonder of a legend they had only heard of becoming a living reality. It was to be a glorious return.

There were very many Dwarrow showing enthusiasm and taking the Bornholm's command as a relief of serfdom. While Haggersath and his companions had to be pleased to see such support in returning and rekindling the eastern realm, it was never the Bornholm's intention to create a migration. He was more likely thinking they would take the other choice and forsake that blasted Giftgiver and his insufferable Haseti of fools and beggars and accept assimilation to the might of the Strongmedjie.

When this news reached the Bornholm's ears, his roused anger would rage and curse the easterlings. He would bluster and shout at his court. He would remind them how very generous he had always been when their lands abated. His wrath could light a bonfire underwater. He expected them to grovel and thank him for his openhandedness. Instead, nearly one-quarter of the Dwarrow were in celebration, preparing to make their journey home. Celebration! An insult!

It wasn't just the Bornholm that saw this movement as an inconvenience. With the road about to be clogged by hundreds of eastern loyalists, it was hardly business as usual. A sole traveler making their way to a new future might blend in as part of the pilgrimage. However, a vaunted enemy caught in this crowd would indeed be in great peril along the same road. Jarlsalt knew this all too well, as he hid his face in his cloak and scurried about. He was that enemy.

He had to make a quick and quiet exodus without notice. Ducking and slinking away through the assembled throng was easier than he had expected. Most of the crowd had gathered in anticipation of seeing the Giftgiver and his Haseti. They gave no notice to some cloaked traveler burrowing through them, who must obviously be searching for friends or family to journey with. Soon Jarlsalt reached the perimeter of the outer dwellings and found the southern road that led along the mountain range.

His mind fought to be in the moment, to be wary of his danger. But emotional confusion reigned, and his mind was a flurry of heated hatred and confusion. Not the son of the Bornholm? Gnomôk spawn? He had known his mother, although very briefly. She brought him home from his birthplace in the desert, so far to the south, but he never saw her again once they reached the mountains. He was raised by Swievalde's household as the 16th son.

It was, however, a lie. A lie like his whole life had been. He looked at his own hands as he continued his aimless flight from Strongmedjie, gaining as much distance as he could in this short time. He was Dwarrow through and through—and yet he saw his skin tone for the first time without clouded vision. Without prejudice skewing his views—those he had been taught to have, to live by his whole life—he saw. He *was* different!

He nearly stumbled in his haste. He was out of the dense part of dwellings and near to the most remote homes, the ones tended by the farmers. Anger welled up from inside. Humph! He fought the tears stinging his eyes. So what if he was different? They would be sorry for shunning him. He would come back and foist a retribution. Once finished, he would not leave one bearded Dwarrow standing.

Over and over, he daydreamed, and he kept up the frantic pace. He teetered back and forth on short, rapid steps that gave his gait a comical appearance of being overly rushed. His legs should have ached by now. His breath should have given out. But something drove him hard. He did not tire or feel fatigue, only a growing hatred. It welled up from deep inside him. He had touched it before, but it never stirred like it did now. He was on fire with thoughts of nothing but revenge through violent destruction. Oh, they would pay. They would all pay. He fussed and muttered, fuming as he ran.

It was well into the night when he moved off the road to rest. He did not want to stray too far. Basilisks and possibly wyverns would be attracted and find him an easy meal. A sole traveler on the road was always a target. Off the road, the greater the distance into the wilds of Tisroc, the greater the danger. Jarlsalt went without a fire and gnawed at the dried goat he pulled from his pack. It was creamy with fat and had a heady herbal flavor from the fennel pollen and lemon peel used in the curing. It was coated with big grinds of black pepper that covered the musky goat gaminess. His flask on the left side had a good vintage, half-sweet white wine; its grapes had been picked once the noble rot set in. It gave the wine an unmistakable note of harvest at winter's first breath, the beginnings of decay. Nothing else created that flavor. How fitting it was that these things nourished him at the onset of his life's disintegration. On the road, this was a meal fit for the son of the Bornholm.

Bah! He almost spat it out. But he was too hungry. All that running drew up a strong appetite. Finishing the goat, he pulled out a hard cheese that tasted like salted apples and carved a few pieces off, eating them directly off of the knife. He was tired. After he tucked the cheese back, he felt the fatigue set in. He was far enough off the road not to be seen. Sucking loose grinds of the peppercorns, he spat them out. He covered himself completely with his cloak and slipped off to sleep.

His sleep was fitful. He woke in a cold sweat, sure that a basilisk was stalking him while he rested. Basilisks were dull and gray reptiles three to four meters long. They were similar to lizards, with oversized, long heads lined with multiple rows of flat teeth for grinding. Moving casually upon six legs, they would hunt

Dwarrow or Gnomôk. They did not eat meat often, but when they did, those were their favorite meals. Jarlsalt hated them. He had always been afraid of being turned to stone by its gaze. After one was ossified, the slow creature would take its time consuming its victim until sated. Its flat teeth and incredibly strong jaws were perfect for grinding rock and metal—and, of course, their favorite snack: precious gems.

His worry vanished, forgotten—almost forgotten— as he looked and saw no basilisk stalking him. Only the night sky, silent and calm. He plucked out from his breast his little prize. The Destiny Stone. This would be a prize meal for a basilisk, to be sure. It held a glitter in the night, capturing the cold light of the heavens. There was a strange heat inside the Destiny Stone. Odd—it should have been cool to the touch. It was warm. He just now took note; it had been warm every time he held it. He could see flickers of red deep in its depths. It gave him a sense of comfort, of desire. It fed his yearning for revenge!

He was not sure how long he held the Destiny Stone. It had to be long, because the first rays of the morning refracted and glared in his eyes, making him aware that he had spent the remainder of the night peering in a trance. He tucked away the Destiny Stone. He was no longer tired. His short sleep must have been very deep. He was really quite fully refreshed. Getting to his feet, he looked south where his path led. The road was to his left just over the mild rise. Scruffy shrubs and grasses were all that grew in this part of Tisroc. The barren terrain was still not his home. Now, he had discovered it had never been. He was born of the desert sands to the south.

For some reason, he looked to the west. There on the flat earthen rise, a little more than a stone's throw away, he saw it. A basilisk. It sat on the sandstone ledge basking in the heat of the Sun as it rose. He let out a shudder and began for the road to the east, away from the beast. He wanted no part of that creature's world.

He continued this new ritual of running, eating, sleeping, and staring through the rising of the next four moons. He fed his self-pity and filled his mind with hate during the day so he neither heard nor saw where he went. No heed was paid to the coolness of the air or the winds whipping at his face. He just trudged on, his thoughts endlessly rolling through life's memories, seeking answers—then, disappointingly, receiving nothing that soothed him. At night, he slept but found the Destiny Stone in his hands each sunrise. He did not get much sleep, but he was not tired in the morning. It was as if the Destiny Stone was filling his rest with its red fires. He made his way without awareness or intent, just a blind, driving force leading him forward by his nose.

His movements were not as random as they seemed. He was steadily southeast bound. Something pulled and corrected if he strayed, and strayed he did, many times. It was as if the presence of his concentration—or, better yet, *a presence in his mind*—kept the pathway consistent. Unaware of his surroundings, he walked, he ran, he progressed ahead. Unaware, too, of the stalkers he had picked up, tracing his path.

On the fifth sunrise, Jarlsalt woke in his off-road camp once again. He hadn't seen a basilisk since that first day, and he was calmer than before. But he knew he was being followed. Although one of those great lizards could not match his pace during the day, a basilisk would tirelessly continue through the night if it did follow. They did not sleep with the Sun and the moon as most other beings did. They slept when they did. And when they did, it was for a long time. Even so, he felt it wasn't the basilisk. He was too far south.

The night before, Jarlsalt had again reached for the Destiny Stone. Each night, it warmed his hands and gave him a feeling of belonging. He felt the Destiny Stone was meant for him. The fire inside the Destiny Stone called him. His travels were at the whim of the Stone. And it wanted him to go south.

CHAPTER 47

A Fitting End

Jarlsalt had reached the turn in the road that made its way east. This was the same road he had traveled with that fool Giftgiver and his band of shaggy-bearded dolts when they went on his fathe—*ahhhhhh!* He shook his head at the learned error. As when *that bastard Bornholm* sent them on that doomed venture to sate his shallow greed. But now he turned south, away from the road and into the dusty borders of Tisroc studded with patchy, short brown grasses. The Desert of Cinders, the land of his destination, might be a day away or less. He thought he heard a faint chittering sound behind him. He turned. Nothing.

That was when a sharp crack across his legs made him fall, rolling down off the slope's grassy patchwork of a shoulder. He tumbled, slamming from knee to back to knee again, over and over. Blurred images chased him as he rolled down the ravine into the gully below. When he finally came to a halt, he tried to orient, but they were upon him in an instant. Foul-smelling, hairy rats surrounded him, so many clawed hands taking firm grasps of him, drawing him up.

"Bah!" He spat at the closest to him. "The lot o' ya will be sorry ya did that."

He reached for his short blade, but it wasn't there. He could see it resting up the slope, its ruby winking at him mockingly. His putrid luck, it had come out during his tumble. He found the haft of one of his hatchets—too late. A kvalid was on him already, and its furred foot caught him full across his face as it chittered chidingly. He spun around like a haymaker had twisted him full-on. He landed with a hard thud on the turf, his hatchet sent flying off into the hard-packed dirt. Warm and salty with iron to flavor it, he tasted his own blood.

He needed to get up but found his limbs not responding, and he lay there bleeding into the thirsty clods of earth where his face came to rest. That was when he felt himself being dragged once more to his feet. Jarlsalt was brought to standing, face-to-face with the leader. Its brown-furred weasel snout twitched, and six whiskers moved as the kvalid sucked its teeth. The animal's greasy stench emanated from the matted fur and overpowered Jarlsalt's senses. Slowly, it looked him over like it was shopping in the bazaar outside the gates of Strongmedjie for a rug or fine fabric. It pulled and touched his clothes and then his face with its filthy clawed hand. A stench of rotted meats swam over as the kvalid exhaled hot, rancid breath into his face.

The thing chittered at him, its canine-like maw of sharp, yellow-brown teeth shaking up and down slightly. He had never noticed this small trait before. He had always just plunged his jeweled sword through kvalid when he was in close quarters and moved on to the next. He was never in a position to suffer their will.

The rat glanced down to his belt and tapped at the broach under his belt with its javelin tip. It clinked with the sound of the trusilver-mounted gemstone he had pilfered from the floor of the forge at the Towers of the Horne. He did not answer the nasty beast. What good would a broach, a Dwarrow gift, do for the likes of this cretin? It reached for Jarlsalt's cloth-wrapped packet. Jarlsalt defied the weasel and clenched it into a tight fist, resisting but relenting when a sharp blade behind him pressed into his kidney. The kvalid leader pulled the mounted gemstone free of the cloth and took it into its blackish calloused palm. A new fear twisted in Jarlsalt's guts until he felt he would vomit. Instead, he fell to his knees before the rat.

Holding the gemstone, a blood-red garnet flashing from its perfect octagon cut, up to glint in the Sun, it hissed. Behind, the others chittered excitedly, watching as their leader turned the broach over, held up for all to see. Apparently satisfied but not much impressed, it pushed the broach into a pouch on the inside of its braided belt. The kvalid leader stamped the heel of the spear at the foot of Jarlsalt, perhaps indicating it wasn't satisfied. Miserable and kneeling, Jarlsalt held his hands out, palms up in a submissive gesture to show he had nothing. Jarlsalt kept his hands out to the sides, hoping it dissuade further intrusion or detainment. The kvalid reached for his satchel, tearing it from his belt.

Opening it and taking coins from the inside, the leader growled, tossing them off in the grass, unwanted. It shook the sack, dumping the odds and ends that were all Jarlsalt still owned over his head, the personal effects beating onto his face. Then the kvalid, beginning to show what had to be anger, turned the empty bag inside out and slapped it back and forth across Jarlsalt's abused face. He wore many cuts that openly bled.

Then it froze and looked back and forth between the bag and its besieged bearer, staring at his breast. Panic suddenly unmasked on Jarlsalt's face. The Destiny Stone! It was neatly tucked there, and this animal had its wolfish gaze fixed upon it.

Jarlsalt went to stand, but a javelin haft came around hard on his temple, sending him to the dusty ground, head spinning. He groveled and felt the claws at his breast taking it, taking the Stone. There was no struggle; he could not move. The abuse and exhaustion combined with a resignation of evaporated resolve. He rolled onto his back, the light of the Sun momentarily blinding him through his dazed head. The lead kvalid's teeth were all bared, pencil-thin lips pulled back. Was that a smile? If it were a smile, it would be a humongous grin. Glittering in the Sun, clutched in its clawed hand, was the Destiny Stone.

Like they had been called to a feast, the other kvalid immediately dove in on him, searching for more hidden treasures. A terrible frenzy of razor-tipped hands ripped and tore his belongings from him with harsh abandon. Pain came in all directions as the claws ripped his clothes and tore through his skin. He cried out in anguish.

The chittering continued. He twisted and wiggled, losing most of his shredded clothing and all his personal items to the rabid pilferers. Blood and flesh flipped and tossed in the air until the rats saw he was without further possession. Their interest in him waned, and he took the moment to escape.

He rolled, slipping away until he was able to gather his feet underneath him. With a short distance between himself and the voracious attackers, he sped as quickly as his stunted thighs would carry him. Fear fueled his flight. He had no energy, but if he could not run now, death would find him. He could visualize those toothy maws ripping into his remaining flesh and devouring him alive, his death more terrible than his wretched life had been.

At first, they looked his way as he fled. He was naked and had nothing they wanted, but Jarlsalt was not going to stick around to see if they wanted to eat him. He expected javelins to come, seeking his heart, but none came. Still, he ran like never before until the chittering was left far, far behind.

He slowed to a stop and fell to all fours. His chest burning with fire, he gulped air like his life depended on it. And it did. His head swam. What a day, he thought. What a week. No, what a life. Why? Why?! Who could have cursed him so?

His escape was complete. There had been no pursuit. But those nasty rats, they took it all! He was left by the kvalid as he was born of the sand—naked.

He looked at his grimy self, at his wounds. Bleeding flesh hung loose on his ribs. That wasn't good. He may not survive this. He leaned over and vomited. He was starting to feel the severe pain. His wounds were too many and too grievous. There was no help for him. He was alone and broken so badly that he knew there was no hope at all. He knew it was here that he would die.

It was a fitting end, he thought. His life was a total waste, and now it is finally over. *Take me. I am ready.* He lay back on the dry, dusty dirt and mercifully passed out.

CHAPTER 48

Nose Tracker

Nothing was left by the natural scavengers. There had been a struggle, and by the few things left, it seemed the Dwarrow who had been assailed could have been only one or two. By contrast, the dead kvalid raiders were easily a dozen or more. This was what Nef-Rekja had said. He would know. Nef-Rekja had a nose for tracking things. That was literally what his name meant, nose tracker. His slender, mousey, brown beard often dragged along the dirt when he examined the signs, with his long, pointed nose sniffling, nearly touching the ground. His scraggly hair stuck out randomly from his soft, mustard-yellow stocking cap. Nef-Rekja carried only a large, serrated knife across the front of his wrinkled muslin tunic. On his left side, tugging so hard on his belt that it drooped, hung a brownish orange bag loaded with stones he had meticulously collected for use with the sling, which dangled off his hip.

He pulled his nose off the ground and looked up at Mevindh-Gulbard.

"He is not here." His muffled voice sounded bored. As if he was just too tired to speak but did it anyway.

"Yes, that be obvious," Mevindh-Gulbard said in an answer strained with patience. "Pray tell, do you know where he do be?"

He nodded. Mevindh-Gulbard motioned for him to speak, but all he did was stare at him, waiting. Still a beacon of patience, Mevindh-Gulbard leaned over slightly and made a clear and audible whisper. "Could you be more specific?" Then, hoping he had made his point, he stood erect once more.

"Oh, yes." Nef-Rekja nodded, very willing to please. But the skinny, frumpish Dwarrow just stared with glassy, amber-brown eyes wide as could be. Mevindh-Gulbard waved his hand, motioning for the tracker to continue, but all he got was a crooked yellow-and-brown-toothed smile, his teeth so cramped in his narrow mouth it reminded him of too many pillars in an overcrowded hall.

Now Mevindh-Gulbard was sure this was either the stupidest Dwarrow in the company or he was intentionally trying to be vague. But what good would it do for a Dwarrow fleeing the Strongmedjie for a new life in the Towers of the Horne to anger the Giftgiver's very own Gulprąst? So, he assumed the former.

"I be a little short with understandin' ya. Show me what ye mean. Show me where he has gone. That, or tell me plain, like I be an idiot."

"Right, yer Preistiness." The nose tracker pointed south, up in the sky. "Over there."

He had gotten used to the nose tracker's mangled term. Nef-Rekja may have been a brilliant tracker, but the cost Jikseon took for the skill left the annoying little Dwarrow with endless social and cognizant difficulties. Mevindh-Gulbard suffered the term "preistiness" since correcting him made no change at all. Nef-Rekja's endless grin grew even wider, increasing his ungainly lack of charisma. He made an odd clicking motion with his jaw, which made a light snapping noise as it ticked.

"He be dead then," Mevindh-Gulbard deduced. Nef-Rekja must have been alluding to the heavens— albeit he seemed to direct his attention south rather than the more traditional motion of straight up. No reason to go after a dead Dwarrow. Mevindh-Gulbard turned to take his small contingent back to the main caravan.

He didn't get three steps in when he heard Nef-Rekja continue speaking, as if the conversation had not concluded and the Gulprąst was still before him. "Mebbe. But I don't think so."

Patience was becoming tested, now that Mevindh-Gulbard was almost angry. He whirled on the rumpled-clothed tracker. "'Mebbe'?"

"Yeah," was all the thin tracker said. And then, "But I think not." Nef-Rekja nodded, reaching an understanding with himself.

Mevindh-Gulbard closed the gap between them in just a couple of steps, saying, "How can ye know?"

"Oh, that be easy," he said, his smile retracting at the flared nostrils in Mevindh-Gulbard's face. Mevindh-Gulbard waited a few seconds, but he wasn't about to play this game anymore.

"Why do you think the Dwarrow fled, an' where do you think he be livin'?" He knew he looked menacing. He didn't like to look this way, but it was one of those times where it would be better to. "Be concise."

"I dunno what c-con-conchise means," he stammered out, now withdrawing in the face of a dangerously angry Gulprąst.

Taking in a breath and letting it out very slowly, Mevindh-Gulbard forced himself to calm down. He would get nowhere frightening this toad. He took in another deep, soft breath and forced a pleasant "preistiness" smile upon his face. Then, when he was sure he would not intimidate, he asked, "Please, nose tracker, explain how ye know this Dwarrow be livin', and where he may be. I saw ya point to the sky, an' thought ya meant—"

"No," he interrupted. "I was pointin' at them birds up o'er there."

Mevindh-Gulbard squinted. Yes, there were four, five, six birds circling to the south. They remained in the same area, just circling.

"Ahhh, well done, me expert tracker. *That* be using yer nose." He laughed, and Nef-Rekja's smile returned. Mevindh-Gulbard patted the thin shoulder of his tracker and took his scouting party south, where the vultures were waiting on death to deliver their meat.

As they closed on the spot where the birds circled, they saw a Dwarrow splayed on his back in the dusty turf with many slashing, gash-like wounds. Mevindh-Gulbard was sure the vultures had made attempts to begin their feast, but perhaps the injured Dwarrow shivered or waved them off. They had not begun to consume him yet. Not much, anyhow.

Mevindh-Gulbard kneeled by the shredded body and began to examine him. A sudden recognition came flooding in. He pulled back for a moment. He knew that ruddy, pointed face, the oily beard now mussed. His shredded skin was still intact enough to know it was Jarlsalt! He touched the mutilated Dwarrow. He was barely breathing and hotter than a forge at full tilt. He would not survive long.

"Good," Mevindh-Gulbard said under his breath. The Gulprąst was tempted to let the crows and vultures fight over the Dokkur Dvergur's remains. But the fate of the wretched traitor was in the hands of the Giftgiver. It was not his decision to make.

"Do that be the 16th son?" asked one of the escorting soldiers behind him.

"Aye," said another. "But the title don't be nothin' fer them birds up there." She pointed to the vultures above, which were not put off by the group's arrival.

Ignoring them, Mevindh-Gulbard placed one hand on the dried, bloody mess that was Jarlsalt, and a soft, familiar warmth flowed through him and into the wrecked body. He pulled out the golden beryl gift that Haggersath bequeathed to him in the other. Eyes flickered below him as the half breed gasped, drawing a ragged breath into his parched throat. The Gulprąst's broach began a soft yellow flicker. He saw Jarlsalt's senses returning. Jarlsalt's dry eyes gave a start as he focused on Mevindh-Gulbard, recognizing him.

Mevindh-Gulbard pressed on him. "Be calm. You will not die by my hand, though you do not deserve saving."

The dirty scoundrel fell back and rested until he concluded enough healing had occurred to allow the injured half breed to be stable. Jarlsalt needed both food and water if he was to travel. The Gulprąst called out for a waterskin. Nef-Rekja was there surprisingly quickly with a skin near bursting with the liquid. Jarlsalt smiled weakly and took it from the nose tracker.

"Ahhhh, me thanks," Jarlsalt croaked out.

He took a long draught, and as it hit his dry, raw throat, he seized up like the sear of hot metal had touched his bare skin. He fell over to the side, coughing—he expelled the liquid and emptied the contents of his stomach, belching up blood in the mix of it all. On his hands and knees, he didn't seem to be able to draw breath; he shook, open mouthed and not finding a gulp of air. Mevindh-Gulbard caught the unmistakable medicinal waft of Vallhah, the scathing Dwarrow liquor, and sent an annoyed glare at the nose tracker.

"Water!" Mevindh-Gulbard said at the rumpled Dwarrow, who was incredulous, holding his hands to his sides, palms up in innocent confusion.

"I picked it up where the rats be leavin' it. I'll drink it, if'n he don't want it." He snatched it up before it could leak out of the dropped bag. Another of the soldiers offered a skin. This time, Mevindh-Gulbard checked it first. Water. He waited for the vile Dwarrow to recover, then thrust the water at him.

"This be the right stuff. Drink. We be movin' to catch the caravan as soon as ye are done."

Jarlsalt tentatively took a sniff, looking darkly sidelong at him. Satisfied, he drank a bit and rested. Better, thought the Gulprąst. He knew to go slow. If he went too fast, it would come up just as violently as the Valhalla did. Looking up, Mevindh-Gulbard saw the vultures had given up hope of weeks' worth of feasting and had moved off to find another tasty meal. The Gulprąst motioned at Jarlsalt as he stood, and his rescuers pulled him to his feet. He was unsteady at first. They reluctantly aided him in moving back toward the north and east.

It took some time to arrive, but Jarlsalt gained strength and speed as they went. Mevindh-Gulbard had used a healing charm in the shape of an ordinary pebble. It carried a latent healing potential that released its power over time. He knew it was the most effective healing method. There was far more efficiency with this than with a single impulse heal. When they closed on the caravan, a scouting party came out to meet them.

"Looksee here at what manner of murderin' scum ye did find," said none other than the billowy-bearded Rock-Biter, Grölle. He had his ferskeyttr with him.

"Methinks the Giftgiver'd be mighty glad ta lay eyes upon ye. I understand yer not the Dwarrow ye thought ye were, eh?"

This brought a hearty round of laughter from the Dwarrow. Mevindh-Gulbard did not laugh with them. He was focused on the opportunities and problems the swarthy traitor brought with him. He was intent on getting the prisoner to Haggersath as soon as possible. Jarlsalt said nothing, but snarled at Grölle.

They led him back to the road, where a caravan of hundreds of Dwarrow was traveling eastward. He was handed some goat jerky and a water skin to keep, as well as some fresh clothing to cover his wounded body. They could not leave the Dokkur Dvergur completely alone, so Mevindh-Gulbard made it his own duty to watch him. Only he would bear the responsibility, until Haggersath directed his will.

CHAPTER 49

Truth and Lies

The caravan moved slowly, and Mevindh-Gulbard prompted and herded Jarlsalt along the way. It wasn't until the second day that a familiar face showed up to see him. Flaxen bearded and grim faced, Haggersath approached without extensive salutation. His mood was cool and direct.

"Ahh, Gulprąst, what manner of treatment be this for a captain of the Bornholm, eh?" he demanded, making a scornful jibe at the traitor.

"I'd been expectin' ya." Jarlsalt wiped the gritty sweat off his cheek with a heavily scarred hand. "Ya be the leader o' this lot? Or do it be one o' these other fucks that took the mantle from ya?"

Haggersath chuckled softly. "Never do ya learn from yer mistakes, eh?"

"You'd be a fool ta think that he would," Grölle said to Haggersath. He turned then to Jarlsalt and added, "Ye need to know yer place. An' yer lucky the Giftgiver is leadin' us. If it had been yer precious Bornholm, ya'd been left in the sand back there."

"An' if it be Grölle leading us, or—even better—Bolfath, ye'd be in chains, or spittin' yer guts out on the road," Mevindh-Gulbard said, upstaging the captain. "But if ye like ta keep even ground with the others here, ye'd best be forthcoming with these questions we be askin' of ya." He wanted to be sure that Jarlsalt understood his life hung in the balance. He would be judged by his answers, and not just their words and meaning.

Jarlsalt's arrogance deflated, and his shoulders drooped a bit. They knew he was deposed. "All right then. 'Ave at yer query. I'll be quick ta answer ya."

"Wise choice, Dokkur Dvergur." Grölle stressed the name, causing Jarlsalt to wince as if he'd been slapped.

Mevindh-Gulbard became serious now. "What happened to yerself on the road here? Why'd we find ya without supplies and left ta the vultures, naked as the day ye were born?"

Jarlsalt looked askance, his face twisting as he considered his plight and the repercussions that revealing the truth might bring forth. Mevindh-Gulbard watched him closely. Haggersath would expect his Gulprąst to recognize any untruths the scandalous Dwarrow might try to pass off.

After a brief hesitation, he began, slowly, "I was attacked by a band of kvalid rats on the road. They took me by surprise." Mevindh-Gulbard was able to keep a straight face, although he shared the amusement the others showed at this part of the tale. Before long, he allowed a corner of his mouth to flicker up in half a smile. "I tell ya true, there be mebbe a hundred of them furry bastards." Mevindh-Gulbard knew that was an embellishment but did not show his annoyance to the prisoner. "An' they had tralkvalid with them too. They took everythin' I had, despite me fightin' them like a windstorm upon the mountainside."

He ended the fabrication on the biggest lie. Mevindh-Gulbard just looked at him, unmoved. Haggersath waited. Mevindh-Gulbard was expected to sift out the truth of it. "The kvalid came and took yer belongings," Mevindh-Gulbard said. "I got that. Now, where were you expectin' ta go? Ya have no home in the west, an' there only be death fer yer actions in the east. Where would an outcast like yerself be travelin'?"

Jarlsalt frowned. Perhaps he knew he could not fool the Gulprąst with tall tales of heroism. He replied softly under his breath, "South. Only south is left to me."

Mevindh-Gulbard smiled now. The truth had unexpectedly spilled out of Jarlsalt. "Aye, south. But that be the desert lands of the Gnomôk. An' you, you be a half breed—which explains much." He eyed the traitor and surmised his dilemma. "The Gnomôk wouldn't want you either, I expect. North be closed to ya too. The Bornholm sounded quite sure that he'd like nothin' more than ta take yer head fer display." He recited the obvious to show Jarlsalt there was no need to explain his grievances. They knew them already, and didn't care. "But none of that be yer fate. Ya must answer fer yer treachery in the Horned Towers and the massacre ya did there. We be walkin' ya back to the Horne. An' once there, yer life will surely end—if the Giftgiver calls fer it."

Hate blossomed on Jarlsalt's lips, and fire seared across his brow. "No!" His hands waved erratically, like he was on fire. "No! It cannot be this way, never!"

Mevindh-Gulbard looked for the answer from Haggersath, and Haggersath gave a nod. That was a signal that they were finished with him until they reached the Towers. The guards seized Jarlsalt and clapped irons on his wrists. He was dragged away, and the inquisition team began to leave—when there came a final desperate, shrill cry.

"No!" he stammered out, "T-t-th-the rats! T-Th-they t-took it." Mevindh-Gulbard looked unmoved. "The rats, damn you!"

Grölle stepped in to take custody now that Haggersath was through with the traitor. "Yes. We know, and we don' care 'bout yer baubles and pitiful dinkling of golden coin. Be off with ya, ye filthy lecher."

"B-but they t-t-ook," he whimpered, struggling and gurgling like a tantruming child ignored by a parent. He screamed next with a voice not his own. This voice carried an echo upon it, like two people talking at once and saying the exact same thing. Or when an ale barrel was empty, and you spoke your name into it for the effect. It snapped their attention to him. *"Walk away, yellow-beard, but they took your precious gift."*

Mevindh-Gulbard stopped in his tracks. Haggersath gripped his arm with the strength of genuine urgency.

"Yes, I stole one of the gifts you made, rock lover. The rats have it!" the strange voice continued. It was too soothing, too strong to be Jarlsalt's, but there was no one else present. He laughed at the Dwarrow, and his ungainly humor filled their reluctant ears.

Mevindh-Gulbard did not notice that Haggersath had let go of his arm. He was not aware until he saw the Giftgiver's fist smashing the taunting traitor to the dirt. "You traitorous, lying fool. You have no idea of the madness yer actions bring." Haggersath grabbed him by his ill-fitting garb and brought Jarlsalt's scabby face close to his.

"Yes!" the voice taunted back to him, gurgling with glee. But Jarlsalt's face did not display what the voice showed. His was a look of fear, eyes wide and cheeks quivering. He was afraid, despite the words he jeered out. *"Do you not know? They have it, and they will take it to the Rotte-Hojle."* Jarlsalt was flung hard to the dusty turf at the armored foot of the Giftgiver.

Mevindh-Gulbard stood watching. Haggersath was in a rage. He would not be kind anymore. The dark Dwarrow had crossed a line.

Haggersath's face took on a red color, and he spat, "Blast yer meddling, Dokkur Dvergur. Yer black mind be damned. Tell me: What way did these rats take me own gifts o' Jikseon?"

Jarlsalt twitched at his feet, his face curled in a perpetual scowl. He had a mixture of fear and hate on his face. *"They be east of the road, but your rabble cannot catch them. Look to your wagons. A basilisk moves with greater celerity. They will make their home in less than a fortnight, and you will be here tending your flock."*

"What be their number?" asked Haggersath.

Mevindh-Gulbard wanted to know if he had indeed seen tralkvalid, as he claimed earlier. He was beginning to think there might have been a bit more truth in the story after all. He risked the Giftgiver's wrath at him interrupting and asked, "Did ye say they had them bigger buggers with then too?"

"Indeed, yellow priest, yes," answered the scowling outcast. *"They are escorted by tralkvalid, yes—and I saw some twenty. I can only hope that there are more."* And then he laughed again.

Haggersath regarded him with deep concern. He looked at Mevindh-Gulbard, seeking validation. Letting the Giftgiver know he believed at least some of this rhetoric, he nodded to Haggersath. It rang true. But the voice was as if another spoke through him. There was real malice in the mocking tone. He was hoping that Haggersath held the same concern in his mind. He made a mental note that he would ask about it when they were out of the prisoner's earshot.

"You'll keep yer head fer the moment. But when we find these thieving weasels, and they don' have the broach gift ya claim they do, I'll let Bolfath have his way with ya—any way he likes it!" Haggersath had made his judgment.

Jarlsalt's eyes changed. He lacked the brashness and imperious tenor that spoke down to them just moments ago. What he said now seemed oblivious to his predicament. "So if they do be havin' the gift ye made in the forge, I can leave?" he asked. "I be free ta go, all fergiven' and such?"

The whole lot of them let loose mixed snickers. Nef-Rekja broke out in all-out belly laughter. It took a moment or two for the noise to die down enough to continue.

Mevindh-Gulbard and the Giftgiver stared at him, watching as sweat gleamed over Jarlsalt's forced, expectant smile. Haggersath nodded. "Ahhhhh, no. Not at all, ye murderin', lyin sack o' goat dung. Ya gets what a fuck like ya deserves. But I'll make it fast an' clean, so's ya don't shit yer pants."

Jarlsalt gulped and shivered, and Haggersath turned, sparing no more time for the liar. Mevindh-Gulbard walked next to him. "Do we pursue the kvalid fer the gemstone gift?" he asked Haggersath.

He nodded as they walked, telling the Gulpąst his mind. "Aye, tell Captain Grölle I want him ta take his ferskeyttr an' one other. We be needin' ten soldiers too."

"I be comin' with ya," Mevindh-Gulbard said, expecting his skills to be needed.

"Aye, an' Bolfath. We be needin' axe work, and there be none better than he fer that," Haggersath agreed, smiling with teeth a shade darker than his flaxen beard. "The rest of the caravan be followin' the Stonescraper. Tell him ta clear out the Towers and make ready fer our return. When he gets there."

"Aye, Giftgiver, it will be done as ye like," he affirmed, hinting at his own smile under his wiry mustaches.

The caravan had passed out of sight down the road under Diwolde Stonescraper's stewardship. He was just the choice for organizing and managing the continuing migration of those loyal to the eastern Dwarrow. It was a rebuilding of a nation, going home now to the Towers of the Horne.

Meanwhile, Mevindh-Gulbard had joined Haggersath's expedition to recover the lost gift.

CHAPTER 50

Noshid, the Mad God

Jarlsalt was left unbound. It was at the insistence of his jailor that he be allowed freedom of his limbs in order to move quickly. Fear of what would happen seemed to be enough to keep him in line—especially with the giant Bolfath looming over him. They had made him the jailor of that inbred beast. Ha! He was a half breed too. Put the two defiled together, where they belonged. But Bolfath was touted for his imperfections. Jarlsalt was an outcast, hated. His guts twisted at the thought, and he choked on his own breath. It caused him to stumble, and he would have fallen if he had been shackled. Small thanks for small wonders.

His nerves were frayed. Every time he dared glance at the bodyguard, he was met with a hungry, vicious smile, teamed with a cutting stare. Both would have to wait for the inevitable, but both of them knew the outcome.

Jarlsalt saw the company the Giftgiver had composed for the pursuit of the gemstone pendant that had been skirted away in the hands of the rats. Haggersath took his Haseti along with him. The lone missing member was that blasted Grýttr, Diwolde Stonescraper, who continued as the leader of the loyalists to the Horned Towers. Jarlsalt counted eight Rock-Biters. So he brought two ferskeyttr, one led by Grölle. That one had been a thorn in his side ever since making captain; he was always seeking a way to make himself look good in front of the Giftgiver, which often meant antagonizing Jarlsalt. Also in the escort were ten regular soldiers. He was expecting a fight. Meanwhile, the trek had turned from heading due east to bending somewhat southward.

It made no sense for Haggersath to insist on dragging him along. Yet here he was, traipsing over the low smatterings of shrubs and dried grasses, giving chase. There was no reason for this except to execute him with fewer eyes to witness Bolfath's brutality. He did not trust the promise the Giftgiver relayed about taking him back to the home of the eastern Dwarrow for an "honorable death." It was an eastern Dwarrow lie.

They had traveled for the greater part of three days and reached the tall grasses of the Plains of Sorka. In the direction they were going, the Rotte Hojle had to be only a couple days more ahead. If they wandered too close, this little foray that the straw-bearded fool put together would not have strength in numbers; Jarlsalt knew the closer they would get, the larger the packs of kvalid patrolling their grasses would be. Big enough a patrol, with the kvalid being at home in these grasses that towered well over their heads, and they might find themselves overwhelmed. Kvalid this close to the Rotte Hojle would let none escape alive.

They halted once more. He overheard a strange Dwarrow with a long, thin face and a nose to match say to Haggersath, "Yes, great giftyness. Jus ahead o' us." He could see the satisfied smile on the rumpled Dwarrow they had used as a tracker.

"How many?" asked Haggersath.

"Excellent question," the tracker said with the same bland expression of pleasant ease.

Then he was quiet. How odd this Dwarrow was. Jarlsalt had never seen him before today. Feeling an itch, he looked down at his arm and began plucking bloated ticks off his limbs. The tall grassland was a miserable place.

"I'll be havin' an answer," Haggersath stated plainly. "Tell me how many rats are in the nest."

"Oh, nest? Where?" said the tracker, his confused head turning this way and that. His long, thin beard whipped like a snake under his chin. He scratched his beard and thought so hard he twitched—then, the pleasant, satisfied demeanor returned to his long face. "Is this a riddle?"

Haggersath turned red. Jarlsalt stifled a snicker. Mevindh-Gulbard stepped forward and interceded, "Nef-Rekja."

The tracker's head swiveled to the Gulprąst, still carrying his annoying smile like it was painted on. "Your priestiness?"

Mevindh-Gulbard asked him, "How many kvalid are you tracking?"

"Two," he said without a flinch.

Rolling his eyes, Mevindh-Gulbard continued to unravel this mystery. "And how many travel with the two kvalid you are tracking?"

"Sixty-one."

Haggersath looked at his Gulprąst, eyes wide with astonishment. Jarlsalt could not help enjoying the frustration the nose tracker brought to the eastern Dwarrow.

"Why ya little weasel…" Grölle started.

"Calm now," Haggersath said to Grölle.

"I be the nose tracker," Nef-Rekja corrected with energy. "I be no weasel."

"So ya say, mebbe around sixty, then?" Haggersath asked in confirmation.

Nef-Rekja's forehead closed forming a vertical set of wrinkles. "Sixty-one. I am the nose tracker, there is no mebbe."

Haggersath smiled coolly at him, then he looked at the waiting Dwarrow around him. "I want Captain Grölle ta take this nose tracker and yer two ferskeyttr directly into the meat of this rat patrol." Haggersath then told his captain, "Grölle, yer boys will lead the way in. Bolfath, ye stay with me and Mevindh-Gulbard." Then he pointed to Jarlsalt. "Two of ya stay and drag him in close so's he don't run while we be busy with rat cleansin'. The rest o' the boys watch the ferskeyttr flanks."

Having their orders, the Dwarrow efficiently moved out, disappearing into the tall grasses.

"There they be," Grölle said. His ferskeyttr would lead the attack. Haggersath had only selected his Haseti to accompany him for expediency. A ferskeyttr could handle three or four times their number in a fight. The vanguard led by Grölle would manage thirty or more of the rats at the front. Haggersath and Mevindh-Gulbard were dangerous, and Haggersath doubled the group's efficiency. And then there was Bolfath—Bolfath could wreck numbers uncountable just on his own. Again, his group could handle more than half of the rats alone. That left four regular soldiers to watch the rear and three on each of the flanks—more than enough for the lightly armed weasel raiders ahead of them. This would give warning of any other force or surprises that always happen in battle.

"An' that liar cannot count," Grölle added as the noise of a battle began. "There only be half what he claimed and not a one bigger than rat scum!"

Dwarrow war cries. Chittering of kvalid. Sounds of steel meeting wood. Scrapes and clangs of metal finding metal. The tall grasses hid everything but stopped nothing.

With the battle plans laid out and Grölle's ferskeyttr already engaged, they moved in to find the rest of the kvalid raiders. It was easy for the Dwarrow to hide in the tall grasses. Advancing seemingly unnoticed, their helms and hackles bobbed and danced undetected. Hunching low, even Bolfath was difficult to see. They would make short work of the rats and their crude weapons.

Jarlsalt was efficient in battle and had laid many battle plans of his own before, like this one. It was a solid scheme. He sat between the two sets of guards, who eyed him with suspicious scorn, and waited, listening to the battle, hoping for their chance to get in the action. Jarlsalt scoffed inwardly. Battle was not their task. If they had been under his command, he would have reprimanded their thinking. Set their priorities right. Instead, he smiled.

And then fate stepped its pretty little head in. The wind changed direction, and the chittering changed cadence. Jarlsalt still could not see a thing, but he heard Dwarrow cries of surprise and gathered that when they fell upon the spot where the kvalid had been, they found the rats were gone. Those rats had sharp noses, and they would know where the Dwarrow would be and how many, *without seeing them!*

Then, out of the tall grasses they came, stabbing with their javelins and trying to pierce the hard travel armor of the Dwarrow. The prodding iron javelin points danced with rapid strikes at the Dwarrow. Jarlsalt's guards were engaged. As he expected, they forgot him for the moment. He took the chance and plunged into the tall grass, leaving the fighting guards behind him.

Bah! He ran straight into Grölle's Rock-Biters, all four of them. The ferskeyttr took no injury, because of their excellent armor and battle skills. They were dealing with kvalid dashing all around them. Lucky for Jarlsalt, he was in their rear and went unnoticed.

He slipped back into the grass, away from them—
and ran right into Nef-Rekja, tumbling both of them
over. He was at the heels of Haggersath's group. Blast
it all! His legs were all tangled with the nose tracker's.
But thankfully, Haggersath's Haseti was hard-pressed
as well, dealing with a stronger attack than Grölle's.
Mevindh-Gulbard swung his bejeweled mace, taking
a kvalid across the snout, chipping teeth and spraying
blood. At least a dozen kvalid were making their
hit-and-run assault, but the Dwarrow were having no
trouble holding their ground. Dwarrow battle cries of
surprise behind him told Jarlsalt that Grölle's ferskeyttr
was probably getting flanked. This assault had not gone
well with the wind changing; the surprise was gone,
and, lacking the numbers of their enemies, they were
now on the defensive.

Jarlsalt looked at the nose tracker, who did not
seem to be anxious to fight with either him or the
kvalid. They just looked at one another. Around them,
Haggersath and his Gulprąst were alone, turning in
place dizzyingly, trying to avoid another surprise attack.
Somehow, Bolfath and the ferskeyttr had separated.
Fighting in the rocky hamlets under the shadow of the
Silfr Mountains was one thing, but now this overgrown
grassland was home to the kvalid, and they were very
comfortable making their quick strikes to whittle the

Dwarrows thin. But Jarlsalt saw the bloodied corpses of rats beginning to pile up. It came at a hard cost.

With a roar, Bolfath burst through the grasses and spun around, flashing his axes in a horizontal whirlwind, surrounded by no less than five chittering kvalid. He nearly caught Mevindh-Gulbard across the head—a lucky near miss. Squeals filled the air, and hot blood sprayed the group as three of the weasel-like creatures lay dead or dying at his feet. He did not escape untouched but stood ready for more with a javelin protruding from his left thigh and a glancing cut across his smiling cheek. He was in bloodlust and, of course, had never been happier.

The next strike came at Nef-Rekja and Jarlsalt. A javelin glanced off a seemingly wild swing of Bolfath's axe, preserving the nose tracker's neck. He grasped his neck, testing it to make sure it was intact. The remainder scattered from Bolfath, running back to the grass cover. Nef-Rekja leaped to his feet and followed the Haseti into the grass after them.

Jarlsalt found himself alone again in the grass forest.

Shouts from the Dwarrow continued to pop from different directions, with periodic yelps by injured kvalid. Their chittering was everywhere. Jarlsalt moved through the grass more cautiously than before. Danger lurked in every place. The kvalid did not care a goat-shit whether he was eastern or western; a Dwarrow was a Dwarrow, and they were all enemies to be slain. And if he was thought to be a kvalid in the tall grass, one of those easterners might lay him low. A wayward javelin. A swipe of a hatchet. A slip of a long blade. Who knew? What a mess this fight was. Nobody knew where anyone else was, and if you found somebody, they might kill you before they figured out who you were. A mess, all right.

He tripped over something in his path and almost went to the ground. Righting himself, he turned to find that he had tripped on a kvalid body lying there. He was going to leave, but then he saw a weapon in the grass. A short sword that spread to a fat blade at the tip. He did a double take to get a closer look. Was it…there! A huge ruby in the hilt end. Yes. His sword!

Jarlsalt recognized the gravely wounded kvalid leader before him in the grass where he lay, waiting on death. All kvalid looked the same to him. All except this one. He could never forget the slathering breath and snapping jaws of his tormentor.

"Well met." He smiled down sardonically. "I see ya be gettin' what's what." He nodded approvingly at the leader's demise.

He stepped on the blood-matted, furry arm and wrested his sword from the dying kvalid. He took the scabbard and fastened it home on his hip, then held the blade at the throat of the raspingly gurgling weasel.

"Time's come fer ya. Now where'd ya put me blood-red gemstone an' me pretty Stone?"

It looked at him with rheumy eyes, spying death over Jarlsalt's shoulder. He was going glassy. Jarlsalt reached for his old satchel at the rat leader's belt, sure that it held the Destiny Stone. Its clawed hand gripped his arm, pulling him close. He caught a raking strike from the other hand to his chest, cutting deeply into recently scabbed wounds not yet healed. He cried out in pain; the weak chitter the leader let out had to be laughter. He felt the squeeze of the constricting claw as the sharp talons dug deep into his chest and gripped around his ribs from inside him. He felt blackness coming. The pain was so great; it was mercifully taking him away. But then a boiling anger washed out the pain. Jarlsalt shoved his sword hard through the neck of the kvalid leader, ending his fetid breathing.

Blood oozed out and drowned the grass beneath its neck. Its grip on his bones released and slipped from his rib cage. Jarlsalt touched his chest, and his fingers felt shredded, soft, warm, wet meat. There was pain, but not so much as the shock of it all. He was bleeding profusely. Feeling lightheaded, Jarlsalt slumped down and sat in the grass beside the dead weasel. He rested a moment, blocking out the sounds of battle all around him. Not again, he panted to himself, begging. No, not again.

He was so tired. Exhaustion was sudden, and it dragged at him to collapse right there, just as he had done in the desert mere days ago. It would be so easy. No more worry or troubles. So easy to just…

And then it came. In his chest, where the wound was, brewed a fire of heat, warming him with a touch of energy. He looked at the satchel he had caught his death trying to acquire. He took the bag off the dead kvalid and rummaged around the contents. Something clinked against glass. He pulled out the garnet pendant. He chuckled lightly, but it hurt to do so. Then he drew another soft breath, relaxing. He knew it was in there; he heard it clink against metal. What else could it be? He looked again; it was there, in the bottom, among other oddities the kvalid kept.

He drew forth the Destiny Stone.

Yesss! the voice in his head hissed with glee. The fire grew in his chest. He opened his ripped tunic and saw the deep, bloody rake in his body. Blood oozed too fast; he would not survive this wound. It would take his life, and soon. The gashes were deep. His blood loss was a river and would not be mended. He lay back on the grass, yielding to the oppressive pressure playing across his broken sternum. *I'm dying*, he thought with total dismay. *Here, in this horrible place, I'm dying.* He could feel the Destiny Stone's warmth in his fingers. It was likened to his bosom.

He peered into the Destiny Stone—it was calling to him.

> *"Come, my son, let me in. I alone can save you now. Face your destiny, for it is paired with my own."*

He was transfixed. Even had he wished, he could not pull his gaze or mind away from the command.

> *"Release your will to me."*

He panicked and tried to escape the grasp the Stone had upon him.

> *"Do not flee. You are my chosen. I am you—I am Noshid."*

He was as if struck, but his will melted in awe in the face of his god—of his mad god. Of Noshid.

CHAPTER 51

Greed and Luck

Haggersath was struck in the melee, but it was not by spear or club or another mundane weapon. It was by an awareness that froze him in mid-fight. Bolfath saw him stop and moved to guard him, as his first job demanded. He did so with his bearlike ferocity.

"By Jikseon's majestic beard! *It be here.* An' so close too," yelled out Haggersath, his eyes unfocused, his mind pulled in the direction of the Destiny Stone. It was very close. He had chased to recover the pendant gift, but *this* was far greater! With the Destiny Stone, he could finish the work on the gifts. He could feel the draw of power upon the Destiny Stone. Something or someone had hold of it—*and they were using it!*

He tasted the sheer force of magic and turned in the direction he had left that traitorous lout, Jarlsalt, with the two pairs of soldiers as guards. An orangish glow emanated from the grass in that area. Fire leaped up, licking the sky for several meters. They needed to cut through these rats and get the Destiny Stone. The gemstone pendant would have to wait.

"Mow the rats down like they be blades of grass an' follow me," he bellowed with intensity that laid bare his urgency.

Pulling away from the trap set by the kvalid, they retreated in the direction of the Destiny Stone—but their path was cut off when two huge tralkvalid broke through the grass in front of them.

"Oho! Now me play begins!" Bolfath declared with giddy excitement. He moved without hesitation.

Bolfath smashed through the guard of the first, who did not expect a Dwarrow to carry such strength. His axe bit deep, shearing off its weapon arm at the shoulder. But big as the bodyguard was, the tralkvalid were bigger. The other barreled ahead, swinging its iron-banded mace with enough force that its glancing blow knocked Haggersath to the ground. It then leveled Mevindh-Gulbard over with a charge of its great hairy shoulder.

The Gulprąst gagged at the reek of oily residue when the beast's rancid pelt wiped across his face. With a backward spin, Bolfath caught Haggersath's assailant with consecutive strikes of his two axes. They bit deep into the chest with a wet, hard *thunk*, and immediately, *thunk* again. He flashed his heavy axes like a dance of death, finishing the overgrown weasel with a clean decapitation. Blood spattered everywhere, making the grass walls a celebratory green and red.

Haggersath wondered, rising to his feet, why Grölle and his ferskeyttr hadn't rushed to assist in the attack. Once upright, he could focus and hear. Noise to his left sounded hard with battle; Grölle's unit was still fully engaged. How many of these blasted rats were there?

He felt the Destiny Stone yet again and started off in the direction of the orange glow, the direction where the Destiny Stone lay. It was here. He was smiling now. He would get to the Stone and take it back to finish what he had started. The gifts. He came to a clearing where at least ten kvalid were slain at the feet of a rather bewildered-looking Nef-Rekja. He held a bloodless knife in his hand, shakily pointing it over his head with a downward grip. Not very effective in a fight like this one, despite the array of carnage around him.

The odor of burning grass made Haggersath look up again to where the Destiny Stone was. Furiously, a ball of fire burned with wild immolation over the grass, several meters overhead. A calm figure sat amid the conflagration, legs crossed and floating over the grass, suspended in the air.

Another attack coming at them in the grass took his attention. More kvalid poured through the tall thickets of grassy forest. Where were all these kvalid and their greater cousins spilling from? It was far more than the party they identified in their pursuit. They must be closer to the Rotte Hojle than they thought. There would be no end to the rats hauling themselves out of their home to protect it from "invasion." They had to make their way out and leave the gemstone pendant. He would never find it with this endless stream of kvalid.

But the Destiny Stone—he could not abandon the Stone. No, not again. He did in Strongmedjie because there was no way to overcome the Bornholm in his own hall. Here in this grassy plain, the kvalid were formidable but a much more manageable obstacle. They would not get a more favorable chance.

Bolfath waded through the kvalid with ease, a slaying machine of the first order—unstoppable. Mevindh-Gulbard had regained his feet and fought off two more. Haggersath swung his hammer to take one up the length of its body, and it fell away, smashing upon its front like soft flesh popping through bones. He missed the next on the way back down, where his hammer hit a stone head-on, rattling his arm. A chip flew up and gashed his forehead. He lurched rearward, losing his helm, bringing his hand to the wound on his head. Blood seeped into his eyes. He was momentarily stunned, and the rat caught his calf with the javelin. He went down backward. Of all the luck, he thought. But before he could right himself and get his trusty hatchet free to block, Bolfath cut the bugger in two.

He looked on at Haggersath, whose vision was blurry. Had the hit on his head done more than cut him? His free hand went to his cut again; it came back wet and red. Bah! It would bleed, but it would heal. Where had his goat-horned helm fallen off to? He'd never find it in this blasted grass. He was still dazed.

Something pulled at the Giftgiver's mind. He thought it was the Destiny Stone, but it wasn't. The sense of awareness to the Destiny Stone was gone. He touched his forehead, and seeing the blood on his hands, he was seized. He fell onto the grass, searching feverishly for the chipped rock that struck him. He had to find it. The time had finally come. The gifts no longer mattered. The Destiny Stone would need to wait. Nothing could deny his desire. It was bound to happen to him, but why now, of all times? Why now?

He had been chipped. It had to have been a rock with mangeesum to cause his blood to boil so. Mangeesum? In a stone upon the Plains of Sorka? Unheard of! Yet here it was so. He had been chipped, and the fever had taken him.

Mevindh-Gulbard acted, taking charge. Haggersath heard it happen like it was far away, though it was only a couple of meters from him. Haggersath moved on all fours, seeking the chip. He must find it. Nothing else mattered now.

The Gulprąst issued orders behind him. "Grölle, get yer boys headin' south before we be overrun. Bolfath, keep our rear clear so we kin get away from the Rotte Hojle."

Bursting through the grass, on top of them came more creatures. Haggersath looked up and saw Mevindh-Gulbard's mace pulled back to strike.

"Wait! Gulprąst!" the creatures cried. "Hold yer mace, blast it!"

They weren't kvalid; it was two of the soldiers left to guard Jarlsalt. They were battered and wounded, both. The Gulprąst lowered his mace but not his wrath. "The other two be dead," one said. "We lost the Dokkur Dvergur. He—"

"Ferget him!" Mevindh-Gulbard cut in. "Grab the Giftgiver and make haste behind Grölle's ferskeyttr. Don' let the rats touch him."

Shifting with pointed precision, they followed Mevindh-Gulbard's orders as one. Cutting a path clear to the south, away from the onslaught of the kvalid, away from the flame-enveloped image floating over the grasses. The Dwarrow retreated the field without the pendant gift, without the Destiny Stone, but Haggersath smiled as they dragged him along. He smiled at the small, bloodied rock chip in his hands. He would have a son to lead the Horne when his time was done.

CHAPTER 52

Pure Malice

J arlsalt felt himself pushed to the corner of his own mind. He had no control over his body. He had no control over his thoughts. He was merely allowed to be an observer. And he observed. He saw a wall of pure flame, red and hostile, that held his soul in check. It flashed a face—no, two—no, no, *three* faces as it shook its head in his mind's eye. He beheld the wildly angry, somber, and insane laughter that could belong to no other. Was this what death looked like? He knew he teetered on the doorstep.

Face-to-face with Noshid, the mad god. His god. His god was not Jikseon, as he believed all his miserable life. He would not be accepted by the Gnomôk and was despised by the Dwarrow. An offer came, now, at the end of it all, for true acceptance—and it was coming from Noshid.

"Join me, little one." Noshid beckoned to Jarlsalt. *"You shall be my Hospitium."*

He could not refuse. He didn't want to. He would accept this offer. He wanted it. This could make him what he had always wanted: a friend in the power of a god, even if only at his death. He would command— no! He would *impose* respect and fear and death. Vengeance would be his. He released, welcoming the Destiny Stone, embracing Noshid, his god.

Jarlsalt felt the power of the Stone of Destiny unleash its fire, and they were engulfed in red magic. It coursed through his body, burning and yet somehow healing his wounds. Pain, intense pain. He was agony. It was one with him.

"Yes, yes! Come to me. Join me."

His flesh melted and was remade in the joining with the divine. He and Noshid as a single being. He would have died if not for the joining. Noshid could not manifest in the world of Thear without a candidate conceding its whole being to him. But now, with the Destiny Stone, it was happening.

Noshid's laughter echoed in his head. His mind was slipping, and his consciousness was abating into dark nothingness. He was wholly consumed—but he began to see again. It was not yet truly an awareness of anything. Not like before. There was no recognition. He saw, but he did not understand.

Slowly, very slowly, things took their places. He saw the blue of the sky above. He saw the tall green grasses below him. He was…floating, high over the grasslands. It required no thought, no effort. It just was. He saw creatures below, furry beings with sharp-toothed maws, slavering and chasing others whose metallic hair gripped their broad chins and who wore heavy steel garb in ringlets and plates. *Dwarrow*, he remembered, as if it was something in the distance from long ago. Yes, that is what they were—and the others, *kvalid*. They fought in the grasses below him. It was not his concern.

He felt the hot Stone in his hand—so hot it was burning and healing his palms in a never-ending cycle of pain. But with each moment, the power of the red fires of Noshid returned to him. He…he was Noshid— once, but no more. He had gathered power into his being. Once he was called Jarlsalt, but that was before. He became greater than a mere mortal. Not Gnomôk. Not Dwarrow. Not even a fallen god. He was something else. Something new to this world.

He drew on the Destiny Stone, absorbing more and more burning and searing with exponential pain as he lapped up everything the Destiny Stone would yield. It was too much power; it was too much. Unbearable.

He screamed silent words in the air, and fire flew out from him. In the sky above, flames of red leaped off the Sun itself, almost in protest. He let the Destiny Stone respond by burning grass and kvalid without sympathy. The Dwarrow had retreated southward, avoiding the death pyre.

His will slammed into a blue wall within the Destiny Stone. It barred his way with icy accusation. Cold it was, refuting the fires he flared against the wall. It was indomitable. It refused his entry further and began to force him back, back, out of the Destiny Stone.

It held, a whisper of frost with the breath of final winter.

> *"Yield, Noshid. It is not for you. You and your foul vassal begone!"*

He would not be denied! He fought back—as red and blue magic struggled in the Destiny Stone. It became blazing hot, flaring to melt even rock and vaporize ice. Only a being like himself, made of a melding of god and Gnomôk and Dwarrow, could withstand the torridity. He began to penetrate the blue wall. Fissures spewed and hissed gases of steam in his face. He would overcome the impediment.

Soon, all the gemstone's power would be taken. He could feel the power of red magic—he held much of it already, drawing it out as he might. Yellow quietly moved away whenever he tried to grasp it. Once he broke the blue standing in his way, he would tame the yellow and harness it.

"Your greed will destroy us all—you fool!" the cold void of blue bit at him. *"Get out!"*

He laughed.

> *"I will take as I please. I will destroy you and all you have made. Has this not always been my promise to you, Christiemay?"*

He pushed again, but he knew, of the three colors of magic in the Destiny Stone, red was least invested by the gods.

And then it broke through. The Destiny Stone snapped a great crack, and the fire went out. No more magic spilled forth from the Stone. It was cold and dead in his hands as he floated, a dull white, cloudy with black-lined fissures throughout the crystal, like the webs of spiders. It was dead and empty, devoid of power, useless now to anyone.

It did not matter. His transformation was complete. He dropped the empty, fractured crystal to the grass far below him.

He had drawn every twinkle of red magic from the Destiny Stone until it burned out and cracked. Where the blue and yellow had gone, he did not know, nor did he care. He was now greater than any living being on Thear. His was a melding of a god and its chosen minion. Each of the gods sought to make their favored complete through the magic in the Destiny Stone. Jikseon's bearded Dwarrow failed through their greed and shortsightedness. Morningsong's pride-filled Sylvan failed, unable to see success through their own hubris. *Ha!* Bruss's race of Man, so concerned with their daily lives, never even knew the race began. Christiemay and her blue-magic menagerie, lost in their own fantasies of ice and flowers, waited too long to join.

Noshid, the mad god, had won through fire and pure red magic. Cast to Thear all those eons ago and forgotten by the others, Noshid gathered his chosen— no, his *avatar* and became one with Jarlsalt. He could remain on Thear now, unlike the other gods, whose appearances were limited and intangible. The land could not bear them for long, and the Sun would extinguish their essence if they tried to stay. But Noshid had found a way to remain in physical form. No longer a thought or ghost on Thear, he was real. He was powerful. He was filled with hate. Hatred of everything. Pure malice.

He was *Pyrofўlakis*, demigod of fire and revenge. His would be the revenge Jarlsalt craved. His would be the destruction Noshid promised at his inception.

He had won, and the Race to Destiny was over.

Here ends Book One:
The Race to Destiny

The story continues in Book
Two: The Shattered Stone

Glossary

Explanation of Names and Terms

Aieren, a Gaelean noble who leads the Sylvans tasked by Morningsong to save the Daoine Maithe by gaining and using the Destiny Stone.

Aìte Longotahce one of the two remaining cities of the Daoine Maithe. It lies on the northeastern edge of the remaining forest.

Augabragð 37th Bornholm of the Strongmedjie.

Belusan Qûmhachdach A noble male Sylvan companion of Aieren's quest.

Berillian Mountains are a gentle range that runs up the spine of the Pyrainian peninsula.

Bihander a large sword more than a meter long requiring two hands to wield.

Bargveoor Dodher the tallest mountain in the Silfr Mountains. Home of the Stromurjotonn.

Bolfath He is Haggersath's bodyguard. 150% larger tha the largest Dwarrow. Suspected of being a rare half breed.

Borgar-hlid the thick as wide as tall bodyguard of the 38th Bornholm of Strongmedjie.

Bruss The god of the waters and pure yellow magic. Creator of the race of Man.

Christiemay The goddess the air and pure blue magic. Creator of many magical and mundane creatures. Filled the world with the wild creatures.

Cranne huge 'dog' sized pasty bluish white bugs. Sort of a blue magic consuming tick. They tend to hide in the tall grasses of the northernmost regions of the Plain of Sorka.

Cridhe Tùsail "Ancient Heart or Deep Root' the names of the First Tree who laid way for the Daoine Maithe with Morningsong

Crúimthier of the Silroh of Christiemay. Wears a dark blue sapphire to enhance his blue powers. He serves Christiemay as both a messenger and a battle mage.

Daoine Maithe the forest that provides the Sylvan their magic. It is almost gone from existence and is headed to extinction. Once it covered nearly one third of Thear's lands.

Desert of Cinders The parched desert land created when Noshid was cast to Thear in the form of a comet.

The Destiny Stone An artifact of world altering power created by the gods to save their race creations from prophetic destruction.

Diwolde Stonescraper one of the few remaining Grýttr he is in Haggersath's haseti. He understands stone as a living part of the world.

D0kkur Dvergur a perverse Dwarrow probably half breed or having Gnomôk blood. Any Dwarrow who commits offenses against the race of the Dwarrow so grievous they may be ostracized.

Dvalig Stonementor One of the greatest of the Grýttr. He was the master builder o that directed the building of the Towers of the Horne.

Dvaligbjarg is also called the Crag of Dvalig. It is the walled yard inside the Towers of the Horne.

Dwarrow Tallish metal-bearded race created by Jikseon of the land. Stout and hard like the rock they sprouted from, they live in the northwestern mountains of Thear.

Einvald the 1st son of the 37th Bornholm destined to become the 38th Bornholm.

Ferskeyttr is the complex combat formation used by the Rock biters to great effectiveness in large melee situations. They fight as a group in fours.

Fhalá 30 cm long Sylvan knife for 'bloodletting'. Used as a side arm they are straight and single edged. Instead of coming to a point, the bladed side curves up in a steep arc near the tip.

Forungr The Warning Tower. This is the first tower of the Towers of Horne. It is used as a garrison and place for guests as well as the support and storage of the people in the Towers.

Galean, the mundane creatures the Sylvan become once magic leaves their being.

Garm Fire born canines of the Desert of Cinders that often serve as combat dogs for the Gnomôk.

Gifr volcanic humanoid-like creatures made of cooled lava on their exteriors, but their insides are molten, and they 'bleed' freely once fractured. They are servant creations of Noshid. Tall between 2 to 3 meters and sturdily built.

Glaive a pole arm with a curved bladed scythe that often has a barb on the other. The shaft will usually have a haft along its mid and or lower length to maintain a solid grasp during combat.

Glenia Fìor-ghlan a female Sylvan companion of Aieren. She competent with abow and quite good at healing with red magic.

Gnomôk Short swarthy creatures made with fire and sand. Champion race of the god Noshid. He made them with the single purpose of defiling and destroying that which the other gads had made.

Grambol Doomsayer A Dwarrow in Haggersath's company who can sense magic and treasure. He may also draw divinations. He is so old even Grambol has forgotten his age.

Grimmr 25th son of the 38th Bornholm and officer in the armies of Strongmedjie.

Grýttr the Dwarrow who learned a sort of magical engineering specializing in stonework. The oldest and most industrious have gone nearly extinct with the fall of the Horned Towers.

Gulprąst a sort of magical warrior priest prized by the Dwarrow. Their magic in healing is unmatched throughout Thear.

Haggersath Giftgiver A Dwarrow of the line of Giftgivers who ruled the mountain city, the Towers of the Horne. He is tasked by Jikseon to save the Dwarrow by returning the Destiny Stone to the Towers of the Horne and forging gifts reminiscent of those great gift in the past.

Háseti a trusted council of friends or core leadership group in Dwarrow circles.

Hrajaar heavenly place where Dwarrow who have fallen in battle go after death to be at Jikseon's call should he need those warriors once more in the name of his peoples.

Himiniodurr Horne to the Sky the great mountain that the Konungr was chiseled from. It is the most important peak to the Dwarrow. It is under this peak that the greatest Dwarrow highway runs.

Homestead Tree the three huge trees that are each the center of each Sylvan city.

Hospitium the chosen vassal of a god, obligated to allow a symbiotic possession which may serve the god more than it might the host. Still, it requires both to exist.

Hugat Maela Primary advisor and herald to the 38th Bornholm.

Hyljaleid the secret Dwarrow path network under the Silfr Mountains—ages old—known to few Dwarrow. Much of this knowledge was lost after the fall of the Horned Towers.

Ishard King of the Vannflott.

Jarle the line of Dwarrow that are potential leaders of the of Strongmedjie.

Jarlsalt 16th son of the 38th Bornholm and a member of Haggersath's company. He commands the warriors in the party and is often at odds with Haggersath because he was charged by the Bornholm to lead form the ranks.

Jikseon The god of rock and stone yellow and red magic. Creator of the race of Dwarrow.

Kindjal a curved wide-tipped sword that hooks back on itself, often used by the people of Galee.

Krath a ruined Dwarrow city in the Silfr Mountains. Overrun by kvalid.

Konungr, the Kings' Tower the inner Tower of the Horne housing nobles and the forge as well as library and other items vital to the Dwarrow.

Kvalid Ferret bodied rat faced creatures from the Rotte Hojle in the center of the Plain of Sorka. They infest any uninhabited area in northern Thear. Holding clan societal behavioral and only moderate intelligence, they use crude or pilfered weapons.

Lhiannan shee woodland fairies who preys upon those who carry the grace of the Daoine Maithe. She consumes their 'magic' through seduction of desires leaving the victim 'empty' and having no wish to live they die of thirst and hunger.

Malas 'The great spatterer' Borgar-hlid's maul and primary weapon. He uses it with great pleasure, often making his unfortunate victims unrecognizable. The weapon has been passed down from bodyguard to bodyguard of the Bornholm. Mostly a symbolic artifact since few have the strength to wield it.

Mangeesum A blue veined ore created with the falling of Noshid and the creation of the Desert of Cinders. Its rare properties allow the binding of magic to inanimate objects through designed processes. If a male Dwarrow is bloodied by chance or purpose by and edge of stone with this

Man The race of created from the waters by the god Bruss.

Mevindh-Gulbard the Gulprąst in Haggersath's party. Has yellow magic deals mostly with healing and protection.

Morningsong The goddess of the forests and flora and all things fae. She is made of red and blue magic. Creator of the race of Sylvan.

Mulńtirna Ban-dia the southernmost of the two remaining forest cities of Daoine Maithe.

Noshid The god fire and pure red magic. Creator of the race of Gnomôk.

Ogrekaru near giant sized furry creatures who used to inhabit the northeastern plains outside of Sorka and the hills near the south of Daoine Maithe.

Osjalfradr the chief Gulprąst of the Strongmedjie. Part of the court of the Bornholm.

Pyrofýlakis is the being created when Noshid used the Stone of Destiny to join his essence with Jarlsalt to be able to wield power and remain indefinitely on Thear.

Reòiteag deigh ice spider colonies that infest some of the caves in the Silf Mountains. They operate as a single entity and entrap then devour travelers. Often they animate a victim whom they do not consume to set traps and make an appealing cavern for shelter to trap the victims.

Rock-Biters elite Dwarrow warriors.

Rommaith Glè-luath a male Sylvan companion of Aieren who is fading towards becoming Gaelean. A tremendous warrior from a very old and respected family.

Rotte Hojle a depression that leads to a hole in the land which is the origin lair of kvalid and their ilk. It lies in the center of the Plain of Sorka. It appeared after the Daoine Maithe retreated from the area.

Runeweaver Weiders of black rune magic that is unnatural in the lands of Thear. They guard the Destiny Stone.

Saurr-modr is the great active volcano in the north end of the Desert of Cinders. Believed by fire dwellers and the Gnomôk as the Thear bound home of Noshid, the mad god.

Scian a 30-centimeter-long single edged slender curved blade used by the Sylvan as their primary side arm.

Sgiathach are slender silver ice serpents from the far northeastern Silfr mountains. They have long graceful bodies like snakes and two sets of smallish wings. Made of pure blue magic they rely on it for flight and survival. Their touch is like ice.

Silfr Mountains The massive rugged sharp peaked mountain range that stretches completely across the northern edge of Thear.

Siolvarin ale preferred drink of the Dwarrow. Strong toasty grain ale with a hoppy note at the finish.

Silroh the order of 'wizards and special servants to Christiemay. These messengers once lost touch with their purpose and were frozen in glaciers for a penance.

Skökull Captain of the guard in Strongmedjie and 3rd son of the 38th Bornhilm.

Sorka the large plain that covers the center of Thear.

Stromurjotonn Fierce storm-ice giants of the northern most Silfr Mountains.

Strongmedjie The last surviving city of the Dwarrow and current ruling house. Home of the Bornholm line of dwarrow.

Sunspots and evil taint upon the sun from Noshid's ill will at the creation of Thear and its peoples. The source of a foul magic.

Svigalae Upright fire lizards who wield red magic and serve Noshid as his higher-ranking army leaders.

Sylvan Tall long surviving race of very magical creatures made from and bearing features reminiscent of trees. Bark like skin. Leaved often for hair. Created as the champion race of the goddess Morningsong.

Thear The flat map like world created by the magical colors if the Sun's power.

Thrargan Last ruler of the Towers of the Horne. Betrayed by Thrazur.

Thrazur 36th Jarle of the Bornholm who allowed the fall of the Horned Towers so he could be the uncontested leader of all the Dwarrow.

Tisroc the land of the Dwarrow in the northwest part of Thear.

Tralkvalid a much larger strain of kvalid which lead by brute force. Smarter and stronger than their smaller cousins, they can be fearsome enemies.

Trō-lekær large war pets that resemble great white bears used by the Stromurjotonn as loyal companions.

Trusilver is a hard silver alloy that has many uses. Makes unequalled armor and weapons that harbor abilities in red or yellow magic.

Toradh Dunne the largest lake on Thear. Crystal clear icy waters in north central Thear up against the Silfr Mountains.

Towers of the Horne (or the Horned Towers) Once greatest city of the Dwarrow now in ruins. Home of the Ring-givers.

Vallhah is a strong peat-based spirit with anise overtones that the Dwarrow are fondly partial to. About 40% alcohol.

Vannflott the race of ice giants who live in the depths of Toradh Dunne.